THE TRAITOR'S WIFE

A novel of Bess Raleigh

Anna Rossi

Copyright © 2018 Anna Rossi

All rights reserved. No part of this book may be reproduced in any form or by any electronic or mechanical means including information storage and retrieval systems, without prior permission of the copyright holder.

Anna Rossi asserts the moral right to be identified as the author of this work.

This book is a work of fiction. Names, characters, places, and incidents either are products of the author's imagination or are used fictitiously.

ISBN-9781730748158

Cover Design by Rocking Book Covers

For Peter, Dani and Ingrid

* * *

* * *

CONTENTS

~PROLOGUE~ 9
~PART ONE~ 13
Robert Cecil 20
Bess 23
Robert Cecil 34
Bess 36
Robert Cecil 41
Bess 43
Robert Cecil 59
Bess 61
Robert Cecil 82
Bess 84
Robert Cecil 100
Bess 102
~PART TWO~ 108
Robert Cecil 128
Bess 129
Robert Cecil 135
Bess 144
Robert Cecil 163
Bess 164

Cal	188
~PART THREE~	192
Robert Cecil	215
Bess	218
Cal	230
Robert Cecil	233
Bess	237
Robert Cecil	253
Bess	256
~PART FOUR~	262
Bess	267
Robert Cecil	275
Bess	279
Robert Cecil	300
Bess	304
~PART FIVE~	307
Robert Cecil	320
Bess	323
Robert Cecil	338
Bess	342
Robert Cecil	344
Bess	347
Robert Cecil	349
Bess	351
Robert Cecil	363
Bess	367
Cal	372
Bess	376

~PART SIX~	386
Cal	399
~PART SEVEN~	416
Cal	447
~PART EIGHT~	454
Cal	460
Bess	467
Cal	478
~EPILOGUE~	485
Author's Note	493
The back-cover picture	499
The two poems mentioned	500
About the author	501

* * *

* * *

~PROLOGUE~

BESS

Old Palace Yard, October 29, 1618

On the eve of his execution, I dreamed I attended the playhouse – the Globe, with its neat thatched roof.

Not only was it, in the nature of dreams, open in the heart of winter, when any audience would freeze to death and such places of amusement are, of necessity, closed, but I went alone (a practice I would never dare, awake), well-bundled in disguise – thick, coarse shawl over a servant's moth-eaten gown.

I sat upstairs, in the second gallery, with familiar faces all about me – one-time friends and enemies who knew me not, although I wore no mask – who laughed and talked together but frowned upon me; drew fashionable skirts and perfumed sleeves fastidiously away, muttering I should be down among the groundlings instead of mingling with my betters.

Yet many of the groundlings recognised me. Those rowdy, jostling strangers, paying a pittance to stand in the yard before the stage, tilted up their weather-beaten faces and exclaimed and pointed in disapproving amazement to see Lady Raleigh here at such a time. One red-cheeked woman shouted angrily to me above the ringing voices of the players – 'A loyal wife would be in church, praying for 'er 'usband's soul on the night afore 'e dies!'

Warm with embarrassment, I looked down at her dumbly, not knowing what had brought me here. The merriment, the noise, the hissing and booing at the actors who played villains, the throwing of rotten fruit, only served to bewilder me. And no matter how well the players sang, pranced, strutted, postured, they made no sense, their words and actions seeming to come from several popular plays strung willy-nilly together. Then one of them –a stout man – stepped forward and announced:

> *'The graves that hide us from the parching sun*
> *Are but drawn curtains till the day is done.'*

I stood up to shout: 'Those are not lines from a play! They're from one of Walter 's poems.' But the fiddles struck up for the jig at the end, drowning my voice. The notes sounded wrong, discordant; jarred wincingly upon the ear. And as I pushed my way down from the second gallery, slipping and slithering now on the ice-encrusted steps, the audience were hostile, aggressive, thrusting backs and shoulders deliberately in my way, preventing me from passing.

When at last I reached the ground, they hemmed me in still closer, forcing me to a halt. I could scarcely breathe and when I did I was rendered faint and sick from the stink of unwashed gowns and sweating armpits. Then a tall man shifted his position and I saw with horror that I was not at the Globe at all but caught in the press of people in Old Palace Yard, unable to move or turn my face from the scaffold while my companions cheered and applauded my husband's severed head as it rolled, lips still moving, away from his twitching body across the bloodied straw ....

I awoke in tears.

And now, in the early morning of this most dreadful day, my nightmare becomes reality. I sit straight and stiff as a poker in the black coach parked near the palace of Westminster, the real and solid scaffold clearly visible through its window.

The Abbey bell tolls seven. Soon they will lead him out. What is he thinking as he devours his last breakfast? (For he will eat, I am sure of that; will force down every bitter morsel to prove he has nerves of steel.) Of his family? Of me? Is he tortured by regrets? Wishing he'd steered a different course – married some rich, powerful woman who might have saved him from the block?

Twisting my wedding ring, I gaze out bleakly at the crowds gathering for the spectacle. Watch without registering the executioner donning his black hood. See instead the splendour of Greenwich Palace; the splendour of Walter Raleigh, dancing with the Queen –

✱ ✱ ✱
✱ ✱ ✱

~PART ONE~

BESS

Greenwich Palace, Christmas, 1584

Look at them, strutting a measure, flirting in time to the music. Billing and coo-ing like turtle doves, in appearance more gorgeous than peacocks.

Dressed to complement each other in shades of violet silk, myriad jewels flash from their clothing, their ruffs are encrusted with gold. Diamonds sparkle around her throat and in her red-wigged hair. His great, gilded, pearl droplet-earring glints with his every movement.

She's fifty if she is a day (fifty-one, they tell me), and he more than 20 years younger. Yet he looks at her adoringly as if she is a girl. And, worse, she acts like one – simpers and smiles and plays the coquette.

Wipes a bead of sweat from his high forehead with her own handkerchief after a sprightly galliard, sniggers behind her fan with him during a pavan. *Sluttish behavior for a Queen of England!*

'Water', she calls him, with her fondness for nicknames. A pun on his first name, on the way he pronounces it in his soft, West Country accent and on his passion for exploring the ocean. And perhaps therein she sows the seeds of my dislike, for water is not my favourite element. I drank a cup of it years ago, before my nurse could prevent me and before it was boiled for beer-making; came down with a nasty fever. So perhaps it is inevitable I should look on this proud, arrogant, black-bearded Captain Raleigh with distaste; this soldier/sailor man of action who yet dances gracefully and writes poetry and is Elizabeth's first favourite.

'He's the tallest, handsomest man at Court,' my friend Audrey Shelton breathes, squeezing my arm in rapture. 'Slender yet very obviously muscular, do you not think? And his glossy black hair curls naturally, did you realise that? Without the aid of tongs?'

'It gives him the look of a slimy Spaniard,' I mutter back, and she laughs, used to my contrariness. She always wagers on Raleigh in a fencing contest, a tennis tournament, while I stubbornly wager against him and lose money in the process.

She laments, for the hundredth time, my hostile attitude. 'For he's done nothing to provoke your displeasure.'

I shrug. 'He irritates.' (Mostly because he appears so sure of himself and his privileged role at Court while I, a novice, feel out of place and awkward.)

Not that my 'hostility' troubles him, for he fails to notice it, or me. Oh, he dances with me now and then as he dances dutifully with all the Queen's Maids when she orders it, talks vaguely of trifles, smiles on me with the tolerance an adult affords a pretty child (I look young, I am told, for my nineteen summers). But his mind is occupied with more important personages than uncertain, untitled Bess Throckmorton, dullest (he makes me feel dull) Maid-of-the-Privy Chamber...

And, perhaps, after all, our sovereign names him well because more sophisticated women than Aud Shelton insist that when they gaze up into those smiling, brilliant brown eyes their silly legs, beneath their farthingales, do indeed turn to water. While they strive, pink of face, to appear unaffected for fear of angering the Queen, who brooks no competition. Fool! Does she imagine any of her grovelling 'gentlemen' remain faithful out in the shrubberies? Behind securely locked doors at the end of little-used passages?

The musicians and the dancers finish with a flourish; Water hoists the Queen aloft. The dance demands it but surely his beringed hands are placed too intimately on Royalty's silken seat?

'Will it please you to parade with me or partake of some refreshment, Morgan le Fay?'

I smile to hear my own childhood nickname – turn to see my brother Arthur bowing before me, forestalling several interesting-looking gallants who retreat in disappointment or swivel instead towards a gratified Audrey. I make my curtsey demurely but dimple at him.

'Are you looking to set me at my social ease, brother, or ensuring I do not shame you by mixing with the wrong company?'

He flushes. 'You're too new to be discerning and there are certain – undesirables – from whom I would protect your reputation...'

Raleigh among them? Hardly. Arthur associates his sister with lesser fry. He has a respect for the glittering favourite. They both began elbowing their way up through the Court at roughly the same time, by means of minor positions - Esquires of the Body Extraordinary - so moved in the same circles. I inevitably glimpsed Raleigh while I was growing up and while he was still small beer (he did not notice me then, either) in Arthur's London lodgings, in the homes of mutual friends, always beautifully attired, always in the midst of some attentive throng, talking animatedly (and being talked about).

His adventures have been many, according to Aud Shelton. 'He's sailed the seas with recklessness and fought bravely in France and Ireland.' she reminds me often.

'What of it?' I shrug. 'So have others.'

My mother, unsurprisingly, disapproves of him. At last we agree on something. 'Hardly the stuff of which true courtiers are made,' I overheard her sniff once to her chief gossip. 'Too rough and wild by far. More of a pirate, I should say, like that relation of his, Francis Drake. They both send ships to rob and worry the Spaniards – they'll have us at war one day. Raleigh Senior was a mere Devonshire squire, though you'd never think it to see his son flaunt about. I'm surprised the Queen dotes on such an upstart.'

I share her surprise. True, Raleigh's half-brother was Sir Humphrey Gilbert, the explorer who drowned last year. And his great aunt was governess to Queen Elizabeth when she was a girl and well-beloved of her. But my father served King Edward and then Queen Mary before becoming Elizabeth's trusted ambassador in France and Scotland while my paternal grandmother was related to Queen Katherine Parr, Elizabeth's favourite stepmother. I stress this not to boast, merely to state the case.

For if Captain Raleigh is a nobody compared with us Throckmortons, small wonder the noblemen at Court resent the sudden elevation of a conceited country bumpkin who has done nothing to earn his good fortune save charm the Queen. And one has only to glance at the jewels upon his shoes to see how wealthy she has made him.

I say something of the sort to Arthur as we stroll in the Long Gallery between dances, he most presentably black velveted and russet satinned; I afloat (tightly laced) in a froth of white and silver. In the distance, the violet Queen reclines on silken cushions while the violet Raleigh kneels close beside her, telling some long-winded rigmarole that makes all around them laugh. Though much of the laughter, no doubt, is forced. When the Queen laughs, we all laugh. It is politic.

My brother, I think loyally, fair-haired and fresh-faced, is almost as tall and handsome as Raleigh. But in my heart of hearts, I know this is not quite true.

To my surprise, Arthur seizes me by the elbow, pulls me into a window alcove and speaks sternly.

'I'll not have you join the Raleigh-baiters, Bess! He toils hard for his royal favours whatever the envious say. The Queen values him for his brilliant mind – he has sound ideas on the colonisation of Ireland and the New World. And he puts his ideas into practice, unlike some. Also, remember my warning when you were sworn of the Privy Chamber – proud talk about our family is inappropriate here. We are lucky to be admitted, considering all.'

I shrug his hand away. 'Father was highly thought of ....'

'We can be proud of Father, yes. But discreetly. Remember the Catholic Throckmortons. Remember Francis ....'

I shudder. 'Do you expect me ever to forget him?'

Foolish, scholarly Francis, son of our father's brother. Most courtly families have the legacy of at least one 'traitor' to keep tactfully quiet about; a victim of circumstance in this time when we are all supposed to be Protestants, but many still lean backward to Popery.

Well, Cousin Francis leaned so far he toppled over. He got caught up in a wicked plot to kill the Queen and put her cousin, the captive Mary, on the throne.

It failed, of course. He was racked in the Tower until he confessed, dragged to Tyburn and hanged until he was almost dead; cut down and still alive while his privy parts were sliced off, his bowels and heart wrenched out. His screams, it was said, could be heard across the river.

I can never bring myself to look at his poor head, mouldering on a pike on London Bridge. And I knew him but slightly, while Arthur was close to him. Glancing at my brother's set face, I wish I had not reminded him of these nightmarish events which occurred a few short months ago, before I came to Court.

Remorsefully, I promise to guard my quick (but thoroughly Protestant) Throckmorton tongue and am rewarded by a warm smile and an invitation to dance the Volta.

I note that the Queen has - briefly, no doubt - discarded Water's partnership in favour of the middle-aged Earl of Leicester, whom I know too well for comfort. He is godfather to my brother Nicholas (nearest to me in age) and he also gives me an encouraging smile as Arthur and I take up our positions at a respectful distance.

I return it warily. Thirteen years ago, my father died in Lord Leicester's house, after enjoying a salad supper. Rumour still holds that the Earl poisoned him, but my mother, knowing of their great friendship, has never believed it. Do *I* believe it? I keep an open mind....

Surreptitiously, I look for Captain Raleigh in his distinctive violet silks. Spy him as he leans languidly against a fireplace with his friend, the little hunchback Cecil, watching the Earl who, many say, is the Queen's one true love from her girlhood, whom no-one will ever equal. A sardonic smile lights Water's haughty face. He's thinking, no doubt, that the ageing Earl, balding, florid and heavy, is a poor substitute tonight for dashing Raleigh.

ROBERT CECIL

Greenwich Palace, Christmas, 1584

Watching the male dancers twirl and leap on their straight legs and nimble feet, I'm clad, rather aptly, in turquoise, colour of jealousy. And as we lounge against the fireplace and the Queen's ladies curtsey to their partners but bat their eyes at tall, handsome Raleigh – glance with scorn or sympathy at me – a familiar stab of envy sours my admiration for this 'good friend' of mine. He is everything that I am not, and I can never decide whether to love or hate him.

'Hate him,' my father advised this morning, at our daily meeting in his private chamber. But then, William Cecil, Lord Burghley, despises and distrusts all the Queen's favourites, this current one especially. He encourages my friendship with Raleigh with one aim only – to learn, through me, his every move and thought.

'Because Raleigh could be a threat to us, Robin, if he becomes too powerful,' he went on, in his deceptively mild voice. 'Oh, he may be nothing now, but he's clever and he has the Queen's ear like no pretty favourite before him, not even Leicester. He could not, of course, begin to rival my position as first statesman, but he could prevent you from rising in the way I intend you to rise if he continues to charm her. I've had word spread far and wide regarding his great extravagance at Queen and country's expense, so he's resented in the streets as much as he is at Court. But I need you to take note of every petty rumour that could be held against him, any jest he makes that could be misconstrued, any woman he smiles upon that could serve to lower his standing with Her Majesty.'

I nodded gravely and promised to do my best. But part of me loathed myself, for while other men jeer at me behind my back and the Queen calls me 'Pygmy' to my face, Raleigh is ever kind in the most sensitive of ways.

He treats me as an equal despite my younger years, large head and twisted spine. He slackens his pace when I walk awkwardly beside him, dragging my weak foot. Invites me to hawk or partridge-net, knowing they are the only sports of which I am capable. Sits, whenever he can, in my company, sensing it makes me uncomfortable when he towers above me.

'He is a puffed-up popinjay in his silks and laces,' my father sneered, residing behind his desk like a thin black crow in his sober gown. 'An arrogant upstart.'

Some call the Cecils upstarts, but it would not have been wise to refer to it. Not just then, when my father's careworn face softened, and he treated me to his warmest smile.

'You may be small, Robin, and your body may be twisted, but you have a large brain in that head of yours. You're better equipped, at one and twenty, to help govern England than most men twice your age. You'll step into my shoes, one day, so long as we keep down the Raleighs of this world. Ears to the ground, my son, and we'll have him. He's intelligent – too intelligent - not like the dunderheads that have won the Queen's heart before him. But he's also too eager to rise, too outspoken for his own good. He's bound to stumble soon. One way or another, we'll bring him down.'

'We will,' I agreed, because I always agree with my father. 'We'll have him. We have only to wait.'

BESS

Greenwich Palace, January, 1585

Raleigh, I hear from several sources (all of them male, of course), is fast becoming the most hated man in London. But, mindful of my promise to Arthur, I keep discreetly silent about my personal opinions on all things.

Apart, that is, from the night we yawn through a play – 'Felix and Philiomena' – a dull piece enacted by the Queen's own troupe and mistakenly meant to be a comedy.

'Flat as un-spiced ale and far less palatable,' I complain to a group of ladies as we depart the hall at Greenwich, rustling in the Queen's wake, or so I believe. 'Only the performing dog showed any life.'

An almighty blow about the ear near unbalances me.

'When we wish to hear your uneducated view, Throckmorton,' barks the Queen, 'be sure we'll ask for it!'

At her side, her newest favourite grins like a schoolboy.

I most certainly hate him.

* * *

How does the song go?

The one my Catholic cousins sing?

> 'On the twelfth day of Christmas
>
> my true love sent to me . . .'

Something or other – I forget the exact nature of the gift.

Whatever, earlier today, the twelfth day of Christmas, the Queen bestowed on Raleigh a most coveted gift, the honour of a knighthood.

Some of the older courtiers whispered it was a wonder she didn't tickle his neck during the glittering ceremony as she had apparently shocked the Privy Council by tickling Leicester's years ago when bestowing his Earldom. Today she was the soul of decorum, but her eyes sparkled with a pleasure to match Raleigh's own. He has already been given the use of Durham House, a palace on the north bank of the Thames, for his London residence, along with lucrative wine monopolies, cloth monopolies. The rumbles of discontent among his betters grow ever louder and are joined now, so I'm told, by the murmurings of those beneath him; by the ordinary folk who dislike paying taxes to the youngest son of a tenant farmer.

Understandable, I think, but do not say.

* * *

Greenwich Palace, April, 1585

Arthur is in trouble! How ironic! Especially as his very own tongue has tripped him up and landed him there.

I should not be gleeful as the matter is serious but it's hard to resist a smile.

Arthur is not the eldest of my five surviving brothers. I say 'surviving' because there was a sixth – Henry, who died young. William was the first-born but he is a little . . . special. Sweet William, I call him, and sweet-natured he is, gentle and full of affection. However, doctors told my mother years ago that his mind would be forever locked in childhood.

Therefore, ever since my father died when I was six and Arthur fourteen, Arthur has looked after and looked out for all of us (nursing, I believe, a special regard for me, his only sister, and poor William, who lives mostly with my mother and stepfather in Leicestershire).

Arthur takes his responsibilities seriously, quickly reprimanding his siblings should we point so much as a toe from the straight and narrow. So how has he fallen by the wayside?

It happened soon after my twentieth birthday at the beginning of this month. It was my first at Court and everyone was very kind, the Queen especially. She gave me a little fur muff which I vowed to cherish always and shall, as I have grown to like her better, seeing more sides to her now. On this, my name day, she played a special song to me on the virginals; packages arrived from my family; Arthur, knowing my passion for Italian fashions, presented me with a lovely feathered fan while the other Maids and Ladies showered me with so many unexpected and thoughtful gifts I was overwhelmed.

Then all was spoilt when the Earl of Leicester summoned Arthur to him and told him gently that our stepfather, Adrian Stokes, had died. Arthur came to me, white-faced, and we were both shocked and upset. Following my father's death, my mother wed Adrian with near scandalous haste, but it has turned out well for my brothers and me. A rich widower with no children of his own (he was married to the Duchess of Suffolk, mother of the tragic Grey sisters), he has been kind and generous to a fault. We have all grown fond of him – I, especially, who can barely remember my important but much-absent father – and have long since come to look on his fine estate at Beaumanor as our home.

'He looked so well when he and our Lady Mother visited Court three weeks ago,' I wept to Arthur. 'What can have happened?'

Despite my concern for my mother, I could not up and leave my duties without warning, but Arthur at once rode off to see her, promising to send me word of the funeral as soon as possible. Imagine his bewilderment when he found, on arrival, instead of the house of mourning he'd expected, all as usual and our stepfather alive and well!

He was merely thankful at first, of course, as was I, when I heard the news.

But his relief soon turned to anger against my Lord Leicester for causing unnecessary grief. Returning to Court a few days later, when I was busy attending the Queen, his furious words about the fool's errand on which he had been sent were reported to more important ears.

The next I hear, my brother lies imprisoned in the Marshalsea.

What did he actually *say*? Everyone is asking this question but no-one seems to know, apart from the Privy Councillors who held court against him, and they all remain tight-lipped. But they have treated the matter seriously, sentencing Arthur to two months, a long confinement for a small offence. Worse, he is committed a close prisoner.

Arthur rightly considers this last ungentlemanly and such a commotion has followed. He has written protesting letters to everyone he can think of, including Leicester himself, who has scorned to reply. His friends visit him daily to sympathise, my brother Robert has been to see him and my mother has turned up at Court to plead for him, a task she cannot relish, preferring to command rather than bow the knee. He refuses to see me (I suspect he is too embarrassed) and languishes still in his gloomy, barred and shuttered cell, angry and humiliated.

Poor Arthur! I am very worried on his behalf. Lord Leicester (who must surely have been misinformed about the state of our stepfather's health, and did not intend to give offence?) is too important a personage to annoy.

I find myself in a dilemma. Should I speak to the Queen? Speak to Lord Leicester? Add my pleas to the others? Is it expected? The wisest of the Queen's ladies advise against. Her Majesty, they say, prefers her Maids to stand aloof from these kind of difficulties, whoever is involved. And, of course, I am hampered by not knowing the nature of Arthur's insults ....

※ ※ ※

Help has arrived from a most unwelcome quarter.

Early this morn I was strolling the palace gardens with Audrey Shelton, feeding the peacocks between duties and discussing

Arthur's troubles for the hundredth time. He has now taken a mild chill and my mother is worried he'll die from it.

Aud has an adored elder brother of her own and is sympathetic to my plight. She was insisting that it would be best to pluck up courage and approach Her Majesty (all well and good for her, she's related to the Queen through the Boleyns and might be received more kindly) when who but Sir Walter Raleigh approached *me*.

He appeared suddenly on the gravelled, box-hedged path before us, his great height obscuring the sun. He was dressed magnificently, as always, in peach-coloured satin, his doublet slashed with silver and trimmed with pearls. An ostrich feather nodded in his hat, offset by a great sparkling jewel, while the enormous cartwheel ruff about his neck stood up stiff and immaculate, in contrast to mine, which I knew drooped about my shoulders from the recent fall of rain.

'Could he be about to spread his cloak over a puddle for us?' Aud whispered to me and we both suppressed a giggle. Kate, my maidservant, heard from a worker in the Palace laundry that the latest sneering ballad sung in the streets about Sir Walter claims he flung down his jewelled cloak 'at a splashy place' for the Queen to walk upon.

If he truly executed this extravagant deed of gallantry, which I very much doubt since no one of my acquaintance witnessed it, he did not consider Aud and me worthy of a similar one. Today he left his cloak where it belonged, draped rakishly over one shoulder. But he swept his hat from his thick dark hair and bowed deeply, acknowledging us both with a courtly greeting and a brilliant smile before addressing himself to me.

'Mistress Throckmorton, might I have a private word concerning your brother?

His eyes are strangely fascinating, when they concentrate on you alone – very dark and bright and compelling – set deep in his fashionably pale face.

Audrey moved away beyond the sundial to sit on a stone bench flanked by two gilded heraldic beasts (her knees were failing her after that smile so it was just as well a seat was near) and I was left alone with 'Water' who quickly came to the point.

Arthur, it seems, has now written to Raleigh. How could he? Has he abandoned all dignity? And the Queen's favourite has graciously done his best to improve my brother's position.

'I have relieved the restrictions of close arrest,' he told me. How he enjoys rubbing our noses in examples of his influence. 'And have arranged for your brother's physician to attend him. But I regret the two months sentence has to stand. The Queen is annoyed and Lord Leicester furious.'

I wanted to say a quick, haughty 'thank you', gather up my skirts and move on. But frustrated curiosity got the better of me.

'Can you tell me why my brother has been imprisoned? The nature of the insult?'

For a moment he hesitated, then replied rapidly, lowering his voice. 'I have not his exact words, but it seems it had something to do with a salad supper. Does that make sense to you?'

I was amazed. 'You mean the salad supper my father ate years ago in Lord Leicester's house? Died soon afterwards?'

He nodded. 'I believe your brother said something to the effect that Lord Leicester had, perhaps, sent your stepfather a similar salad supper which your stepfather neglected to eat. Therefore surviving when Lord Leicester expected him to be dead.'

So Arthur, despite my mother's assurances, also harbours doubts about my father's death resulting from 'natural causes'. But to hint as much... He who advises caution in others!

Everyone knows Lord Leicester is sensitive on the subject of poisoning, for my father is not held to be his only victim. He is also suspected by many of poisoning the late Earl of Essex in order to marry his widow. Both 'murders', among others, were recently mentioned in a scandalous book by an anonymous author thought to be a Jesuit priest, which, though banned by the Queen, is still, to Leicester's fury, being widely read. No wonder he wishes to make an example of Arthur! I stared at Raleigh, horrified.

He was speaking again, in the soft West Country accent the Queen claims she could listen to for hours (and does).

'Our wits desert us sometimes when out of temper and in vino veritas. So it surely was with Arthur. But worry not, sweeting. He won't be ill-treated. I've gained permission for his own servants to wait upon him and he'll soon be out and about. It is not such a dreadful punishment.'

How I hated to be in his debt and how dared he call me "sweeting"! 'You'd be an authority, of course,' I said maliciously, 'having been imprisoned in the Marshalsea yourself.' For brawling beside the tennis court, years ago, according to Aud.

If I'd hoped to disconcert him, I failed. He looked startled for a moment, then threw back his black head and laughed, his white teeth gleaming, the huge pearl drop he wore in his right ear swinging madly.

'Name me a man of prominence who was not imprisoned there at one time or another. It's the fashionable place for young gentlemen. But when I was there I enjoyed myself, thanks to another Arthur. My cousin Arthur Gorges was admitted also, having challenged a nobleman to a duel in the Presence Chamber, and we wrote fine poetry together.'

'Fine' it would have to be, of course, I thought sarcastically, if written by Raleigh. Yet, against my will, I love his poems. I have even copied his 'Farewell False Love' into my commonplace book from the manuscript circulating at Court and re-read it often. But I would never have told him so...

I thanked him stiffly for helping Arthur and, signalling Aud, made my escape. But not before he had taken his leave of us with another elaborate bow and called me Audrey.

'No – I am Audrey,' piped up my friend Shelton, blushing. 'Arthur's sister is Elizabeth.'

'Indeed?' he said, his dark eyes mocking mine. 'But then, there are so many Elizabeths, it is easy to mistake them.'

I knew he had not for a moment mistaken my name. He remembered it well enough; had set out to annoy.

'Did he slip you a love poem?' Aud asked enviously, digging me in the ribs with her bony elbow as I hurried her away, 'with a note, asking you to meet him? That is his usual practice when he's interested. And the way he looked at you ....'

'If he had dared,' I told her crossly, 'I would have torn it up. Thrown the fragments in his face!'

'Like the actor who played the heroine tore up the love-letter in that boring play we watched,' nodded Audrey. 'Only he – that is to say she – pieced the fragments together again and then ....'

I let her prattle on. My stupid heart was thumping from the encounter. I would have preferred the Devil himself had come to Arthur's aid rather than smug, sophisticated (disturbing) Sir Walter Raleigh.

* * *

Hampton Court, a few days later.

Angry rumbles of thunder resounding through the palace. Rain pelting against the leaded windows. Flashes of lightning illuminating the Paradise Chamber where the golden glow of candles, in their hundreds, already casts a flickering brilliance over the jewelled Persian hangings, over the Queen, in cloth of silver, receiving foreign ambassadors.

Fountains tinkling, lutes and viols playing, fragrance of thyme and meadowsweet rising from the rushes on the floor.

And, suddenly, a mingle of musk, rose and ambergris – Raleigh's perfume – as he brushes past me in the press; slips a folded paper into my hanging pocket in full, blatant view of that most important of Elizabeths who sits upon her diamond-studded throne and is, luckily, short-sighted....

I tear it up, of course. What else can I do with Aud Shelton gawping on? No other soul notices but Aud has the eyes of Argus. More, I fling the pieces to the ground, so that Raleigh has to stoop hastily to gather them up – to grovel to retrieve them among silken skirts and stockinged legs whose owners glance down in amazement. When at last he straightens, flushed, his eyes are glittering. But not with anger, with amusement. Again he looks at me and laughs, his dark beard quivering. Again I'd hoped to embarrass him and again I'd failed.

Does nothing throw the man? His hide's tougher than that of an old stag my stepfather killed after years of hunting him down.

ROBERT CECIL

Hampton Court, 1585

God's teeth, my aching back! It always plagues me most when my mind is troubled. Raleigh invited me to go hawking, but I declined. It was all I could do to speak civilly, for he's turned his amorous gaze on *her* now, on the maid I have long fancied – Elizabeth Throckmorton of the bright face and laughing eyes.

For months I've been hesitating. Holding back from speaking to her brother Arthur for fear she might reject me. Her brother (who's landed himself in gaol of late, the fool) would favour the match, I feel – he's in awe of my father and aware my prospects are good. But though she'd likely let me down gently, with a regretful smile and some kindly words, she might also giggle with her friends in private.

'What!' I can hear her cry, 'marry a hunchback? Oh, his face is pleasant enough but – a *gnome*? A sorry little creature who drags his feet and scarce comes up to my shoulder? He's surely taken leave of his senses to even think on it!'

Even so, I've been on the verge of risking her ridicule, but – too late. Now I'll be obliged to sit back in torment – to watch as Raleigh moves in and dazzles her as he dazzles all women.

'Early days,' my father mused, when I reported the shameful scene in the Paradise Chamber. 'If a romance develops we'll inform the Queen and he's finished. But it may fizzle out, of course, amount to nothing'

It may, but I doubt it. The hopeful day-dream is over for me. I see that I was indeed a fool to think on it.

BESS

Nonsuch Palace, Summer, 1585

My brother Arthur has been released. Thinner, paler, and more than a little sheepish, he's joined the Court here in Surrey, where we're residing with the Queen, on Progress. He refuses to discuss his imprisonment with me, saying it is behind us and best forgotten.

He has other things on his mind.

He has struck up a correspondence with one Anna Lucas, of Colchester. She came to visit him at Nonsuch with her mother, Lady Lucas, a bossy woman, and appeared pretty and pleasant enough but rather overwhelmingly love-smitten. Her eyes followed Arthur wherever he went and her voice became shrill and excited in his company. I watched her with amusement mixed with a touch of scorn. Will I ever be such a fool over a man? I cannot imagine it.

My mother, who has also journeyed to Nonsuch, is delighted with Anna and very hopeful. She thinks it high time Arthur takes a wife. Unfortunately, she is even more eager for me to wed. An ambition I do not share. Arthur, as head of the family, is comparatively easy to manage. A husband might be less so. And I am enjoying my freedom, if one can call waiting on the Queen freedom. I'm in no hurry to change things.

This attitude annoys my mother, who thinks Arthur should take a firmer stance with me. My father, she says, would have seen me betrothed long since. She frequently reminds me of my childhood friend, Mary Sidney, sacrificed on the marital altar at fifteen.

Twenty, sings her repetitious song as she walks with me in the delightful Inner Courtyard before returning home, is too old to be unattached. (She's probably afraid I'll get deflowered in a shrubbery.) And I have, like Mary before me, been sent to Court to ensnare a husband.

Pausing beside a white marble fountain dominated by a white and gold plaster horse, she looks at me critically. (She always looks at me critically.)

'No-one could call you pretty, and you're over-tall for my liking.' She is petite and doll-like and makes me feel like a giant. 'And I wish you'd lighten that mousey hair, make it more fashionable. Still, your eyes are good - it's a pity they're hazel, rather than blue, but they're large and lively. You're vivacious, slender, you sing well and you dance beautifully, but you need to watch your tongue. Men don't like clever women and on occasion you show too much wit.'

That tongue again! I use it to voice an old grievance.

'You seem to forget I have no dowry.'

Thirteen years ago she lent my marriage portion to the Earl of Huntingdon - £500 left to me by my father. Arthur is still furious about it and is still attempting to get it back.

As ever, she shrugs this off. 'You still have a small farm, somewhere or other, that was also bequeathed to you. I had no dowry at all when I married your father. It worried him not. And that is precisely why Arthur took such pains to make you a Maid of the Privy Chamber. The Queen is indulgent to her Maids – look at Mary Sidney Herbert, married to an Earl! If you show yourself eager to marry, she will provide you with a handsome wedding gift and herself find you a husband.'

I wince. I've no doubt she will – an unattractive one. Mary's Earl is plump, thrice-wed and over forty.

Six short months at Court have taught me how matters stand. The Queen, though she pretends otherwise, is no champion of the married state.

'She's the Virgin Queen from fear,' Lady Warwick confided one day as we distilled rose water for Her Majesty's casting bottles. 'She shudders away from carnal intimacy – can't abide the thought of it. And is it surprising, when her father sent her mother to the block before she was three years old? What example of matrimonial bliss is that?'

'For the past seven and twenty years,' put in Lady Scrope, carefully boiling sweet marjoram and benjamin to make dry perfume, 'her ministers have been pressing her to wed – to produce an heir and secure her throne and the succession. So she's dallied with foreign princes for the sake of keeping peace with other countries. Dangled the carrot of the English throne in front of their greedy eyes. Led them gaily on by their noses and appeared to consider them, one after another, as her consort. But she has never, I'll swear, had serious intention of marrying, of entrusting her person to a husband.'

And now she is too old, ran the unspoken, treasonable thought between us. She can never bear a child. A fact that both relieves and frustrates her, makes her unreasonably difficult over the marriage arrangements of others.

She hates her clerics to marry, even though it is now permissible by law. While her 'favourites' fall immediately into disgrace should they dare to take a wife. They must never show desire for other women, must only shower attention on their Queen in that extravagant, adoring, flirtatious yet essentially chaste fashion which, I have come to realise, is pure fantasy – a stupid game that flatters Elizabeth's vanity.

But thus it follows that when she does find husbands for her Maids, they must be men she least fancies about her. Worthy, often, and sometimes with wealth and a grand title, but the duller of wit, the plainer of face, the better.

Not an inviting prospect.

'I'm going to remain a spinster and a virgin always, like Her Majesty the Queen.' I vow to my horrified mother, who would almost prefer the shrubbery.

❋ ❋ ❋

Raleigh was today appointed Lord Warden of the Stannaries. (Pity the poor tin miners, whose interests he's supposed to protect. He'll probably rob them blind.)

After the poem incident, he's gone back to treating me with polite indifference. Which, I tell myself as I respond in like manner, is exactly what I wish.

So why do I experience this vague sense of disappointment?

ROBERT CECIL

Whitehall Palace, Autumn, 1585

'Raleigh's to be made Lord Lieutenant of Cornwall, by royal command,' my father fumes, arriving back from an audience with the Queen and banging a pile of papers down on his desk. 'And she wants soon to create him Vice Admiral of the West! However many titles does the wretch aim to collect?'

I shrug uncomfortably, fresh and richer from a hand of cards Raleigh let me win. 'He tells me his ambition is to become a Privy Councillor.'

My father, a religious man who seldom swears, utters an oath. 'Over my dead body! Have you *nothing* on him, Robert?'

I shake my too-large head. 'Nothing yet.'

'He's definitely not gone further with the Throckmorton girl?'

I manage to keep the lilt from my voice. 'Definitely not.'

'Well, at least Her Majesty is beginning to value *you*. That's something, for which to be thankful.'

'Yes'

The Queen looks upon me kindly now – calls me her 'Elf' which I consider marginally better than 'Pygmy'. But she still hangs on her precious 'Water's' every word and he's earned another name among his sneering critics at Court. 'Sir Oracle', they call him and mutter in vexation because she will not allow her Oracle to cease clinging to her skirts and travel to the colony he's attempting to found in the New World, although she's bestowed on it the title of Virginia. He confided to me recently that he felt weak and insipid as his nickname Water, waving others off to the land of milk and honey discovered by his own scouts through his own efforts, then returning meekly to be the Queen's lap-dog.

'If only we could persuade her to pack him off to Virginia,' my father sighs, stroking his white beard. 'He might solve our problems by providing a hearty dinner for the New World savages.'

BESS

Whitehall Palace, Autumn, 1585

The flags are out! The trumpets sound! Sing loud in happy triumph!

Even if you're *not* sure of the words, which the other Maids and I most certainly are not, in this hastily-devised and rather silly celebratory masque in honour of Sir Richard Grenville's exploits to the New World.

Disguised as dark-skinned native women, our faces stained with walnut juice – all black wigged, furred gowned and befeathered head-banded - we brandish flower garlands and warble patriotic homage to Thetis, the Sea Goddess (Elizabeth Tudor, naturally, enthroned at the front of the audience). We lavishly salute her for piloting her sailors to Virginia, bringing us Christianity.

The Queen, who personally couldn't care less whether the New World savages turn Christian or not and would, surely, prefer them to remain pagan were she really a Greek goddess, applauds our antics enthusiastically – hastily followed by the rest of the Court and proud Grenville himself.

Raleigh's sun-bronzed relation has already performed *his* party piece – taken his drained Venetian wine-glass between his teeth, crushed it into fragments and swallowed them down. Ugh! He travelled to Virginia in place of 'Water' and is the hero of the hour after recently arriving back in Plymouth Harbour with riches galore. Not only has he successfully settled the new colonists on suitable, fertile land but he has snatched Spanish prizes on his way home – captured the poorly-armed Santa Maria, which 'happened' to be carrying a cargo of gold, silver, pearls, sugar and spices.

Rich pickings for the investors, among them Secretary Walsingham and the Queen, hence our present merriment.

And a new triumph for Sir Oracle, whose prestige has never been higher. Raleigh grins from ear to ear as jealous Lord Leicester is forced to congratulate him smilingly but with a murderous glint to his eye, his tall stepson, the young Earl of Essex, hovering awkwardly at his elbow, unsure whether to be gracious or surly.

Word has it that Leicester plans to take gangly young Essex along with him and his nephew, Sir Philip Sidney, to do battle against the Spaniards. They are being troublesome in the Netherlands and the Dutch need the aid of an English army.

'Perhaps he thinks to oust Raleigh by making a man of Essex - turning him into a suitable rival,' I suggest to Aud.

'An impossible task,' she giggles, handing me an embroidered napkin.

Still in our fur-trimmed costumes, we attend the Queen; arrange a goblet of small beer and a dish of her favourite comfits on a gilded table beside the royal chair, while the more lowly benches are cleared for general dancing and Her Majesty converses with Grenville, maybe asking for a lesson in crunching glass, which she should be good at, considering the sharpness of her tongue.

From the corner of my eye, I see Essex making his clumsy way towards me, but he is forestalled by Philip Sidney, who neatly side-steps him and bows exquisitely, his high-crowned damask bonnet sweeping the floor.

I hesitate,.

Devoted brother to the girl I dressed fashion-dolls with long ago (Mary Herbert, Countess of Pembroke – that tender-aged bride held up to me as an example), and not-so-devoted husband to another old friend, Frances (nee Walsingham), he has never been a favourite of mine. He's a demon on horseback in the tiltyard and as clever and poetical as Raleigh. But his complexion is off-putting. As a child, he caught the pox from his mother, who caught it nursing the Queen. And he takes himself so seriously – he is apt to lecture rather than converse. Boring!

Yet it seems churlish to refuse him since he makes hay, obviously, before sailing to bloody war (and tilting in dire earnest). Therefore I sigh as I sink into a curtsey, thinking unkindly that Philip should never wear red, it ill-becomes his pinched and pitted face.

'I enjoyed your masque, sweeting. It was very palatable,' breathes a soft Devonshire voice in my ear. Raleigh, in a flurry of cream satin, leading out the Countess of Warwick. He eyes me wickedly. 'But your costume is wrong, save the feathers in your hair. Did no-one tell you Virginian squaws cavort in their birthday suits? Now there's a sight I'd relish!'

My face, I'm aware, as we all spring into a galliard, out-scarlets Philip's doublet.

* * *

November 1585

It was my mother's oldest retainer, Joseph, who brought the letter. His lined face was ever transparent, so I knew before I opened it that it contained bad news.

My stepfather, Adrian Stokes, has now indeed taken sick and died. (Could Lord Leicester have been visiting a soothsayer who made error of her dates?) No mistake this time, alas, and no dark whispers of poison from any quarter.

Arthur and I are both granted permission to ride to Beaumanor for the funeral. Yet we are not our usual selves as we canter the frosty miles. We are a little strained and awkward together, unable to share our grief which seems muted, unreal; as if we betrayed too much emotion at the dress rehearsal and come dry-eyed to the performance.

Even as I watch the coffin being lowered beneath the flagstones of the chapel, I keep thinking that it must again be some bizarre blunder; expect warm, broad-shouldered Adrian to come striding suddenly in to join us from his precious stables where he sat me on my first decent pony and taught me to ride as proficiently as my brothers.

But he does not, of course. The estate now passes to his own thin, cold-mannered brother, who is already here to claim it. And suddenly my eyes stream embarrassingly as I bid farewell to the dogs and horses and falcons, to the small but pretty chamber which was always kept especially for me.

Kind Adrian has left me some remembrances; an elaborately carved bed and other furniture to be given to me on the occasion of my marriage (hah!) Also a fine gilt cup I coveted when I was small. More importantly, my mother is well provided for. She need never want for anything.

'You see, it is as I told you,' she finds time to say to me (callously, I feel) before she removes herself and my brother William to her London house and I return to Court and the Queen's Day tilts. 'A good marriage can leave a woman secure.'

※ ※ ※

August, 1586

Our security here at Court has been shaken to the core – I shall never breathe freely again! At any moment the Queen could be assassinated and take many of us with her!

The idiot Queen of Scots has yet again been involved in a Papist conspiracy to overthrow Elizabeth – together with a wretch named Babington who sought Elizabeth's murder and has come perilously near to carrying it out.

We are horror-stricken to learn his followers were actually discovered within the Royal Household! We might all have been daggered in our beds!

The Queen, the only one cool as a cucumber, has whisked us off to Windsor Castle. She says we'll feel safer here but we're still as nervy as a herd of deer, while, in the City, the bells ring and the bonfires blaze in thanksgiving for her safe delivery.

Babington and his cronies are to be despatched in the barbarous manner of my cousin Francis, and Raleigh, it is said, will be given Babington's estates and made richer than ever. Some say he helped Walsingham ensnare the traitors.

Elizabeth is forced at last to put Mary of Scotland on trial. But she has vowed, privately to us, her ladies, and openly to the Privy Councillors, never to execute an anointed Queen and a descendant of her own Tudor blood.

'She's getting soft as sugar paste in her old age,' snorts Aud Shelton. 'Respectable beheading's too good for the Scottish whore. As well as instigating all these plots she had her English husband murdered, remember, so she could marry her kilted lover. She should be hung, drawn and quartered along with the rest.'

'And her breasts cut off and burned in front of her!' agrees the normally gentle Meg Radcliffe. 'Elizabeth will never be safe while she lives and neither will we. When Lord Leicester returns from the Netherlands, he'll make the Queen see sense.'

But Leicester was not the first to return . . .

* * *

November 1586

'We've lost the most noble knight who ever lived,' sobs Aud Shelton.

We stand together on Tower Wharf, watching Sir Philip Sidney's ship dock from his final journey. Draped in black and with black sails, it contains his embalmed body. And we, of the mourning crowd come especially from Court, also wear black; clutch our cloaks tightly about us in the biting wind.

Blood red, he wore, when I danced with him. Symbolic? I am filled with guilty remorse for being reluctant to partner him in that last galliard. But how was I to know he'd be laid low by a Spanish musket?

'Why do men thirst for war?' hisses Lady Warwick in my ear, her teeth chattering. 'Women do not. Women have more sense, anticipating the pointless slaughter, the terrible loss of husbands, fathers, sons and brothers. Men only see the patriotism and the glory.'

Tell me what is glorious about riding out on foreign soil at the head of an army – being cheered, admired and trumpeted – and returning in a box?

The trumpets today play melancholy airs, mingle with the soulful wail of pipes and viols as Mary, Countess of Pembroke, white-faced and trembling and looking uncannily like a female, clear-skinned version of Philip, oversees, with Sir Walter Raleigh, her brother's coffin being lifted ashore.

I am only too conscious that I could now be mourning Arthur, who fought in the Netherlands in '78 and desperately tried to be part of this present scuffle. Thankfully, the Earl of Leicester is not a man to forget an injury (oh, that salad supper!) and brusquely turned him down. Arthur, to get over his disappointment at being allowed to live, spent last summer getting married to Anna Lucas and is now busily setting up home with her in her parents' house in Colchester. 'You'll be the next bride', everyone vowed to me at the wedding feast. I managed not to groan.

'Bess – thank you for coming.'

Frances, Lady Sidney, staggering under the weight of her outsize belly, is being helped on to terra firma; clasps my hand briefly as she passes. I squeeze her hand in return, trying to convey support. Small and dark and timid-seeming, she's amazed everyone by travelling all the way to Arnhem to nurse her wounded husband back to health, despite being months gone with her second child. Only to fail, of course, since the wound turned poisonous, leaving her with this morbid business of bringing back his corpse.

'He'll become a national hero now,' weeps Aud.

It seems he's one already for the wharf is thronged with ordinary black crows as well as us Court starlings. Respectful men and youths with hats doffed; tearful women and little maids throwing Christmas rose petals atop the passing coffin. No matter that they've only, most of them, known Philip from a distance – a shining, mounted figure processing through the streets before jousting on Accession Day. This particular day he represents all the young soldiers killed in the Netherlands and these humble tributes mean as much, if not more, than the shower of eloquent praises produced by the poet-courtiers, Raleigh among them.

Raleigh has hailed Philip as the 'Scipio, Cicero, and Petrarch of our time'; proclaimed, among other grand and lengthy things, that there, on the battle field

'.... didst thou vanish shame and tedious age,

Grief, sorrow, sickness and base fortune's might
Thy rising day saw never woeful night,
But passed with praise from off this worldly stage.'

Yes, I *have* copied it out.

At present, and as usual, Raleigh is much to the fore; bossily directing the men who shoulder the coffin, taking Mary of Pembroke's arm as she stumbles in her distress. His sombre black attire is brightened (naturally) by slashes of silver satin, by the enormous pearl and diamond buttons that fasten his doublet and sparkle on his elaborately frilled cuffs. In addition to the Babington estates he's been given land in Ireland – he can afford a few more jewels. Yet his tailor needs to improve the quality of his thread for, even as I watch, one of the doublet buttons pops off and falls to the ground – rolls steadily towards my feet.

Before I can bend to pick it up a ragged boy darts forward, quick as a flash, and snatches the prize; is about to pocket it when Raleigh turns and sees him. The boy freezes, pales, and I freeze also and catch my breath. I've seen beggar boys hanged for less. But Raleigh merely smiles his brilliant smile and turns away again, allowing the boy to disappear, much the richer, back into the crowd.

I rather like that. It provides one cheering moment in a dark and depressing day.

* * *

February, 1587

The Queen has signed Mary of Scotland's death warrant but, weeks later, will not allow it to be used.

Burghley, Walsingham, Leicester and the rest are all tearing their thinning hair – alternately begging or bullying her into final action but to no avail.

Her temper is foul and her language worse. Yesterday she slapped Aud Shelton for being slow to fasten her stomacher (Aud's face yet bears the mark); hurled a warming pan at me for bringing her the wrong wig. I ducked, but it damaged a tapestry.

If our nerves suffered over the campaign in the Netherlands - and they did - it was naught to what they suffer now. Not even Raleigh can coax a civil word from his 'Moon Goddess' who, when she is not screaming obscenities at her councillors, hides away in her bedchamber and will not be persuaded to ride, dance, hunt, hawk, make music, play at cards or even walk the gardens. Which means her Maids and Ladies cannot either.

We sit glumly about with our embroidery frames in whichever palace we occupy 'till we are driven colour blind by the brilliance of the thread, our conversation becoming shorter, sharper and more quarrelsome. Then, today, a door flies open and guards jump to attention as our Mistress emerges without warning, dressed for her afternoon ride.

Needles and silks cast carelessly aside, we leap up, like a flurry of demented swans, and rush to change. By the skin of our teeth we make it to the stables in time to accompany her.

The joy of it – galloping across the expanse of Greenwich Park in an exhilarating wind! My mount is faster than the one to which I am accustomed (no time to choose our favourite mares) but even so I cannot keep up with the Queen who is flying ahead, her hat askew, her troubles left behind in the council chamber. Or so she thinks.

She is riding recklessly, closely followed by Raleigh, then Essex, laughing over her shoulder at Leicester, sadly outpaced.

When suddenly, alongside me - a figure in Tudor livery astride a sweating grey. He flies past Raleigh and Essex, trying to catch up with the Queen who sees him and slows her mount, gesturing to us all to do the same. As our horses stamp and snort and prance, the man happily pants out his news.

Glad tidings, your Majesty! The Whore of Scots has today been brought to the block in Fotheringay Castle!'

I am so amazed I gasp aloud and many others with me. All these weeks Elizabeth has anguished over that hideous death-warrant. And now someone (who?) has dared take the decision out of her hands!

The Queen knows who. Oh, the fireworks as she swivels in her saddle and berates a red-faced Leicester, who stammers something along the lines of the biggest threat to her Majesty's throne having been removed. She almost spits as she curses him and the rest of her council (who, luckily for them, are not present).

White with anger she rants, raves, then finally weeps; wheels her mount ferociously about and heads back at breakneck speed to the Palace, everyone hastily following suit.

Everyone except me, whose spirited bay mare takes fright at the commotion; thunders off in the opposite direction and, being impossible to control, leaps log, stream, ditch, before eventually throwing me over her head and on to mine.

And who forsakes the royal party and gallops after me? Gathers me up, helpless and dazed: props me against a tree like an undignified rag doll? Loosens my ruff, my cloak, my bodice? Prods me all over to see if I've broken bones? Mops the small wound on my forehead and waves his perfumed gloves beneath my nose until I cough and splutter, gasp for breath?

To add to my embarrassment (I am an expert horsewoman who prides herself on never falling), Raleigh is unbelievably tender and kind. He lifts me on to his own fine, jet black stallion as carefully as if I am the Queen herself, leaps up behind me and trots me gently back to the Palace. We'll send a groom, he says, for my borrowed mare, who looks to be heading full tilt for Land's End. Meanwhile, I must see a doctor when I get back; make sure I've done no damage.

Damage? There is damage aplenty!

I am disturbed by the nearness of his body pressed close to mine; by the warmth of his arms about me, holding the reins; by the heady, familiar smell of musk, rose and ambergris arising from more personal areas now than the beautiful gloves upon his hands…

When we reach the edge of the park, I insist he sets me down so I can continue to the Palace on foot. Imagine the faces of Aud and the others should I return in such a fashion, held tight against Raleigh's chest.

He complies readily, dismounts and swings me to the ground. But instead of releasing me, he holds me for a moment, looks down into my eyes with that wonderful intense gaze and says softly; 'Bess – little Bess – thank God you were not badly hurt! When I saw you lying there among the snowdrops ….' He bends and kisses me, long and hard upon the lips. And before I have time to recover, to summon breath to protest, he is up in the saddle and gone, clattering round to the stables without a backward glance.

He sends one of the Queen's physicians to me in the Maids' quarters – old Doctor Lopez, a Portuguese Jew (turned Christian, of course) with a lovely bedside manner - who patches up my cut, proclaims me fit but shaken (small wonder) and in need of rest. This time I find the words to protest and it is Lady Warwick's turn to insist. She herself helps me undress, ignoring Kate's twitterings and flutterings.

Beneath my pillow I discover a poem (how on earth did he smuggle it there?):

Now what is love? I pray thee tell.
It is that fountain and that well
Where pleasure and repentance dwell.
It is perhaps that sauncing bell,
That tolls all in to Heaven or Hell;
And this is love, as I hear tell.

Yet what is love? I pray thee say.
It is a work on holy-day;
It is December matched with May;
When lusty blades in fresh array,
Hear ten months after of the play:
And this is love, as I hear say.

Yet what is love? I pray thee sayn.
It is a sunshine mixed with rain;
It is a tooth-ache, or like pain;
It is a game where non doth gain;
The lass saith no, and would full fain:
And this is love, as I hear sayn.

Yet what is love? I pray thee say,
It is a yea, it is a nay,
A pretty kind of sporting fray;
It is a thing will soon away;
Then take the vantage while you may:
And this is love, as I hear say

.

Yet what is love? I pray thee show.
A thing that creeps, it cannot go;
A prize that passeth to and fro;
A thing for one, a thing for mo;
And he that proves must find it so:
And this is love, sweet friend, I trow.

Pinned to the poem is a note, asking me to meet its author. In secret. Tomorrow.

* * *

'Take the vantage while you may ....'

The arrogance of the man! Does he truly expect me to rush into his arms at the snap of his bejewelled fingers? To sneak away and meet him in a cold, dusty, pokey little hidey-hole of a disused chamber beneath the Small Gallery stairs?

I decide I will teach him a lesson; fail to turn up and let him cool his heels and his ardour waiting in humiliating vain. I snigger with satisfaction as I picture him impatiently pacing, should there be room enough to pace.

Yet, surprisingly, he seems not to take offence. Merely persists with more poems and more notes, all appearing riskily and mysteriously under my pillow, expressing his undying hope. So that I am forced to go eventually. Not for any romantic reason, you understand, but simply to inform him that his pursuit is pointless. To order him to discontinue it; to end this foolishness.

And, naturally, our temperaments being what they are, it is not the end but the beginning . . .

* * *

When Philip Sidney is buried in St. Paul's Cathedral, given a magnificent funeral and laid to rest in a vault of the Lady Chapel, my thoughts dwell not on the prayers and tributes of the slain hero but on the merits of Sir Walter Raleigh, who walked in the mourning procession and whose very name, now, sets my pulse a-race.

Suddenly I understand how Anna feels about Arthur, how Frances Sidney felt about Philip; can think of nothing but my stolen moments with Walter. For, of course, they have to be stolen – engineered with the utmost secrecy. How else can we get to know each other when the Queen will not even allow him to dance with her Maids without permission? And on the rare occasions she grants this, she recalls him to her side before the music stops, in case he begins to enjoy himself.

My feelings have changed, but the situation has not. There can be no future in our relationship. But it makes no difference.

Dazzled, bewitched, joyous, I walk on air – live only for the day and refuse to think about a possible unpleasant 'morrow.

* * *

'No woman has ever appealed to me as you do,' whispers Walter, in our draughty little chamber that is scarcely more than a cupboard.

Am I naïve to believe him? To push to the back of my mind thoughts of other Court ladies who have boasted of receiving his billets doux? Shamelessly, I enjoy his practised kisses and caresses; am amazed and a little frightened by my eager response. But I do not forget the warning sounded in that first poem beneath my pillow:

> Lusty blades in fresh array
> Hear ten months after of the play

It seems I have not completely lost my wits for I never permit him to go too far (no shrubbery for me!)

Meanwhile, I am also cautious in other ways. I boast to no-one and select each alibi with care. Walter is equally cunning so, miraculously, no tongues wag about us. In a Court rife with gossip, our romance goes undetected.

ROBERT CECIL

Cecil House, April, 1587

'We can afford to bide our time,' my father says, helping himself to manchet bread.

We breakfast at his London house since he is in disgrace for sanctioning the disposal of Mary of Scotland. Before banning him from Court our Gracious Majesty, the Virgin Queen, hurled her slipper at him in fury – called him, among other things, 'traitor', 'false dissembler', and 'wicked wretch'.

None of which greatly upset him since he's confident she'll soon forgive him and summon him back. Her right arm since she came to the throne, he knows, she knows, and I know that he's indispensable.

'It will pay us to be patient – no need to rush,' he continues, pouring us both wine. He likes to dine at the long table in the great hall, in the old-fashioned style, with his entire household about him. But when we are both at home the first meal of the day is a private affair – he permits no long-eared servant to wait upon us as we talk. 'The longer the seduction continues, Robin, the harsher the retribution. 'Water' plays into our hands at present. Now that he's finally taken the plunge we'll let him swim awhile. Before we watch him drown.'

BESS

Whitehall Palace, April 1587

It's not only the Queen, now, who keeps a possessive eye on her West-Country favourite when we socialise in the Privy Gallery.

'Which of the Court ladies has Raleigh dallied with in the past?' I whisper to Aud Shelton over shovel-board one evening.

Audrey shrugs; darts a look towards where Walter gambles noisily at Primero with the Queen, little Robin Cecil and Arthur Gorges. 'Too many to relate.'

A roar of laughter from the Queen's table and he glances up. Our eyes meet, but he looks beyond me, not daring even to smile.

Love is a sunshine mixed with rain –

It is a tooth-ache, or like pain

He has obviously experienced such torment before, but it is new to me.

✳ ✳ ✳

Arthur and Anna have a healthy daughter. They are delighted, but my mother and Anna's parents were all hoping for a boy.

This latter attitude I find depressing. Girls count for so little, the marriage-market apart. And some of us disappoint even there.

I despatch a courier to Colchester with a pearl and lace cap I have worked for my new niece, and a letter of warm congratulation. Before the fellow departs, I add a footnote regretting that the Queen, still in a fury over the death of Mary of Scotland, refuses to spare me for the Christening.

Which is only part lie. The Queen indeed still rages –she's banished poor, loyal old Burghley from Court - but I have neglected to ask her for leave. Walter cannot spare me, or at least says he does not wish to, and I fear to be absent lest someone more attractive slides into my slippers.

※ ※ ※

Walter has been appointed Captain of the Queen's personal Guard!

Since several eminent men were hoping desperately for the honour, this has caused the usual surreptitious uproar about the Court. But no one dares oppose the appointment openly and Walter is contemptuous of the wild mutterings as to how he's achieved it.

'If any man accuses me to my face, I will answer him with my mouth,' he shrugs to me. 'But my tail is good enough for those who slander me behind my back.'

He is flattered by this latest proof of royal esteem, but I regard it as a mixed blessing. The post, though unsalaried, carries with it enormous trust and prestige, thus proving Elizabeth has no suspicion of our dalliance. But Walter's leisure hours have been short enough as it is, now they will be further curtailed. The Queen's Captain is expected to be near his sovereign at all times. His men (all young Adonises, chosen for their looks) protect her person from poison and the assassin's knife or pistol, their diligence increased since the Babington episode. They escort her to chapel, deliver her messages and surround her on public occasions. If he was her lap-dog before, Walter Raleigh is her right arm now. He boasts to me that he has better access to her than most of her Privy councillors, one of whom he aims soon to become.

With a mixture of fear and amusement, I stand demurely by as Elizabeth admires him in the splendid tawny and black uniform her purse has provided; strokes the rich material flirtatiously; smirks up at him and murmurs how much the colour suits him. If only she knew that, overnight, her precious Oracle has become mine.

I even catch myself occasionally spouting his views to the other Ladies, under the banner of my own flag, of course, since his opinions are clever.

Walter is, in truth, somewhat alarmingly clever. Our relationship is not all a-hugging and a-kissing. We talk much, as lovers do, each time discovering a little more about each other. I tell him of my upbringing at Beddington, my uncle's house, at Beaumanor with my stepfather– funny little anecdotes from my childhood which seem to amuse him. He tells me of his boyhood home in Devon, which his late father rented and which he is attempting to buy. (Surprising, to me, that he should want to – the proud Sir Walter Raleigh, tenant of splendid Durham House, owner of vast castles in Ireland. Why trouble to purchase the reed-thatched farmhouse where he was born and breeched?) But it seems he's a sentimentalist.

'I've been asking the fool of an owner to name his price for the past three years or more, but he won't discuss the matter,' he growls, clenching his teeth on the stem of his silver-barrelled pipe and kicking at a stone like a sullen boy while we stroll, now, in our quiet little wood. He knows all the lonely spots ideal for courting. I dare not let myself wonder how many others he has escorted down these paths. 'I would rather seat myself there than any place else, Bess. There's nowhere in the world like Hayes Barton. I always think of it bathed in sunshine. And I dream, sometimes, of being a tiny boy again, scrambling after my brother Carew along the muddy path that led us through Hayes Wood to our first sight, smell and sound of the sea.'

The sea. His great passion. Not for the ocean itself, he explains, confessing with a grin that he gets sea-sick, but for the promise it holds of undiscovered lands beyond its horizon.

'Lands to be conquered, Bess, in the name of Queen Elizabeth. Lands to increase our wealth and broaden our knowledge.'

His thirst for knowledge seems insatiable. All my brothers, save William, attended university and are well-versed in the classics. But Walter buys every new volume the moment it is published – on astronomy, chemistry, geometry, mathematics, navigation, geography, history, science, medicine, philosophy, literature – my head aches from the variety. He never sleeps, he tells me, more than five hours out of four and twenty because he rushes to his desk before the sun is up each morn to write or study or both.

'I've seen your Durham House study,' I tell him, a touch diffidently, 'from the outside, at least. It was pointed out to me once, from a barge upon the Thames.' (By nosey Aud, of course.) 'It is situated in that high, rounded turret that overlooks the river.'

'The room at the very top,' he nods. 'With a view that sweeps right down to Deptford, where I can spy my ships ride anchor. It's a view to lift the spirits, Bess; to make mundane thoughts take wing!' He waves his silver pipe expressively and I smother a cough, receiving a blast from the foul-smelling weed therein. 'The discourse that goes on in that chamber you would scarce believe....'

And I would not, perhaps, approve of, for his enemies condemn it as 'Godless' talk; call his bosom friend, the Earl of Northumberland, a 'wizard'; refer to his astronomer/henchman Harriot as 'that Conjurer!'

Yet their activities sound innocent enough: -

'Tom Harriot conducts school there, also. As brilliantly as he performs everything else,' Walter continues. 'You could hear a pin fall, he's so eloquent ....'

He puffs contentedly at his precious lighted weed, inhaling the nasty fumes as if they are nectar from the Gods. John Hawkins discovered tobacco more than twenty years ago but no-one was much interested until the ubiquitous Harriot brought back a clay pipe from Virginia, and taught Walter the native fashion of smoking it. Where the Queen's favourite leads, many follow, and Arthur tells me that tobacco pipes of all sizes and materials are fast appearing in men's mouths everywhere, not merely at Court.

'School?' I query, blinking away the smoke. 'You allow children up to your sanctum?'

He laughs. 'Among my books, maps and scientific instruments? Never! Tom teaches the arts of navigation and mathematics to my pilots and captains. When he's not braving the ocean himself ....'

He has already explained to me that Harriot's exacting work, in travelling first with the scouts then with the settlers and cataloguing everything his greedy eyes devoured, from weather, coastline and vegetation to flora, fauna and native life, has been invaluable in their exploration of the New World.

'It makes our efforts different, Bess! Scores of Spaniards, of humble fishermen, even, have been back and forth through those very waters for years. But there's been no detailed record of their findings, such as Harriot's written Brief and True Report -which is anything but brief - and my artist John White's drawings. Nothing to show doubters and other would-be-settlers that it's no Fairytale Land we speak of, but something solid and real and worthwhile.'

Yet, disappointingly, his colony has failed. Those first brave adventurers proved not so brave after all; quarrelled among themselves, made enemies of the savages, then scuttled home gladly with Sir Francis Drake, who was out annoying the Spaniards.

Not that Walter blames them. 'The supplies and reinforcements I sent were delayed at sea. The settlers became disheartened. How can I make the Queen realise I need to lead these expeditions myself? I need to be there in person, to enforce sensible rules, raise morale and maintain peace with the natives.'

I keep silent, not wishing, any more than the Queen, for him to risk life or limb.

I love, though, to hear his tales of Virginia, handed down (naturally) from Thomas Harriot. And, even more, of a lost city all of gold called El Dorado, described to him by a Spaniard he once took prisoner.

He weaves stories more enchanting than any I've found in a book and, I admit, they do have the ring of fairy tales to me.

'Such a wondrous, glorious city, Bess, thought to lie twixt the basins of the Orinoco and Amazon rivers. And it's chieftain and namesake bathes every day in gold dust ....'

I love to watch him when he enthuses thus, his dark eyes sparkling, his face alight as my brother William's at Yuletide.

* * *

When Walter's second band of colonists - eighty-nine men, seventeen women, and eleven children - boldly set sail for the New World to found the wondrous, glorious City of Raleigh (whose chieftain and namesake remained at home to bathe every day in his Queen's approval), I was not at Court to welcome him back from Plymouth Harbour.

Fate found me in Colchester, attending the funeral of Arthur and Anna's baby daughter in the church where she was so recently baptised.

'Arthur and his wife are young,' Audrey consoled me, when I returned. 'They will have other children.'

'But she only lived a month,' I was raw from the recollection of Arthur's stricken face as he carried the tiny coffin. 'And my sister-in-law suffered a long, agonising confinement to bear her. What was the point to it all?'

'New souls are delicate, that's why so many children die. Some say they mislike this wicked world and make their way quickly back to Heaven.'

I tore off my riding dress without waiting for Kate's help, threw it angrily on the bed. 'She had cause to mislike me, the aunt who never troubled to visit her – who wriggled out of attending the poor mite's christening.'

'Did you?' Audrey's narrow face sharpened with surprise and interest. 'Why?'

Because I preferred to be in Walter Raleigh's arms, I almost told her. But common sense prevailed and she jumped to her own conclusion.

'You dreaded feeling jealous of your brother's happiness! Oh Bess, some great lord will ask for your hand soon, despite your lack of fortune.'

I attempted a grim smile. 'He'll be turned down if he dares, I do assure you.'

She smiled back, disbelieving. 'Whoever he may be?'

'Whoever he may be.'

'You don't mean that.'

I did. I do. For any suitor will be other than Sir Walter Raleigh, who cannot and will not dare.

✻ ✻ ✻

'Marry me,' says Walter (in a shrubbery of all places, beyond the formal gardens at Greenwich Palace.)

Naught of the asking about it. It is a command, no less.

I draw back from his arms and stare at him, squinting in the sun's glare. He does not jest. His eyes gleam with excitement, with intensity. My heart pounds.

'You know I cannot!'

His dark brows lower. 'Why not?'

'The Queen will never give her permission.'

'No. So we'll marry without it.'

I gasp. 'In secret, you mean? Oh no, Walter, I dare not.'

He grasps my hands so tight it hurts. 'Bess, we cannot go on like this! I am a man, no lovesick boy! I already serve one teasing, playful virgin, I have no room for another. I need a woman of flesh and blood – one I can truly pleasure and who can pleasure me in return…. And since you will not give yourself fully to me out of wedlock, which I respect, then wedlock it must be.'

So this is his sole reason for wanting to marry me. I say tartly, stung; 'There are other things of importance in a marriage besides pleasures of the flesh.'

He tilts up my face and smiles his devastating smile.

'Of course. And I want them all. Your contrary companionship, a shared house and gardens. Children – your children. Eventually. Though any children will be obliged to spring from those aforementioned pleasures of the flesh.'

I jerk my head away. 'And how long would this 'eventually' be, may I ask? How long after this secret marriage of ours would you tell the Queen?'

He shrugs impatiently. 'Not long afterwards. 'Twould depend. She values my opinions, as you know, and I've the support of Robin Cecil who has the support of his father. The elder Cecil has even been obliged to ask me for a favour or two. I believe they will indeed make me a Privy Councillor soon. And once I have a position of real trust, real value, Elizabeth will not cast me off lightly, marriage or no. She's too good a politician herself to discard the ministers she respects. She might be annoyed ....'

'She will be furious!'

'Furious, then. But not for long. It will be in her own best interests, in the best interests of her government, to forgive us. To accept our union.'

He makes it sound simple. But it is not.

Worriedly, I pluck a leaf from a plant taller than both of us, begin to shred it with precision.

'She may never make you a Privy Councillor,' I point out.

'She will.' He looks smug. 'I am confident of it.'

'Already you are not in quite such unique high favour. My Lord of Essex commands much of her attention.'

It seems we laughed too scornfully at the Earl of Leicester's attempts to push his red-headed stepson forward. They were merely a little premature, since Essex has come storming back from the Netherlands a very different figure from the awkward adolescent who left – handsome, sure of himself, a war hero. The same difficult-to-please Londoners who spit after Walter's coach cheer Essex when he rides through the streets while Queen Elizabeth, of course, is delighted with him.

'The upstart has competition!' crow Walter's enemies.

'But Her Majesty still prefers full-grown lap-dogs to fawning puppies,' he says easily, now. 'And do you not see, Bess, how the Queen's new passion for Essex can work to our advantage? Already it leaves me more freedom to come and go as I please in my off-duty hours. Let the 'Puppy' provide that airy-fairy aura of romance and pretend-courtship I, as the years go by, am finding more difficult to sustain. Let Essex supply the sugary poetry, the endless stream of flattery, while I move on to more important things ....'

'Like marriage. And eminence in the Privy Council. Both, I presume, of equal importance?'

'Yes. Why frown so? I am already a politician, do you doubt my ability to become a statesman?'

'I doubt the Queen's predictability when it comes to choosing her ministers. And I fear you are underestimating the extent of her anger when she hears of your secret wedding.'

'*When* she hears? Then you agree to it?'

'No I do not! Let us wait until you are made a Privy Councillor if it is so much safer.'

'But that may not be for months ....'

'You said it would be soon.'

He flushes dangerously. 'Bess, if you are deliberately trying to anger me, you are succeeding. I had thought you would be pleased – excited. Perhaps you do not *want* to marry me.'

Hurt gives an edge to my voice. He has not once mentioned the word 'love'; not today or previously - only in his poetry which is not, somehow, quite the same. 'I certainly do not want a ceremony behind locked doors, where the priest may not even be genuine and the validity of the marriage can be discounted later, as many another has been.'

'God's blood!'

His hand flies to his sword hilt. His nostrils flare, his eyes blaze. Were I a man, I'd be a corpse!

'So you think I would prove dishonourable?' He almost spits with rage. 'Pretend to marry you, have my "wicked way", then wriggle out of responsibility?'

I glance away uncomfortably. 'That is not what I am saying ....'

'It is exactly what you are saying, wench!' He grasps my chin again, but with a hard, cruel hand, forcing me to look at him. 'I give you an ultimatum. Agree, now, to marry me in secret as soon as can be arranged – you yourself can book the precious priest – or we go our separate ways.'

I am trembling with panic. 'Walter, I cannot! I have not the courage! You may be forgiven because of the Queen's regard for you, but I would not be. I would be banished from Court....'

'So a merry life at Court means more to you than having me for husband?'

'No, of course not, but ...'

'No "buts", Mistress Throckmorton. You have made your choice. I will pester you no more.'

He releases me, bows with exaggerated formality, rams his Captain's hat back on his head then strides off furiously through the undergrowth, the greenery shivering in his wake.

Tears of anger, bewilderment and frustration gather in my eyes as, somewhat fittingly, it begins to pour with rain.

✣ ✣ ✣

Such a miserable summer. At first I wait eagerly for a poem or a note, penned in his erratic script, eloquently contrite, backing down. But as the days and weeks pass without the appearance of either, I begin to accept that his words were not merely uttered in the heat of the moment. We truly have 'gone our separate ways'.

The difficulty is that our particular ways cannot be separate enough. We are obliged to meet face to face daily, thanks to our respective duties. When we are forced to speak to each other, we do so in the coolly formal manner we have always adopted in public, avoiding each other's eyes. I am sometimes sure I feel his burning gaze upon my back, but as I refuse to give him the satisfaction of seeing me glance round, I never know whether or not I imagine it.

✱ ✱ ✱

Whitehall Palace. Autumn 1587

'Bess Throckmorton, you are croaking like a dying frog! What ails you? Surely you do not weep?'

Back from (for me) a wretched Royal Progress, we make music in the Privy Gallery after our mid-day dinner. Or, at least, cease to make it as the Queen lifts her fingers impatiently from the virginals and frowns upon me.

Walter still ignores me and the song the Queen has chosen, expects me to sing without a tremor to her accompaniment on the virginals and Aud Shelton's lute, is Walter's *Farewell False Love*, newly set to music by Chapel Royal organist William Byrd.

Of course I weep, who would not?

I swallow. 'I am sorry, your Majesty, I suffer badly from a head cold.'

'Then why did you not say so, stupid wench, instead of ruining our tone? Audrey, take over the singing. Penelope, take over the lute. Bess, go and rest yourself until supper time.'

'Thank you, your Majesty.'

* * *

Instead of resting, I engage in a better distraction from melancholy, for, on leaving the Royal Presence, I all but trip over my brother Arthur, lurking in the corridor, hoping to see me. We embrace warmly. His duties at Court are only occasional since his marriage and I've missed him sorely.

He peers at me, frowning. 'Tears on your cheeks? Has the Queen been unkind again?'

'No more than usual,' I shrug, doing her an injustice. 'How is Anna?'

His wife, he tells me gloomily, has been depressed and ill since the death of their little daughter – and he proceeds to give me such luridly intimate details of her illness and the physician's bleedings and various attempted cures that I begin to feel decidedly off-colour myself.

To divert him and cheer us both, since he too has a free afternoon, I suggest a visit to the new Rose Playhouse, recently built. 'The performance to be seen there is good, people say. Unusual.'

Arthur is taken aback. He can be a little stuffy over some things, and says he is not sure he approves of ladies attending public playhouses – especially the Rose, which is situated across the river in Bankside, Southwark, home of the bull and bear-baiting (and the stews, housing the whores, which he delicately omits to mention).

'Alas,' he demurs, 'the play is not really suitable. It may be a little – violent.'

'Arthur,' I laugh, taking his arm. 'Have I not watched bear-baiting with the Queen?' (and been secretly sickened by it). 'Do I not go hunting? Hawking? I'm hardly likely to faint at the sight of theatrical blood!'

* * *

We find the new playhouse disappointingly similar to its two older rivals in Shoreditch and Bishopsgate. Wooden in structure, the main part open to the skies, it has the usual well-cushioned Lord's Rooms, the tiered, covered galleries for the middle-class, a yard that slopes stage-wards for the benefit of the groundlings and a shallow stage that juts out like a scaffold and faces southeast to catch maximum daylight.

But the play! It takes away our breath! The verse/speeches soar and the story is gripping. Tamburlaine, the central figure, played by a striking actor called Edward Alleyn, with a thrillingly powerful voice, begins as a Scythian shepherd and rises to be a mighty monarch who, for his tyranny in war, is termed the Scourge of God. He is desperately ambitious and grotesquely cruel. The play seems to delight in his excesses and I have to school myself many times not to flinch. His one saving grace, for me, is his love for his lady, Zenocrate. (Would that I could be loved so faithfully.)

The audience is rapt; even the groundlings, apart from cheering on the violence, are mostly silent. Yet my concentration wavers suddenly and the culprit sits near to us – Sir Walter Raleigh, resplendent in lilac damask – further along our row in the upper Lord's Room..

My face, thankfully, is hidden, since Arthur insisted I wear a large, feature-concealing mask for respectability. But if, while fluttering my fan, I turn my head slightly to the left, I can clearly watch Walter watching the action as, sitting between his cousin Arthur Gorges and Robert Cecil, he smokes his inevitable pipe, his brow furrowed in concentration.

So much for dispelling melancholy! Edward Alleyn has lost his magnetic appeal. I cannot stop picturing Walter as he will surely be later, discussing all he now sees and hears with his companions – but not with me.

I long to leave but am trapped here, pretending to enjoy myself for Arthur's sake, clapping, gasping, groaning with the rest. Until, at long last, the final scene is enacted with promise of the marriage, naturally, of Tamburlaine and Zenocrate, and we all rise to our feet, shouting our appreciation.

'Marvellous!' enthuses Arthur. 'Bravo!'

I murmur to him that I am surprised Tamburlaine did not die at the end, since most of the other characters did, and he replies that he thinks there is to be a second part written.

'Raleigh will know,' he says and, to my dismay, makes to go over to him.

I hang on his arm, slowing him down. 'I have to return to Court,' I plead. 'To the Queen'

But now Robert Cecil is bowing before me, sweeping off his hat to display his thick brown hair, smiling his sweet smile. He really has an attractive face, such a shame he's so deformed. Some say his nurse dropped him as a baby, others swear he was a changeling, substituted by wicked fairies. He enquires did I enjoy the performance, which he thought brilliant. I reply that I did indeed, and agree over its brilliance.

'The blank verse, for me,' he says in his soft voice, 'possessed the haunting quality of music.'

'For me also,' I assure him, and after a few more pleasantries we turn to leave. But not before the little hunchback presses a folded paper into my hand.

'A love note,' he whispers, 'From our mutual friend.'

✻ ✻ ✻

'I'll wed you as soon as you wish,' I gasp breathlessly to Walter between kisses, in a dusty little store-room at Whitehall Palace. After we have been through the timeless dialogue of all lovers making up a quarrel: - 'It was my fault, I was thoughtless, selfish....'

'No, mine. I said things I did not mean...'

'Hush, sweetheart, hush!' He holds me close. Such relief to be in his arms again. 'I love you more than life itself, but you were right to beg caution, we must go on as before for a while. Meantime – wear this for my good intent ....' He slips a huge, ornate emerald on to the third finger of my right hand. 'A stone plundered from the Spaniards and set by Peter Vanlore, the best goldsmith in London.'

I gasp – twirl the lovely thing to catch the light from our single candle. 'It's beautiful! But when will we ...?'

'When the time is right we'll decide together on a wedding date, whisk that ring from your right hand to your left.. Just now we'd best slip out though a garden door – walk and converse in the frosty air – if you are to be a virginal bride.'

Reaching the protection of a leafy arbour our love-making, this time, takes us further than ever before. Yet it is Walter who comes to his senses first and calls a halt. Leaving me trembling with frustration and not a little alarm. I am not sure I can hold out until he becomes a trusty Councillor and is given permission to wed.

* * *

November, 1587

'Of course you have our permission, my dear Bess,' purrs the Queen. She raises me from my knees with her own slender white hands, brushes my cheek with her over-painted lips.

My eyes are drawn to the motto on her personal arms above the royal throne: Semper Eadem (Ever the Same). Hah!

'We pray you find Lady Throckmorton in ruder health than your brother leads you to expect,' she goes on affectionately. 'We've always liked and admired your mother, you know. She fought like a tigress for your father when he was our Ambassador in France and wished to come home. She forced us to listen to her.'

(My mother always says the Queen was deaf to her endless pleas – kept Father abroad the longer because she'd dared to ask for his return.)

The sparkling emeralds about Elizabeth's throat, in her ears and scattered over her lavish white satin gown, make me guiltily conscious of my betrothal ring and I instinctively tuck it out of sight. Which is ridiculous since I wear Walter's jewel on the wrong finger and with several other rings and she can have no idea of its meaning.

'A woman of spirit, Anne,' she continues, still talking of my mother, 'you are very like her, Bess.'

I? Like my mother? I struggle not to look horrified and feel immediately disloyal to my well-intentioned parent. Especially if she is seriously ill. Which I doubt. One cannot rely on Arthur's judgement. Since the death of his little daughter, he has become an alarmist on the subject of health. Hopefully, the trouble will prove no more than a bout of the ague that afflicts her regularly.

✽ ✽ ✽

I am sick with grief and guilt. How did I not notice she was fading away? When I saw her last at Court, I remarked on her thinness and she told me she was deliberately eating sparingly. 'I cannot abide fat older women,' she'd said in her bracing fashion. Why did I believe her?

We bury her beside my father in the Church of St. Katherine Cree, in Aldgate – close by Throckmorton House, which now passes to my brother Thomas.

'Why did I not visit her more often?' I groan to Arthur.

He looks at me ruefully. 'Perhaps because it was a relief to be away from that searching gaze which detected so many shortcomings, real and imagined.'

Perhaps. I always disappointed her – disappointed them both, since my father had wanted a family of sons and my mother had yearned for a fluffy, dainty, submissive puppet she could manipulate, and marry off, with ease.

Will her soul, hopefully in a better place and able to see all things, be pleased about Walter and me? Or will her bones twist and turn with everlasting annoyance in their earthly grave?

I find that she has left me her gowns and her personal linen, none of which will fit, and her considerable collection of jewels. If the Queen notices my emerald, I can now pretend it has come from my mother.

I offer to help Arthur arrange the funeral, but he needs no assistance. With his customary efficiency, he attends to every detail, which includes ensuring the Throckmorton House servants all have black gowns to wear and that my brothers Robert, Thomas and William are able to be present. Nicholas is in Italy, on his grand educational tour, so the news has not yet caught up with him, while poor William cannot seem to grasp what has happened, however many times he is told. Inside the church, he asks me brightly when our Lady Mother is coming home. 'When, Bessie? When?'

Arthur assures me he will now look after William and deal with my mother's remaining practicalities, the payment of her household's wages, her debts and other legacies.

'Her last words to me urged me to find you a husband,' he says worriedly. 'But I will not, just yet, unless you wish it.'

Just yet!

I give him my best scowl. 'I most certainly do not wish it!'

How I wish I could tell him about Walter. But dare not.

* * *

Continuing with my duties at Court, again I am prone to sudden attacks of weeping.

How spineless I've become! The Queen is kind and I experience a rush of tenderness towards her. Losing a mother, it seems, is traumatic at any age, and she's been a long while without hers.

But the one person who can comfort me is absent.

'Raleigh has gone to Southampton,' Aud Shelton reports, 'to meet his colonist leader, John White, who has returned to England to collect supplies for the City of Raleigh. And Leicester is resigning his post of Master of the Horse, which the Queen is giving to Essex. Which won't please Raleigh....'

Indeed it won't. But how dreary the days without him; how brilliant the morning of his return....

Which quickly clouds over. We're quite unable to meet since he's busier than ever, frantically riding to Plymouth and back, rushing all over the country on missions for the Queen. And Governor White is forced to delay sailing with his supplies for no ships are allowed, now, out of English waters. Not with this threat from Spain . . .

ROBERT CECIL

Greenwich Palace, January,1588

As I understand it, war with Spain has been inevitable for years. King Philip believes he has a claim to the English throne through his ancestor, John of Gaunt. When, as a prince, he married our Queen Mary and got a foothold here, helped her 'shepherd' us back to Rome by means of Smithfield bonfires, he no doubt thought it was for good.

But when Mary died and Elizabeth took her place, refusing his hand in marriage, he was forced to slink away, smarting, and watch us turn Protestant again. Now our execution of the papist Queen of Scots has given him an excuse to strike. He vows to punish us for our 'heretic faith' with the fires of his inquisition – to do away with Elizabeth and put his own daughter on the throne in her place.

Elizabeth, though, refuses to accept the inevitable. Tries, desperately, to prevent it. 'Peace,' she cries to my father, back in his rightful place at her side, 'we must strive for peace.'

I have therefore just returned from the Netherlands, discussing peace terms with the commander of the Spanish forces, the Duke of Palma. My father arranged for me to go as an observer – unofficial – as part of my education. Lord Derby headed the mission, but with a crafty show of deference I managed to make my presence felt; strove to prove I have an eloquent tongue as well as a crooked back. Alas, all to no avail. Philip is set on invasion.

Dispirited, we sailed back. To hustle, bustle, excitement and fear.

The Queen remains outwardly calm and so does my father. But behind closed doors the voices of her councillors rise sharp and quarrelsome as they argue the best course of action or defence.

' I'm told the astronomical signs are bad,' my father sighs, as we walk slowly in the privy garden - he limping from gout and I dragging my weak foot. 'That this year of 1588 brings a conjunction of the planets Saturn, Jupiter and Mars – strong portent of disaster.'

Like the Queen, he is a man of peace and so am I. But this is a time for the war-mongers to flourish.

'Her Majesty suggested Raleigh be admitted to the Privy Council,' he says. 'But I convinced her otherwise. He is, however, to join the Council of War in an advisory position.'

I stifle my sigh of relief. No-one in their right mind can deny the Oracle's advice is badly needed.

BESS

Greenwich Palace, February, 1588

'Marry me,' I beg Walter, when at last we meet again in our dusty little cupboard- room, 'before the Armada comes.' 'I want to be your wife. In case ... in case ...

He's hurried here direct from the Council of War, of which he's a valued member - another upward rung, he hopes, on the Privy Council ladder - and is leaving for the West Country almost at once. Unfamiliar in practical travelling attire – all buff jerkined and leather booted – he's different, too, in other ways; alight with a fire, an urgency, that has nothing to do with my various charms and fills me with abject terror. I can smell battle on his breath, along with his tobacco.

His reaction to my proposal is unflatteringly dismissive. 'Sweet, there will be time enough for us to wed after this tinpot scuffle!'

He takes me in his arms. Absently. Were I a plank of wood, I'd stir more interest, being useful for ship-building.

'We'll beat them – send them packing!' (Is he reassuring me or himself?) 'It's pure madness for them to attempt to invade by sea upon a perilous coast, with no port to back them. And we have the best, the fastest, most modern of ships which sail more shallow, Bess; can turn their broadsides twice before greater craft can wind the once.'

He's just been expounding the virtues of the ship he had specially built for him in '86, the Ark Raleigh, which, in a typically grand gesture, he re-christened the Ark Royal and presented to the Queen. Now, it seems, the Ark Royal has been chosen to sail as flagship against the Spaniards at the head of the English fleet – a great honour, he beams with satisfaction. Thankfully, his person will not be aboard her or on his 'Bark Raleigh' or 'Roebuck' (named for the creature on his coat or arms). But this affords small comfort as he now tells me he is to command, with glass-crunching Grenville, the defence troops on shore in Devon and Cornwall. 'A task safe as houses,' he smiles.

I happen to know better. With my own long ears I overheard him admit the other day that our great vulnerability lies in our land defence; that a chance wind might easily deposit a large part of the Spanish army anywhere on the English coast between Land's End and The Wash.

'Our sailors are used to bloody combat, thanks to privateering,' he'd said, sotto voce, to his small, intent audience huddled at the far end of the Privy Gallery. 'But our brave volunteers - the farmers, tradesmen and the rest - are being recruited more for their enthusiasm than their skill. They'll be no match for the disciplined Spanish dogs, if the devils do manage to land ....'

And if they do, if the worst happens, he'll be there in the thick of it, leading his make-shift soldiers as surely as his ship will lead the navy – one of the few skilled warriors, fighting as he did in Ireland, savagely, recklessly, inspiring the amateurs under his command to acts of suicidal bravery with their clumsy pikes, billhooks, bows and arrows–

'No need to be afraid,' he comforts, more lovingly now as he realises I am trembling.

But I know he's lying. Know also that to lose him without properly belonging to him would be more than I could bear.

'Perhaps you don't want to marry me after all?' I challenge him. 'You've changed your mind? My lack of dowry ...'

Now I have his attention. His dark eyes smoulder down into mine. 'If I'd wanted a wife for her dowry, I would have secured one long ago, Queen or no Queen! Of course I've not changed my mind, you maddening wench, but I'm no Privy Councillor either. We agreed not to marry in secret ...'

'On that score I've changed *my* mind.'

'God's blood!' He gives me a small, exasperated shake. 'There's so little time, Bess! The Spanish could sail any day and I'm still working on all strategies of defence in the West Country and further afield – on fortifying strongholds as well as training troops. Also, I have to slip over to Ireland briefly to safeguard my properties there. What time have I to spare for a bride, to even wed one?'

'I don't care how short the time we have together as long as we have some. A few hours will suffice if needs be. For if the Spanish win....'

'They will not win!' He cups my face in his strong, long-fingered hands. 'Bess, the sudden death of their admiral, Santa Cruz, has frightened them to death. Seamen are superstitious and the man was considered lucky as well as competent, important to those under him. They have no faith in his replacement, the Duke of Medina Sidonia. How can they have? He's neither soldier nor sailor – he's been appointed, unbelievably, on account of his illustrious ancestry. He'd have difficulty commanding a Thames wherry, yet they've put him in charge of a navy. Even his mother has no faith in him!'

'My mother had no faith in *me*.'

He grins suddenly. 'Nor mine has much in me, but the issues are different. And don't fear for me, sweetheart, I have the personal good luck of a Santa Cruz ....'

'Santa Cruz is dead!'

'But he died in his bed – a feat I plan to emulate, but not yet awhile. I have his luck and his skill in battle. Sweetheart, after our victory I swear I'll be made an Earl as well as a Privy Councillor and we'll be wed openly and grandly in St Paul's Cathedral, with your good brother Arthur to give you away and the Queen as honoured guest. That's my last word on it.'

Indeed! Well, it isn't mine. And it's surprising how the most passionate of kisses can change a man's mind.

* * *

Greenwich Palace, February, 1588

Lady Raleigh. I am Lady Raleigh.

If I keep repeating it to myself, I might believe it.

This very morn I awoke in my narrow little bed in the Maid's Coffer Chamber, plain Elizabeth Throckmorton, spinster and virgin, and I lie in it tonight a married woman.

It all happened so quickly and romantically – like a scene from a masque or play. Indeed, it was from a play – the dreadful Felix and Philiomena – that we devised our programme of events.

'Why not come to me disguised as a page?' Walter laughed, thoroughly enjoying the plotting once my 'reasoning' had persuaded him that he could after all fit a wedding into his busy defence schedule. 'Like the heroine in that little comedy you so despised? You aped her behaviour before when you tore up my first love poem. It's fitting you should do so again under kinder circumstances. You will come with your maid, of course, who can be one of my pages also...'

'But where?' I interrupted. 'Where can I come to you?'

'Where else but to my London house? My presence there will hardly be wondered at. As for your own arrival, my men are frequently travelling the river between royal palaces and Durham House with news and messages. It should be a simple matter for you and your maid to slip into my retinue, suitably clad. I'll smuggle your wench the clothes and she can smuggle your bridal gear to me. My men will be alerted, naturally. Your wench can be trusted?'

'Kate? With her life. She's already guessed I must be seeing someone, though she has no idea who. But what of your household servants? You have – how many?'

'Forty.' He grinned smugly. 'Each one as trustworthy as your Kate. None of them would ever betray me. Though I suppose it might be wise to give some of them a short holiday....'

'And if Kate serves as my witness, who will be yours?'

'Robin Cecil.'

I was horrified. 'No! He'll tell his father!'

'Of course he won't. Because I have so many enemies, you overlook my many friends. Cecil would die for me twenty times over ....'

'Just the once will suffice if the Queen finds out! Cecil already knows too much, with your impulsive notes at the playhouse....'

He sighed. 'Tom Harriot, then. Now I must make haste...' He was kissing me quickly, almost chastely, buckling on his heavy sword. 'Lest the Spaniards break down this very door....'

'But the date?' I cried. 'We have not yet fastened on it. And convention dictates marriage can only be solemnised...'

'Between the hours of eight and twelve in the forenoon. And never during Lent. I'll select a suitable time and date and send you word,' he laughed over his shoulder.

✻ ✻ ✻

We only just made it before Ash Wednesday and the pious days of Lent. But the accustomed celebrations to mark Shrove Tuesday

– pancakes, a lavish dinner, bonfires, torchlight processions, fireworks, dancing far into the night - worked to our advantage.

Aud and the other Maids, atwitter with excitement, were far too occupied in prettying themselves to pay much heed to me when I pleaded a troublesome stomach. Easy to stay behind with Kate when they rushed off to dress the Queen and join with her in the revelry. A simple matter, then, to dress ourselves – giggling - in our borrowed hose; in tunics emblazoned with the Raleigh crest; to sweep up our hair and pin it beneath concealing feathered bonnets; to creep down a chamberers' staircase and join the Raleigh retainers who waited dutifully on the waterside steps beside the Raleigh barge with its satin awnings and cushions. To step nonchalantly aboard and be rowed upriver to the impressive Raleigh residence which backs on to the Strand.

Durham House. I have visited it several times before, in attendance on the Queen, but never thought to be wed within its battlemented walls of plain grey stone. Originally snatched from the Bishops, as so many palaces have been, it is more fortress outwardly than house, with its Norman towers and turrets and great arched Watergate, boasting for its neighbours the London homes of several officers of state – York House, Arundel House, Leicester House – with the chimneys of Lord Burghley's mansion also visible from the river.

Strange to leap freely ashore without a masculine arm to assist or a tangle of skirts to hamper, though Kate, behind me, stumbled and almost fell. Stranger still to tramp as a body up steps still slippery with sea-weed, through gardens, courts, under another great stone arch, through a heavy side door and up a wide marble staircase to Walter's apartments – beginning, like the Queen's in her palaces, on the first floor to avoid risk of flooding.

There to be met by a bowing, nervous-looking Thomas Harriot, thin and tall and sober in his usual scholar's garb (and most pleasant and mild of manner for one called 'Conjurer') who respectfully detached us from our escort and led us down a maze of corridors to the chamber where our finery was laid out in front of a blazing fire. (Walter's bedchamber, in fact, for I recognised the fragrance of musk and ambergris mixed subtly with tobacco.)

'He must be rich as Croesus', breathed Kate, almost tiptoeing to our smuggled wedding clothes which lay draped across an Italian chest. 'See – carpets on the *floor* as well as on the tables!'

Turkish carpets, by the look of them. Fine paintings and engravings adorned the silver damasked walls, many of them of ships in foreign settings. And a ship made all of glass stood exquisitely on a walnut cabinet. But it was the enormous bed covered with rich green velvet and glistening silver lace and surmounted with white, bespangled plumes that drew my gaze and held it; that set sudden doubts hammering in my mind. Once I slipped between those silken sheets, there would be no turning back. Suppose the priest wasn't genuine? How far could I trust Walter? How far could one trust any man?

'The boat we came on is still moored...'

Kate was also having second thoughts. They were plainly etched on her smooth plump face, unflatteringly framed today by her tight pageboy's bonnet. She was young and romantic and she considered Walter Raleigh a God among men. But now her eyes flickered nervously to the portrait of our Royal Mistress which hung, in all its glory, above the fireplace.

Three strides took me to the forbidding likeness. I lifted down the ornate frame, staggering under the weight, and replaced it – pearls, hawk-nose and all – face to the wall. '

'Make haste, unpin my hair. And find that little wired head-dress of pearls we packed somewhere . . .'

* * *

The look Walter gave me when I appeared rather shyly in his study doorway in full bridal regalia dispelled any lingering qualms; warmed me to the tips of my brocade-slippered toes and made my heart, already racing from the steepness of the turret stairs, thump faster. He was standing by that same window Aud had pointed out to me from the river, far below, with Thomas Harriot and a plump, frowning man in parson's garb whose face looked as white as his ruff and who appeared to be protesting in a high, indignant voice. But his whining ceased at my entrance.

'A sight more lovely than a summer rose!' Walter exclaimed softly, a world of love in his eyes as he came to greet me.

'Lovelier even than the sun dancing upon the sea?' I laughed, sinking into a curtsey. (I tease him often about his frequent descriptive allusions to the ocean).

'Far lovelier.' Straightening from his bow, he raised me upright, kissed my hands; looked down at me, intense and unsmiling, as if he willed me to believe these were no idle, courtly compliments. 'My Bess, you have never looked more wonderful.'

'Nor you.' In silver grey satin ablaze with diamonds and trimmed with the snowiest of lace, a great oval diamond swinging from one ear, he was grander than on the day he received his knighthood.

Yet, for once, I believe I did almost rival him. I had chosen a bodice and kirtle of my mother's, which Kate had managed to lengthen and alter – palest primrose silk, the colour of hope and joy, embroidered with delicate golden roses, its stomacher, sleeves and petticoat encrusted with tiny pearls. It was so rich my mother had never dared wear it to Court for fear the Queen would rip it off her back in a fit of jealous pique; and although it had suited her well, I knew it suited me better, for Kate's scissors had attacked it with youthful gusto, and the décolletage, below my gold-edged ruff, verged now on the indecent. But Walter's gifts of diamond and pearl necklace and earrings and long, ivory lace veil - plundered from the Spaniards, he'd told me with a grin - added demurer touches.

'Come, my golden Venus, this may be no Cathedral but your precious Parson waits.'

Treating me to the mischievous, dazzling grin that had first won me, he indicated with the sweep of one satined arm the makeshift altar (his writing table, with the books and papers cleared, an altar cloth, a crucifix, and two white candles substituted) and the disgruntled clergyman shuffling reluctantly now to stand before it.

As we moved hand in hand to join him, I could not help thinking wistfully that we were both more suitably clad for St. Paul's Cathedral...

The all-important ceremony that has bound us both for life passed in such a blur of unreality I can scarce remember it. Is it the same for every blushing bride? Did we stumble over our vows or say them boldly? Did Walter smile at me when he placed a gold ring on my finger - switched my betrothal emerald deftly from my right hand to my left? Kate tells me that a shaft of sunlight shone through the turret window of the almost circular chamber, forming a brilliant, multi-coloured halo around our two bent heads as we knelt for the blessing – Walter's black as jet, mine fair beneath my veil. But she is full of pretty fancies and may have imagined it.

The Parson, who was not of the Court but nonetheless familiar to me (and therefore genuine – I'm ashamed of my doubts), scuttled scowlingly away after he'd done his lip-service duty and signed the documents Walter presented, pausing only to collect his enormous fee. And Walter, leading me in to the wedding feast, confessed that the wretched man, terrified of offending the Queen, had been forced along at knife-point.

'But surely,' I said in alarm, 'he'll extract his revenge by betraying us!'

'Not he!' laughed my husband, the pirate. 'He's too worried about keeping his throat intact.'

We sat down at one end of a long table in a huge, echoing, marble-pillared hall - just the four of us, rattling around - attended by the smiling retainers who had been my boat-fellows and dining off silver plate engraved with the inevitable Raleigh arms. I recall not one of the sumptuous dishes. Kate was uneasy because Walter insisted she be of the party and she was uncomfortable eating with us, I remember that. But Walter charmed her, of course, and we were soon very merry, even Thomas Harriot, who at first kept glancing over his shoulder as if he expected us all to be arrested at any moment.

Two things marred my own enjoyment: a huge tapestry of the Ark Royal riding the waves, guns blazing, which dominated one wall and reminded me with an ominous pang of the war - are all the paintings Walter owns uncomfortable? And the thought of that green and silver bed awaiting me in the musk, ambergris and tobacco-scented chamber. Despite all our secret love-play, I was still as virginal as the Queen herself (well, almost). Supposing I found the full marriage act distasteful? Or, worse, became so cold and stiff with nerves I disappointed?

But I drank more wine than usual. Walter saw to that while partaking of very little himself. And when at last we got to it, when Walter swept me up in his arms and carried me to it, waving away Kate and Harriot, who'd expected a traditional bedding and were hovering to attend us, I was no longer nervous but more than a little giggly.

※ ※ ※

Big! It was so big! I had never seen a naked man before (only one carved out of marble or stone or painted on a tapestry – none of which can *grow*!) Perhaps I should have expected it to be large considering the size of Walter generally, but my main fear was that it could not, surely, go where I believed it was supposed to go …?

'It won't fit!' I panicked to Walter and he laughed, kneeling like a Greek God above me, surprisingly white and smooth-skinned and unswarthy, despite the blackness of his hair and beard.

'It will,' he assured. 'Trust me!'

It did, surprisingly, and I was glad it did. After the first time, which was painful. But Walter was more, much more, than a once-an-afternoon gallant. 'Wonderful!' he kept groaning. 'Wonderful!' And wonderful it was, for both of us. Mostly, I realise, amateur though I am, because he was tender and considerate and loving – making sure my pleasure matched his own.

I suppose, I thought, I have to accept that he's had years in which to practise. And immediately made myself wretched by wondering who, precisely, he had practised with...

'Have you ever begotten a bastard?' I gasped out in the middle of it all.

He ceased abruptly; looked down at me, disbelieving.

'What?'

'All those other women you must have bedded before me – the loose ones who let you take liberties.... Did you ever give one of them a child?'

He groaned again, not this time with passion.

'Bess, I love you, but you ask some damnably unladylike questions at some extremely delicate moments...'

'But did you?' I persisted. There is so much about him still that I don't know. Suddenly it seemed imperative I knew this.

'Of course not.' He was impatient. 'The first child I father will be yours. When the time is right.' His tedious "right time" again. 'If you're worrying about having one too soon, don't – I've taken care of it.' (How?) 'And now, please, may we return to more important business?'

We returned to it very satisfactorily.

* * *

Later, much later, we rose, slipped on fur-lined robes, mine beribboned with silk and lace – another present from my husband, and sat, silent and companionable, on the window seat, watching the afternoon craft race the swans on the water below, which curved here at a right angle so that we saw, to our right, the sprawling river frontage of Whitehall Palace and Westminster Hall; to our left, London Bridge and the turrets of the Tower. Walter smoked his pipe, his arm around me, my head (much clearer now) nestled against his shoulder. I had never known such a sweet sense of belonging.

Soon, too soon, when the tide dictated, I would be obliged to return to Greenwich - pray God I had not been missed - while he would begin the two hundred and twenty mile ride to his headquarters at Plymouth. But this brief, shining moment was ours. No matter what happened in the future, no-one could take it from us.

He stirred. His pipe, I suspected, had gone out. 'An angel for an angel's thoughts? You're not dwelling on Parma's footling invasion, I hope?'

I was indignant. 'We agreed not to so much as mention the war today! I was just wishing my mother could have been here to see us wed.'

He nodded, reaching for his tinder-box. 'I was wishing the same.' For a moment I was surprised – he had hardly known my mother. Then I realised it was his own widowed parent of whom he spoke.

'But your mother could have come! She's not of the Court – you could have had her brought quietly from Devon and no-one would have known. Why did we not think of it?'

His smile was wry. 'I did invite her, sweetheart. She refused to come.'

'Oh.'

I'd known she was at odds with him. He'd told me so with a slightly bitter laugh. She'd wanted her cleverest son to become a lawyer; had set her heart on his attending university at fourteen. Instead, he'd climbed out of his bedroom window and run off to France with his cousins, to prove his sword in the civil war.

'But at least you came back and went to university later, when you were eighteen,' I had pointed out, 'in an attempt to please her.'

'Yes and left before I took my degree, went on to Middle Temple but studied little law since I used the place chiefly as a stepping stone to Court.'

'But surely she's proud of all you've achieved since?'

He raised a cynical eyebrow. 'Of what can she be proud? She disapproves of colonisation –folk should stay in their own countries, she believes. Privateering she sees as stealing only. I wonder sometimes how she came to produce first my Gilbert half-brothers, then, by her second marriage, Carew and me. Adventurers, all of us. But she frowns most of all on my intimacy with the Queen. She misunderstands our ways of advancement at Court; the flattery, the pretend courtship. In her eyes, I have achieved my wealth through unsavoury relations with a middle-aged woman. She won't accept the smallest gift from me. She sends back money and all else that I attempt to give her, yet she lives in near poverty with but two old servants to wait upon her, and struggles to pay her way.'

'I was thinking,' he said now, stroking my hair, 'that it's a pity her stubborn streak prevented her from being here today because I believe you are the one feature of my life that would please her.'

He kissed my brow, my eyelids, my lips....

Which soon led us, naturally, back to the green and silver bed.

* * *

Now, lying sleepless between the sheets of my own lonely bed in Greenwich Palace, I can hardly bear to recall our parting.

'The Spaniards will lose and I'm invincible!' was his last boast to me in his stable yard.

One final kiss, long and lingering, before he disentangled my clinging arms to spring into the saddle, turned his mount's head towards the Plymouth Road.

I suppose I should be thrilled that my gleaming wedding ring sits, snug and undetected, in my little locked jewellery casket; relieved that Kate and I managed to return while the Queen and Court were still making merry; happy that my nearest and nosiest roommate, Audrey, at this moment snoring beyond the screen that separates our respective beds, has no idea of the juicy scandal she has missed.

Yet all I can do is recall Philip Sidney's black-draped coffin and wonder if I'll ever hold my bridegroom in my arms again ...

ROBERT CECIL

The Palace of St. James, July 1588

'Report's in,' my father pants, stomping into his study with his cane. 'The enemy fleet has been sighted off Cornwall's Lizard.'

I start up, heart pounding. 'Raleigh's beacons..?'

'Have been lit.'

They're meant to flare along the coast from Land's End to Margate, and from the Isle of Wight to the Scottish border – each one alerting the next. Drums will thunder and bells clang in every town and village. Thirty-seven boatloads of soldiers are to be ferried to the Isle of Wight, the Earl of Leicester's army will take up defensive positions at Tilbury. While here, at the Palace of St. James, Lord Chamberlain Hunsdon's infantry are no doubt already closing in to protect the Queen and the rest of us.

Bitterness near chokes me. Volunteers from all over the country will be rushing to join the 'trained' recruits while I, in my puny body, can do nothing but remain here among the women and the men too old to fight.

'Come,' my father urges, taking my arm. 'We do no good loitering here. It's up to us to create an aura of calm.'

His voice is steady but I notice his hands are shaking.

BESS

The Palace of St James, July 1588

Panic in the Ladies' Chamber!

A breathless page reports: ' The Spaniards are sailing *straight for us* in a crescent-shaped nightmare of *gigantic* ships!'

Worse – if it can get any worse – Lady Warwick sweeps in and informs us that the Queen intends to confront the invaders at Dover. Taking us with her.

'Why not stuff us into cannons and *fire* us at the enemy?' wails Aud. 'We'd stand a better chance of survival.'

Thankfully, the Queen is persuaded to change her mind by a frantic Privy Council. Yet we have scarce drawn gasps of relief before she decides to join Leicester at Tilbury. Again, taking us with her.

'Worry's addled her brain!' moans Lady Scrope, pale as paper,

Somehow, we pull ourselves together, begin to sort and list the belongings the Queen will need, feeling a little more normal for the enforced activity.

It is hard to believe, leaving from Westminster Stairs in the Royal Barge as orderly and ceremoniously as ever, that we are actually in the midst of the long-dreaded invasion. Not with the Queen's musicians playing and her loyal subjects cheering; although I hear several wrong notes resulting from shaking hands or faltering breath, and, looking closer, realise the crowd consists entirely of women and children, many of the little boys waving home-made St. George's flags and brandishing wooden swords in imitation of their soldier fathers.

'May God keep Your Majesty safe!' screeches an old woman above the cacophony, almost toppling into the Thames in her enthusiasm to reach the royal ear.

'May God keep every one of us safe,' replies the Queen with a winning smile.

Amen to that.

✷ ✷ ✷

We land at Tilbury to the clamour of trumpets, fifes and drums. With difficultly we cram the Queen and her farthingaled finery into a narrow coach sparkling with great fake emeralds, diamonds and rubies.

'Arranged by Leicester, I suppose,' whispers Aud, 'in a bid to hearten the soldiers by showing them the splendour of the monarch they're defending.'

If so, it works. 'God Save Her Majesty!' thunders from every uniformed throat. And next day, after we've spent a tense night at nearby Ardern Hall, the Queen rides among the troops on a great white gelding (how they cheer!) and delivers such a fine, brave, heroic speech, it brings a tear to my eye. Wearing a steel corselet over a white velvet gown, her wig uncovered and blazing in the sun, a golden helmet and sword carried on a cushion behind her, she looks, from a distance, like some glorious (young!) goddess.

I'm surprised when Lady Warwick shudders and moans 'How can she be so foolish? One fanatical traitor, hiding in the ranks with a pistol, has the chance to accomplish what the entire Spanish Armada has put to sea to do ...'

But only patriots are present today and Elizabeth enslaves them all.

'Let tyrants fear! I have always so behaved myself that, under God, I have placed my chief strength and goodwill in the loyal hearts and goodwill of my subjects; and therefore I am come amongst you, as you see, not for my recreation and sport but being resolved in the midst and heat of the battle to live or die amongst you all; to lay down for God, for my kingdom and for my people, my honour and my blood, even in the dust ....'

As theatrical and stirring as Tamburlaine!

Later, while the Queen is dining with Leicester in his tent, despatches arrive informing her of the Armada's defeat, claiming that God has proved Himself a Protestant by sending ferocious winds to aid us. With the help, some say, of astrologer John Dee blowing from Prague and three white witches blowing from Scotland.

We learn, from Robin Cecil, how Admiral Howard's gallant navy fought unsuccessfully, despite their long-range guns, to break the Armada's formation in the Channel: how the Spaniards, aiming higher up the coast, sailed past Walter's and Grenville's carefully-built fortifications, rendering them needless: how our navy fought them off Plymouth, off Portland, off the Isle of Wight, while Walter's troops marched and galloped eastwards, keeping abreast, only to be rendered redundant when the enemy made no attempt to land at all.

'Through rain-swept days and misty nights,' proclaims little Robin dramatically, standing on a wooden crate in order to be seen as well as heard, 'the great ships moved steadily up the Channel, our guns damaging but not destroying them until at last they anchored in Calais Roads, awaiting Parma and his narrow boats full of reinforcements.'

And it was here that Walter, apparently, joined the fleet; boarded the flagship Ark Royal (that was once Ark Raleigh) and helped Howard, Drake, Hawkins and others set fire ships packed with explosives adrift among the clumsy Spanish galleons, breaking their formation at last. It was here that the Spaniards, battered, burnt and fired upon, turned tail and were chased, eventually, out of sight.

We cheer and dance and hug each other.

But our joy lasts all of five minutes, for another messenger comes at the gallop, shouting that Parma is still sailing – will arrive at Tilbury at any moment - with six thousand horse, fifty thousand foot and many implements of torture.

'Along with seven thousand Spanish wet nurses,' sobs Aud who, in the midst of the panic, has yet managed to milk more information from the terrified man, 'to suckle our orphaned infants after they've tortured and killed all English adults ...'

However, this second report was sent in error, or mischief, for Parma has not arrived.. The reason is unclear. Perhaps he was disillusioned or perhaps the tide was wrong. Whatever, he did not attempt to sail. and we are all safely back at Whitehall, where the feasting and jubilation have to be seen to be believed.

We have come through the ordeal, Lord Burghley tells us, with fewer than one hundred men killed and only one of these an officer. (Thankfully, no relation of mine.)

And Walter? I have only glimpsed him briefly at a distance, congratulating the Queen. She was all *over* him. I wanted to run to him and throw my arms about him; demonstrate my joy and relief at seeing him safe. Instead and as usual, we dared not let our eyes meet for fear of giving ourselves away and, incredibly, he has rushed straight off again without so much as a snatched word, let alone a kiss – sent, with Grenville, to chase or round up the last of the limping Spanish ships and then look to his lands in Ireland.

Bitterly, I realise the Queen's slave has again taken precedence over the bridegroom.

'You know how quickly tongues wag,' comforts Kate, passing me a handkerchief. 'He was right to be cautious, but he'll soon be back, I'm sure. Take heart, Lady Raleigh.'

'Don't call me that!' I snap. 'You were told never to do so!'

She's hurt. 'Never to do so in public ....'

'Or in private! We can't take the risk.'

'But surely, Lady ... Mistress Bess ... you'll soon be able to reveal the truth? With Her Majesty in such good humour over the victory ...'

Her Majesty is, in fact, ecstatic. She's already knighted John Hawkins and Martin Frobisher, and it's said she wants to create Leicester Lieutenant General of England and Ireland.

Surely, after his months of tireless effort, the Queen must reward Walter also? Make him the Privy Councillor she knows he aches to become? And then he can tell the truth and appeal to her better nature. I can be Lady Raleigh openly; our marriage accepted (if not happily), by the silly old woman.

'You're right, Kate, of course you are.' I attempt a watery smile. 'We can endure a few more weeks of this foolery, knowing all will be out in the sunlight very shortly . . .'

~PART TWO~

BESS

Mile End, November, 1591

'Three years?' yelps Arthur, at last regaining control of his voice. 'You have the effrontery to sit there and tell me you've been illegally wed to Sir Walter Raleigh for ... (he smacks his desk and the candles flicker wildly) ... three ... long ... deceitful ...years?'

'It was perfectly legal,' I babble. 'I have a signed document to prove it, and so has my husband. Here, peruse mine if you wish....'

He does wish. Snatching the paper from me he takes it to his study window for the benefit of the light, shakes his head over it and groans; scans it a second, then a third time, as if he cannot trust his eyes.

'A conjurer and a waiting woman for witnesses,' he moans. 'In Durham House, but a stone's throw from Whitehall and Westminster! Deliberately thumbing your nose at the Queen and the Privy Council, to say nothing of your family, of *me*!'

'We felt it to be safer.' I'm still babbling. 'We decided the bolder we were, the less likely to be discovered ....'

'Brazen!' snaps Arthur, shooting me a look so hostile it wounds like a blow in the face. 'It was brazen! Unforgivable! To think that a sister of mine... So this is why you've turned down every suitor I've suggested! Suitors who would have received the Queen's blessing! Suitors who have approached me in good faith – respectably!'

'It would hardly have been respectable if I'd married one bigamously! And had I been free, none of them would have suited me. Dolts, the lot of them, with fat coffers but weak chins ...' My voice falters. So much for promising myself I would remain calm and meek.

'Hah – proud of yourself, are you?' Glaring, he flings himself into the chair behind his desk, a portrait of our father also glaring down at me from the wall behind him. (I hadn't realised they were so alike.) 'You think you've snatched a glittering prize? But when the Queen finds out and withdraws Raleigh's monopolies along with her favour, where will that leave the pair of you? Penniless!'

I bluster. 'Other favoured courtiers have married and still prospered ...

He snorts. 'If you refer to poor little Robin Cecil, he can hardly be compared to Raleigh. He occupies the Queen's respect, not her affection. Also, he very properly asked her permission to wed Lord Cobham's daughter and was granted it.'

And he is not, in fact, 'poor' at all, if one forgets his unfortunate physique, being first knighted, then, three months ago, made a Privy Councillor, the youngest ever. While Walter still waits hopefully.

'For an example of the Queen's wrath,' says Arthur grimly, 'look at Essex....'

Yes, look at him. That was indeed a shock.

I was at my lowest ebb just then, bowed down with guilt, with the effort of carrying on normally. I'd been promoted to a Lady of the Bedchamber, too – respected, trusted – which made me feel worse. Kate, with her determined false cheer, was not much help. I felt I must confide in someone else or go mad. But who? I feared to draw Arthur and Anna into my web of lies, and loquacious Aud Shelton was out of the question. Then I had it – Frances Sidney was at Court following the death of her father, Secretary Walsingham. Frances, I was sure, would be the perfect confidant – sympathetic yet the soul of discretion. In vain, I sought a moment when we could be alone; then it was handed to me on a plate one day when I was sent to fetch a fresh royal head-dress and discovered Frances dressing the newest auburn wig.

I rushed to her but before I could open my mouth, she confided in *me*:

'Oh Bess,' she began at once, 'I have a secret I've been longing to share and cannot keep a moment longer – not from you, my very dearest friend who I know will be the soul of discretion.' She seized my hand. 'Bess – I'm so happy and so terrified! I'm married again – married in secret to Robert Devereux . . . '

I gasped. 'The Earl of Essex?'

She laughed: 'I know I said I could never care for anyone as I cared for Philip, but–'

On she went, describing her new husband's godly attributes while I stared at her in horror. Here she was, calling me her 'very dearest friend', and she was secretly married to *my* husband's worst enemy! Why, the two of them had even been on the point of fighting a duel once, but had been prevented by the Privy Council ....

'Say you're pleased for me,' she begged, 'and that you'll help and support me when the Queen finds out ....?'

I said I would, of course; mumbled something along the lines of congratulation. But the words stuck in my throat. I could picture our loyalties dividing us sadly in the future. Indeed, they were dividing us already for I dared not now tell her my own secret in case she inadvertently let it slip to Essex. Essex, of all people!

The storm erupted soon afterwards. Frances and Essex were both banished from Court and are still in deep disgrace. Essex has gone off to fight in France, but at least he found the courage to break the news of his marriage to the Queen himself before any of his enemies suspected it, which is more than Walter seems able to do ....

'To keep such a secret for *three years*!' Arthur still cannot believe it. 'How is it possible?'

'We meant to reveal it before this. But it was never the right time....'

'Hah! Never the right time for Sir Walter Raleigh!'

'That's unfair!'

I remind myself again that I'm supposed to be placating him, not adding fuel to the raging fire.

I lower my voice. 'I'm simply trying to explain. First the Queen was grieving for my Lord of Leicester and we feared to upset her further ....' (Leicester died suddenly, soon after the Armada's defeat, of an illness, but he was rumoured to have been poisoned, of course.) 'Then Walter was obliged to go to Ireland again, to plant his potatoes and tobacco and reopen the tin mines. When he returned, it was a delicate time because Essex confessed just as we were about to, and Her Majesty's anger, if Walter had followed suit, would have been terrible ....' (Nonetheless, I had urged him to brave it, but he'd flatly refused.)

'It will be all the more terrible now,' predicts my brother, gloomily toying with a quill pen, 'and we shall all bear the brunt of it.. She leans on Raleigh more than ever to cheer her since the banishment of Essex and the death of poor old Hatton ....'

True. She's very much inclined to melancholy, and who can blame her? Arthur and I both wear black out of respect for Chancellor Hatton and, since Leicester's death, we've scarce been out of it with the demise of Lady Burghley from old age, the aforesaid Walsingham from worry, Arthur Gorges's wife Douglas in childbed, Sir Richard Grenville in a sea fight and, most painfully and personally, our own brother Thomas who was taken last year by the plague.

Arthur sighs. 'I suppose,' he acknowledges grudgingly, 'matters could be worse. When Essex confessed, Frances Devereux was great with child ...'

The silence is deafening. Then the pen snaps in his hand.

Helplessly, I watch the horror dawn in his widening eyes; the panic which must surely mirror my own.

I moisten dry lips. Arthur makes a strange, strangled sound in his throat which finally emerges as 'When?'

I whisper: 'In the Spring. When the lambs fall.' And burst into tears.

It proves a good move. While Arthur has no sympathy with a defiant female who flouts the rules, a weeping little sister is more than his kind heart can withstand. At once he is on his feet, overturning the inkpot, which he ignores. I am clasped to his black-velvet chest, being comforted as if I am eight years old.

'Don't worry, Bess, don't worry – I'll help you, never fear,' he murmurs into my hair. And foolishly: 'All will be well.' *How can it be?*

'Now, at least,' he says grimly when I am calmer, 'the Queen will have to be told. Raleigh must realise it ....'

'But he does not!' I sob afresh. 'He says we must wait still longer. He's going to sea! To attack King Philip's silver fleet, sack Panama and avenge his cousin Grenville ....'

Arthur looks pinched about the mouth. 'I think it's high time I had a private word with Sir Walter Raleigh.'

* * *

The interview took place eleven days later – again in Arthur's Mile End house. And has brought me little joy.

Arthur called me into his study the minute they were done; sat pompously behind his ink-stained desk while Walter, handsome and striking as ever in black and silver damask, greeted me with a kiss then settled me tenderly in the carved leather-seated chair I occupied last time and went to lean against the mantelshelf.

'I have shown the deeds of the small farm you own in Mitcham to Sir Walter,' Arthur told me, 'and have explained fully the circumstances of the five hundred pounds loaned to Lord Huntingdon, which I will, of course, endeavour to retrieve before we sign the formal marriage settlement....'

I stared at them both in amazement.

'But surely,' I said, 'you have been discussing more than mere finance? How – and when – do we set about confessing to the Queen?'

Walter looked away. I recognised that stubborn thrust to his chin. Arthur cleared his throat.

'Sir Walter has pointed out to me the great advantages of his sea expedition at this time. If he returns home with a healthy profit from the Spanish silver fleet, Her Majesty will be more likely to pardon you both.'

I could not believe my ears. 'But that will be too late! The babe will be born by then!'

Walter moved swiftly; knelt before me and took possession of my hands. 'Sweetheart, I'm to be Admiral! In full command of thirteen ships! There will be no-one to hinder me, to countermand my orders. This exploit will succeed with flying colours, and then Elizabeth will forgive me anything. She'll admit me to the Council and let you remain at Court. Also, she has already promised me a ninety-nine year lease of Sherborne Castle, in Dorset – a place I've long coveted. We'll be rich, secure, and we'll have a great country estate, Bess ....' His eyes sparkled. 'Surely it's worth a little patience and inconvenience....?'

'Inconvenience?' Wrenching my hands away, I leaped to my feet. 'You call it *inconvenient* for me to grow daily more huge and clumsy and - obvious - with all the Court a-snigger?'

'We'll have you away from Court before anything becomes obvious,' Arthur assured me. His tune well changed after one conversation with my honey-tongued husband. 'My wife Anna can feign illness. You'll come here to Mile End, ostensibly to look after her but, in truth, to lie in.'

'And afterwards Anna will find the babe an excellent wet nurse,' Walter smiled. 'You can return to Court and none the wiser. Until my return.'

Such is the smug, unfeeling reasoning of men. I hated them both.

'*If* you manage to return and *if* I manage to live through the perils of childbirth!' Which poor Douglas Gorges did not. Had he forgotten her already? It would seem so for his smile did not falter.

'Don't be pessimistic.'

Inconvenient! Pessimistic! My temper blazed. I wrenched off my slipper and threw it at him in fair imitation of the Queen. My aim was better than hers. It struck his ear, knocking out his pearl droplet. His ear-lobe, to my satisfaction, began to bleed. He looked astonished.

'I doubt I'll get as far as child-bed,' I screamed as I rushed from the room. 'I'll be forced to lace my stays so tight you'll be rid of me in a few weeks, from lack of breath!'

At this moment I am prostrate on Anna's second-best bed, refusing to open the locked door upon which Arthur and Walter timidly knock. Anna herself is on a visit to her parents' house in Colchester, blissfully ignorant of the dangerous part she is to play in this sorry affair.

'Bess will come round, never fear,' says Arthur's voice soothingly, as they apparently give up and retreat downstairs. 'Meanwhile, we must all make sure our Christmas and New Year gifts to the Queen are among the most expensive . . .'

I pound the pillow! Is money and the protection of their own insensitive skins all they can think about?

I'm tempted to confound their selfish plans by going to the Queen alone. But gossip has it that she once broke a Maid-of-Honour's finger when she confessed to marrying without permission. And *that* poor girl wasn't even pregnant ...

* * *

March, 1592

Things have begun to go awry without help or hindrance from me. On the very eve of the Panama voyage, the Queen, to Walter's disgust, has changed her mind about his Admiralship. As ever, she cannot bring herself to part with him long term, and now orders that Frobisher commands instead; that Walter leads his fleet only as far as the Spanish coast, then turns back.

This pleases me, of course, but Arthur and Walter fume. Frobisher, they growl, is a good seaman but a harsh, unpopular leader – difficult to get men to follow. Anything could now go wrong at sea – even a mutiny. I clearly see their dream of Spanish silver disintegrating by the minute, yet they still insist we wait until the fleet returns before throwing ourselves on the Queen's mercy. And it is not yet even ready to depart, while I, grown cumbersome as a Spanish galleon, sail rapidly towards my delivery day.

To make matters worse, sly rumours of a secret 'Raleigh Wedding' have started to abound at Court. Whispers only, reaching Arthur via third and fourth parties and vague enough – no mention of me or of my 'delicate' condition, thanks to my continued good health and ever more diligent lacing which did not prove too difficult a problem as, until this final month, I remained amazingly small. Worryingly small, I fancy, since Anna kept telling me brightly there was positively no cause for worry, that many first babes are tiny. I could see she was puzzled and anxious. She grew elephantine each time she was with child and even then only managed to produce a thriving daughter on the fourth attempt. Which makes me face the appalling possibility that the cause of all this "inconvenience" could well be stillborn or refuse to suck, like my first tragic niece, and be buried in a few short weeks. Now that it's too late, I am terrified I might have continued dancing and hunting and running about after the Queen too long for the poor mite's safety. But how else was I to remain undiscovered?

Then, last night, three weeks after I came here to Mile End to lie in, Arthur called me quietly down to his study. I'm beginning to detest that room, scene of so many upsets.

My brother was agitated, plucking at the trimming on his doublet sleeve, a habit he employs when especially nervous.

'I have spent the day at Whitehall,' he informed me quickly. 'Thankfully, there is still no mention of your name or of the coming child, but mischievous speculation of a possible Raleigh marriage grows ever louder. And – I scarce know how to tell you this – Raleigh has denied the marriage! Denied *you*, as surely as Simon Peter denied Christ!'

A sick wave of shock jolted through me, but pride helped me conceal it. 'To whom,' I asked calmly after a moment, 'am I denied?'

'To Robin Cecil, in a letter. I bribed his clerk to pen me a copy.' Arthur thrust a sheet of paper under my nose. His hand shook. 'Now that Cecil is State Secretary in all but name – has stepped unofficially into Walsingham's shoes – he was obliged to write a probing letter to Raleigh concerning the rumours. And this is your husband's knavish reply...'

Walter had written from Chatham, where he toils night and day to fit his ships for sea. Frobisher may be in line for the glory, but Walter is left with the effort of preparation. This neat, immaculate copy bore little relation to what would surely have been his original hasty scrawl, and the important part leaped up at me; -

"I mean not to come away, as they say I will, for fear of a marriage and I know not what. If any such thing were, I would have imparted it unto yourself before any man living; and, therefore, I pray believe it not and I beseech you to suppress any such malicious report.

For I protest before God there is none on the face of the earth that I would be fastened unto."

'It seems Raleigh changes shape with the ease of Proteus!' exploded Arthur. *'None he would be fastened unto!* To lie thus, to Lord Burghley's son, can only make matters worse...'

I realised he shook with anger. A muscle jerked in his neck. Laughter bubbled up in me. I gave way to it and could not stop.

His jaw dropped. He threw open the door and shouted for Anna, who came running.

'She's hysterical! Bring aqua vitae...'

'Too strong! It's too near her time...'

'Slap her face then...'

'Don't you dare!' With an effort, I pulled myself together. 'Walter does not lie *to* Robin Cecil,' I explained to them, 'he lies *for* him. To avoid dragging him into trouble alongside us when the truth comes out. When our deception comes finally to light, Robin can produce this letter and pretend ignorance...'

'*Pretend* ignorance!' The muscle looked to jump free of Arthur's neck. 'You mean Cecil already knows about your true reason for being here and our part in it?'

'Walter told him months ago. You know they're very close friends.'

'But – a Cecil! If he should tell his father who then goes to the Queen...'

'Robin will not tell anyone. Having a wife and child of his own now, he is sympathetic. He will do his utmost to quash the rumours before they reach the Queen's ears.'

'I hope and pray you are right!' Arthur pulled at his sleeve so hard a seed pearl came away in his fingers.

I found myself quoting his own habitual words of comfort: 'All will be well.'

But will it?

Common sense forces me to accept that Walter was obliged to protect Robin Cecil who will, hopefully, help him soften the Queen's anger when our nemesis comes. But did he have to go quite so far?

'There is none on the face of the earth that I would be fastened unto.'

This from the husband I have risked so much to be with – have crept away, over the months, the years, to lie within that green and silver bed at Durham House, stupidly trusting in his assurance that his expensive, Italian-made 'Venus Gloves' would keep me from the pickle I now find myself in...

Does he, for all his pretty speeches and love poetry and thoughtful little gifts (the latest was a lucky talisman to help ease my pains at the birthing), truly wish to be 'fastened' to me? To our child? Or will it suit him better to remain in the Queen's favour by continuing to deny us both after this babe is born?

* * *

'Scream!' my sister-in-law advises. 'As loud as you can – it helps.'

I button my lips. I've resolved to be brave, not issue a sound, and nothing, I'm convinced, will help.

I lie on Anna's elaborately covered and curtained best bed this time, writhing in agony. Which suddenly abates.

'A false alarm,' sighs Anna - in some relief since she's coping alone. The midwife has been given leave to slip out for a short while this afternoon to tend her own family while Kate has been despatched on an errand. 'It happens.'

It is happening too often for my liking. This is the third time I've had pains and nerved myself for the supreme ordeal which has failed to come about. And I am all impatience now to get this offspring born, whether or not its father acknowledges it.

'Banish that frown,' commands Anna, helping me to sit up. 'If mother remains tranquil, baby is born tranquil.'

'Screams one minute, tranquillity the next,' I grumble. 'You cannot have it both ways. Which do you want?'

She dumps her daughter in my lap. 'Nurse your niece. Put in some practice.'

Little Mary beams at me. At thirteen months, she is a plump, contented child, her parents' pride and joy. But – their *fourth attempt*! My brow drips sweat, and not only from the heat.

'Surely we can open a window the merest crack? I'm gasping like a salmon newly fished from the Thames.'

They've taken trouble with my lying-in chamber. The best bed boasts hangings fit for the Queen herself; one enormous carpeted sideboard groans with silver plate, another with Anna's cherished Italian pottery; three of Arthur's finest Italian paintings have been brought specially from Colchester to adorn the brightly tapestried walls. 'This child will feast its eyes on beauty the minute it enters the world,' Anna had beamed when I'd thanked her. But then she had sealed up the windows.

'Fresh air is harmful at this time,' she'd told me then as she tells me now, adding; 'I'll dampen the fire a little and fetch you a spiced caudle ...'

I wince. 'Forget the caudle...'

A stomach cramp worse than a sword-thrust (though I've never experienced a sword-thrust) is slicing through me. I all but throw Mary back to Anna as, praise be, the midwife comes bustling through the door, casting off her cloak and rolling up her sleeves; the same woman who laid out three of Anna's babes.

'Pull forward the birthing stool and 'elp 'er on to it. Unbind that talisman from 'er arm . . .'

'No!' I snatch frantically at my precious eagle stone. 'My husband sent me this – it comes from foreign parts and has protective powers...'

'Not worn on your arm, it 'asn't. It must be placed on your lower belly now or 'twill prevent the babe being born . . .'

I am too preoccupied to argue further, busy coping with the ferocious rhythms and tremors the churchmen say Grandmother Eve, in her sinfulness, visited on all her female descendants when she plucked that rotten old apple.

'Bite down on this rag ...' (Anna)

'Push 'arder, for Gawd's sake!' (the midwife) 'That tiddlin' bit of effort wouldn't void a cherry stone ... '

I abandon bravery and scream.

* * *

He is the very picture of health, with Walter's haughty nose and a mop of silky dark hair. He sucks like a tavern drunkard and his lungs are powerful enough to put the royal trumpeters to shame.

'What shall you name him?' asks Arthur, trying to suppress his envy but not quite succeeding. One of his stillborn infants was a son.

'Damerei, after an ancestor of Walter's,' I smile, fondly watching the wet nurse swaddle those restless limbs. Was ever a babe so perfect? 'We agreed upon it before he departed for Chatham.'

He is still in Chatham. His fleet, finally ready to sail, is held back by contrary winds. Yet he has not bothered to visit or even to write a line, despite Arthur's urgent letters.

'Who for godparents?' asks Anna hopefully.

'You and Arthur, of course. And perhaps our brother Nicholas, who is good at holding his tongue? Can you get in touch with him?'

Arthur brushes my cheek with his lips. 'It shall be done.'

Only it was not

* * *

Nicholas could not be traced in time so another godfather was hastily found.

I almost swoon with shock when he bows his long form over my hand on the appointed morning, his red hair blazing in the sunlight streaming through the mullioned windows of Anna's little parlour.

'My Lady Raleigh, congratulations on a fine new son.'

'My Lord Essex, you do us honour with your presence…'

* * *

'Are you mad? Do you wish to ruin us all? *You* were the one who worried about Cecil knowing!' In a fury, I corner Arthur in the passage by the Great Hall. I am already flushed from a confrontation with the bribed clergyman.

'You should not be here, you should still be lying-in,' the pompous man of God had frowningly admonished me. 'Birth mothers play no part in baptism. All essential spiritual work is done by the godparents.'

'I wish to offer up thanks for my safe delivery,' I'd excused my presence haughtily and would brook no argument. One particular godparent might snatch the babe and whisk him away to show the Queen, were I not in evidence.

'It's bad enough,' I hiss at Arthur, 'that Walter is too busy to attend his own son's Christening, but this! What in God's name possessed you? I asked for Nicholas!' I did not even realise Essex was permanently back from France!'

Arthur is unperturbed and almost as pompous as the parson. 'Nicholas has neither wealth nor influence. Essex is a good friend of mine, his lady wife is a good friend of yours, and now the Queen has allowed him home, he'll soon return to favour. His help and soothing words could prove invaluable...'

'Soothing words! To help Walter Raleigh? He'll gallop straight from your courtyard to the Court itself and how he'll enjoy the telling!'

'Nonsense! He'll not stoop to low weapons; he's a nobleman with a sense of honour. He's suffered for his own secret marriage, remember, and is a doting father. He told me he was flattered to be asked. He's always had a soft spot for you, Bess. You must admit he's being most charming...'

Oh, most – handing me a supportive note and a silver Christening spoon from Frances, closing one eye in a merry, conspiratorial wink as he carries Walter's son to the improvised font.

And about as trustworthy as an adder lurking in long grass ...

❋ ❋ ❋

At last – a reassuringly loving (if short) letter from my husband, with a welcome gift of fifty pounds for our baby. Both items are delivered to me at Mile End by Walter's half-brother, Adrian Gilbert, who stands stolid and thick-set and sour-faced before me, a disapproving glint to his eye and a demand on his lips to inspect his new nephew.

Adrian is seldom at Court and I have never met him previously, only seen him at a distance, strolling with Walter. At closer quarters he is not ill-looking; indeed, his features have a look of Walter's but without the warmth, the spark of mischief, the animation of expression that so attracts. I do not take to him at all. He certainly does not appear the sort to coo at babies and, perhaps realising this, he frowningly hastens to explain that Walter - Wat, he calls him - being anxious, has sent him specifically to see us both in person and report on our well-being; also to cast his son's horoscope as there was no doctor present to do so at the child's birth.

I know Walter respects Adrian as a man learned in science and astrology, while Mary of Pembroke thinks so highly of his work she has provided a laboratory for him in her house at Wilton and a pension to go with it. But I would much have preferred Thomas Harriot to carry out this routine task, although I wonder at the value placed by so many on these particular horoscopes. What astrologer, good or bad, would have the heart to tell proud parents that their infant son or daughter's future is doomed? However, I hide my misgivings and receive him graciously, as befits his legal half-sister; allow him to see and hold Damerei who is promptly sick all over him (the child has taste).

When Kate has cleaned up his satin doublet, which will never be the same again, and he has consulted his books and charts and pronounced fortunate stars and planets for Damerei (surprise, surprise), he extracts a small revenge for his smarting dignity. Perhaps he saw me smother a smile, heard Kate hiccup on a giggle? Over the refreshment I have ordered, he asks me did I know that the Castle of Sherborne, where he presumes 'Wat' and I intend to live in due course, has a curse upon it?

I say I did not know and, in truth, would rather have remained in ignorance, but he continues regardless, explaining that it is not the dwelling itself that is cursed but those who would live in it. 'The curse was pronounced by St. Osmund, a former bishop of Salisbury, who promised destruction to any who alienate the estate of Sherborne from the bishopric'. As, of course, Walter has done – with the aid of Queen Elizabeth, who enjoys snatching land from bishops. He then goes on to smile and say that of course there can be no truth in it, he but told me to amuse me!

I am relieved when he departs eventually, more stiffly than he came, after we've bowed and curtsied formally in an atmosphere thick with mutual dislike.

He's quite spoilt my pleasure in Walter's letter. A curse on our heads is all we need at this particular time.

* * *

Curse or no, I am back at Court, all slim and prim and virginal-looking.

My confidence grows daily for I detect no covert nudges, no surreptitious whispers; no-one stops talking when I enter a room suddenly. Aud Shelton, perhaps, seems a shade cool, but she was ever a fair-weather friend, blowing hot and cold as it suited her, and she has turned to other gossips these past six weeks or so of my absence, which is understandable. When I did rather daringly mention colourful rumours which had 'reached my ear' concerning a possible marriage of Raleigh's, she shrugged and said vaguely that there would always be rumours about him and these particular ones appeared to have been unfounded, and no-one knew who the bride was supposed to have been anyway. She'll detest me when the truth is out.

Robin Cecil goes out of his way to be charming. It's a comfort to know he's such a good, trustworthy friend.. And the Queen continues warm - asking solicitously after Anna's health - so it appears I misjudged the motives of the Earl of Essex who must be keeping our secret and who is, as Arthur predicted, almost back in favour now that Walter is at last at sea. He sailed from Falmouth on the sixth of May and will turn back when he reaches a place called Cape Finisterre. I can't wait. Poor Frances, of course, is still forbidden to show her face at Court, but at least she is with her children, which I envy.

Caught up again in this frantic, futile whirl of activity which constitutes serving royalty, I feel I am existing in a bizarre dream. I am not the person I was, yet have to pretend to be, all the while missing little Damerei. Perhaps foolishly, I had not realised the maternal pull would be so strong. My thoughts dwell frequently back at Mile End where my poor child grows and (knock on wood) thrives in the care of his wet nurse.

ROBERT CECIL

Whitehall Palace. May, 1592

'Will *I* go to the Queen?' my father asks. 'Or will you?

'

BESS

Whitehall Palace, May, 1592

Do I imagine it or is the atmosphere around me changing? I realise my conscience is troubling me even more than usual because yesterday Arthur quietly signed and sealed my official marriage settlement in his Mile End study in the presence of Walter's cousin, Sir George Carew - yet another who knows all.

But I'm sure Lady Warwick's smile appeared stretched and strained and Lady Scrope's conversation changed course when I came on them unexpectedly this morning.

The Queen remains friendly, but too much so? I've seen her play cat and mouse often enough. This morning I stuttered when I spoke to her; dropped one of the Royal jewel caskets, damaging several ornamental pearls on the clasp. Yet I was not even verbally chastised. And there was an odd expression in those sharp black eyes of hers – something inscrutable – which filled me with unease.

I can't eat. I can't sleep. I hear, or imagine, whispers everywhere.

* * *

There is definitely something amiss. Returning from prayers today, walking behind the Queen, Aud Shelton snubbed me openly and I did not dare ask why.

Thank God for a message from Arthur informing me that Walter is back in Plymouth and returns to Durham House tomorrow. He says that Anna, dear Anna, has arranged for Damerei's nurse to take him to visit his father and begs me be patient and cautious. But I, whatever the risk, aim to invent a sick headache and sneak over there with Kate.

I cannot miss seeing father and son together for the first time…

* * *

Little Robin Cecil slips me a note when he shuffles past me in the Privy Gallery. (He's afflicted with a splayed foot as well as a crooked back.) The note requests me to meet him in a secluded arbour on the far side of the herb garden.

It is very early. The Queen is not yet fully dressed and I am supposed to be fetching her a clean ruff (she spilled wine on the first while breaking her fast), but I pay one of the chamberers to collect it instead and steal out, jumpy as a footpad, to find Robin awaiting me, skulking among the greenery.

He steps out and lays a hand on my arm. 'Bess – is it true you mean to meet Raleigh at Durham House today?'

I gasp. 'Is it common knowledge?'

'It's rumoured. And rumours of your marriage and child have reached the Queen, who believes them..'

My heart stops. 'She knows? But who...?

He shrugs. 'Does it matter? The important thing is that you escape from here. And not to Durham House.'

'But I must warn Walter...'

'I've sent him word.'

'Then I hope you've told him he must come here at once and see the Queen ... explain...'

'It's too late,' Robin looks grim. 'He should have grasped the nettle sooner. She'll not receive him now. I have advised him to write...'

A kind of desperate courage seizes me. I turn on my heel. 'Then I'll go back and see the Queen myself. She expects me anyway...'

'Don't be a fool!' Robin grasps my sleeve. 'You must run to the stables and take horse to Mile End, to your brother - lie low for a while. If you see the Queen alone, she'll tear you limb from limb!'

I wrench my sleeve from him. 'I won't sneak away like a thief in the night! I've done nothing wrong. It's not a crime to be legally married and I shall tell the Queen so!'

'Such pretty hair, to be torn out from the scalp!' I hear him groan as I march determinedly away.

My determination is short-lived. By the herb garden gate I meet Lady Heneage, wife to the Vice-Chamberlain and ever a forthright woman.

'Elizabeth Throckmorton,' she says without preamble, 'I'm to accompany you to your quarters to collect your belongings. You're relieved of all duties and are to be placed in my husband's custody until further notice...

* * *

June, 1592

'Veritas vos liberabit', my mother was fond of reciting to my brothers and me when, as children, we were loath to own up to some small misdemeanour. 'The truth shall make you free.'

Not always. We are all confined; Walter at Durham House, in the care of our kinsman, Sir George Carew; Arthur and Anna at Mile End; I here at Whitehall, in a couple of pokey rooms as far from the other Maids as possible - lest I infect them with that dread disease called marriage, I suppose - under the dutifully watchful eyes of Lady Heneage and her daughter, Elizabeth Finch.

The Queen refuses to see any of us. And, worse, forbids us to communicate with each other. The only news I hear is brought to me by my elegant jailers and their servants. Beth Finch, herself a happy wife, is much too kind to repeat spiteful gossip to me, but she admits that gleeful wagers are being taken on whether or not Walter will escape a visit to the Tower.

'Of course he will,' she comforts, her long face creased with sympathy. 'It's not a matter of seduction, for Heaven's sake! You'll both be banished from Court for a while, that's all. It's nothing serious...'

But the Lord Chamberlain thinks otherwise. In my interview with him, he referred to 'Raleigh's brutish offence'.

'There's nothing brutal, my Lord Hunsdon,' I retorted, 'about giving one's wife a child. I'm a respectable married woman…'

'You're a shameless hussy who will not say another word!' he bellowed, his great round face the colour of a strawberry. 'You swore on oath to serve and obey your sovereign. You know full well that by wedding you without Royal permission, Sir Walter Raleigh has defiled your honour and degraded the entire Court. You could have gone far, you were one of Her Majesty's favourite ladies. Damn it – you were one of *my* favourites! But you're finished here now. Out of my sight, Mistress Throckmorton – I refuse to call you "Raleigh". Your father must be spinning in his shroud!'

'What a dreadful fuss,' sighs Beth Finch, 'over a wedding ring. If Her Majesty wasn't an embittered old maid who wants to keep every handsome man for herself, it would never have arisen. Just wait it out patiently, Bess. The storm will blow over soon. I heard my mother reply to the Countess of Pembroke, when she enquired about you, that she thought you were soon to be allowed to go to your brother's London home. You'll still be under house arrest, of course, and unable to see Sir Walter. But at least you'll be reunited with your sweet little Daniel.'

'Damerei.' The tears I kept at bay before Lord Hunsdon spurt like a fountain. 'I've almost forgotten what he looks like…'

※ ※ ※

August,1592

'Lady Raleigh– Elizabeth – you *must* wake up!'

I drag open my eyes, stare groggily at Lady Heneage, then close them again.

'Go away. It's the middle of the night.'

She shakes my shoulder urgently. 'It's morning - just. You are commanded to get dressed. An escort is here for you...'

That awakens me. I sit up eagerly. 'I am to go to Mile End? To my brother and sister-in-law?'

She flinches. 'No.'

And then I see two guards, waiting in the doorway.

ROBERT CECIL

Cecil House, 1592

'I can't believe the Queen's cruelty in sending them to the Tower,' raged my wife Lizzie earlier this evening, 'I could understand it if their child had been born out of wedlock but they were lawfully married. It's most unfair. I'm shocked! Disgusted!'

I am a little shocked, myself. I'd expected Raleigh to be imprisoned, of course, but not Bess. The silly wench should have heeded my warning – fled while she had the chance. I felt better, though, when my father, who was dining with us, pursed his lips in disapproval and said his spies had told him they were enjoying a second honeymoon within those stout grey walls.

'The knave's bribed his gaolers. They turn a blind eye when he slips across from the Brick Tower to the one opposite and into his wife's bed.'

'Good,' said Lizzie, pleased. 'Serves the Queen right.'

I'm glad Bess is getting some comfort. Once, I'd have been jealous, picturing them together. But not now that I have my Lizzie, the sweetest, loveliest woman in the world. The moment I saw her at Court, dainty and exquisite as a porcelain figure, I fell in love with her. But never, in my wildest dreams, had I imagined she could fall for me.

'The rest of the time he's treating the place like an office,' my father continued, spearing a piece of mutton on his knife and still talking of Raleigh. 'Busier than ever, apparently, with sailors, sea-captains, ship-builders and the like forever in and out, seeking his advice, his signature on this or that. More than a few courtiers too, I believe, hoping to curry favour in case he's soon forgiven. No chance of that, I could tell them, and if he gets Bessie pregnant again he'll give further offence.'

' I'd like to discover the villain who betrayed the two of them to the Queen,' Lizzie said grimly. 'May he never prosper, whoever he is.'

I applied myself to peeling an apple with great concentration.

Now, snuggled up to me in bed, my kind little wife is still fretting.

'Poor, poor Bess,' she says, 'separated from her baby.'

I refuse to feel guilty.

Not even about the contrite letters and poems Raleigh has sent me, intended for the eyes of the Queen. If I'd troubled myself to pass them on, she'd likely not have read them.'

✳ ✳ ✳

Nonsuch Palace, September 1592

The Queen summons me.

I'm surprised. I've been unofficially doing the job Walsingham was doing for nigh on two years – and doing it well – but the Queen tends to overlook my achievements or credit them to my father. She never asks for me alone. Perhaps there is some mistake and it's really my father she wants?

But when I arrive in the privy chamber I find my father is already with her – leaning on his cane beside her gilded chair.

I sink down on one knee – not easy for one of my disability – but she waves me up impatiently, ignores it when I wobble and almost topple over, face first, on to her jewelled slippers.

'Elf,' she says, when I've righted myself, 'we need your sharp nose and eagle eye. Two of our ships from the Panama voyage have sailed into Dartmouth. It seems Sir Walter Raleigh, before he obeyed my order to turn back, sent his Roebuck and my Foresight a-pirating. They've captured a Portuguese carrack, loaded with treasure.'

'Marvellous, Your Majesty, 'I murmur, wondering what it has to do with me.

'Marvellous it is not!' she snaps, rapping her fan on the chair arm. 'Looters are at her, stripping her bare. No-one controls them. You will journey down at once and rectify this; recover what is rightfully ours, divide the spoils as they were meant to be divided and restore proper order.'

Horrified, I gasp: 'Your Majesty, forgive me, but I know nothing of maritime affairs.

No-one will listen to me.'

Her rouged cheeks glow redder still. 'Little man, you must make them listen! This is not a request but a command.'

I look to my father for support. He looks away.

* * *

Dartmouth, 1592

Madre de Dios – the carrack's well-named.

'Mother of God!' I frequently groan, amidst this utter chaos on the bustling quay, the wind ripping at my cloak and the seagulls shrieking.

Never have I seen such an abundance of riches in one place – pearls, diamonds, rubies, damasks, tapestries . . . But neither have I seen such barefaced villainy. One thieving sailor pushed right past me with a jewelled goblet in his hands. 'Arrest that man!' I shouted to my guards, but his rough-necked colleagues closed in around him, quick as a flash, and by the time they were thrust aside he'd vanished into thin air.

I've had barriers, now, erected around the rosewood chests I discovered dumped on the stony ground beside the enormous ship, overflowing with gold, silver and aromatic spices, but for every looter we apprehend, be he sea-man, merchant, tradesman or profiteer, two more slip through somehow and make off with valuables.

'The crew 'ave not been paid,' one insolent fellow growled to me before I had him marched off to prison. 'You can't blame us for 'elping ourselves.'

They've helped themselves most efficiently, it seems. My men discover wenches in taverns wearing ropes of pearls, beggars with gems in their pockets. Divide the spoils? Soon there'll be no 'spoils' left.

The gaols are not big enough to hold all the offenders, and many have gone to ground. When we hammer on doors, seeking information about the robbers or stolen goods, we are met with blank faces and denials. Even when we ransack the nearby hovels or warehouses we come away with nothing and an appeal to the local authorities brings no joy – they resent my authority, coming from London, and offer no useful advice.

'I despair,' I shout to Sir John Hawkins, who's meant to be assisting but who stands there shaking his grey head, useless as I. 'This is hopeless. What can we do?'

'Write to your father,' he shouts back, sucking on his pipe of tobacco. 'There's only one man they'll heed – one man they idolise enough to do his bidding.'

I sigh, return to my lodgings and take up my pen. No need for either one of us to speak the Idol's name.

* * *

He rides in to a hero's welcome. To resounding cheers and the waving of caps and hats.

Smiling, leaning down from the saddle to clasp eager, outstretched hands, his face is alight with triumph as he catches my eye. He may be hated in London but he's loved in the West Country.

He's pale from his incarceration but dashing as ever, despite dressing sensibly for the task in hand. He looks as much at home in plain brown doublet and hose and leather boots as he does in his silks and velvets and they suit him equally, his only adornment the double pearl which swings from his ear as he dismounts. Sir John Gilbert, his half-brother and the Deputy of Devon (who has neglected to put in an appearance until now, rushes to embrace him, tears in his eyes, and Raleigh turns to embrace me also, warm to me as always.

He sets to at once and works like a demon, paying the crew their wages, recovering treasure. Much of the latter is lost, of course – sold, for a quarter of its value, to the thieving London merchants who rushed down ahead of me. But to my amazement and chagrin many of the cut-throat sailors relinquish what they've taken - gold and silver plate, spices, precious stones as big as hazelnuts – trade it to him willingly for a small increase in wages, docile as lambs, touching forelocks in deference, congratulating him on his release.

'No, not released – I'm still the Queen's poor prisoner,' Raleigh says sadly, enjoying their sympathy, their indignation, the way they glare at me as if I, and not the warden he rode down with, am his keeper, waiting to take him back and lock him up. I deem it wise to hover in the background as much as possible, a dagger 'neath my cloak, just in case one of them takes it into his head to do away with me. Not that I'd stand much chance.

Noticing, Raleigh beckons me nearer, indicates that he'll protect me, and instantly the old resentment flares. I'll protect myself, I thank you. But soon his smile, his laugh, his easy charm win me as they always do when in his company and I find that, against all odds, I'm enjoying myself.

He insists I leave my present lodging at the uncomfortable inn and stay with him at a house a little east of Plymouth, owned by his friend, Christopher Harris, a very hospitable fellow. The three of us pass the evenings merrily, drinking and card-playing far into the early hours.

Raleigh asks after my Lizzie and I ask after Bess. His face darkens and he says she's as well as she can be, shut away in the Tower.

'It's a shame you're not allowed to meet,' I say innocently and he laughs then, and winks broadly.

'We manage. But she pines for our son, our little Damerei, and that I can do nothing about.

I, too, long to see him. It's a fine thing to be a father, and I've held him but the once.'

I nod in sympathy. 'Our young Will is the apple of my eye.'

I find I'm smiling at the mere thought of him - beautiful little Will, with his straight back and sturdy legs. Thank God, he'll never see shocked pity in the eyes of his parents' visitors when they look upon him. Never have to hide himself away with books while other boys his age enjoy strenuous sports.

Among his other duties my father is Keeper of the Wards - attends to the upbringing and education of rich but fatherless boys. Therefore I grew up with several fine, strong lads sharing my home and my lessons; learnt, very early, to endure the cruel teasing, the unkind taunts they made about my puny figure behind my father's back. I endured it with a good-natured smile upon my lips, bitterness in my heart and a determination to do better than any of them.

So far, I've succeeded. And I aim to do better – to become as great a statesman as my father. I may be barely five feet in stature, but I'm rising in the world. And in order to continue rising, I have to harden my heart when Raleigh, at his most affectionate, throws an arm about my shoulders and asks:

'Can you do nothing, Rob, to speed our release from prison? The wretched plague has reared its ugly head again in London. Sensible folk have fled to the country and my wife and I should be among them. Now that you're State Secretary in all but name and a Privy Councillor to boot, surely your word carries weight?'

I shrug. Look regretful. 'I'm doing all I can but it's difficult.. There's no official record of your offence, no charges made against you that you might clear yourself by answering. It's all down to the whim of the Queen, so nothing but royal forgiveness will free you for good.'

He grimaces. 'So I really must, when our work here is finished, return to the grim old Tower? And Bess, my sweet Bess, must remain there?'

'I'm afraid so, yes.'

'And you did pass on my letters?''

I look him straight in the eye. 'Of course.'

※ ※ ※

The last evening of his freedom finds us working out the shares by candle-light, sitting companionably side by side at Harris's desk in his cosy little study.

I pride myself on having a head for figures but Raleigh's quicker still at this complicated reckoning – at the division of these vast sums, the lion's share of which he insists must go to the Queen, despite the fact she put the least coin into the venture.

'May fattening the royal purse soften the royal heart,' he says, but his grin fades when we hear a familiar voice raised in the outer passage and an urgent rap on the door announces, of all people, his brother-in-law Throckmorton, travel-stained and ashen of face.

'Walter – God help me – I'm the bearer of bad tidings ...'

Raleigh leaps to his feet, his own face whitening. 'Bess? Has something happened to Bess?'

Throckmorton swallows, shakes his head. 'Not Bess, Walter. It's Damerei ...'

BESS

The Tower of London, November, 1592

Walter has returned to his prison quarters and is allowed to visit mine, but I find no comfort in it. Nothing seems to matter. He is hurting too, of course, but it doesn't seem to matter. People send letters. I don't open them; don't listen when Walter reads them to me. So people are sorry? Am I supposed to be glad that they are sorry? No letter comes from the Queen. That doesn't matter either.

I blame my brother Arthur. Have blamed him from the minute he told me the news.

'If you hadn't asked Essex to be Godfather, we'd never have been betrayed,' I told him bitterly. 'I'd have been looking after my child's welfare myself by now – not imprisoned in this horrible place away from him, unable to protect him.'

He tried to take my hands but I pulled away. 'Bess,' he pleaded, his pale face going whiter still, 'It wasn't Essex who betrayed you ....'

'Of course it was! Who else?'

He spread his palms; he didn't know. 'But I swear it wasn't Essex. And, on my oath, Bess, we didn't know Damerei's nurse had visited sick relatives in the city. We'd have dismissed her had we known. We thought she was responsible – far too sensible to put the poor little thing at risk ....'

'But she wasn't, was she? And now they're both dead.' Of the plague! She gave my little one the plague!

'Bess, I beg you....' He looked dreadful. His eyes were full of tears. 'You're upset, of course you are, but don't blame me. I can't bear it....'

'Get out! Get out, and don't come back ....'

He *has* been back. He went to Dartmouth to fetch Walter and then he came back. Several times, and with Anna. I refused to speak to them – refused to look at them. Now, mercifully, they appear to have given up.

✤ ✤ ✤

We are released from the Tower but banned from Court. Who cares?

We take horse for Sherborne, to spend Christmas quietly.

Walter's servants are overjoyed to see him and make a great fuss of me. I can't respond. Despite all their efforts with seasonal greenery, holly berries, huge fires and warm hangings, the old castle is cheerless – draughty and uncomfortable. I look around at the handsome features Walter proudly points out and can only think; It has a curse upon it.

Walter is amazingly kind. He's gentle and considerate. He showers me with jewels, with all manner of gifts. I summon a stiff smile for him but leave the boxes, the caskets, the packages, unopened. He holds me close. I can't respond. He whispers that we will continue to sleep in separate chambers; that he will wait - as long as it takes – for me to heal.

'Heal?' I demanded once. 'Heal? I do not have a cut finger that will heal with a touch of salve!'

He made no answer – just looked sad..

* * *

It seems that Walter, in desperation, sent secretly for his mother and, to his surprise, she's arrived – journeyed, on her slow old mare, from Essex in this bitter weather. Where a marriage, a birth and a baptism failed to bring her, a melancholy daughter-in-law succeeds…

She's thin as a stick, brisk, stern; ordering the servants about in a manner you'd think they would resent, yet they scurry to do her bidding. And she's as tender to me as Walter.

'We all lose children, Bess, my dear,' she says softly, holding both my hands in her old gnarled claws. 'It's the order of things. But we have others that live, that thrive, that don't replace but that compensate. You will too, I promise – strong, wonderful sons to inherit this lovely place .'

I only want Damerei.

* * *

Kate confides, as she's dressing my hair. 'Early this morn I rode out to Cerner Abbas with two of Sir Walter's servants. They wanted to show me the giant, Helith, carved into the hillside there. He's a Green Man, they say, a fertility god. The local couples make love on his great you-know-what when they want to start a family. I brought back a little clod of earth for luck. We'll put it under your pillow, wrapped in silk, and you'll soon have another beautiful babe to comfort you.'

Will they never realise this kind of talk is hurtful?

* * *

'Has she not wept at *all*?' I heard my mother-in-law ask Walter. 'If she could, it would release her – make her feel better.'

* * *

January,1593

Walter plans to return to London. Alone. Well, he was bound to eventually tire of his drooping wife and there are plenty of people here at Sherborne to look to my wretched welfare. He can leave with a clear conscience.

He might be banned from Court but he's still required to sit in Parliament, which opens on the nineteenth day of February. He doesn't seem to mind that he's been demoted. As a symbol of his 'disgrace' he has not been returned as a knight of the shire for

Devon but as member for the little borough of St Michael, in Cornwall.

'Scarcely more than a village,' he says, 'with few electors. But at least I'm still there, Bess, and I'll make my voice heard in the House of Commons, never fear. There's more than one road back to royal favour.'

It won't be an easy road. The Queen's still full of anger towards him. Despite his careful division of the shares, his generosity to her, she made sure he lost money in the end on the Madre de Dios, on the entire Panama venture. And she still won't see him, of course, or acknowledge any of his letters.. We're lucky the old hag has left us Sherborne and Durham House – not snatched them back in spite.

I turn away with a sigh; gaze out of the window at the bleak winter landscape Walter is planning to alter – to transform into 'wonderful gardens' and 'glorious country parks'. But I can summon no more interest in his plans for Sherborne than I can in his futile efforts to return to Court.

'You don't mind my going?' he asks. 'Don't mind my leaving you here?'

I turn back. 'Of course not.'

It doesn't matter.

✳ ✳ ✳

The night before he's due to depart, I find a locket beneath my pillow, tucked under the little silken purse which contains the Cerne Abbas earth.

It's a beautiful locket – gold, shaped like a heart – and when it springs open I find I'm looking at a miniature of a beautiful baby.

My beautiful baby. My Damerei. And Walter's. He must have had it painted months ago, as a surprise for me.

And suddenly I am weeping – a great, noisy torrent of tears that will not be stemmed. I'm running to him in the room set aside as his study; clinging to him, kissing him, and he's clinging to me, kissing me back.

After a while I whisper: 'Take me with you to London.'

He does. But first he takes me to bed and I come truly alive again.

✳ ✳ ✳

Durham House, March 1593

Being official mistress here is gratifying but strange. I sometimes feel I will never get used to giving orders, receiving visitors, swishing about openly in silken skirts in the very building where I once crept clandestinely around back staircases and servants' corridors to reach Walter in the master bedroom.

Dwelling so close to Whitehall Palace yet knowing myself forbidden, is stranger still. Not that we are starved of company. Robin and Lizzie Cecil are quick to visit, of course, but I had feared other old friends would shun us for fear of offending the Queen. Happily, this is not the case.

A number of Courtiers are pleased to follow the Cecil's' example – dine with us and entertain us in their London houses in return. Harriot's School of Navigation continues to flourish in Walter's study, and Walter's special circle also gather there regularly to put the world to rights - Arthur Gorges,

Northumberland and Tom Harriot chief among them, but many others also. I smile to see the wide variation of intellectuals, scientists, explorers, artists and, inevitably, poets, who cross our stone-pillared threshold and head eagerly, with their pipes of tobacco, up the stairs to the turret room (my bridal chapel).

During the hours Walter shines in Parliament, several of my women friends who sent letters of sympathy when I languished in the Tower descend on me, among them Frances, Countess of Essex.

'You do not suspect my Robby of giving you away to the Queen, do you, Bess?' she asks anxiously when she's enquired after my health and we're sampling cakes and wine. 'Because I know he would never do such a wicked thing.'

What can I say? I have no proof and I am fond of Frances who would never harm a fly, so I smile and shake my head - through my very silence, let her think I believe in his innocence. But I will always be convinced our betrayer was Essex. He wanted Walter out of the path of his advancement and well he's succeeded. The Queen has ever loved playing them off against each other - when the one is brought low, the other must be raised high, like two children on a see-saw. So, to spite Walter, she's chosen this particular time to make Essex a Privy Councillor. Essex who, to my mind, hasn't a brain in his head! How galling for my clever Walter. But he'll be back at Court soon, everyone says.

Frances is still not welcome at Court for the sin of marrying Essex, but she will always be welcome in my home. Just let her precious, venomous 'Robby' attempt to set foot in it.

* * *

From his lowly parliamentary seat in the Chapel of St Stephen in the Precinct of the Palace of Westminster, Walter is busily raising his voice on a wide range of important issues. So far, I understand, he has urged the increase of taxes, but only from the rich, for the continuing sea war against Spain; offered sensible advice over the government's handling of the Puritans and issued a sound economic warning against the ever-growing, and very unpopular, number of Dutch merchants in London.

'Whether or not they agree with his policies, Walter's impressing everyone with the strengths of his argument,' Arthur Gorges, Member of Parliament for Dorsetshire, reports enthusiastically to me at Durham House. 'He's proving he's still a man to be reckoned with. He's even planning a written paper to the Queen on the succession – supporting her in her decision not to yet name an heir. This is the path back to favour, Bess, I'm convinced, and everyone who matters says the same. She'll send for him soon, you'll see.'

But if Walter has impressed the Queen, she shows no sign of it. Meanwhile, I show signs of a different nature....

* * *

Last evening we dined with Walter's great friend, Henry Percy, Earl of Northumberland, at his London house – the man ignorant, frightened folk call 'Wizard' because of his scientific experiments.

A less likely wizard I have yet to come across. He's younger than Walter (my age), rather sweet and shy, especially with women, and has a pronounced stammer, with which Walter is endlessly patient. He's terribly rich - his house is wonderfully furnished - but he seemed more interested in proudly showing me his huge, well-stocked library than any other priceless treasures. Walter says he has a marvellous brain but then, most of Walter's friends are clever. Why on earth did he marry *me?*

We returned very late, but after weeks of near breathless hope, I could wait no longer. The minute we'd dismissed Walter's manservant and Kate, I said brightly, brushing my well-brushed hair again with studied casualness:

'It appears the Cerne Abbas Giant has done his duty well - with the aid of a certain West Country knight, of course . . .'

Walter paused in the act of unbuttoning his velvet night robe, stared over at me from his stance beside the huge green and silver bed of our consummation (no separate chambers now).

'The Cerne Abbas Giant?' he said slowly. 'Bess, can you possibly mean....?

I nodded, suddenly unable to say more.

He reached me in two strides, gathered me up in a bear hug then set me down carefully, his eyes searching my face. 'You're happy?'

'He will never replace,' I whispered, blinking back tears, 'but he will be a much treasured blessing. He or she.'

'He,' said Walter, dashing away his own tears with an impatient hand. 'This will be another son; we'll have a daughter next time. The Cerne Abbas Giant and I will see to it.'

'And he must be born at Sherborne,' we said together, and laughed.

* * *

The week before Parliament dissolved, my brother Nicholas paid me a visit, bringing my brother William, who was so overjoyed to see me again he kept stroking me, much as one would a puppy. Poor Sweet William – the older he gets (he's forty summers!) the younger he seems to act.

' Bess,' Nicholas began, 'about your quarrel with Arthur ...'

'I know, I *know*,' I said quickly. 'I cannot face him yet.'

'But...'

'I'll write to him from Sherborne.'

* * *

July, 1593

The Abbey bells ring out for us as we ride through Sherborne town; people line the streets to wave and cheer. At the Castle, the servants stream out into the main courtyard and on to the drawbridge to bow and curtsey and wish us well – as if it is my very first time here as Walter's bride (I feel it is).

The ancient walls of my new home glow golden in the sunshine; summer wildflowers abound in the park and on the slopes of the drained moat; swallows swoop overhead, skylarks sing. To the north-east flows the shining River Yeo; to the south, rich meadowland slopes gently up to a glorious forest of oak, beech, ash, birch, elm.

'A child born here will be fortunate indeed,' I exclaim to Walter, as he waves the groom away and carefully helps me dismount, as the bailiff, John Meere, and his wife step forward, smiling, to welcome us.

* * *

I've kept my promise to Nicholas; penned Arthur a grovelling apology and sent it off via one of Walter's couriers.

Arthur is prone to sulking. He may not even reply.

* * *

Today Wood, our courier, returns – seeks me out in the chamber I am attempting to turn into a makeshift nursery and gives me a letter addressed to Morgan Le Fe in my brother's spidery hand.

Arthur writes as if naught was amiss between us, causing me to break down in a flood of tears. Kate, alarmed, thinks I've received bad news.

He adds a postscript; Anna intends to leave their daughter Mary with her nurse and travel to be with me at my lying-in. Hmm. With misgiving, I remember that stifling chamber in the Mile End house; my sister-in-law's rules and regulations.

A mixed blessing?

* * *

September,1593

Both Anna and Arthur have arrived, exclaiming in delight at the beauty of Sherborne. We explain to them that we're finding the Castle too draughty and uncomfortable, despite the improvements we've made to it, so Walter is planning to build a new house on the other side of the park. It turns out that Arthur also plans to build a modern house on his land at Paulerspury in Northamptonshire (inherited from my father) so he and Walter have much in common. Walter takes him on a tour of the site for our new building, and they spend hours marching around the park, heads close together, deep in discussion about the ideal positioning of doors and windows, the best possible marble, the expense of elaborate water courses. 'Arthur,' says Anna sourly, is spending money like water. When he isn't losing it at cards.'

I smile to find my relatives unchanged; Arthur complaining of his ailments (he's recently taken the waters at Bath); Anna complaining of Arthur.

I've missed them.

✳ ✳ ✳

After supper Walter and Arthur played at Primero. Arthur lost heavily.

✳ ✳ ✳

October, 1593

Sir Walter Raleigh and the Cerne Abbas Giant make an excellent team. This morning I was delivered of a beautiful healthy boy.

I am triumphant but exhausted – as much by the constant argument as the ordeal itself.

First Walter shocked Anna, Mrs Meere and the midwife, by staying in the birthing chamber (he clutched my hand so tightly he almost broke my fingers as well as strict convention).

'Indecent!' snorted Mrs Meere.

'Unheard of!' moaned Anna.

Next he threw the windows wide and dowsed the roaring fire.

'You'll be sorry, Sir Walter,' the midwife warned. 'Mother and babe will be taken off with a fever if you do that.'

'Mother and babe will be taken off with the Sweat if I do not!'

I caused further uproar by dismissing the wet-nurse. I have insisted all along that I do not want one but Anna engaged a woman behind my back. I intend to keep a nursery maid but will feed this child myself.

'The native women in Virginia feed their own young,' Walter said. 'And their offspring grow up strong and straight as saplings.'

The midwife clenched her hands in exasperation and turned away.

'Oh, if the savages in Virginia do it, it's bound to be right,' I heard Anna mutter.

'Have you chosen a name yet, my lady?' asked the midwife, softening a little before she left,

'We intend to call him after his father and paternal grandfather,' I said firmly, dreading contradiction. But Walter laughed and agreed.

'Little Wat,' he said, stroking the tiny dark head and dampening it with fatherly tears.

Little Wat is to be christened on All Saints' Day in the pretty little church of Lillington, a few miles south of Sherborne. Against convention (again), I shall attend.

Walter's mother has been invited but has sent a message to say she cannot come, Anna and Arthur are to be Godparents. Also Adrian Gilbert (Walter's choice).

No-one remarks on Little Wat's likeness to his brother, but there are times when I have to prevent myself from calling him Damerei. On such occasions I snatch him up and hold him close and weep. For joy and sorrow equally.

※ ※ ※

We find we're nervous parents. We pluck the child from sleep just to make sure he's breathing. I un-swaddle him when I feed him to check for disease blemishes.

And as for superstition . . .

No-one must rock the cradle without the baby in it.

Wat must not glimpse his reflection before he is one year old .

. .

※ ※ ※

I have been forced to re-employ the wet-nurse – it seems my milk is too thin to satisfy my greedy son. I shocked the nursery maid by coming out with a string of curses I picked up from the Queen.

※ ※ ※

January, 1594

'We bask in contentment here at Sherborne,' I write to all my friends in Town lest they think we pine to be back at Court. 'By comparison, London, to our minds, grows worse and worse...'

I take mischievous pleasure in signing myself E. R. – just like the Queen. How it will annoy her if she is shown it!

In truth, we are too busy to reflect on what we are missing but 'contented' ill befits my husband, with his passion for improvement. I am fully occupied and besotted with Little Wat (who is smiling now - his nurse says it's wind, but I know it is not), with Little Wat's father, with the day to day running of my large household. While Walter being Walter, manages to be involved in a dozen different pursuits at once.

As well as overseeing Meere overseeing the estate, bullying the builders, breeding and training his horses, his falcons, he is striving to add the leases of three manors to our list of properties – quarrelling with the Bishop and clergy of Salisbury in the attempt. On top of all this he still fulfils his duties as Lord Warden of the Stannaries, Lord Lieutenant of Cornwall and sundry other posts.

His couriers and agents wear out the London Road, their saddlebags bulging with his pleas, commands and complaints (which are often on behalf of other people - widows, seamen, our less fortunate Sherborne neighbours - who appeal to him for help over all manner of issues. Last week he wrote to poor Robin Cecil four times in one day.)

Sometimes his patience wanes and he takes horse for London himself, thunders there and back in the space of a few days. And however late we are abed and however energetic behind the drawn bed curtains, he continues with his habit of rising early each morning to study and to write creatively. The servants say his energy is frightening. I overheard one maidservant claim it came from the devil and instantly dismissed her.

He is happy, I believe. I hope. He calls Sherborne his 'Fortress Fold', his wife and (smiling) son his 'heart's delight'. But contented? Never. This restlessness worries me.

* * *

February,1594

I have just written to Robin Cecil - secretly! I slipped the letter into a courier's saddlebag when Walter's back was turned.

Walter has thrown me into a panic by talking of "perhaps" voyaging to Guiana; of "calling" at Virginia along the way in the hope of finding his lost colonists from the City of Raleigh. He speaks of crossing the Atlantic as if it costs no more effort than rowing the width of the Thames in a wherry.

'I owe it to poor John White to go myself,' he said.

I share his concern for the colonists, of course – everyone does. It was a full two years after the Armada before Walter was able to obtain permission for Governor White to return with their supplies, and when he finally did there was no sign of them. All those men, women and children who'd sailed so bravely from Plymouth had disappeared into thin air!

John White, living now on one of Walter's estates in Ireland, is a broken man His daughter, son-in-law and baby granddaughter are among those lost. Most people believe them to be dead – eaten by wild beasts or slaughtered by natives or Spaniards - but Walter refuses to accept this. He thinks they may have simply moved to another island, abandoned the one on which they were last seen (Roanoke).

Now, it appears, he believes he is the man to find them where lesser men have failed.

With dismay, I recall the tales I've heard of the New World – of the native tribesmen who are not gentle like the ones Harriot brought to London but murderously ferocious. Of the crocodiles, the snakes, the poisonous insects. All this on top of the hazards of the journey itself. And as for Guiana – even further away...

He's been day-dreaming of that golden city again – the place he calls El Dorado. I knew it had never truly left his mind but I didn't believe he'd ever set out to discover it in person.

'It's the way forward, Bess,' he insisted last night in the privacy of our curtained bed. 'I have to do something drastic to win back royal approval and I'm determined still to wrest a piece of the New World for England. Guiana presents wonderful possibilities for both. It's a place ripe for colonisation, while the gold it is believed to yield will soften the Queen's heart in a trice, if I can find it.'

'But what about your affairs here? What about Sherborne? The tin mines?' Wat and me?

Naturally he'd leave people to look after everything, look after us, he said. There would be Robin Cecil, Tom Harriot and my brother Arthur, in London. The Pembrokes, Carew, Adrian Gilbert and John Meere close at hand. And in any case, his plans were by no means certain yet. He'd have to find and convince several investors, request Letters Patent granting him permission to explore on the Queen's behalf...'

'It will be many months, sweetheart,' he promised, stroking my hair, 'before we're parted. If it happens at all.' *But he wants it to happen – is intent on making it happen!* 'Meanwhile, not a word to anyone. It's our secret – and Robin Cecil's.'

Until his plans are further advanced!

We made love with a rather desperate passion and I managed to hold back my tears until he'd fallen asleep. Then, tossing and turning, I decided to implore Robin, for my sake, to help my husband back to his old position of Captain of the Guard rather than further his plans for sailing towards the sunset, golden or not.

* * *

'Here we have a walled rose garden with an ornamental fountain at its centre,' enthuses Adrian Gilbert, spreading his carefully-drawn plans over the beautiful round walnut table we've bought in anticipation of our move across the park.

I die a thousand deaths each time Adrian stabs hard at a chart with his quill while making a point. 'Here a cherry orchard,' (another stab) 'and here a water feature' (yet another!) 'that will be smaller than a lake but bigger than a pond, teeming with rare, jewel-coloured fish, ringed with exotic plants from your new found land of Virginia and in constant, rippling movement from the waterfall drawn over rocks from the River Yeo...'

He steps back a pace and waits for Walter and me to make admiring noises. Which we do – genuine ones. Adrian is performing miracles in landscaping our new gardens, improving the old ones. When Walter claps him on the back and calls him a genius, he beams. But when I give him a sisterly peck on the cheek his smile fades and his eyes harden. A little later I spy him surreptitiously wiping his cheek with his sleeve.

* * *

At Walter's request I have been sitting for a portrait – well, standing for one. For hours at a time. My legs ache from the effort, I can scarce move my poor stiff neck.

And after all this I hate the result. My gold-embroidered gown and kirtle, my ropes of exquisite pearls, my wedding earrings, the jewelled ornament in my hair – all are executed beautifully. But my face! It looks as wretched as I feel.

Walter is surprised at my reaction. He loves the painting – says it has 'character' and pays more for it than he'd agreed.

No word from Robin Cecil. I expect he thinks I'm a bad, selfish wife who should keep her nose – long, according to the portrait - out of her husband's business.

* * *

Hancock, Walter's secretary, knowing how worried I've been, whispered to me today that Walter is arranging for one of his captains – Jacob Whiddon – to make the voyage to Guiana. I'm ecstatic.

ROBERT CECIL

Whitehall Palace, March 1594

Raleigh's friends at Court never cease to sing his praises. They aim to persuade the Queen to reinstate him. The Pembrokes, George Carew, Percy of Northumberland, Arthur Gorges, others ...

Someone has even put forward his name for admittance to the Privy Council.

'And Her Majesty appears to be wavering,' my father says. 'Any ideas, Robin?'

I stroke my beard thoughtfully. 'I believe there's some talk in Sherborne of him being an atheist ...'

BESS

Sherborne Lodge, March,1594

A great bustle and clattering of hooves in the courtyard while we're at supper.

I'm pleased when Carew is announced. Walter's' only full brother is a most welcome guest when he visits from his home near Salisbury or from business on the Isle of Portland. (When Walter was in favour, he secured for Carew the Governorship of Portland Bill and the wardenship of Gillingham Forest.)

Not in the least like Walter, Adrian or John, the oldest Gilbert brother, in looks – being fair, with ruddy cheeks - he's good-humoured and affectionate. He and his kind wife Dorothy (a dragon to some but a friend to me) have done much to help us settle in this part of the world. Dorothy has recommended good servants, offered sound household advice, while Carew has introduced Walter to all the local landowners of note and they regularly go out hunting and hawking in a very amiable party.

But Carew is looking far from amiable today.

'I've come straight from Dorchester, from socialising with Sir Ralph Horsey,' he says grimly, waving away my offers of refreshment with an impatience quite unlike him. 'Wat – you will scarce believe this, but Ralph has informed me unofficially that an inquiry is to be held soon at Cerne Abbas, by the Commissioners in Causes Ecclesiastical. An impudent investigation. Into *your* doings!'

Walter lays down his knife and stares. '*My* doings?'

Carew paces. He's obviously too angry to accept the cushioned stool a maidservant pushes forward. 'Your activities, sayings, the company you keep, the people you employ, your beliefs . . .'

I gasp and dismiss the servants. Walter thoughtfully dips his fingers into the silver fingerbowl; wipes his mouth on a napkin embroidered with his coat of arms.

'Would the Reverend Ironside of Winterborne Abbas be part of this 'inquiry?' he asks mildly.

'He would.'

They exchange a measured look. Walter's lips twitch. Carew's stern expression relaxes. They burst out laughing.

'What *can* all this be about?' I demand at last, irritated. 'First it's bad news, then it's a great jest. Explain, please.'

'They think Wat's a witch,' Carew sobs, hiccupping.

'A witch?' How can they laugh?

'Well, an enemy of the church, at least. A non-believer.' An atheist? I freeze in horror. 'All on account of a little harmless amusement.' And they're off again, crying into their wine.

'Amusement?' I could slap them both.

'Forgive us.' With an effort, Walter controls himself. 'Back in the summer, when you were large and exhausted, expecting Little Wat, Carew and I went to dine one day at Sir George Trenchard's ...'

I nod. I remember. 'At Wolveton House, near Dorchester.'

'Ralph Horsey was also invited. And a few others, including the Reverend Ironside.'

'Who's a pain in the . . . A pompous old fool,' Carew puts in, grinning. 'He was boring us all into a stupor until, when we were a little merry with wine, Wat diverted us by starting to tease him – asked him to exactly define "the soul". Unsurprisingly, he couldn't and Wat ended by tying him up in verbal knots. He didn't like it. He had a face like thunder when he left. It was marvellous.'

Again they collapse.

'So marvellous there's to be an official inquiry into your religious beliefs,' I say tartly.

'So it would seem. It's no laughing matter, in truth.' Carew mops his streaming eyes and plumps down on the stool at last.

'It is! It cannot be taken seriously, Bess,' Walter insists. 'At the root of this so-called inquiry dwell a bunch of vindictive clerics, still bristling with anger over the Queen's gift of the Sherborne lease – they mutter to all and sundry that I *"bewitched"* her into giving it to me, although they know the Bishop of Salisbury was well paid for it. There can be no repercussions from this foolishness, I promise you. No substantial evidence of 'heresy' on my part can be put forward because none exits.'

'It will never stand up,' Carew agrees roundly. 'I was angry – *am* angry – because of the sheer indignity, the disrespect it implies towards Wat and his position in these parts. But Sir Ralph Horsey and other good friends will also have to serve on this commission. They will never allow such nonsense to proceed. It will be laughed out of existence.'

I wish I could share their confidence. But this smacks, to me, of more sinister plotting. *Someone* must have sent or taken an account of Sir George's private dinner to an authority in London or such an inquiry would never have been authorised. Ironside, furious at being made to look foolish? Or has Essex planted a spy in these parts? I dare not voice my suspicion. Walter thinks I blame every mishap on Essex now. (I suppose I do.)

'You've neither of you said or done anything else that could be held against you?'

Carew looks sheepish. I glare at him. 'Well?'

He shrugs apologetically. 'We were once in Blandford and needed a post-horse urgently. We were obliged to borrow the nag belonging to old Jeffreys, the parson from Weekes Regis. He protested strongly – said he must get home because he had to preach a sermon the next day...'

'And?'

'I told him not to worry; said his horse would be back first and could preach for him - the text would be the better for it.'

This time it is I who laugh, albeit against my will. 'Surely they are not using that at the inquiry?'

Carew's grey eyes twinkle. 'I believe they are.'

✽ ✽ ✽

I can breathe again, after a fashion.

Through lack of evidence the three-day inquiry has come to naught. Neither Walter nor Carew was examined in person and most of the people who were called to answer questions were biased clergymen.

All the same, it was a nasty business. Lord Thomas Howard, Viscount Bindon (no friend to Walter), headed the commissioners; made sure he listened grimly to every silly rumour and choice morsel of tittle-tattle. The Lieutenant of Portland Castle, a protégé of Walter's, was accused of tearing pages from his bible on which to dry his tobacco; his servant, a man named Oliver, of telling two God-fearing townswomen that Moses kept fifty-two concubines.

Poor harmless Tom Harriot's name was dragged up again (the Conjurer), and that of studious, Henry Percy (the Wizard Earl), both of whom were said to be bad influences on Walter. Carew, whose 'horse incident' was frowned upon, was also abhorred for having innocently remarked 'There's surely a god in nature' while admiring the beauty of Gillingham Forest – implying, according to his accusers, that he worshipped pagan gods. And, of course, Walter's special interest in 'the soul' was much debated.

The inquiry may have broken down but it is not forgotten. Where there is smoke there must be fire, people are saying. I'm sure many of the more ignorant parishioners of Sherborne now firmly believe Walter to be a witch. He received frightened sidelong glances from several members of the congregation when we took our places in our prominent pew in Sherborne Abbey on Sunday last, amid much whispering. One tiny, trembling child even shrank back against her mother's skirts as we passed, it pained me to notice; let out a little squeal when Walter's cloak brushed her arm.

Further embarrassment lay in the knowledge that the parson who was conducting the service, Francis Scarlett, had given evidence – had eagerly passed on to Lord Bindon and the others a few more exaggerated stories he'd received second or third hand. He was very awkward when he bowed to us at the door afterwards, his face as colourful as his name. Walter deliberately made him more uncomfortable by being extra charming.

'A nine days wonder,' he said cheerfully as we strolled home arm in arm We like to walk to the abbey on Sundays, weather permitting - much to the disgust of our escort, forced to walk also. 'A squall that will soon blow over.'

Will it? I can't help being frightened by this unjustified 'atheist' slander which cannot be other than harmful.

The taint of it will certainly not help Walter get back to Court.

* * *

April, 1594

Carew again comes galloping unexpectedly into the castle courtyard, grim of face. Please – not another inquiry!

Walter, perhaps thinking the same, goes out to greet him. Carew dismounts, embraces his brother emotionally. Their mother is dead.

* * *

'Damn her independence!' swears Walter.

We've learned that she missed Wat's christening, turned down our other invitations because she was ill. Self-sufficient to the last, she wanted no-one to know – threatened her servants with dismissal if they breathed a word.

Walter is grief-stricken, full of regret and guilt for the visits he could have made, the things he could have done had he only known.

'That's how I felt,' I tell him, 'when my mother died. It's how every son or daughter feels, no matter how good they've been. And you tried hard to be wonderful to your mother. It's no fault of yours that she wouldn't let you help her, that she rejected your gifts and your money.'

She's left a very practical will addressed to "Dear Sons", lumping them all together, asking them to make sure her bequests to servants are dealt with, that various small debts of money are paid. She's left nothing personal to any of them, and no personal message for any of them.

I, who met her so briefly, seem to have understood her better than her youngest (favourite) son. I know that she adored him, took pride in him. I could see it in her eyes whenever she looked at him. But he wanted her to show that pride and she could not, she kept it hidden inside. So he will never believe in it. I vow I'll never be like that with Little Wat.

* * *

Walter's mourning for his mother has somehow become mixed with his mourning for the Queen, for their lost friendship and the reality of his disgrace..

Each day since the funeral in Exeter (my mother-in-law was buried in the Church of St. Mary Major, beside her second husband, Walter's father) he has become more withdrawn. He has lost interest in me, in Little Wat - even in the new building. 'What use in spending good money on it when it's only on lease, however long?' he snaps when I venture to mention it. 'We shall never be allowed to own it.'

He bites my head off each time I try to talk to him reasonably and seems permanently angry - railing against his banishment from Court, his suspension from his post of Captain of the Guard, from any hope of advancement. All in a manner most self-pitying.

More often, and worse, he won't talk at all; sits for hours in his cramped, makeshift study seeing no-one, writing to no-one. His quills lie idle, his books gather dust as he slumps in his leather-covered chair and stares blindly out over the rain-soaked park. The weather seems to echo his desolate mood. He doesn't even come to bed.

This new, depressed Walter is far removed from the husband, the lover, I know.

'He'll snap out of it in his own good time.' comforts his brother Carew. 'I've seen him like this before. Best leave him in peace,'

'Best leave him in peace,' advises Kate.

'Best leave him in peace,' shrugs Adrian Gilbert.

But, sitting there alone, he's not at peace! I remember how he helped me after the death of little Damerei and wish desperately to help him in return. Yet how?

* * *

The rain still comes down in torrents but for me the sun has come out for there is a spring to Walter's step. I don't know what has cheered him and, in truth, I don't care! Suddenly he's everywhere – shouting orders to the builders, offering advice, jesting, laughing. His couriers rush in and out with more correspondence than ever, their bedraggled horses steaming and stamping on the wet cobbles of the courtyard.

Merrily, we brave the elements and go hunting, hawking, in company with our neighbours. We play with our son. We entertain. We make love again – in our marital bed and, daringly, in the dripping green woods under the protective branches of a great oak tree. I am full of happiness and hope. I want that sister Walter promised me for Wat.

I ask Kate to obtain some fresh, chalky (muddy) earth from the site of the Cerne Giant – to again fill the little silk purse and place it beneath my pillow.

'But don't tell the Reverend Ironside,' I implore her, laughing.

* * *

We're in! Who would have thought moving ourselves and our belongings such a short distance in the pouring rain could be so exhausting?

I've agreed many times today (with Kate, with the nurse maid, with William the butler, with Smith the cook and Smith the cook's brother, with Mrs Meere, with brother-in-law Carew, half-brother-in-law Adrian, helpful Thomas Harriot and a dozen others) that everything about the new house, to be called Sherborne Lodge, is absolutely wonderful – a huge modern kitchen, still-room, buttery and brew house in the basement which runs all the way under the house and courtyard; a proper nursery for Wat; another turret study for Walter, a sitting room for me; airy rooms for visitors; the Raleigh initials engraved on the window of the Great Parlour; the Raleigh arms emblazoned on the ceiling of the Great Chamber; the Raleigh motto carved into one imposing fireplace, my unimposing portrait in pride of place above another (ugh!).

But I'm too worn out to appreciate any of it. We began our exertions at dawn and it is now past midnight. As I collapse into the gilded bed that has been sent down from Beaumanor (the one bequeathed to me by my stepfather that once belonged to the Duchess of Suffolk - at last I have somewhere to put it), I am aware of Walter's voice still giving orders, supervising this, that and the other. I'm too tired to take in exactly what. Then – 'Lady Raleigh will tell you where to stow that,' I hear him say in the corridor outside the Great Bedchamber. As his head appears round the door, I part the bed-curtains and throw a well-aimed pillow at it.

'Lady Raleigh will not! It can wait for the morrow.'

Perhaps his energy does come from the devil after all.

※ ※ ※

I knew I was too happy. Hancock was mistaken. Walter still intends sailing to Guiana.

'But I thought you'd sent Captain Whiddon in your place!'

He looks surprised. 'I sent Whiddon to spy out the land - to find out exactly how far the River Caroni is from the sea; whether or not it's near the mouth of the Orinoco. His report will help me when I depart with a fleet.'

'I'm sorry,' Hancock mouths from behind his small oak desk.

* * *

A reply from Robin Cecil after these long months! Second-hand, from his wife.

I sympathise greatly with you, dear Bess, as a wife and mother, but Robin regrets he cannot help. He says the Queen remains stubborn in her un-forgiveness towards you both, and he believes in Sir Walter's proposed voyage to Guiana – he is investing in it himself and so is his father.

He instructs me to beg you not to worry, since Sir Walter is a traveller of great experience and wisdom.

Meanwhile, I am sending you the recipes you once asked me for and –

I crumple the page and throw it away. I've been fond of Elizabeth since the day she arrived at Court, but I'm in no mood to read her domestic news and solicitous enquiries, however well meant. I was foolish to write. As for Robin investing – words fail me!

* * *

Everything is arranged. Jacob Whiddon has returned with a good report - if you discount the fact that seven of his men were slaughtered by Spaniards in Trinidad. Copying the pilots of the first Virginian voyage, he has brought back a native to be trained as an interpreter. This "savage", a gentle, giant of a man whom Walter has christened Harry, has developed an admiration for me and follows me everywhere – I can scarce turn round without falling over him - yet when I complain to Walter he only laughs and tells me to be sure to talk to him as incessantly as I talk to everyone else!

Together we plan a magnificent Christmas at Sherborne – gifts for the servants, feasts and presents for the families of the estate tenants to make up for the bad harvest, masques and revels for our own friends and relatives, fireworks in the park, even a boat race on the river, weather permitting. My native, I tease Walter, can be our Lord of Misrule. But even as we write out the guest list, Walter's Letters Patent arrive from the Queen.

He reads them with a wry smile.

'She's left out "trusty and well-beloved" which she has always used before. Now I am simply – coldly - "our servant Sir Walter Raleigh". But,' his eyes sparkle, 'I'm empowered to take possession of any territories not already in the possession of a Christian king...'

And he's instructed to 'annoy and enfeeble the king of Spain and his subjects' – fancy words for waging war on the Spaniards at every opportunity. She *wants* me to become a widow!

'I'll have your armour cleaned,' I say, a catch in my voice.

'Please,' he murmurs absently.

His mind's already sailed. Merry Christmas!

✳ ✳ ✳

Cecil House

The Cecil's have organised a special 'Bon Voyage' dinner party.

'To speed Raleigh on his way and assure Bess she has people to care for her while he is gone,' Robin smiles.

Annoyed as I am with him, I smile back. He and Lizzie are so kind, so affectionate. Who could have nicer friends?

And there's an old one in attendance.

'Bess...'

I swing to face Audrey Shelton for the first time in three years. Cautiously, we take stock of one another.

'You haven't changed,' she decides.

'Nor have you.'

'Not quite so slim, perhaps, but it suits you. And definitely more elegant. I 'd die for that shade of silk – not exactly blue, not exactly green - so unusual! Part of the spoils from a plundered foreign ship, I'll be bound?'

'Yes, as it happens.'

'And those wonderful pearls and diamonds?'

'A wedding gift.'

'Ah, yes.'

Her thin, pointed little face is more animated than ever, giving the illusion of prettiness when she's actually quite plain. Her slanted eyes sparkle, her hair is still girlishly long and flowing, the rich brown glint of it complementing her peach and silver gown. She looks much younger than her age (three years my junior).

'You're not yet wed?' I know she isn't.

'Not yet, but I hold out hopes.' Her eyes flicker over my shoulder and I turn to glimpse Thomas Walsingham, cousin to

Frances and once patron to poor Marlowe, passing by. Surely she doesn't care for him? A cold fish, I've always thought.

She can still read my mind. 'Now you've captured Water, I don't have a lot of choice.' And suddenly we're laughing, embracing, confessing how much we've missed each other.

'Bess, I'm sorry I treated you badly. I was hurt that you hadn't confided in me, afraid of angering the Queen and, well, plain jealous, I suppose. I regretted not writing to you when you lost...'

'It doesn't matter.'

'I grieved for you. But now I hear you've another little boy . . .'

'Walter Junior. Aged two.'

'Looks like his father?' She's wistful.

'Just like.'

'Then he must be beautiful.'

'He could not be beautiful if he took after his mother?'

'I didn't mean – '

I chuckle. 'I know you didn't. And you must come visit us at Durham House – see beautiful Little Wat for yourself.'

'Oh, I couldn't!' She flushes as I raise my eyebrows. 'Bess, please understand. I can't afford to vex the Queen. I've high hopes of being promoted to Lady of the Bedchamber soon and . . .'

'Of course.' My voice, I'm aware, is like ice.

'But then again . . .' She brightens. 'No doubt Sir Walter will soon get back to Court if he discovers El Dorado. And maybe the Queen can be persuaded to forgive you also, although she's never forgiven Frances of Essex, has she? But Dorothy of Northumberland thinks she might be forgiven now that she's married again – the Queen has never much fancied Henry Percy, if you recall, his stutter irritates her. So it could happen. And

Penelope Rich is still welcome at Court even though she's practically living with her lover, Lord Mount joy, and has a child by him as well as offspring by Lord Rich –'

'Unhappily married women always appeal to the Queen,' I point out, 'which makes my return the more unlikely.'

She nods. 'I know, but still – if your friends all got together; signed a petition and gave it to Lord Burghley to present – '

To Lord Burghley, I note. Not to Audrey herself. 'I've few true friends,' I tell her coldly. 'Friends who are pleased to know me whether I am in favour or out of it.'

'But...' Her flush deepens.'

'It was interesting meeting you again.'

I sweep past her, nose in air. If she crawls to Durham house on her bare knees now, I'll have the door slammed in her face.'

✳ ✳ ✳

February,1595

Doublets, shirts, trunk hose with canions. Stockings, suspenders, hats, ruffs. Have I selected enough? Dean, Walter's manservant, hovers resentfully. He's been with Walter for years and dislikes me taking over this task, but it's the duty of a wife, surely?

Cloaks lined with fur, cloaks lined with silk. Two chests of books to install in his cabin. Writing materials, an abundance of them.

'What else?'

Dean sulkily turns on his heel. If I need help I can fish for it.

I consult my list of medicines: - syrup of wild chicory, lettuce, pomegranate juice and water-lily flowers in case his ague comes back; distillation of marigold to soothe his eyes when he's overdone writing and reading; my infusion of basil to calm his stomach (he's confessed rather shamefacedly that he suffers from sea-sickness.)

'The silver tobacco case or the gold?'

Walter shrugs indifferently. He's pacing the floor in anguish. His ships are becalmed, held up in the Thames - he should be away by now.

And there are other worries on his mind.

He halts in mid-stride. 'Bess - should I not return...'

'I don't wish to hear!'

Childishly, I put my hands over my ears, but he crosses to me and gently prises them away.

'Sweetheart, you must, for the safety of your future and Little Wat's. Tom Harriot holds documents that will absolve you from paying back the investors. And there is a will inside my rosewood chest. In an ivory box. The key is in my study desk, in the concealed compartment. Only open it if...'

'I shan't need to open it. Come see the lute I've chosen for you to take..'

✽ ✽ ✽

'It's time.'

Confused, I squint at Walter in the candle-light, realise he is shaking me awake in a bed that isn't ours – in a room that isn't ours. Then I remember that, of course, we are guests in the home of Christopher Harris, Walter's deputy Warden of the Stannaries.

His house is at Radford, just outside Plymouth, and convenient for the docks.

Walter stands over me impatiently, fully dressed. 'You need to hurry, Bess.'

'But it's not yet daybreak!'

'It's midnight, and the wind's right. Are you bringing Wat or leaving him with Nurse and Kate?'

'Bringing him.'

A woman with a child in her arms looks vulnerable. Perhaps, at the very last minute, he will not be able to leave us, after all...

✳ ✳ ✳

Harry the Native bows deeply and sadly over my hand on the frosted dockside, illuminated, rather strikingly, by moonlight.

'But you must be glad, surely, to be visiting your own warm country?' I shout, my voice thin against the bitter wind and the noises of departure, my teeth chattering. He shakes his head, mimes he would rather stay with me. He can now speak several English sentences but is too overcome to remember any.

It's hateful, bidding farewell to the sea-captains known to me. I've grown fond of them all. And here's Laurence Keymis, the loyalist (and nicest) among them, kissing me fondly, stroking Wat's rosy cheek.

'You'll be off voyaging soon, young man,' (Over my dead body).

Even Edward Hancock is numbered among the three hundred adventurers. He looks scared to death.

'Take care. Take great care,' I order everyone but am struck suddenly dumb when Walter comes to me for the last time.

'We'll be back before you know it, sweetheart,' he promises, kissing me soundly on the lips, ruffling Wat's hair so hard he begins to cry. I can only nod and summon a stiff smile – refrain from clutching his silken doublet in a futile attempt to hold him back.

Wat howls the fleet out of sight as if he recognises the dangers facing his father, and I feel like howling also as tall, black-gowned Tom Harriot takes the child from me, then offers me his arm. Together we battle against the wind while directing our steps back to the inn to wake Kate and the rest of our escort, break our fast and depart for Sherborne.

A Sherborne bereft of Walter. For how long?

'They'll return in triumph,' Tom comforts, in his kindly manner. 'And we'll survive.'

He might, but will I?

✼ ✼ ✼

March, 1595

News of Walter's progress, amazingly soon! On his way to the Canaries he captured six Portuguese ships well stocked with fish. He ordered his men to take a small amount of fish, wine and water from each then let them go and sailed on. Later, one of these ships was captured by another English sea captain who brought her back to Plymouth as a prize.

The Portuguese coxswain, through an interpreter, reported that Raleigh was 'merry and healthy' and this Sunday, in Sherborne Abbey, the parson offered up a special prayer that he remain so. My 'Amen' was so fervent it might well have been heard in London.

* * *

May, 1595

News again – in a letter from a Captain White. My husband, he reports, overpowered a Spanish ship laden with firearms. Later he captured a Flemish ship, gaining twenty butts of wine. Again, he and his crew were 'well and merry'. I'm not surprised.

* * *

August, 1595

A message from Carew – Walter's ships have arrived in Plymouth! Great excitement in Sherborne. This morning I visited the Abbey to give thanks. Now I am writing to Robin Cecil, to Arthur Gorges, to George Carew, to Henry Percy, to Mary Herbert ... I'm tempted to write to the Queen, but I suppose she'd rip it up unopened.

* * *

They have not returned in triumph.

For me, of course, it's a triumph to welcome my husband back into my arms. But over forty men have perished – among them poor Captain Whiddon. And although resounding cheers greeted them at Plymouth and the surviving adventurers and seamen are excitedly broadcasting news of gold mines, diamond mines, the exact whereabouts of El Dorado, they have not found El Dorado – the terrible flooding of the Orinoco River forced them to abandon their search. And they have brought back only a handful of diamonds and very little actual gold. As for visiting Virginia –

'Storms again drove us back.' Laurence Keymis sighs, munching on a leg of chicken. He's brown as a berry but terribly thin and he cannot seem to stop eating. 'We turned for home with great reluctance, regretful for the poor lost colonists.'

My biggest regret is for John White and the other relatives, their renewed hope cruelly dashed.

※ ※ ※

Walter is as thin and brown as Captain Keymis. And hungry also - for me as well as for food other than the seaman's diet of hard biscuit with salt beef. He gulps down Smith the Cook's new-baked bread and fresh roast mutton with enough heartfelt compliments to have the man beaming from ear to ear, then rushes me off to bed, bringing a beam to my face also. But when I snuggle down after our reunion, confidently expecting a long, intimate talk behind drawn bed curtains, he leaps up and starts dressing - obliged, he tells me, to make a trip to London to see Lord Admiral Howard and Robin Cecil.

Husbandless again (did I dream his arrival?), with the help of (thin, brown) Edward Hancock I'm working out a menu for a lavish Welcome Home Supper which the Guest of Honour has promised to attend . . .

* * *

'Two main courses,' I instruct Smith the Cook, 'each consisting of sixteen choices of meat which must include larks, brawn, and venison pasty'. All Walter's favourites.

'Virginian potatoes, my lady?'

'Of course.' We exchange a grin. None of us like them but because Walter has planted them in Ireland and sermonises on their merit, we feel obliged to make a show of eating them. 'Followed by fruit, many sugared dishes and a special march pane confection depicting Sir Walter's fleet sailing into Plymouth Harbour.'

Turning abruptly to leave the kitchen, I collide painfully with a bowing Harry the Native. Smiling through gritted teeth, I extend my hand to be kissed. It will be worn away - we've been through this ritual countless times since he got back. Behind him, smiling and bowing and waiting to kiss my hand, is our new guest Leonard the Native – another dark-skinned giant brought to England to train as an interpreter – and behind Leonard, waiting his turn, bows proud, handsome Prince Cayoworaco. And behind him, smiling also, is the Prince's servant – a kind of page, I suppose – who looks very young to have travelled across the ocean,

Cayoworaco's father, apparently, is King Topiawari of Arromaia, who, at one hundred and ten years old, walked a round trip of twenty-eight miles to pay homage to Walter in Guiana.

I could do without the homage. I just wish they'd stop walking on my heels.

* * *

Alas, my supper was not the success I'd hoped. It turned a little sour when Robin Cecil reported (over roast swan) that some of Walter's detractors have accused him of never leaving England at all - of hiding himself the entire time in an obscure little cove in Cornwall, waiting for his fleet to sail back and collect him. Witnesses can be produced, we heard in amazement, who claim to have seen him there!

Lizzie, usually so tactful but she'd had more wine than usual, made things worse by telling us that other mischief-makers whisper he sailed only as far as the Barbary Coast; traded there for gold ore then brought it back and pretended it came from Guiana.

'And, no doubt, I was seen there also, bargaining to my back teeth,' Walter growled, making a face of disgust over the food he'd just swallowed before he realised it was potato.

In fact, the small amount of gold he *has* brought back is intended merely as a sample, to prove to the Queen and the Privy Council the richness of Guiana – and even this is being derided, according to Carew.

'Rumour has it that it's fool's gold, no more than pretty rubbish,' he put in apologetically, daintily retrieving a piece of mutton from his beard.

Walter kicked a leg of my precious dining table and swore.

'Some of my sailors,' he admitted, 'did pick up all that glistered in Trinidad. I assured them the stones they found were of no worth but they refused to believe me and brought them home anyway. Now they've had them "valued" to their cost, thus devaluing the gold I myself have brought, which is certainly genuine – Westwood, Bulmer, Dismuke of Goldsmith's Hall, Palmer of the Mint have all confirmed it. Have they not, Robin?'

Robin Cecil murmurs that they have indeed. But he looks a little discomforted. Walter's gold is not of sufficient value to satisfy the investors, of which Robin is one and his father another. And it is certainly not impressive enough to gain the forgiveness of the stubborn Queen, who still refuses to see Walter so that he can tell her of his discoveries and present his case for colonising Guiana to her in person.

'But what can you do then?' I asked, frustrated. 'All this expense, effort and loss of life seems to have been for nothing.'

'If the Queen won't listen to his golden tongue,' Carew grinned, 'he'd best take up his golden pen.'

And this Walter has done – to silence his critics and gain the attention of Elizabeth he has started to write an account of his *Discovery of the Large, Rich and Beautiful Empire of Guiana, with a relation of the great and gold city of Manoah.*

I am reading it page by page as he produces it. Find myself awed, amazed and horrified in turn. Part of this new land he so lovingly recalls sounds like Paradise, with wonderful coloured birds, red deer, emerald-green fields and crystal mountains. But a lot of it is a tangle of horrid, insect-ridden jungle and dangerous swamps - one of his native guides was eaten by an alligator! Some of his men died in agony after being struck down by poisoned arrows. Amazons, whom I've always thought to be mythical, live along a river named for them. And Raleigh was told stories of a fierce tribe of gigantic men with eyes in their shoulders and mouths in the middle of their breasts! Ugh!

'Yet you left hostages there!' I cry accusingly. 'In exchange for Leonard, and Prince Cayoworaco and his page, you left a servant of one of your captains and a cabin boy in this terrible, frightening place!'

'Volunteers,' he smiles, 'Not hostages. They begged to be allowed to stay – Francis Sparrow to draw maps of the area and young Hugh Godwin to learn the native language. And as for the Prince's page, he'll soon settle in. He's very bright. He's already learning the English tongue with Harriot, who says he's unbelievably quick at picking it up. He'll make an excellent interpreter for us on future voyages.'

'But he's so young,' I protest. 'He can't be more than sixteen summers.'

'No more than eleven. He's tall for his age.'

'Eleven! You should certainly not have brought him. What of his mother..?'

'The old Chief told me he's an orphan; said he was eager to come.'

'Even so...'

My voice tails away; he's not listening. He's reaching out for me and his eyes are narrowing with that warm, familiar, come-to-bed look.

So wonderful, having him home!

CAL

It was my older brother the alligator killed. I watched it happen, though none of them knew it. None of them saw me, up among the branches of a tree. Not the Great White Chief they call Sir Walter, or any of his men.

I blame the Great White Chief. It was he who persuaded my brother to act as their guide along the Orinoco river, on their search for the Golden City. My brother was frightened. He was not the warrior I would have liked him to be. He didn't want to go with them, they bribed him with a strange flat object with many little spikes – a comb, I know it to be now, but I didn't know the name of it then. It was silver (I know silver, I've seen rocks of it in the mountains) and it flashed in the sunlight. It attracted me, too. I would have liked one but I was afraid to go near the strange men. I thought they were Spanish and they might tie me up and torture me. The Spaniards have tortured many of my people.

My brother did at least attempt to fight when he fell into the water and the alligator took him. He struck at the monster's eyes with his knife, as we've all been taught to do, but the alligator dived deep, and when it surfaced again and made for a distant rock, my brother hung limply from its jaws. Just as well he'd drowned, I thought later, before he was devoured. But at the time I howled with grief because, although he was no warrior, he was my only surviving relative and I loved him.

There were more of us once, of course – more brothers, sisters, cousins, aunts, uncles, my father, my father's wives; all wiped out either by the sickness that affects my people or by the wars we, the Orenoqueponi, fight against the Carib groups who dwell on the main river.

My mother never lived with us. She was an Amazon Warrior Woman, according to my father, though my brother said this was nonsense. But I believe it because I am tall – much taller than others of my age – and Amazon women are said to be tall, as well as strong and fierce. My father told me the women captured him, and he was made to mate with my mother. Not a hard task, he told me, because she was very beautiful. He was forced to remain among the Amazons until after I was born. If I'd been female they would have kept me with them, but as I was male they gave me to my father and set us free – sent us both back to our own tribe.

I'm proud to be the son of an Amazon; it makes me stronger and braver than most. I couldn't wait to grow up and become a warrior, fighting the Caribs.

Imagine my horror, then, when the Lord of our tribe, Topiawari, chose me to serve his son, Cayowaraco – to sail back, with the great white chief Sir Walter, to the white man's country way across the sea. I did not dare protest, and there was no-one to argue for me.

I wanted to shed unmanly tears but, being the son of an Amazon, I squared my shoulders – broader than most – and pretended to be brave.

On the ship, though, I was a coward. The white sailors laughed, watching me tremble and shake. I told them I was afraid of the Water Spirits, which made them laugh the more, showing their ignorance, for the Water Spirits wreak evil on mankind. One is male, the other female and their bodies are scaled, like fish, but their heads are like those of people, their feet like land animals. They delight in wrecking ships, then eating all on board. In terror, I watched for them, but they chose to leave us alone.

Now that we're safely on this cold and colourless shore they call England, where the Sun God rarely shines, my Lord Cayowaraco orders me to behave with grace. I must smile and bow and grovel to Chief Sir Walter, to his lady and his friends, to the man teaching me their ugly tongue. I must never show I am unhappy to be so displaced, snatched from my homeland and brought to this great, stone, frightening building with many huts they call rooms, to be studied and displayed like a dumb animal.

I could eat well here, but I dislike much of their food. I sleep on a hard bed instead of a soft hammock and I cannot wear my loincloth because it is too cold. I am forced to wear clothes that itch and irritate, though I refuse to wear the uncomfortable things they call 'shoes'.

I day-dream, sometimes, of stealing a knife from the kitchen and killing the Chief in his bed, but where would that get me? Hanged, I suppose. Not good.

I like the Chief's Lady, who has a kind smile, but I hate his servant, Dean, who calls me a savage and laughs at my mistakes.

Perhaps I should knife him instead, but that, too, would get me hanged.

'You'll get used to it here,' says Harry, in our own language.

I despise Harry for fitting in. He would lick Chief Sir Walter's boots if asked to do so – lick his behind even, and enjoy doing it.

Harry! What sort of name is that? As bad as Charles, the name they have given to me. Dean laughs at me because I cannot say it without spitting. Spitting is all it is good for. I would like to hear Dean pronounce my real name. None of them can say it. They do not even try. But Charles!

'Cal,' I say. It is all I can manage. Spit? They are fortunate I do not vomit.

'Perhaps he's trying to say Hell,' laughs Dean. 'Maybe that's what we should call him – Hell.'

I've learnt what they mean by 'Hell'. 'It is Hell living in England,' I try to snarl at him, but the words are too difficult yet. They come out wrong and he laughs louder. Maybe I *will* knife him. Maybe it's worth a hanging.

~PART THREE~

BESS

Sherborne Lodge, January, 1596

We've received an invitation to dine at Essex House. But not from Frances. From her husband, the Earl of Essex himself!

I rush to tell Walter, busy with his own letters.

'We won't go, of course.'

He lays down his quill. 'Why not?'

'You know why not. You and he are rivals! Enemies!'

He looks smug. 'We're quite friendly at the moment. When I was last in London we had several pleasant meetings. There's a business venture afoot which could interest us both.'

'But – you wouldn't get involved with him, surely? Not after the way he betrayed us? After the Cerne Abbas inquiry..?'

He sighs. 'Bess, I've told you a hundred times we have no proof Essex was behind any of that. And even if he was, things change. It's time to be diplomatic, to think of the future. I'll need him on my side if I'm ever to return to Court.'

I laugh in his face. 'On your side? Best watch your back!'

* * *

Frances welcomes us with open arms, Essex thumps Walter between the shoulder-blades, kisses my cheek (I try not to flinch).

After the lavish five-course meal, when the men disappear to smoke tobacco and we're left alone, Frances sighs and reaches for my hand.

'You must be as worried as I about the coming expedition. But at least the planning of it has brought our husbands closer, which should enable the two of us to see more of each other.'

I frown, perplexed. 'What expedition?'

She stares at me. 'You don't know? He hasn't told you? Oh, my dear...'

It seems Walter's current 'business' is an undertaking with Essex to sack Cadiz.'

* * *

Back at Durham House I pace the floor and rage at him. How could he become involved in such a scheme without telling me? How can he plan to leave his wife and son again so soon?

He does not attempt to defend himself – just watches me with an aggravating little smile on his lips until I stalk from the room in disgust.

* * *

'Sweetheart, I wasn't at liberty to tell you,' he murmurs into my hair in the early hours. 'The planned attack on Cadiz is a military secret.'

'But Frances knew . . .'

'Frances should *not* have known. Her husband was indiscreet.'

'Essex trusted her.'

'You know I trust *you*. But we swore to keep our mouths shut. Apart from not letting the Spaniards know we're coming . . .'

'Am I likely to inform them?'

' . . . there are a thousand things to organise, to discuss. The Queen has not yet given her permission. If she does, much good can come of this, Bess.'

I've been lying with my back to him. Now I relent – turn over. 'You'll be reinstated?'

'Perhaps. At least I shall be in the forefront of things again.'

His eyes are very bright but very earnest, willing me to understand.

If he wasn't going to Cadiz, I suppose he'd be fretting to return to the swamps and the alligators in Guiana.'

* * *

I do see more of Frances. Because she is still banished from Court and Essex still thriving there, for most of the time she lives quietly with her mother, either at Walsingham House in Seething

Lane or at Barn Elms in Putney. Both houses are on the Thames and therefore easily accessible to me by boat from Durham House Stairs.

While our men-folk are engaged in councils of war, we worry together.

'Although I can see why the assault is necessary,' Frances admits. 'Robby says the Spaniards are readying another armada to send against us.'

'And it's rumoured they're sending soldiers to encourage a new Irish rebellion,' I nod. 'Walter's afraid they plan to use Ireland as a back door into England. Even Robin Cecil and his father agree firm action is needed.'

We grimace at one another in perfect understanding. However supportive our words, we hope the Queen, with her horror of war, will argue against the policy that attack is the best form of defence – crush the very idea of this brave new venture with one stamp of her jewelled heel.

* * *

She hasn't, though. She's granted her permission for the attack on Cadiz, withdrawn it, then granted it again.

So now it's official; Lord Admiral Howard and the Earl of Essex are to have joint command, Lord Thomas Howard is to be Vice Admiral, Walter will serve as Rear Admiral, while Sir Francis Vere is appointed General of the Troops.

Walter and the Lord Admiral are travelling daily up and down the Thames, readying the ships, the victualling. Essex is already at Plymouth, marshalling the army.

* * *

Today Anna visited me in floods of tears. It transpires my brother Arthur has asked Walter if he can sail with him as a gentleman-volunteer.

'He doesn't even know where the fleet is *going*, yet he's determined to go with it!' she sobbed. 'Please, Bess, entreat Walter to say no.'

I promised I would. Only to discover he's already said yes.

* * *

'Remember, Bess - my will is in the rosewood chest . . .'
'In an ivory box. I know.'
'The key is in my study desk . . .'
'In a concealed compartment. I know.'
'Only open it if . . .'
'I know. I *know*!'

* * *

Plymouth, June,1596

A great throng of people with flags and banners, seeing off the fleet. And such a fleet- the largest and most glorious ever to depart England. Frances, Anna and I catch our breath when we see it.

'Well over a hundred ships,' Essex informs us charmingly, his red beard glinting in the sunshine, the jewel in his hat blazing fire. 'Manned by eight thousand soldiers and one thousand, five hundred sailors.'

The four English squadrons (the fifth is Dutch) are to be led by Lord Admiral Howard in the *Ark Royal*, Essex in the *Due Repulse*, Lord Thomas Howard in the *Merhonour* and, of course –

'Raleigh in the *Warspite*, one of two brand new galleons belonging to the Queen,' says Essex, waving a silken arm.

Both he and Walter are dressed in their splendid best – attempting to out-do each other in the most exquisite silks, velvets and lace. (Although Raleigh, I think proudly, in blue and silver, his pearl earring swinging, is much the more handsome.)

No Captain Keymis this time, to kiss me goodbye. Walter has sent the poor man back to Guiana to make further exploration. And I find now, in these last moments, I am as bereft of speech as I was before the Guiana voyage.

'God keep you safe!' I manage to whisper at last, as Walter clasps me to him.

All too soon the drums roll, trumpets sound and the great ships begin to move with pennants flying – brilliant crimson for My Lord Admiral, tawny-orange for Essex, blue for Lord Thomas Howard and sparkling white for Sir Walter Raleigh; each ship also fluttering the proud flag of Saint George.

'Arthur?' cries Anna, beside me. 'Can you see Arthur?'

'No.' I'm straining frantically now to see the *Warspite*, but it's already lost to me. Anna begins to sob in earnest as we watch the last billowing sails slip over the horizon.

* * *

Sherborne Lodge

No news since the fleet departed. I've heard not a word and neither has Carew, Adrian Gilbert, or anyone else we know. I've written to Robin Cecil four times in the past week, in the hope a report has come through, and am just taking up my pen for the fifth time when William, our steward, bows before me:

'Captain Keymis is below, my Lady.'

'Thank God!' I gather up my skirts and am halfway down the stairs before I remember that Laurence is back from Guiana; he'll know nothing of the attack on Cadiz.

All the same, it's good to see him. He may not be the best looking of Walter's captains (he has a cast in one eye), but he's certainly the most pleasant. Also the cleverest. He was a Fellow of an Oxford College before he left to adventure with Walter. He's a genius, I'm told, like Tom Harriot, but I confess his wide smile and warmth of manner are the qualities I value most.

Today he's affectionate and charming as ever – presenting me with ribbon lace he's picked up from some trading ship, making much of Little Wat, producing comfits and toys from pockets that seem bottomless. Yet there's a subtle difference I cannot quite fathom. Do I imagine that his smile is strained, his laugh forced? Thinking he's exhausted, no doubt, from the terrible voyage, I despatch a protesting Wat back to his nurse and ring for refreshment. But he barely touches the food although he gulps down the ale with such speed I ring for more.

He tells me his report from Guiana is not encouraging. The natives, he says, were disappointed because they'd expected Raleigh, not Keymis, with an impressive force to fight the Spanish rather than a few men in a single ship. He did manage to find a better route up the Orinoco River, and he was told of a wonderful new gold mine (which will greatly interest Walter). But he has no gold at all to show for his efforts and tells me ruefully that he has 'emptied Raleigh's purse'. The worst news of all is that the Spaniards 'are everywhere'.

'Much further up the river than they were on our last voyage.'

'But there is something else?' I ask shrewdly, still aware of his unease. 'Some other news you're holding back?'

He springs abruptly to his feet and paces the floor. I cannot imagine what is troubling him so much. Eventually he stops and turns – speaks gently.

'Have you news of Raleigh?'

My blood runs cold. 'No – have you?'

He sits beside me, takes my hand. 'I feared to come before because I could not decide whether or not I should tell you this –'

'Tell me,' I breathe. 'Quickly!'

His grip on my hand tightens. 'There's a rumour around the docks – only a rumour, mind– that the Cadiz assault was a disaster. That the fleet has been badly battered and that Raleigh . . .'

'Yes? Yes?'

Both his eyes wander from mine. 'That Raleigh has drowned.'

✻ ✻ ✻

People rush to comfort me; Anna, from Mile End, my brother Nicholas from London, Carew, from Exeter ...

'It's only a rumour,' they say. 'Nothing more.'

But a rumour that's all over London, not only around the docks.

'I'll write to Cecil,' I decide, calmer than all of them, cold and numb and unreal. 'Robin Cecil will know the truth.'

'I'll go to him in person,' offers Nicholas. 'Be back with good news, you'll see ...'

He spoils his display of optimism by pausing at the door –

'Did Walter make a will?'

✷ ✷ ✷

I kneel before the rosewood chest in an agony of indecision.

If I lift the lid, take out the ivory box, remove the document that rests within and break the Raleigh seal, I am admitting I think it's true. And of course it cannot be. I would know if he was dead. I'd feel it. Wouldn't I?

✷ ✷ ✷

It reads much as I'd expected.

I scan the familiar writing on the thick cream parchment quickly, guiltily.

His estates in Ireland, the Sherborne lease, to pass to Little Wat after proper provision for me, etc, etc. Minor gifts to the servants, to casual friends. Instructions that his debts should be settled by debts outstanding to him. His best horse and saddle to my brother

Arthur. His best rapier and dagger to Cousin Arthur Gorges. Further bequests to Robin Cecil, Tom Harriet, Cousin George Carew and Adrian Gilbert – even to John Meere. His ship the Roebuck to be sold and the profits to go to ... The sentence leaps up at me – dances before my eyes. *"I will that my reputed daughter begotten on the body of Alice Goold, now in Ireland, shall have the sum of five hundred marks."*

✷ ✷ ✷

'Bess ...?' Nicholas bursts in, unannounced.

I'm in my closet – half-dressed. A shocked Kate hastily throws a robe about me to preserve decency. Nicholas fails to notice, strides forward to clasp my hands.

'Bess, Cecil's heard at last! Raleigh's not only alive but a hero! Not a shadow of doubt! Official despatches say Cadiz is in English hands and Raleigh's action was so praiseworthy those who were formerly his enemies now hold him in high esteem!'

'Bess?' He's staring at me, concerned. Why don't I swoon? Laugh? Smile, at the very least?

I manage to smile – stiffly. My face, I'm afraid, will crack. But he does not detect the effort it costs; smiles back jubilantly, embraces me, calls for the best wine.

'Arthur?' Anna arrives at a run, her skirts clutched high. 'What news of Arthur?'

'Safe, and another hero.' Nicholas hugs her close. 'Knighted by Essex for bravery.'

'Oh!' Anna turns pink, has to sit down. 'I'm Lady Throckmorton!'

Nicholas turns back to me: 'Bess, dearest Bess, you must be so relieved!' (Am I? I suppose I must be. Somewhere beneath this terrible, consuming anger). 'But it isn't entirely good news. Raleigh was injured in action, a deep gunshot wound in the thigh, The bullet struck up from the deck of the Warspite. He'll need nursing; it will take time to heal.'

Picturing him in pain does not soften my anger. I too am injured. Sick with disappointment, with disillusion.

✻ ✻ ✻

Mile End, August, 1596

He's as beautifully dressed as ever in a robe of deep wine velvet, but a thick, bulky bandage encases his wounded leg and he looks pale, thin and ill, lying on the couch in Anna's parlour. His eyes light up when I enter the room.

'Bess – my Bess – how good it is to see you!'

I make no move to rush into his outstretched arms. Just stand there, looking at him.

His eager smile changes to a frown. He drops his arms to his sides, struggles to sit up, to reach for his cane and rise. 'What is it? What has happened? Little Wat? Is he sick?'

'Wat is well.' My voice is cold. 'I can see that you are not. You'll need nursing, I'm told. Perhaps you should sail to Ireland? Get Alice Goold to nurse you.'

'Alice Goold?' He drops back on his cushions, stares at me, appalled. 'What...? How...?' I watch him make a supreme effort to collect himself. After a moment he says quietly, flatly. 'You read my will.'

I shrug. 'They told me you were dead – drowned.'

'Yes. And now you wish I had been?

I make no answer. He flinches. 'Bess ...'

'When?' I ask.

'When what?'

'When did you 'beget' this daughter on ...' I almost spit the words, 'the body of Alice Goold'?'

'I ...'

'On our wedding night you swore you had fathered no bastard. I asked you and you denied it. Did you lie?'

He answers so softly I cannot catch it. 'What?'

'I said I spoke the truth. Bess – is this necessary? It was a long time ago. .. And you and I have been so happy . . .'

'When?'

He sighs. Looks away. 'In eighty-nine.'

And we were wed in eighty-eight. I'd been praying that, against the odds, he would tell me it had happened when he was a young soldier in Ireland – long before we had properly met. My own legs feel weak, suddenly. I grope for a stool and sit down. Well away from him.

'Bess...' His gaze is direct, honest (hah!). 'We'd quarrelled, if you recall. I'd gone to my lands in Ireland distressed, angry, hurt. You'd told me you wanted an annulment. That you didn't recognise our marriage . . .'

'Because you wouldn't confess it to the Queen. The time "wasn't right".'

'It wasn't.'

'But it was only a lovers' quarrel! I didn't mean it!'

'I know that now. I know you better now. But at the time I thought you meant it, I thought we were finished.'

'So you fell into the arms of the first woman you saw? This Alice Goold? Or was she your mistress all along? Is she still your mistress now?'

'Of course she isn't. It was my one lapse. I came back ....'

'With Edmund Spenser – you persuaded him to bring the first book of his poem The Fairy Queen to the Court to show Queen Elizabeth. Secured him a fat pension for it. And I couldn't wait to congratulate you - fell into your arms like a fool. Begged for your forgiveness!'

' I came back and we made up our quarrel. I regretted Alice Goold. Regretted breaking my marriage vows. I swear to you, Bess, I have never done so since and I never will again . . . '

'Why should I believe you? Probably no woman is safe from you. To think I pitied Frances for the dalliances of Essex. . .'

'Bess, I am not like Essex! I will never betray you again....'

'How can I believe you? Ever trust you again?'

He stares at me. He looks exhausted and defeated but I feel no sympathy. He brushes a hand across his eyes, 'I don't know.'

'When did you last see her?'

'My daughter?'

His daughter! Wat's sister!

'Not your wretched daughter! This Alice Goold!'

'In eighty-nine.'

'But...?'

'She died, giving birth to my .... the child.'

'Oh.' Even my bitter tongue is silenced for a second. 'But the will said "now in Ireland".'

'You misread it. That applied to the child. The child is in Ireland, with her grandparents.'

'I see. And who was this Alice? A servant girl?'

His eyes flash. 'Of course not! She was the daughter of the Attorney General of Munster. A gentlewoman.'

'And you were in love with her?'

'I loved – and still love - you. I was fond of her, she was infatuated with me. She ...' he looks uncomfortable, 'she threw herself at me, but there were others..'

'So she was a whore!'

'No! Just a little . . . free with her favours. At first I denied the child, thinking it could not be mine. But, later, when I saw her...'

'She looks like you?'

'Yes. And like my mother.'

How I've longed for a daughter who looks like him.

'Bess...' He's pleading. Proud Sir Walter Raleigh. 'I beg your forgiveness – please! These months at sea I've thought of you, longed for you. I cannot get down on my knees because of this damned wound but I am grovelling just the same. Don't let this spoil what we have ...'

I rise, shake out my skirts. 'It's already spoilt, Walter. It was ruined from the moment I read your will. I know you often keep secrets from me – business matters, military and naval matters - but I thought our personal relationship was based on truth, on honesty, on respect. I cannot respect you now. I will do my duty as a wife - see that your leg is dressed, that you are well fed and that all your comforts are as usual. But don't expect things ever to be the same between us.'

As I close the door I hear him swear, hear the thud and clatter of his cane as he hurls it at the nearest wall.

I hasten to tell Anna's servants my husband must occupy a separate bedchamber 'Because his wound makes him restless at night.' No-one believes it, I can tell from their faces, some amused, some concerned.

And, in the evening, the atmosphere thickens.

'I'm not sure I shall use my title,' muses Arthur, at supper.

'Not *use* it?' Lady Throckmorton chokes on her mutton. 'What can you mean, not *use* it? You won it, did you not?

'You must have been very courageous,' I murmur, trying to appear interested.

Arthur shrugs. 'Not especially.' He looks at Walter, hoping he'll deny this, vouch for his courage. Walter does not, his face sour as the sauce in the jug beside him. 'Everyone who fights in a war has to have a degree of courage, naturally,' Arthur continues. 'But Essex created over sixty new knights, you know, and considering it's possible to count on one hand the number Lord Admiral Howard created after the Armada, this leaves us open to ridicule. At Court, a Cadiz knighthood is regarded as a great jest by everybody except the Queen, who's furious – she thinks Essex did it for popularity, to increase his own following, rather than bestowing the honour for merit. I'm uncomfortable with it. It would seem more dignified to ignore it...'

'I am *most* comfortable with it and I am going to ignore *you* until you say something sensible!' retorts Lady Throckmorton, banging down one of her prized Venetian wine glasses with such force she breaks its stem and departing the room in a huff.

Now wife speaks only to wife.

Husband only to husband.

In an atmosphere cold as the Thames in winter.

'This situation,' I overhear Kate whisper to Anna's maid, 'is unbearable. How long is it going to last?'

* * *

Arthur and Anna are reconciled. He's keeping his title (no great surprise) but Anna has postponed the celebration dinner she's been planning. What point, when the Raleighs remain so low in spirits, so disagreeable?

'Perhaps in a little while, when Walter is feeling better .. ?' she suggests, her eyes inviting me to confide. I cannot.

I stare bleakly out of the window at Little Wat, playing with Anna's Mary at battledore and shuttlecock, They look like two pretty little girls in their gowns, ruffs and caps, cheered on by Cal, the boy from Guiana. Until Wat hoists his skirts and relieves himself in a flower bed to the disgust of his nurse and the giggling delight of little Mary and tall Cal. Once I would have found this amusing, but not today.

Alice Goold's daughter must be six years old - one year older than Damerei would have been, had he lived.

'You should go ahead without us, you and Arthur. Things are unlikely to improve.'

* * *

Audrey calls, with unwelcome chatter – too fond of her own voice to notice my cool response.

'The Queen is in no mood to reinstate Raleigh despite his brave efforts,' she reports indignantly. Good. Serves him right. 'And it's a sin because the crowds in the streets might cheer Essex but everyone at Court knows Raleigh was the true hero of Cadiz. It was he who changed the plan of attack, you know, which led to its success. And it was he who captured two merchant ships, bulging with treasure. But the Queen is so angry, Bess, you wouldn't believe - not only on account of the Essex knighthoods but because she expected more treasure. She concedes the sacking of Cadiz may have averted another Armada, but the Spanish Admiral fired the rest of his ships in his own harbour rather than surrender them to us and then our fleet missed the Spanish treasure fleet on the way home. To crown all, Howard, Vere and Essex allowed plunder from the town of Cadiz to escape into the hands of the common soldiers. So she's annoyed with everyone ... . But how foolish I am, sitting here in Anna's parlour telling you all this when Raleigh will have told you already, of course, to say nothing of Arthur ...'

'Of course,' I nod.

He's told me nothing. While Arthur's stories, his re-living of the battles, have floated over my head.

But it wouldn't do for Audrey, of all people, to know how matters stand ...

※ ※ ※

'Bess, your husband needs you ...'

In a sudden burst of temper I fling the torn petticoat I am mending for Little Wat across the room (he pesters to be breeched but is far too young, of course). 'Anna, I know your intentions are kind but will you *never* stop pestering me - never accept the fact that my matrimonial difficulties are none of your wretched business?'

'I accept it this minute,' she retorts, tossing her head. 'I fully accept it is none of my business that *your* husband sits in *my* husband's study looking stricken because he has just received news that his brother has died - even though I am the one who is going to have to comfort him because his own wife, obviously, has no intention of doing so.'

She slams the door on her way out. After a stunned moment, I rush to open it – shout after her down the stairs.

'Not Carew? Anna, tell me it's not Carew?'

Her voice floats up to me. 'It is poor Sir John Gilbert who has passed away. Not that you're interested...'

The oldest of his Gilbert half-brothers. He thought the world of him.

* * *

'In the winter of my life' he had described himself in the forward of his Discovery and I had laughed at him for no one, surely, could ever think of Sir Walter Raleigh as old.

But today he looks near to it - shrunken - slumped in Arthur's leather chair beneath the frowning portrait of my father. And defeated.

'What else can go wrong?' he is demanding wearily of Arthur as I enter the room.

'My dear, I'm so sorry. I, too, was fond of John...'

He turns to me, his eyes brimming. 'Bess...oh, Bess...Forgive...'

'Don't say it.' I rush to him. 'It doesn't matter. Nothing matters, only that you're safely home and we're together again.'

It could have been Walter who died!

* * *

'By what name is she called?' I ask in the night, clasped in his arms.

It's a complete change of subject. In his grief for John Gilbert, he's been reliving his boyhood with Carew - telling me stories of their admiration for John and his brother Humphrey, describing how the Gilberts taught the younger boys to hunt, fish, hawk, swim and row almost as soon as they could walk... But he answers immediately.

'Alice.'

After her dead mother, my rival. But she looks like her father.

Mistaking my interest, he holds me closer. 'Someday I would like you to meet her.'

I pull away at once. 'Never! I never want to set eyes on her!'

He cradles me again. 'Then, sweetheart, I will make sure you never do.'

* * *

Cecil House, January, 1597

Walter's health has improved but his limp is pronounced.

'It pains me to see it,' I sigh to Lizzie Cecil as we sit embroidering baby clothes in her lying-in chamber.

Walter is at Sherborne, attending to estate matters, but Lizzie is awaiting the birth of her third child and has begged for my company. A very private person beneath her social gaiety, she has not invited the usual crowd of women friends to surround her during her confinement so I feel flattered that it's me she wants – despite my envy, for Helith the Fertility Giant has disappointed me again this month. And today came news that Arthur and Anna's reunion after Cadiz has borne fruit – or, at least, will do so in six months' time.

New babies all around, yet it seems I'll never give Wat a sibling. I can't understand it. I'm strong, healthy. And Walter is extremely fit in *that* department, if not in others.

'I can't believe his jaunty, energetic stride has gone forever,' I continue now, 'that he will never dance again, never more win wagers for me at tennis...'

I break off, biting my lip as well as my silken thread, for Robin Cecil has never been able to dance, to play tennis, to joust or to hunt. He enjoys, with Walter, the gentler sports of hawking and partridge-netting, but that is all he can manage.

'Forgive me,' I begin, 'My stupid tongue...'

Lizzie waves my apology aside with an understanding smile. 'Robin's case is quite different. He sympathises greatly over Walter's disability – says it must be hard to put up with for one who has been so agile, that what you have never enjoyed, you can never miss. He jests that at last he can keep up when they walk in the gardens.' Her smile fades and she frowns down at the tiny cap she is decorating with seed pearls. 'But I confess I worry, Bess, before each birth, in case Robin's condition should be hereditary. Both times so far he has been thrilled to be a father – enormously proud of the straight, sturdy little bodies of first Frances and then Will. He has never said but I know he feels it proves to the world that he is a normal man. If I should give him a child that isn't quite perfect, it will break his heart ...'

'Of course you'll give him a healthy child,' I say stoutly, but I experience a twinge of worry. She looks so small and fragile, despite her enormous bump. I wish she would wear my lucky eagle stone but she's refused it because Robin and his father, Lord Burghley, are firmly against such 'superstitious nonsense'. 'Frances and Will are surely evidence that Robin's – affliction – cannot be passed on ...'

'Will is small for his age. Much smaller than Wat.'

'Every child is smaller than Wat. And quieter. And better behaved.'

She laughs. 'But none is more loveable. Bess, if anything should go amiss with me, you will look out for Will? I do not fear for Frances, who is doted on by Robin's sister-in-law, but Will is more vulnerable, more sensitive of manner and constitution. And he does not greatly care for his aunt while he adores both you and Sir Walter ...'

I shake my head at her. 'You know I would look out for him should circumstances demand it. But they will not. These are just the morbid fears of your condition. Come, enough of sewing - let me beat you at chess before the daylight fades.'

* * *

She should have worn my amulet. Late last night the midwife woke me, saying her pains had started, and just after dawn her life blood drained away giving birth to a tiny daughter whose back is as crooked as her father's. Poor stricken Robin held his wife's cold hand and wept for all three of them. Neither the mid-wife nor I could persuade him from the bedchamber. We had to enlist the help of his equally stricken father.

* * *

Walter has written a beautiful letter of sympathy to Robin, who showed it to me this morning and confided;

'He has always had a better way with words than I, but I once wrote a good letter to my sister-in-law before asking for Lizzie's hand. I feared all women must think me repulsive and I would only cause embarrassment by proposing. My sister-in-law assured me that Lizzie loved me and I really believe, by some miracle, that she did, Bess. She never seemed to notice my deformities, although she must have done.'

His 'deformities' grow more noticeable by the minute, his poor shoulder more hunched, his lurching walk more awkward. And his face, usually his redeeming feature, white and twisted. It is terrible to see him – the capable, brisk statesman – so lost and wretched.

I put my arms around him and held him for a long, sad while. What else to do?

ROBERT CECIL

Whitehall Palace, March,1597

'Work,' my father says. 'Work is the only solace.'

I nod. Lizzie lies at rest in Westminster Abbey beside my mother; my daughters are in the care of my sister-in-law; my son is at Sherborne with Bess Raleigh. I have only work left to me.

My father understands the need of it since it was his salvation when he lost my mother. But he and my mother had years of happiness, Lizzie and I fewer than ten. More time together than many, friends say, thinking to comfort. Cold comfort to a frozen heart.

My sweet Lizzie worried that I worked too hard. She was pleased when I was, at last, sworn in as Secretary of State because she knew I coveted the post and was already doing the job anyway. But she drew me away, whenever she could, into a happy social life. Now that she is lost to me – buried – all happiness is buried with her. So I bury myself, also, in official business up to my ears.

Raleigh and Essex are, at present, part of that business.

Essex, of course, was furious at my official appointment, which took place when he and Raleigh were engaged in the sacking of Cadiz. We have been at odds since boyhood, when, as one of my father's wards, he was also one of my chief persecutors – mimicking my shambling walk to the amusement of the others. Today he resents and fears my rise to power and I dislike his position as first favourite, even though I know her Majesty values my opinions far above his, realising, as I do, that he will never make the statesman he wishes to become.

He fears Raleigh, I've always believed, even more than he fears me, dreading Walter's reinstatement lest he elbows his way, again, into the Queen's warm affection. And yet the two of them have returned from Cadiz appearing the best of friends. They have discovered a certain camaraderie, I suppose, after seeing action together, but I find it hard to believe that Essex, always so jealous, has changed this much towards his greatest rival. Surely their mutual admiration cannot last?

'Come what may, let us use their sudden friendship to our advantage,' my father says. 'We have need of them both, just now.'

True.

Philip of Spain, smarting from Cadiz, is thirsting for revenge. He sent another armada against us last winter which was, thankfully, wrecked by storms in the Bay of Biscay. But it can only be a matter of time before he tries again. Our spies tell us that his invasive fleet, what is left of it, has taken refuge at Ferrol. And so, much as we Cecils, along with the Queen, abhor the expense of war, it would seem only logical to wage an attack that will finish the Spanish once and for all – damage their ships so soundly they can never again set sail.

And for this we need strong commanders. Chief among them Essex and Raleigh, who appear to work well together.

'You must hide your pain, Robin,' my father says, 'and appear merry. Invite them to dine, take them to a playhouse. Be charming to both. Win them both. Keep them together until we've seen off the Spaniards.'

I have always been charming to Raleigh. Charming Essex will be a little more difficult.

BESS

The Rose Theatre, 1597

'How wonderful to see the three of them so friendly,' Frances marvels during the interval, calling my attention to the sight of Walter, Cecil and Essex, their heads together, discussing the play, a performance of *Richard the Second*.

Is it? I remain sceptical.

Walter and Robin have been close for years, of course. But Essex? He and Walter look handsome and splendid in their suits of silk and cloaks of velvet. Poor little Robin, sitting beside them in his sober gown, his hair newly grey from grief, looks old enough to be their father.

'Please be careful,' I beg Walter in our coach returning home. 'I still don't trust Essex.'

'Perhaps you should.' he grins, tweaking my ear. 'He's promised to get me an audience with the Queen.'

I pull a face. 'I'll believe it when it happens.'

* * *

Durham House, June, 1597

The longed-for miracle has come about. But whether it was with the help of Essex is debateable, for it was our loyal friend Cecil who led a limping Walter into the presence of the Queen. Essex was absent from Court; unable, I suspect, to face the sight of his rival being forgiven - which he very charmingly was. The Queen smilingly reinstated him as Captain of her Guard. And, that same evening, they rode out together and had what he gleefully describes as 'very private conference'.

'What does that mean?'

'Why, just that we talked much as we used to in the old days.' His eyes glow. He looks handsome, eager, boyish even.

'You did not ask for my reinstatement?'

'Bess, how could I? I will, but it's too soon. You know that.'

I do. Yet I can't help being unreasonable. 'But what did she actually say to you?'

He is annoyingly vague. 'She was very gracious. Very kind.'

I'll wager she was. I'll wager he flattered her madly and she flattered him madly back and they put their heads together and chuckled over some silly classical jest or pun and held hands and made spectacles of themselves and—

And I'm angry and jealous and peevish because he's back at Court and I'm not and I feel shut out.

(And I couldn't make a classical jest to save my life.)

* * *

In bed, during the after-lovemaking talk that has become our habit, he confides the sort of details I wish to hear.

'She's looking terribly old, Bess – close up, beneath the paint.'

The white, complicated mixture I used to make and apply so carefully. These past five years I've only seen her at a distance – in her barge on the Thames; parading, in pomp, to St Paul's. Hard to believe I was once close enough to paint her face.

'You won't be composing poetry to her, then?'

He smiles. 'Oh, she still likes to be flattered as if she were eighteen summers. Sad, in truth. On the one hand, she's a fine intellectual – one of the most brilliant people I've ever known - on the other, a lady whom time has surprised.'

Gallantly put. In other words, mutton dressed as lamb.

'Audrey told me she's banished all the mirrors from her privy chambers because she can't bear to see her reflection.'

'She's still full of energy, though. Much of our ride was taken at the gallop. And she still hunts, they tell me; competes at archery, takes long walks, dances her courtiers off their feet.'

He moves his stiff leg with a small wince of pain. At least he's unable to partner her now in a galliard. Or dance with her nubile young Maids. Unkind, I know, to be glad of it.

Not that he'll be at Court for long. Without quite meeting my eyes, he tells me he's off to annoy the Spaniards again.

With Essex, his new bosom friend.

* * *

Sherborne Lodge, July, 1597

Medicines, books, quills, ink ...

Dean, the manservant, sulking again as I tick off the endless items.

We say our farewells at home, for a change. Little Wat gets over-excited enough, without seeing off the fleet. Also -

'It's something of a muddle, Bess, with Essex in charge,' Walter confesses ruefully

'Come back soon, Sir Walter,' entreats Will, on the verge of tears. 'We'll miss you here.'

'Kill all the Spanards, Farver!' commands Wat, dry-eyed, jumping about with enthusiasm. 'Every – last – one!'

'God keep you safe,' is all I manage. With difficulty

* * *

Determined not to mope while Walter's away, on top of my household duties I entertain the neighbours and am entertained in return, am invited to dine, to hunt and to hawk. I sing, read, and ride with the children, and, in September, write to my brother Nicholas asking if my brother William can come to stay. I've long felt guilty about Sweet William. Arthur and Nicholas have looked to his care since my mother died. Our brother Robert has gone abroad and seldom gets in touch, while I rarely take my share of the responsibility. Time to put this to rights.

As I'm laying down my pen, Kate rushes in – calls me urgently to the window. I go in trepidation. What now?

Our steward, Meere, has a strange, hip-swinging, rather effeminate way of walking. There he is, making his way to the stables - blissfully unaware of a grinning Wat and Will in single file behind him, swaying their skinny hips and walking with the exact high, mincing step.

Meere glances up and we duck down hastily, hands over our mouths. Meere doesn't care to be laughed at.

✻ ✻ ✻

Nicholas arrives in due course, not only accompanied by William but by an elegant young woman I've never met. Smiling from ear to ear, Nick introduces her – his betrothed! Her name is Mary More and she is pretty and pleasant – she makes me promise to attend their wedding, planned for next January.

'Say you will, Bessie! Promise, promise, promise!' shouts William, who seems, sadly, more child-like than ever.

I hasten to make them welcome and am at pains to appear merry – but Robin Cecil has sent a letter via Nicholas, enquiring about his son Will's health, and the postscript has depressed me: "No news of Raleigh and Essex."

Soon after my guests have departed, though, leaving William behind, I have another visitor –

'Bess, I had to come in person...'

Frances, to my astonishment, has journeyed all the way down to Sherborne. She whirls, ahead of my footman, into the Great Parlour where I sit practising a new piece on the virginals. I strike the most horrific chord.

Rushing across the room, she snatches my hands from the keys and holds them tightly in her own cold ones.

'Lord Mountjoy has written to Penelope Rich from the fleet,' she gabbles, 'He says Sir Walter is to be court-'martialled'.

'Court-martialled? Walter?'

I stare at her stupidly, half-registering how unlike her elegant self she looks – her black hair straggling down below her hat, her travelling dress smeared with mud . . .

'Mountjoy says . . .'

She is interrupted by a great commotion - my brother William, rising clumsily, knocking over a small table. He's been hiding in the shadows, enjoying the music. He likes me to pretend I don't know he's there.

'People who get court-martialled are killed, Bessie!' William shouts, kicking the upturned table, waving his arms wildly and bursting into noisy sobs. 'Arthur told me! I don't want Walter to be killed!'

My head reeling, I pull away from Frances to go to him, put my arms about his waist (the furthest I can reach - he is very tall). 'Walter won't be killed, Will,' I soothe. 'Only the guilty are put to death. Whatever this is about, Walter will be found innocent, I'm sure.'

'Will he, Bessie? Truly?' Abruptly, he stops crying, turns his big, bearded face hopefully towards Frances. 'Will he? You think so too?'

Frances nods, gives the ghost of a smile. 'Of course.'

'Then why are you looking so miserable?'

I try to laugh. 'She isn't miserable, Will, just tired. She's travelled a long way. Would you seek out Smith for me, ask him to organise some refreshment for both the Countess and her escort? And then go and find Little Wat and Will Cecil – weren't you teaching them how to play tennis yesterday?'

'Tennis – yes! I like tennis, Frances, I'm good at it.' He beams, bows (belatedly) and lumbers out, bumping against another small table on the way..

'I'm sorry, Bess,' Frances is on the verge of tears. 'I didn't realise poor William was staying with you. I would never have...'

'It doesn't matter, he's forgotten it already. Now – tell me...'

* * *

She knows very little more. Only that Walter's (alleged) offence is 'disobeying orders'.

'Whose orders?' I demand. But I know, of course.

She colours.. 'Well–my Robby's, I suppose, as commander-in-chief. Oh Bess, I'm so sorry. What are we to do? They've been getting on so well of late. Yet they must, from the sound of it, have had a very great falling out...'

I nod grimly, thinking this is the chance Essex has always wanted – the chance to destroy Walter for good, hang him aboard ship, make sure he never returns to England, to the Queen. To me.

I know Frances is a true friend to Walter but I cannot prevent my voice sounding cold, accusing:

'What can we do? With your husband's blessing, the death sentence may already have been carried out.'

※ ※ ※

We sit together by the fire, long into the night. Worrying. Praying. Hoping for news. Surely, surely, I'm bound to hear something from someone.

As soon as it is light I take up my pen and scribble a note to Robin Cecil, in case he should hear first. But when I rush down to the stables to give it to a courier, a messenger gallops into the yard bearing no comforting news from Raleigh but a letter from dear, thoughtful Cousin Gorges.

I sink down on a nearby bench, to read it.

My dear Cousin Bess,

'*Whatever you may hear, I wish to assure you that your husband has committed no crime. The fault lies entirely with Essex as commander.*

It's true that fate was against us early in this voyage, with a series of accidents beyond any man's control, obliging us to abandon our planned attack on Ferrol.

The Warspite's mainyard broke in two, making it impossible to tack about in the face of an easterly wind; the Repulse sprang a leak, which took time to repair. But from the start Essex has wavered - issued conflicting orders, changed those orders, changed them back, changed them again.

To cut a long story short, eventually our squadron became distressed for water, so Raleigh asked if we could wait a while at Flores, to obtain more. Essex agreed and sailed on.

But loading casks of water is a long, laborious task, Bess, and the work had hardly begun when, to our astonishment, a message came from Essex ordering Raleigh to meet him immediately at Fayal, the chief island of the Azores. We could, he wrote, continue to get water there before launching a joint assault.

Raleigh was not best pleased but we up-anchored and went.

Yet when our ships entered the roads of Fayal there was no sign of Essex and his squadron We were amazed, but there was nothing for it but to drop anchor and wait.. Then the Spanish forts opened fire and many of us urged Raleigh to fight but he refused, knowing that Essex would want the glory of the first attack.

I know he worried that the Spanish might think he hesitated out of cowardice, but he nonetheless waited THREE WHOLE DAYS, during which we gnashed our teeth watching the Spaniards strengthening their defences along the shore, removing most of their valuables. On the fourth day, his patience snapped – for all we knew, Essex and his ships could have been sunk by pirates. When our boats, out seeking water, were fired upon, Raleigh gave the order to land.

We easily took the town, for the Spaniards had fled from it to a high fort which Raleigh decided to take the next day. But next day Essex arrived at last – summoned Raleigh aboard the Due Repulse.

We all expected he would be praised and thanked for accomplishing an English victory - the one success so far of our expedition. Instead, Essex, near hysterical, accused him of a gross breach of orders, of flouting the articles of commission which decree no captain shall land troops without the General's presence or express permission, under pain of death.

Raleigh pointed out that he was no mere captain – that as Rear-Admiral he was a principal commander, and could not be court-martialled at sea. Furthermore, in the absence of Essex and Lord Thomas Howard, he was obliged to take command, to take action as he saw fit. He was courteous but definite. He said repeatedly that he had neither intended nor given offence to the Earl's honour.

All this calmed Essex down somewhat and Raleigh returned to the Warspite. But the Earl's supporters persisted in trying to blacken Raleigh's name and he was for several hours still in grave danger of being court-martialled and hanged from a yardarm (which would have caused a mutiny, Bess, for those of us who love Raleigh would not easily have allowed it).

Thankfully, Lord Howard arrived with his squadron. He persuaded Essex to accept an apology then persuaded Raleigh to make one, telling him that he knew he had acted correctly, but that it was, sadly, necessary to appease the Earl's wounded vanity. Raleigh apologised graciously, Essex accepted the apology and was at once very merry and friendly again.

But when, after all this formal nonsense, Raleigh urged our long delayed attack on the high fort we found the Spanish had fled. We have therefore been forced to burn the city and sail away with no ransom and no prizes.

Our objective now is the Spanish treasure fleet but I confess I've lost faith in this voyage. If only Raleigh was in sole command . . . But what use in wishing?

Just know you have no cause for alarm, Bess. Whatever rumours you may hear in England to the contrary, Essex is treating Raleigh well and they are the best of friends again.

Your affectionate cousin

A. Gorges

PS: I know you will be discreet regarding this letter, which should not have been sent at all.

Burn it, he means, but I shall have to tell Frances something of its contents.

* * *

'I knew my Robby would relent,' she smiles, on taking her leave. A lie. I related an edited version of Arthur's letter to her and she almost fainted with relief. 'It's his followers, Bess, who cause the trouble. They're all so jealous of Sir Walter.'

And Essex is not, of course.

* * *

November, 1597

Walter, praise be, is safely back in his 'Fortress Fold'. But what a struggle to get here and how right was Cousin Gorges to be pessimistic!

Thanks to more bungling on the part of Essex, they failed to capture the treasure fleet (said to be the richest that has ever sailed), more terrible storms battered them on their way home, scattering their ships in all directions – Walter's Warspite and George Carew's Mary Rose both sprang leaks. And when Walter crawled at last into St. Ives and Essex into Plymouth, they were met with greater panic than in eighty-eight for news had arrived, in their absence, that those huge Spanish battleships from Ferrol, successfully repaired, were again on their way to invade us – with no prepared English fleet this time to oppose them. Worse, the new Armada's first aim, it was rumoured (brother-in-law Carew came in person to alert me), was to seize Falmouth..

Essex rushed up to London to consult with the Privy Council over supplies and finances while Walter was again left to frantically organise coastal defence.

At Sherborne, we barricaded his precious diamond-paned windows and shook in our shoes. Thankfully, however, further news followed that the invading fleet had been broken up by the very same gales that had so hindered Walter and Essex..

'Once more God blew and our enemy was scattered,' marvelled Kate, scurrying off to give thanks in the Abbey. 'Once more He proves Himself a Protestant'.

What has Essex proved himself? An inadequate leader of a failed voyage? An untrustworthy 'friend'?

'I occasionally fear for his state of mind,' Walter told me, in the privacy of our closely-curtained bed. 'He's so excitable at times, beyond all reason. There are qualities in him I respect - admire even. But no matter how warm he now appears to me on the surface, I know I can never trust him again.'

I never trusted him from the beginning.

CAL

I have grown to trust the Great White Chief. He is a warrior! I was wrong about him. His fancy clothes, the pearl in his ear, misled me.

It was a while before I realised it. I still distrusted him when he marched me to the tall grey building they call a church. I trembled and drew back when he took me inside because I saw it had a table they call an altar. I thought I was to be held down on it and sacrificed to the white men's Gods, so I pulled out a knife I had snatched from the kitchen and threatened him with it. He did not flinch or even back away. Instead, he stood his ground and explained, quietly and calmly, that white men only worship one God, and that I was to be offered to him peaceably, in a ceremony called Baptism.

'And you won't cut throat?' I asked. 'You won't spill blood?'

'Not a drop,' he promised, with a warm smile that lit up his eyes and reminded me, suddenly. of my father's. He held out his hand for the knife and, almost without realising, I gave it to him. 'Our Holy Man.' he said, will pour a little water on your head, make the sign of the Cross on your forehead, and you'll become a Christian with a proper Christian name.'

Charles! I can say it at last – I can say most of their English words. But I pretend I cannot say this 'Charles'. 'I am Cal,' I still insist, and they laugh and give in to me.

I am more settled in their big house and sometimes they take me to their other big house beside the busy wide river they call the Thames. I like the Great White Chief's Lady more and more – Lady Bess, I call her now. And their son, the Little Wat, reminds me of my youngest brother who died moons ago, of the sickness. But, most of all, I like to serve Chief Sir Walter who takes more interest in me since my baptism. He asks me questions about my life in my homeland, praises my English which he says is 'remarka' something, and says he will take me to the place named Court, one day, to meet the Great White Queen.

My young Lord, Cayowaraco, who I served, has gone back to our homeland to be King – the old Lord, his father, has died – and I feared I should have to go with him. (I would like to visit my homeland but am still afraid of the ocean, where the Water Spirits live.) But the Chief Sir Walter said no – I was to remain here 'for the present.'

Dean, who is kinder to me since I charmed away a boil on his finger, told me of the White Chief's bravery on his latest voyage to attack the hated Spaniards.

'Sir Walter was first into the surf from the landing boat at a place called Fayal, cane and all,' he said proudly, 'and led his men straight into the field of Spanish fire. Look – '

I gasped in admiration as he showed me the holes in the Chief's shirt and breeches, shot through with musket bullets.

Being the Son of an Amazon, I am happy to serve such a Great Brave Warrior, to give loyalty and protection to his family. I smile now, with sincerity. I soothe the White Chief's bad leg, using special ointment known only to the men of my country. I run errands for the Chief's Lady, I watch over the Little Boy Wat. And when I've finished praying to the Gods of the Golden Sun and the Blessed Moon, I pray to the White God in His grey church every Sunday.

ROBERT CECIL

February, 1598

Back in his old place Raleigh might be, but his career is at a standstill. The Queen, charmed again, keeps suggesting that he apply for this or that important post, but I am adept at finding arguments which persuade her to change her mind.

'It's vital the man believes he will advance, though,' my father warns, from his bed. He's become very frail, of late, and is forced to do much of the country's business propped up against soft pillows. 'Essex grows ever more troublesome, with his erratic behaviour and lust for power. He will never truly support you. You still need Raleigh on your side as a valuable ally'

I know it, and I dangle the hope of higher office before the eyes of my handsome friend, much as a carrot held out to a donkey but just a little out of reach.

Meanwhile, I am sent by the Queen on a mission to France – mainly to preserve our Anglo-French alliance by dissuading King

Henry from making a separate peace with Spain. Also, his country owes us money and Elizabeth (diplomatically, of course), wants it back. With a fine show of reluctance I agree to Essex acting as State Secretary in my absence. He has no talent for the job and I'm hoping he will make a mess of it.

My stay in France is uncomfortable. The weather is vile; I do not trust King Henry's geniality and his everlasting requests for me to join him in wolf-hunting is irritating, to say the least. Any fool can see that I am not built to hunt a mouse – long hours in the saddle are not for the likes of me. I find his pestering insulting, especially as I cannot obtain a straight answer to any matter of business. After three pointless months of waiting about, I am forced to return home in a foul mood with the French debt unpaid and no more knowledge of Henry's foreign policy than I had when I departed England.

When I visit my father, I see at once my worst fear is to be realised - his hold on life is slipping away. The change these past weeks have wrought is undeniable. He is naught but skin and bone. His face has a yellowish tinge and his hand, when he clasps mine, is claw-like. Panic grips me. I am not ready to lose him yet.

Ever the realist, he knows he's dying. For the last time, he offers me sound advice. Through the power granted to me by my own high office, he whispers, I must strive to bring about England's peace with Spain and the smooth settlement of the lawful succession after our good Queen's death. Swallowing the lump in my throat, I promise to do my best.

The Queen herself arrives, incognito, sits beside his bed and feeds him a little broth. I am touched to see tears in her eyes.

When she leaves, I send for Thomas, my half-brother (my father's first-born and heir, but never his favourite. I know I have always been that), my sisters and all the grandchildren, including my son Will, who is at Sherborne Lodge.

To my dismay, Will comes reluctantly. He is fond of his grandfather, but it appears he now prefers the company of the Raleighs to that of the Cecils. He can barely wait to return to them and I overhear him confiding to my brother:

'I love my father, Uncle Thomas, because it is my duty. But he's always busy and he's not – well – entertaining the way Sir Walter is, or so glamorous.'

Glamorous. No. I can never be that. If Lizzie was here she would urge me to be extra warm towards our seven-year-old son, to use charm of my own to win him. But if Lizzie was alive he would not be staying with the Raleighs. As it is, hurt causes me to be cold and distant, driving him further from me.

My father is buried in St. Martin's Church, Stamford, near his family home, but there is a service for him in Westminster Abbey. Raleigh attends, of course, looking 'glamorous' in his mourning attire, a rich lining to his black cape, jewelled buttons on his black doublet, the pearl in his ear gleaming. He embraces me with warmth and sympathy – understanding, like no other, the depth of my loss. But even as I grip his hand in gratitude I see my Will hovering at his heels like a puppy eager for a word or a pat. When he begs to go 'home' with Raleigh I insist he remains with me, even though I know, he knows, and Raleigh knows, I shall have little time to spare for him.

Lord Buckhurst becomes the new Lord Treasurer but I keep my position as State Secretary and the Queen relies on me for advice and counsel, much as she relied on my father. She cannot say or hear his name without weeping, though, and I doubt she will ever hold me in as great affection.

At Court there is speculation that Raleigh will be made a Privy Councillor – even that he may be given a peerage.

I smile when I hear mention of either, nod and say it is possible.

Possible that pigs might fly.

Meanwhile, as ever, there is trouble in Ireland . . .

BESS

Sherborne Lodge, 1598

Kate saw the messenger first, from my bedroom window.

'He's coming through the park, my lady, riding hard. And he's wearing the royal livery.'

As soon as I was decent (Kate was helping me dress), I picked up my skirts and hurried down the stairs. Walter met me in the passageway.

'Bess- dreadful news from Ireland! I've been summoned back to Court to give advice.'

It seems the rebel leader – the bloodthirsty Earl of Tyrone – has won a battle against us at a place called Yellow Ford; killed two thousand of our English soldiers. And now the native Irish are running amok – murdering all the English they can lay hands on, The slaughter, the Queen's messenger said, is truly terrible . . .

I turned about. 'I'll come with you to London . . .'

* * *

Durham House, 1598

'Babies dashed against walls, wives forced to mop up their husbands' blood before being killed themselves ...'

Marriage has failed to curb Aud's gift for dramatic narration (she's caught Thomas Walsingham at last). She sweeps theatrically about my withdrawing chamber in Durham House, waving her arms, wringing her hands...

'And did you know that Edmund Spenser, the poet, has had to flee from his estate in Kilcolman? His house was fired and his youngest child perished in its cradle. His wife is said to be mad with grief ...'

'Poor, poor things!' I've only just finished reading Spenser's fifth (brilliant) book of The Faerie Queen.

'My Thomas says Raleigh's estates must also have suffered.' She seats herself at last, sips her wine and looks at me searchingly.

'We haven't yet heard the full extent of the damage.' Walter will lose lands, money – a whole township, probably, in Tallow. Many of his tenants will be forced to flee, if they haven't already - abandon their homes, like the Spensers. But the thing that most upsets him is the waste. 'All those years of effort gone for nothing, Aud. Walter says there's no point in being bitter, but I feel bitter for him. He's tried so hard to establish an English colony. Much harder than most of the other English landowners ...'

She nods sympathetically. 'That horrible Earl of Tyrone will take some stopping now. Thomas says he doesn't envy whoever they choose for Lord Deputy - the repercussions of this tragedy will probably go on for years ....'

* * *

A small but disturbing 'repercussion' occurred the very next day.

'There's a young woman asking to see you, my lady. With a child.'

Frowning, I looked up from my tapestry work. 'A young woman? Has she no name?'

'She won't give a name but she seems respectable. She says you don't know either of them but the child is niece to Sir Walter.'

I was puzzled. I know all Walter's nieces.

'Show her in.'

The woman, a nursemaid, was indeed a stranger to me. But the child I knew at once.

* * *

Walter, still in his Court finery, paced his study angrily. Guiltily.

'Yes, I did send for her and, yes, I should have told you. It slipped my mind.'

'Slipped your mind?'

'Amid all the commotion, confusion, the paperwork I'm having to deal with the meetings I'm obliged to attend. You don't seem to fully realise the extra burdens this Irish disaster has placed upon my shoulders ...'

'And you don't think the unexpected arrival of your daughter might be a burden upon mine? Your daughter by Alice Goold?'

He came swiftly to me and held me close. 'Bess,' he said softly, 'she's eight years old. How much of a burden can she be?' I stood stiffly in his embrace. He kissed my hair. 'Her grandparents are old, tired – unable to cope with this latest upheaval. I thought she might need mothering. And who better for the job than the best mother in the world? You've always wanted a daughter and you said you'd like to meet her one day. We could hardly leave her in Ireland at such a time, my darling. Now could we?'

Babies dashed against walls! Wives mopping up . . .

'Of course we couldn't.' (But he should have told me.)

'And I knew you'd take to her on sight. Such an enchanting little maid – the female image of Wat!'

His eyes glowed with pride, with love. I found I couldn't tell him that after his 'enchanting little maid' had swept her curtsey (prompted by her nurse) I'd tried to embrace her. And she'd raised her pretty head and spat at me, full in my face.

✷ ✷ ✷

We've brought her back with us to Sherborne. Alice, named for her mother, has her own room, her own pony, grand new clothes.

But the last thing she wants is 'mothering'. Especially from me. She hates me. She hates Wat. But adores Walter.

I've told all the servants that she's 'a distant relative of Sir Walter's'. She addresses her father, Wat and me as 'Cousin'.

'But I doubt they believe it,' snorts Kate. 'She's too much like Sir Walter and our dear little Wat. To look at, that is.'

'She's beautiful.' The same black hair that curls naturally, without the aid of tongs. The same brilliant dark eyes that change in a flash - they dance for Walter, smoulder for me. In her father's presence butter wouldn't melt. But out of it . . . I refuse to complain to Walter. She's so young, still. Adjusting to strangers in a strange place. Neither does Wat, who's no tell-a-tale. But I'm sadly aware his 'Cousin Alice' is no substitute for kind, gentle little Will Cecil.

'Will she go soon?' my son asks me quietly, imploringly.

Am I unkind to hope so?

✼ ✼ ✼

Wat's prized wooden soldiers have been found broken – every one. His coloured ball is flat as a pancake, a puncture in it.

My peacock-feathered fan has gone missing. Also my best scented gloves.

'She needs a beating, that one,' says Kate darkly. 'I'll tell the nurse...'

'We have no proof and she denies it,' I point out. She's far too sly and clever to be caught.

'You should tell Sir Walter.'

'Give her a little more time. She'll perhaps settle down. I'll buy Wat more soldiers..

'And that solves anything?'

✼ ✼ ✼

Ink – all over my newest gown and its matching petticoat.

Kate is anguished. 'This time we *must* tell Sir Walter.'

I set my teeth. 'We won't. I'll not play the wicked stepmother. Give her time and enough rope. She'll hang herself.'

* * *

She's done so. But Kate was right. I should have spoken up earlier. I would never have forgiven myself if . . .

But I jump ahead.

This morning Kate and I, fresh from gathering plants in the herb garden, came face to face with Walter, thundering, with his cane, down his turret stairs.

'Little Wat! In the river!' he gasped, at my startled enquiry, and rushed out into the park, Kate and I hot on his heels.

The native boy, Cal, met us, plodding up the grassy slope, a limp, pale Wat dangling in his strong brown arms. I screamed.

'He is good, my lady – stunned. A small cut – he hit head on rock when he fell in river. . .'

Walter, white-faced, took Wat from him. 'He did not fall in. Alice pushed him in – deliberately, behind the back of her nurse. I saw it, from my study window. If Cal had not been near . . .'

He talked severely to Alice, ordered her nurse to beat her. Then he questioned the servants, each member of the household, Mrs Meere, Kate, as to her behaviour.

'Pack my niece's belongings,' he instructed the nurse coldly, 'I'm taking you both to stay with my brother Carew and his wife. We leave in an hour.'

* * *

'I feel a failure,' I groaned to Kate as we watched the little party ride off, a sulky Alice perched on the front of Walter's saddle. 'I wish I could have won her. She's to be pitied, in truth. No doubt she's been taught to resent the fact that Walter married me and not her own mother; to resent Little Wat...'

Kate gave a sudden chuckle. 'I pity her if she tries spilling ink on one of Lady *Dorothy's* gowns!'

✻ ✻ ✻

I worry about 'Cousin' Alice for a while, in the care of strict, forbidding Dorothy, but I'm afraid she is quickly forgotten when Walter returns and bursts into my sitting room, all smiles.

'Bess, sweetheart ...!'

I'm at my writing table with Hancock, checking the household accounts. Even as we look up, startled, Walter pulls me from my stool and drags me round in an unsteady, limping dance.

'What? What?' I'm breathless, laughing, delighted to see him so happy.

Hancock, laughing too and ever tactful, makes to leave us. Walter waves him back to his seat.

'For your ears also, Hancock. I've just come from the Queen – received assurance I was expecting...'

My heart stops as suddenly as my feet. 'You're not going to Guiana again?'

He laughs. 'Better than that!' I grimace at Hancock – 'better'! 'Her Majesty has granted us the freehold on Sherborne. We can rip up the lease, Bess. It's ours! Every stick, stone and blade of grass!'

'But that's wonderful, sir!' cries Hancock.

'Wonderful!' I echo, hugging Walter. I know how much he's wanted this – deserved it – after the planning he's put into Sherborne Lodge; the time, effort and money he's spent on the building, the gardens, the estate. Then I draw back, distrusting Queen Bitch. 'It's not one of her empty promises? She truly means it?'

He flicks my cheek affectionately with his ringed finger. 'Letters patent are being drawn up. It will take a few months to become official but, yes, our Fortress Fold will indeed be ours – to pass down to Wat, to our grandchildren, our great-grandchildren... There'll be Raleighs here for centuries to come.'

A lovely thought!

✶ ✶ ✶

Durham House, March, 1599

'Mother, Mother - Come and look!

Little Wat explodes from his schoolroom that overlooks the Strand.

I am already on my way, drawn by the shouts, the drums, the trumpeting.

Seizing my hand, he drags me to the window. 'It's my Lord of Essex and a lot of soldiers.'

I look down on a vast, cheering crowd, on the new Lord Deputy of Ireland, smiling and waving at the head of his army, off to subdue the rebels.

'He talked himself into it!' Frances had groaned to me. 'He argued against the suitability of every candidate put forward until he was the only obvious man for the job. Part of him wants to go, he says it's a post that can cover him in glory. But part of him is terrified that – well - that others will advance at Court while he is away.'

She flushed and lowered her eyes. Chief among the 'others' is Sir Walter Raleigh, who can only benefit from her husband's absence for Essex has dropped all semblance, now, of friendship – reverted to his old, sneering, jealous rivalry.

No-one is quite sure why, least of all Walter, but I've heard from Arthur Gorges that the very mention of Walter's name makes him fly into a temper. And he insulted him publicly and deliberately at the Queen's Day Tilts last November.

Walter dressed his retinue splendidly, as always, their helmets, this time, sporting plumes of orange tawny. But no sooner had he settled his men around the Queen than Essex paraded into the tiltyard with a much larger following – displaying two thousand plumes of exactly the same colour. It was meant to demonstrate his superior grandeur, his contempt for Walter. But it only succeeded in angering the Queen, who showed her annoyance by leaving early.

'Essex tells everyone Raleigh has been poisoning the Queen's mind against him,' Cousin Gorges said, 'but it's more likely he, as a Privy Councillor, is responsible for blocking Raleigh's advancement.'

Quite. So I can't pretend I'm sorry to send him off to fight the Irish barbarians. Although I am, of course, concerned for Frances, who is with child again.

She confessed the fact awkwardly: 'I've hesitated to tell you...'

'Don't be foolish,' I scolded. 'I'm pleased for you. I don't begrudge others more children.' (Well, I try not to. Even Aud, now, has given Walsingham a son and will likely produce babies like a doe produces rabbits.)

I've finally thrown away the sachet of earth from beneath my pillow - merely thank the stars I managed to birth Little Wat. May God keep him safe in this precarious world.

'God save your Lordship!' cries Wat now, hopping excitedly from one foot to the other and echoing the shouts of the crowd below.

God will need to save him, according to Walter.

'Ireland needs a hand that is sure and steady,' he'd frowned, shaking his head. 'Essex would not be my choice, but I wish him well.'

Generous, when Essex wishes Walter nothing but harm.

Whatever his inner turmoil, the Earl looks confident today astride a wonderful mount, smiling and waving at his admiring public, the sun shimmering on his breastplate, his sword-hilt, tinting his red hair to a blazing halo.

But scarcely has his vast retinue clattered out of sight, still surrounded by a cheering crowd and bound for Chester, the first mustering point, than the sky darkens forbiddingly and there follows a great downpour of hailstones and heavy rain.

'A bad omen,' Kate says darkly.

* * *

May,1599

Frances has retired to Chartley, her husband's house in Staffordshire, Just as well, for the present Court gossip would greatly distress her.

Walter looks grim, comes and goes busily yet tells me little. But Aud, as usual, is more forthcoming, calling at Durham House regularly to fill me in.

'According to Robin Cecil, Essex is blundering about in Ireland like a prize fool, proving his lack of ability.'

'Instability', I can't resist saying, pausing to throw some bread to the swans. We are strolling in the part of the gardens that slope down to the river, and I am reminded, suddenly, of the day we were feeding the peacocks at Whitehall Palace, all those years ago, and Raleigh came to find me - beginning, in a way, our attraction for one another.

'Many would agree with you,' Aud stoops to detach a twig from her skirt. 'Cecil says the Queen expressly forbade him to make Henry of Southampton his Master of Horse yet that was the very first thing he did on his arrival! And he's been dithering about – marching south instead of north as he was commanded, storming castles of no importance, losing battles he should have won. Queen Bitch, I have it on authority, keeps writing him furious letters, but instead of placating her, he simply writes furious ones back!'

Blaming Walter, I've heard since – even at this distance! Accusing him, with Robin Cecil and Henry Brooke, Lord Cobham, of dripping more "poison" into the royal ear, of willing his campaign to fail when everyone knows it's in Walter's best interests for him to succeed. Walter, after all, is the biggest landowner in Ireland – it is his tenants that are being murdered or rendered homeless. And what is Essex doing about it? Creating more knighthoods than he did at Cadiz, in an effort to hold his army together. Men are deserting left, right and centre, apparently, and who can blame them?

'They should have chosen Mountjoy to command,' is all Walter will growl when I question him about it. 'I told the Queen so, but Essex argued that Mountjoy was too bookish and she listened to him!'

❋ ❋ ❋

September, 1599

'My Lady, you have a visitor. The Lady Walsingham...'

Again, the balancing of my accounts is interrupted. Again, Hancock excuses himself and, today, is not bidden to remain.

When he's closed the door behind him, Audrey waves away my offers of refreshment, shakes out her skirts and perches on the edge of a chair. 'Have you heard the latest about Essex?'

'No. Walter is at Nonsuch with the Court. I've heard nothing.'

'You soon will.' She leans forward. 'Bess, Essex has made a truce with the Earl of Tyrone against the Queen's wishes. And further against her wishes, he's sailed back home.'

'Sailed back? With his army?'

'He's left his army to fend for itself and arrived back with a handful of followers, hoping for the Queen's forgiveness. And, Bess, this is the thing– he rode through the night and arrived at

Nonsuch Palace at ten this morning – forced his way, without warning, into the Queen's bedchamber ...'

'No!' My mouth gapes, I can't close it.

'He did!'

We stare at each other, aghast. Then we burst into helpless laughter. After dancing late the night before, the Queen would not be dressed at such an hour, Still in her nightshift, she'd be without her face paint, her wig, her jewels; her grey hair – thin and wispy – straggling over her shoulders. Only the most trusted of her ladies are allowed to see her thus.

'She'll never forgive him!' I gasp at last.

'Never.' giggles Audrey, wiping her eyes. 'Oh, I wish I'd been there!'

* * *

'He thought to be forgiven, at first, because the Queen received him kindly,' Walter said grimly. (He's furious and embarrassed because his guards did not prevent Essex from entering the privy chambers, made a mockery of his security.) 'She was probably in shock, as well as greatly alarmed, but she appeared very calm and composed. She let him kiss her hand, then bade him go and tidy himself – he was covered in stinking mud – told him she'd send for him later. You should have seen him dining with his friends, Bess, in the outer hall – a-swagger with confidence, like a dog with two tails! He truly thought all was to be well again...'

But in that second interview, the Queen revealed her fury. She's banished him from Court but not to his own house. He's under close arrest at York House, the home of Lord Keeper Egerton. It's but a stone's throw from our own Durham but we never glimpse him. He's not even allowed to walk in the small walled garden, let alone receive visitors, least of all his wife, now staying with her mother and safely delivered of a baby girl.

As soon as I could, I hurried to Walsingham House, taking a tiny gown I'd embroidered for the new arrival.

'Robby has been charged with "contemptuous disobedience of the Queen". said Frances, still abed and looking ill. 'Will he ever be allowed to even see his new daughter, Bess?'

'Of course he will!' I assured her, cuddling the said daughter and trying not to feel envious.

But will he? Who knows? He's still calling Walter his enemy and blaming him for all his troubles with the Queen. He can't seem to accept that he's his own worst enemy. As Walter says, he's brainsick.

* * *

February, 1600

Lord Mountjoy has been appointed the new Lord Deputy of Ireland and has already departed for the Isle of Bogs (Walter's name for it) with far less pomp and ceremony than did Essex, still a prisoner in York House.

'At least it must be safer there now, since Essex has obtained a truce,' I say to Walter, who laughs scornfully.

'Never believe it! The terms of the so-called "truce" were not even written down. It's impossible to agree a "truce" with Irish rebels.'

* * *

March, 1600

This morning I went again to see Frances, who looked much more herself. Essex, she said, also much recovered, has been allowed to return to their house on the Strand.

'But he's still in close confinement under a new jailer, Sir Richard Berkeley. And I'm only allowed to visit him "occasionally and by day".'

'What do the authorities think you can do at night that cannot be accomplished by day?' I demanded. Imagine the indignity of being locked out of your own home – Sir Richard is in possession of all the keys and over a hundred of the Essex servants have been turned out to seek "other employment".

She smiled wanly. 'At least Robby can now see his son and new little daughter. And he's much heartened by the crowd outside, on the street. People parade daily with banners of protest; shout and cheer and demand that the Queen forgives him.'

So, despite his failure in Ireland, he's still very much the public hero.

Also, it seems, his wild talk about Walter being his enemy is widely believed. Nasty ballads are being sung in the streets to this effect while today, to my horror, some of the protesters paraded outside Durham House and a stone was cast through one of our windows. It's a miracle no-one was killed.

I'm relieved when Walter says he needs to attend to estate business and we take horse for tranquil Sherborne.

Which is not, as it turns out, so tranquil after all ...

✳ ✳ ✳

Such a to-do this morning.

Walter went unexpectedly into his estate office and found John Meere, our bailiff, copying his signature!. Expertly, too, so not for the first time. Heaven knows what mischief his forgeries have caused.

A terrible scene followed, with Walter dismissing Meere and Meere refusing to give up his post, saying Walter cannot make him leave because he originally stated in writing that Meere, if he lives, will hold the position of bailiff for *fifty years*, so he still has forty-two years to go.

Walter ignored this. He had Wood and a footman throw the rogue out and has already appointed a new bailiff –a mild-mannered man who seems honest enough.

Mrs Meere was dismissed along with her husband, but not before she said some very insulting things. And I thought her such a pleasant woman!

Are we not to get peace *anywhere*?

ROBERT CECIL

Westminster Palace/Sherborne, 1600

With Essex banned from Court Raleigh pesters me more than ever. Letter after letter arrives from his estate in Dorset. He is after the job of Vice Chancellor which, of course, cannot be permitted.

So I suggest to Her Majesty he be offered Governor of Jersey. As I expect, he seizes it gratefully, this sop to his pride, this sideways step. No significant post from a political point of view, it yet carries status and he's eager for any 'advancement' after so many disappointments. I daresay one of his energy and enthusiasm can do much good there, so my conscience remains untroubled.

He will be obliged to return from the Island regularly, to see to his other duties in the West Country and here at Court, but it will keep him out of my hair for weeks at a time, Heaven be thanked.

Before he sails, he invites me down to the pastoral joys of Sherborne, where I enjoy a pleasant respite from my own duties. Raleigh, full of gratitude, is the most delightful host; we gamble at cards, hawk in the park, discuss gardening and building (I am considering buying land in Dorset). Bess is her usual charming self and the only jarring note is the behaviour of my own Will. Back living with the Raleigh's and much at home with them, he is faultlessly polite to me but displays little warmth. Young Wat Raleigh, boisterous as ever, shows me more affection.

Ah well. I'm sorry I've let you down, Lizzie my love, if you're watching from Heaven. Successful statesman, failed father. I suppose one cannot have everything.

Yet again, one cannot do *without* everything, and I beg your understanding on the other matter. My only excuse is that seeing Bess and Raleigh so happy still, so comfortably intimate in their domestic setting, brought home to me my loneliness. I know it is wicked to take a mistress, I know I am cursed, I know my father would be ashamed of me but I am hoping – praying – that you will find it in your heart to forgive me.

I do not wish to be married again. I could not bear to be married again, for I could never attain the happiness I enjoyed with you. But she was *there*, will be there again on many an occasion, warm and comforting and ready, as you were, to overlook my deformities and pleasure me – be pleased, I believe, in return. She is married, yes, and has a son to boot, so it is a mortal sin of which I am aware. But her husband, as you may recall, is a cold fish unwilling, it seems, to provide much satisfaction beneath the sheets now that he has an heir. Whereas I . . .

Forgive me, Lizzie. Don't think me disloyal. *Please.*

* * *

January, 1601

Raleigh is doing well in Jersey – a big fish in a little pond – improving and rebuilding fortifications (we can never discount the danger of yet another Spanish Armada). But I've sent for his urgent return. He's needed back in London to support the Privy Council, to support and guard the Queen, who is shouting for her Oracle's presence and advice in these troubled times.

For it's come to our ears that Essex, released to his own house but still forbidden the Court, is simmering with resentment. His friends advise him to lie low, tell him he'll be forgiven in time if he remains patient. But when was Essex ever patient? My spies report he's intriguing with James of Scotland, regarding the succession. How dare he meddle! He's filling Essex House with all manner of hotheads and malcontents - ruffians with a grudge against the government.

Can he be planning a rebellion of sorts? Can even Essex be such a fool?

BESS

Durham House, Ash Wednesday,
February 25, 1601

Essex died this morning.

He laid his red-gold head upon the block a mere two hours before I arrived back from Sherborne, with Little Wat and Will. Arrived back to a London numb with shock, for few believed the Queen would see it through. She'd forgiven this erstwhile favourite so many times before, surely, surely he would be forgiven again?

But this time he'd gone too far. He'd ridden into the city with two hundred followers at his back, shouting that Walter, Cecil and Cobham, 'The Queen's evil advisors', were plotting to take his life – inviting the people to take up arms, join him in storming the Palace, taking the Queen hostage and dictating his terms, which included Walter's death, Cecil's death, and the naming of the Scots King as heir to the throne.

Whether or not he had secret hopes of claiming the throne himself is unclear, but the Londoners failed to rise for him – scuttled into their homes and locked their doors. Applauding their hero when off to war was one thing, open rebellion against the crown, another. His supporters began to panic, to melt away when the city gates were locked against them. There was some fighting at the Ludgate but the trained bands defeated the rebels and Essex was forced to flee – back to his own house by way of the river.

He surrendered later that evening and, the following morning, was taken to the Tower,

Throughout his trial, he sniped at Walter; at Cobham and Cecil too, but particularly at Walter. When my husband stood to take the oath, Essex spat: 'What use is it to swear the Fox?' And blamed him repeatedly, persisting in his claim that Walter and his followers had planned to murder him in his bed, forcing him to take up arms. Thankfully, no-one believed him.

Walter, as Captain of the Guard, was obliged to be present at the execution, but he withdrew to the Tower's armoury, he tells me on his return, feeling Essex would resent his presence.

'He died bravely, Bess, repenting of his sins and insisting he would never have harmed the Queen. And I'm told he asked for me, at the end – wanted to make his peace - but, God forgive me, I was too far away to hear. He had to die, the Queen would never have been safe while he lived. But it was such a waste, There was once much to admire in him.'

He looks strained and there are tears in his eyes. His emotion startles me. Then I recall their closeness before the assault on Cadiz, at the beginning of the Island's Voyage, the enjoyment they shared in each other's company. If the Earl had been less jealous, less ambitious (less mad?), perhaps they could have been true friends

But I can't weep for Essex. At the finish it was his life or Walter's. I can only grieve for Frances. How would I feel in her place? If it were <u>my</u> husband, Wat's father, lying headless in his grave in the Tower's chapel?

✳ ✳ ✳

Today two of my cousins arrived at Durham House. I was in the blue chamber playing chess with Wat and Will when they were announced – Muriel Tresham and Anne Catesby, daughters of my uncle, Robert Throckmorton. I had not met up with either of them for years but was not surprised to see them now. I guessed at once that they had come to plead for their sons, both of whom had been followers of Essex.

Kate took the boys to play elsewhere while we talked. Plump Anne wept pitifully throughout but Muriel, thin as a stick, remained dry-eyed though very pale and tense. Both spoke of their offspring as if they were innocent, misguided youths.

'They joined the rebellion out of ignorance and blind adoration for its leader,' Muriel said.

I reckoned quickly. Robert Catesby must be all of twenty-nine summers, Francis Tresham a few years more.

'Grown men,' I pointed out. 'Responsible for their own actions.'

'Just in search of a little excitement,' sobbed Anne. (They certainly got that.)

'Surely Sir Walter can help them – speak for them?' begged Muriel. 'They are law-abiding, as a rule . . .'

I had to laugh and, after a moment, Muriel joined in. Sheepishly. All my cousins are staunch Catholics, making them recusants for they refuse to worship in a Protestant church or pay their penalty fines. As a result they spend half their lives in prison. Law-abiding can hardly be applied to any of them.

'But this is different!' Anne wept. 'They could hang! And be drawn and quartered!:

True enough. Sir Gelli Meyrick and Sir Henry Cuffe have already suffered this fate at Tyburn, while Sir Charles Danvers and Sir Christopher Blount have followed their hero to the block.

'I beg you to be charitable,' Muriel clutched my hand. 'My Francis is good at heart, if a little wild and extravagant.'

To say nothing of being unstable and untrustworthy, I could have added. But I've always had a soft spot for Robert Catesby – handsome, popular, charming – an asset at a dinner party.

'We'll pay anything,' wailed Robert's mother. 'Any fine asked. But we need Sir Walter's intervention on their behalf. Please, Bess – you can persuade him. They'll never give trouble again. He won't regret it.'

I hope he won't, for of course I agreed to help. I looked at their terrified faces and, as a mother myself, how could I refuse?

* * *

Walter, urged by me, spoke up for my relations but there was hardly any need for there have been no more executions. Only a few of the lesser conspirators have been punished with imprisonment. The rest, Catesby and Tresham among them, have been released for various fines. Let us hope they have learned their lesson.

* * *

I force myself to dress in black and visit Frances (what comfort is there to offer?) She sits, stone-faced and tearless, while others weep and flutter around helplessly in her mother's house at Barn Elms.

Her affection has never wavered, despite the anxiety Essex caused her, the grief over his infidelities. 'He was a wonderful husband and father,' she says. 'I shall never marry again because I shall never meet his like.'

I embrace her and hold my tongue. She said the same when Philip Sidney died.

* * *

Durham House, March, 1601

Perched on a stool beside the fire, I'm stitching at my embroidery. Walter sits opposite, reading and smoking his pipe. We pretend not to hear the din from along the Strand. Essex is still the people's darling and they're blaming Walter for his fall and death – banging drums and singing cruel ballads in the streets to this effect. Essex is their 'jewel', their 'valiant knight of chivalry' while my Walter is 'Machiavelli'. They're claiming he provoked Essex with his wicked enmity, that he sat in the armoury and smoked his pipe – laughed and jeered and jested throughout the Earl's final moments.

Poor Little Wat, playing with his soldiers, is upset by the ballads and obvious hostility, but Walter only shrugs and asks what did I expect?

~PART FOUR~

ROBERT CECIL

Whitehall Palace, September, 1602

All the talk, lately, is of the succession. Forbidden, of course, by Her Majesty, who still refuses to name an heir, and so discussed cautiously in trusted circles. Elizabeth is getting older, how long can she last? Who should follow her? Who has a claim? James of Scotland? The Infanta of Castile? Lady Arabella Stuart? All have their supporters, especially James of Scotland.

Many eminent courtiers are writing to James of Scotland, licking his arse in the hope of securing their futures. Writing in secret, they fondly believe, the fools. I could name each and every one of them – report them to the Queen if I wanted to make trouble.

However, their putrid efforts do not worry me since I have myself been corresponding with King James for some considerable time and with a degree of satisfaction on both sides. He now trusts me to bring about his smooth succession, while I trust him to retain me as first statesman when he gains the throne...

There are pitfalls to be avoided, though. This morning, riding with Her Majesty in her coach, my heart stopped. We were returning to Whitehall from Greenwich and, as we lurched into the courtyard and drew up, we both saw a messenger arriving with a package. The Queen leaned from a window and hailed him while I sat, for a moment, numb with shock. The package, I knew, would almost certainly contain at least one letter from Scotland. Addressed to me. James and I used a code in our correspondence but it was a simple one, easy to break. Even as Elizabeth reached out a gloved hand, I came to life – shot out an arm and snatched it, screwing up my face in disgust.

'Ugh! It smells vile, Your Majesty! Don't touch it! I will personally make copies onto pristine paper before bringing them to you to read.'

The Queen nodded, shrinking back in her seat and fumbling for the pomander which hung at her waist. She has a horror of unpleasant odours.

Just as well she inhaled the scent of violets for I was now sweating like a pig.

Too close a shave, that one.

Raleigh presents another danger. When the Scottish emissaries first approached me, seeking my future support, they also approached Raleigh. Luckily, the short-sighted ass turned them down, saying he must remain loyal to Elizabeth and could look no further while she lived. He then came to me, pleased with himself, and I applauded him, pretending I had said the same.

He doesn't seem to realise one can be loyal to the Queen now, as I am, but also have an eye to one's future prospects by reaching out to James.

I worry, though, that Raleigh could change his mind, see this for himself; win James with his charm, his golden pen, and oust me in his favour.

So, as a precaution, I make sure to blacken him in my correspondence – telling James that the man is a heretic (anathema to a pious king), an untrustworthy troublemaker who looks to others for our future ruler.

And, to back me up and press the point further, I am encouraging Henry Howard, a known mischief-maker and an enemy of Raleigh, to write in the same vein (which he does with poisonous enjoyment). Even I am shocked by some of the things he pens. He calls Raleigh *'that great Lucifer'* and even slanders *'Lucifer's wife'*, my lovely, innocent Bess.

Too strong, by far. Howard is an unpleasant man, hard to like.

But, in this instance, his co-operation is all in a good cause.

※ ※ ※

March, 1603

'Do you think the Queen is dying?' my mistress asks, rising from my bed one afternoon, pulling a robe around her white and perfect nakedness.

'Hush!' I caution. Unwise to even think it, let alone to give it voice.

Yet I fear it is the truth. The Queen, after all, is sixty-nine summers and has caught a chill from which she seems unable to recover.

The astrologer, John Dee, advises her to beware of draughty Whitehall, and so, on a fittingly grey and rainy day, we of the Court remove to Richmond, the warmest of her palaces.

The royal physicians, anxious to please, insist their patient has a 'sound and perfect constitution and will live for many years'. To me, however, she looks to be fading fast, but when Raleigh asks me worriedly if I think it 'safe' for him to visit his Cornish miners on urgent business, I encourage him to do so.

'Her Majesty's will is stronger than her health,' I assure him. 'She'll hang on a while yet.'

Trustful as ever, he leaves for the West Country, and so is neatly out of the way when the end comes. The Queen recognises its arrival yet refuses to go to bed. When I attempt to persuade her, saying she must rest, she reacts with scorn.

'Little man, little man, the word 'must' is not to be used to princes.'

It's pitiful to see her, this once mighty Queen of ours. Too weak to stand, she sits on cushions on the floor of the Privy Chamber. My puny arms have not the strength to lift her and, in Raleigh's absence, no other dares try At last, Lord Admiral Howard strides in, sweeps her up easily and carries her to her bedchamber.

My colleagues, the Privy Councillors, now break out in a sweat regarding the succession – is she coherent enough to name an heir? She is not, but for this I am prepared. In her last moments, I put my lips to her ear and ask loudly:

'Your cousin of Scotland, Your Majesty? Is he your choice?'

And when, in the manner of the dying, her hands wander, I cry: 'A sign of approval! Look, her fingers are forming the shape of a crown!'

※ ※ ※

We of the council and nobility who attended the bedside at Greenwich, depart at dawn for Whitehall Palace.

At half ten in the morning, on a green outside the gates and heralded by trumpets, I fulfil my last promise to my father, read aloud the proclamation declaring James of Scotland King of England. The same proclamation (drafted by me some weeks ago), will be read throughout the land.

BESS

Durham house March,1603

Robin Cecil, it is said, has worked miracles. The Queen was beyond speech at the end, yet he got her to declare James of Scotland her successor.

No civil war, no riots, no disorder. We can all breathe sighs of relief.

'It will be good to have a king again,' Kate beams. 'Everyone says so. He might be a foreigner but at least he's not a Papist. And he and his Queen Anne have a daughter and two sons. No scratching around for an heir from now on.'

In the excitement over the new monarch, no-one, it seems to me, is shedding tears over the demise of our late Queen.

Apart, that is, from Walter, who was devastated to be absent from her side when she died.

'She grew old, cantankerous, and mean with her purse,' he says, wiping his eyes. 'But she was always a great lady and a great queen, with a fine wit and a good deal of common sense. It remains to be seen if this new king can live up to her.'

'Perhaps he'll make you a Privy Councillor at last,' I comfort, 'and allow your wife back to Court. You're travelling to meet him on his journey from Edinburgh? I've heard many are going.'

'Too many,' he scowls. 'Cecil doesn't want the King to be overwhelmed.'

'Oh, but I'm sure Robin means you to go,' I insist. 'I'm sure he thinks you'd be foolish not to pay your respects and make yourself known.'

* * *

How I wish I had not urged him.

King James was staying at Burghley House, in Northamptonshire, the home of Robin Cecil's half-brother, when Walter caught up with him. And where, to his astonishment, he was received sourly.

'Rawley? Rawley? I've heard rawly of you, mon!' The King drawled, in his broad Scots accent - made it clear in a hundred small ways that my husband was not in favour.

I am at a loss to know why. Most people take to Walter on first meeting him –handsome still, beautifully dressed, charming - he wins folk even against their will. Unless they are jealous, of course, like rival Courtiers. But why would a king be jealous of a subject? 'I've heard rawly of you.'

'What is the King like? In his person?' I ask.

Walter grimaces. 'Dirty. He never washes, not even his hands, just wipes them on a damp napkin. He's a coward – so terrified of assassination he wears padded doublets. He eats with the manners of an animal and he likes young men better than women.'

I recoil in horror. This man is to rule England?

❋ ❋ ❋

April 28, 1603

No shortage of tears today. Enough weeping to flood the Thames. Bell-ringers clear a path through the vast, sobbing crowds to make way for the funeral procession as it winds its way to Westminster Abbey; first the paupers, then servants from the royal household, heralds with the Dragon Standard and the Lion Standard, Children of the Chapel in their white surplices, singing sweetly, the Mayor and Aldermen of London, gentry, knights, bishops, nobles and, finally, the hearse, pulled by four horses draped in black, red and black plumes nodding on their heads. The coffin, covered in purple velvet with a life-size wax effigy of Elizabeth on top, dressed in the robes of state and complete with crown and sceptre, is greeted with gasps of awe. I watch Walter limp by, proud and tall in black hat and long black cloak, guarding his Queen for the last time, his men behind him, halberds pointing down.

And surprisingly I, too, find myself weeping – especially when I see Mary of Pembroke, Aud, Penelope Rich and other friends, black-hooded heads bowed, following their mistress as we once all followed her into chapel. Queen Bitch, we'd called her, and bitch she was, at times. But there were also times when she was kind, gracious, amusing. I should be there among them, honouring her, instead of standing beside Kate and Hancock, lost in the crowd. I have always believed she would soften one day, invite me back to serve her. Now she never will.

And how will Walter fare without her, at the dirty hands of our new King?

* * *

May, 1603

I have my answer – badly. James has taken away his Captaincy of the Guard – given the post to a lice-ridden Scotsman.

'It was only to be expected,' Walter says. He's pretending nonchalance, but I notice his hands are shaking. 'Sir Thomas Erskine held the position in Scotland. The King wants his own men about him. Understandable.'

But other Englishmen are prospering - Henry Percy and Cousin Gorges made Privy Councillors, Robin Cecil to be given a peerage ...

* * *

I gape at Walter in disbelief. He says we are to vacate Durham House – to be thrown out of here like people of low-standing behind with the rent.

'But ... I don't understand! Queen Elizabeth took the lease from the Bishop of Durham and gave it to you twenty years ago. And you've spent thousands on improvements ...'

'The Bishop of Durham wants it back!' Walter bellows, waving the letter in my face, his own so crimson I fear for his health. 'And King James is happy to give it to him. We're ordered to get out within seventeen days!'

I grope for a chair. 'This cannot be happening . . .'

'I'll be damned if I'll let it!' Walter marches to his desk 'I'll write to the King's Commissioners.'

* * *

They have extended our eviction to Midsummer Day. Which leaves us three and a half weeks to empty the house of furniture, hangings, linen, paintings – all our belongings and those of our servants - load them onto carts and wagons and despatch them to Sherborne which, being fully furnished itself, will have no room for them.

'Appeal to Cecil,' I beg Walter.

'I already have. He's as sick as we are, but can do nothing.'

* * *

I refuse to begin packing, refuse to give up.

'We'll appeal,' I say to Kate, 'to the Queen.'

'But my lady,' she stutters, 'the Queen is still in Scotland.'

'Not for long. She's travelling south, to be crowned with the King. A handful of ladies are riding to meet her. We will go too.'

Kate pales. 'All the way to Edinburgh?'

'Not *all* the way. Aud and some others are to meet her in Berwick, on English soil.'

'But where is Berwick?'

'Much nearer.' *Is it? I must ask Aud.*

* * *

Where would I be without dear Edward Hancock? Quietly, he persuades Wood to drive the coach, to arrange overnight stays, changes of horses.

'You'll be telling Sir Walter?' Wood asks me doubtfully.

'Of course,' I assure him. (I'm leaving a note.)

We travel fast, stopping only when we are forced to, but even so many women pass us on horseback – ladies from the Court, desperate to be the first to greet the Queen, win her favour.

'Perhaps,' says Kate, 'she'll choose you for a lady-in-waiting. Then our fortunes will rise again.'

'Perhaps,' I agree, 'if we ever arrive . . .'

* * *

Berwick. Queen Anne's Presence Chamber

Such a crush! So much competition! Too many ladies falling over themselves to be noticed in the house where Her Majesty lodges. Way down the tapestried hall is Penelope Rich, talking and laughing with a woman who can only be the Queen. But never will

I get there – I haven't a hope, with an elbow in my ribs, a riding boot upon my foot...

'Bess...'

It's Aud, shouldering her way determinedly towards me, grasping my arm in an iron grip . 'Come with me!'

* * *

The Queen is fair-haired, with a very clear complexion and a rather large nose. When I make my curtsey, stumbling a little from nerves, she smiles graciously. Until Aud speaks my name. Her brow creases in alarm. (I've heard rawly of you!) And when I state my case she avoids my eyes, speaks in good but careful English.

'I would like to help you, Lady Raleigh. But if the King wants your London house...'

'The King does *not* want it,' I say desperately. 'He's giving it to the Bishop of Durham who has other houses...'

'But if the King is intent on giving it...' She shrugs. 'I fear I can do nothing. I have no influence.'

'We thought perhaps it might help if you selected Lady Raleigh as a lady-in-waiting,' Aud puts in valiantly.

The Queen pales. 'The King would not permit it. I am sorry. I can do nothing.'

She turns back to Penelope Rich, takes her arm and they move away.

'My Lady Rich rode all the way to Edinburgh,' whispers Aud. 'She's very well in!'

While the Raleighs, it seems, are most definitely out.

* * *

July, 1603

Some of our belongings have been sold, others moulder in outbuildings at Sherborne until we decide their fate.

I, meanwhile, stay with Arthur and Anna at their house in Mile End. They are here for the coronation.

Walter moves around with the Court, sharing the lodgings of Cousin Gorges now he no longer has his own.

'Why does he bother?' demands Anna, 'When he's been so insulted?'

I sigh. 'I suppose he still hopes to get back into favour.'

'He's better out of it, with a king such as this,' she snorts. 'I've heard there's little in him to admire.'

ROBERT CECIL

Windsor Castle, July 1603

God in Heaven, this king is not what I expected!

I throw down my quill in frustration, push papers aside on my desk and sink my head in my hands. Why labour like a pack horse while all James wants to do is hunt?

Fresh air is good for his health, he says, with scant concern for mine, forced to burn these midnight candles, strain my eyes writing endless letters imploring him to return and sign documents demanding his attention; wasting time dispatching couriers deep into the countryside to find him as he pursues stag or boar, drinks and dribbles and makes merry at his various hunting lodges with his toadying Scottish favourites.

Hard to believe this is a man of fine intellect who sprinkles his correspondence with Latin and quotes the Scriptures word for word. A man who counts himself a scholar and yet acts like a bumbling squire while I and the other councillors are left to run his country.

Rather accept this is a man hard to respect and even harder to love.

He claims he hates London, with its foul odours; hates the Londoners still more, who crowd and jostle and cheer and stare whenever he appears in public. One day, he vows, he'll give them something to stare at – he'll pull down his breeches and show them his arse.

When I think of the late Queen on Progress, God bless her, so gracious to her public, so appreciative of their adoration . . .

Oh, she could curse in private but was never uncouth. She set standards of behaviour and of hygiene, thank the Saints – I was never obliged to scratch, after leaving her presence, remove lice from my clothing, my very skin, as I do after audience with James.

At least James has one saving grace he shares with me – a desire for peace. Raleigh's thirst for assaults on Spain is met with scorn. Yet still my fine friend hangs about the Court, unable to believe his day is done. His blood must be boiling with anger, with humiliation, but he hides it well. And who knows? He could still prove a danger, with his damnable charm, his persuasive tongue. James is a weak man, beneath his padded doublets, his strutting bow-legged walk.

If Raleigh could sway Elizabeth, who was strong . . .

A gentle tap on the door interrupts my contemplation. I sit up at my desk, straighten my wretched shoulders as best I can, retrieve my quill and look busy.

'Come.'

My man from the Tower enters and bows. 'Sir Robert.'

I do not recall his name. His eyes, ears and intelligence are all I require.

I indicate the chair opposite. 'You may sit.'

He does, and imparts new information over the cup of wine I pour from my silver decanter (a gift, ironically, from the Raleighs).

His update interests me.

My spies recently foiled a plot instigated by my brother-in-law, George Brooke, to kidnap the King and force him to be more tolerant to Papists. Under arrest, the fool is gabbling wildly in an attempt to save himself.

Now, it seems, he has implicated his older brother, Henry Brooke, Lord Cobham, in a more serious conspiracy altogether – a plot to assassinate James and replace him on the throne with his cousin, Lady Arabella Stuart.

I have little regard for George Brooke, a hothead short on brains. He's done for himself and will hang, no doubt of it.

But . . . I push back my chair, rise, pace . . .

The involvement of Cobham, my Lizzie's favourite brother, gives me food for thought. Left out of the Privy Council, like Raleigh, ignored by James, like Raleigh, he is, naturally, as discontented as Raleigh, though he makes more noise about it. He is also, of course, a close friend to Raleigh, they are much together.

Can I make use of this?

※ ※ ※

Windsor Castle. July,1603

The king is going a-hunting – no surprise. What else would he be doing on a glorious summers day?

He's taking his time about it – he always takes his time, does James. Led in circles by the royal grooms, the horses await him, stamping impatient hooves. The Courtiers, dressed for the chase, await him, trying not to stamp their impatient feet. Among them, Raleigh awaits him, standing on the terrace smoking his silver pipe. He's more richly clad than any of them, the jewel in his hat shining in the sun as he leans towards the chattering youth beside him, the savage youth named Cal. The sight of Cal irritates me. It always does. A typical affectation of Raleigh's, to have him dancing attendance – tall and straight and foreign-looking – drawing all eyes to him in fascination and in turn, of course, to Raleigh.

'Sir Walter –'

'Robin!' Raleigh turns at my approach, smiles with his usual warmth.

I cannot meet his gaze.. 'I'm sorry to interrupt your hunting plans, but your presence is required in the Council Chamber. To answer a few questions . . .'

BESS

Mile End, July, 1603

Walter? In the *Tower?* Accused of *treason?*

My head is spinning. They are saying that, with Lord Cobham, he was involved in a plot to kill King James and his two sons – put Lady Arabella Stuart on the throne as a kind of puppet monarch, with the help of Spanish gold.

'But this is nonsense!' I cry in bewilderment. 'Insane!'

'Of course it is.' My brother Arthur looks white and stricken.. 'But rumour has it that Cobham's admitted it. Implicated Raleigh.'

I knew Cobham to be disillusioned with King James. He has been overlooked, like Walter, by this new monarch who prefers Scotsmen and pretty boys to old favourites of Elizabeth. He often complained loudly of his treatment when we were still at Durham

House. Spoke wildly, sometimes, and was listened to but laughed at by Walter who sympathised but never took him seriously. Now his foolishness has somehow dragged them both into this ugly mess.

I spin on my heel: 'Kate, summon Wood with the coach, then bring my cloak. We must go to Sir Walter...'

Arthur catches my arm. 'They won't let you see him.'

'Of course they will. I am his wife. And we must send word to Robin Cecil. Robin will help us.'

'It was Cecil had him arrested.'

'No!' I catch my breath.

Have all our friends run mad?

✽ ✽ ✽

At the Tower, the guards are adamant.

'We regret, Lady Raleigh, that Sir Walter is allowed no visitors. More than our lives are worth, to disobey.'

'It's Walter's life that will be forfeit if this affair goes to trial,' I moan to Arthur.

For treason trials are a mere formality, the death sentence assured. Yet whatever wicked thing Cobham was planning Walter was not involved in it, so surely he cannot be brought to trial?

✽ ✽ ✽

I hardly dare even think it, but there may yet be cause for hope. The coronation of King James and Queen Anne is to take place tomorrow at Westminster Abbey. The crowds are likely to be curtailed for fear of the plague and I shall certainly not be among any brave souls who venture out to cheer on the royal procession. I'd be tempted to throw something at it. But Anna has reminded me that the new monarch, in a ritual act of benevolence, is expected to give leave for certain prisoners of the crown to be pardoned and released.

'Surely, Bess,' she says, 'surely Sir Walter will be among them.'

'He's done no wrong to be pardoned *for*.' I point out angrily.

But I'm on tenterhooks of hope. Please God, please!

* * *

He was not released and I'm frantic! They still won't let me see him *And he's attempted to take his own life!*

He stabbed himself with a table knife while dining with the Tower Governor. The weapon was too blunt, thankfully, to kill him – the wound bloody but not deep. So his enemies, Arthur says, are calling it a mere gesture, a touch of play-acting to win sympathy.

Ridiculous! I know he did it with real intent, for little Wat and me. He fears they'll convict him out of jealousy and hatred. If he'd died before being attainted, his goods, his property, would not be forfeit to the Crown.

'But he deeded Sherborne to Little Wat some time ago,' Anna says, puzzled. 'Sherborne is safe, whatever happens.'

I shrug. 'He no longer trusts the Privy Council to play fair. How can he, with Cecil at its head?'

Cecil the false friend. Cecil the Serpent!

But I care not for money or property. Only for Walter. Thank Heaven he did not succeed – that he's still alive to fight this injustice.

* * *

I've been forced to write to Cecil the Serpent with a show of friendliness, imploring him to help us, and this morning I went again to the Tower with Kate and Arthur – demanded to be allowed into Walter's cell. But permission, once again, was refused. No amount of tears could move the gaoler, no amount of gold was bribe enough. Send a letter, the man said, and he would pass it on.

I cannot hold Walter in my arms in a letter - look him in the eyes and make him promise never to attempt such a thing again.

* * *

Will I ever stop weeping?

Today I received a letter from Walter – a terrible letter, meant to be delivered after his death.

In it, he bids me farewell, assures me of his innocence, asks me to take care of Little Wat, to be kind to his daughter. He urges me to marry again but for practical reasons only, never for love. He cannot bear the thought, he says, of my loving another man as I loved him. Then he lists financial matters that will need my attention.

They blur before my eyes.

Thank God he is still alive.

* * *

Cousin Gorges has been released. He visits me here at Arthur's house. No evidence was found against him, he says, he was arrested only on account of his closeness to Walter.

'But so was Edward Hancock!' I cry. 'Yet he remains in the Tower.'

Gently, he takes me by the hand and sits me down, tells me that Hancock, having been mistakenly told that Walter was dead, has hanged himself in his cell. 'He was devoted to Raleigh, I believe.'

And he was always so kind to me. Poor, gentle, loyal Hancock.

I weep afresh.

* * *

August, 1603

Pulling myself together, I write letters to all I can think of – bombard the King, the Privy Council, old friends, old enemies, even foreign ambassadors. But help is not forthcoming. It seems the law is bent upon its course.

People call on me here at Mile End to offer their support before they disperse to the country with the royal party, fleeing the plague. Many shake their heads and regret that their hands are tied. Others seem to consider Walter as good as dead and buried.

I'll-never-marry-again Frances (nee Essex, nee Sidney) brings her new husband, the Earl of Clarincade. She hugs me close and whispers consoling words, but I know she pictures Walter's head upon the block in imitation of Essex.

Mary Herbert is more heartening:

'We'll save him, never fear. I shall invite the King to Wilton, ply him with wine and plead with him for Raleigh's release.' (She's confident her charm will succeed where mine has failed.)

Aud says her husband will also appeal to the King. 'And I'll appeal to the Queen.' (Who, no doubt, will be as much help to me as she was at Berwick.)

Thomas Harriot is shaken and irate. 'How can they think it of him? It's mad! Insane!'

But the one who touches me most is little Will Cecil, who arrives in floods of tears. 'My father says he loves Sir Walter but cannot uphold a traitor! Sir Walter is no traitor nor could ever be! Lady Bess, I hate my father!'

I hate him, too, for *he's* the traitor. But I need to comfort Will. 'You must not hate your father, Will, for he has been misled.' The words stick in my throat.

* * *

'He cannot be brought to trial,' I tell Walter's brother Carew, as we pace together in Arthur's walled garden. 'Not Walter. It's unthinkable.'

He sighs. 'Sadly, it would appear unavoidable. But if we can't prevent a trial, Bess, there might be a way of having one, yet still saving his life.'

I stop in my tracks. 'How?'

He tugs his beard, a trick he has, when thinking. 'If he could be tried in the Star Chamber... I was talking of it with Cousin Gorges and he agrees that it is a court which does not strictly obey English common law. There is no jury, it is presided over merely by the Privy Council and two judges appointed by the King.'

'But how does that help? Cecil leads the Privy Council and if the two judges are appointed by King James who hates Raleigh...'

'The Star Chamber Court cannot impose a death sentence.'

'What?'

'Wait. Before you get too excited, there would be a sting for Walter. To be tried in the Star Chamber is an acknowledgement, before the trial even begins, that the offender is guilty.'

I am jubilant. 'Cecil intends him to be found guilty, anyway, you and I both know that. At least, this way, we could save his life. But – how can we ensure he is tried in the Star Chamber?'

'We have to petition. But that, alone, is not enough. There will have to be a bribe – a large one...'

'Oh.' My coffers are nearly empty.

'Come home with me, Bess. Dorothy will welcome you with open arms and Walter and I have contacts in nearby Salisbury. We'll raise money there; get help with the petition. You have nothing to lose and everything to gain ...'

I reach up and kiss him on the cheek. 'It will take but a short while to pack...'

✽ ✽ ✽

At Carew's house a weeping Dorothy rushes out to greet me. Behind her hovers a striking dark-haired girl who eyes me warily.

Alice – tall for twelve summers and, in looks, more like Walter than ever.

I greet her just as warily. She drops a reluctant curtsey – a mere bob which is barely respectful, then quickly vanishes into the shadows of the hall.

She has not then, I think, outgrown her hatred of me.

When I see her again, at supper, she avoids my eyes, speaks only when spoken to; leaves the table as soon as manners permit.

But later, when Kate is preparing me for bed, there comes a tap on my door and here she is. She stands, for a moment, tongue-tied, looking at me a little desperately. I ask Kate to leave us together and bid Alice take a seat. She shakes her head, not moving. I can think of nothing to say that won't annoy her, so the silence drags on painfully. Then she bursts out:

'Will he die, Lady Bess? Will they kill my fath...Cousin Walter?'

I shake my head. 'Not if I can help it. I aim to save his life.'

She blinks away tears from her big brown (Raleigh) eyes. 'Can I help? Please?'

I nod. 'Of course you can.'

* * *

With the help of Carew, Dorothy, and several of their friends, we raise the princely sum of five thousand pounds, yet our petition is turned down. On Cecil's orders? Or by command of the King himself?

* * *

September, 1603

Back at Mile End I again take up my pen, with Alice sitting beside me applying the Raleigh seal. She begged to come here with me; wishes to be near her father even though she won't be allowed to see him. Kate thinks I was mad to agree, but how could I refuse?

'*Be kind to my daughter,*' he'd written.

We are still not at ease in each other's company and are overly polite, but we are united by our love for Walter where it once pulled us apart.

'There's still hope, isn't there?' she asks now.

'Of course,' I reply. I must try to believe it though it gets harder by the day.

* * *

October, 1603

The plague rages worse in London, so the trial is to be held at Winchester – on the seventeenth of November, the old Queen's Accession Day.

I am desperate to speak to Walter, to tell him, face to face, that I believe in his innocence, that no jury can convict a truly innocent man.

'Surely they will let me see him before he is taken from the Tower,' I say to Arthur.

He shakes his head. 'I doubt it.'

'If they won't I shall disguise myself as a serving woman, stop the coach on the road – throw myself in front of it.'

Arthur smiles pityingly. He doesn't believe me.

* * *

November, 1603

Penned in the vast crowd lining the road, I dance up on my toes when his coach comes into sight. It's surrounded by guards on horseback, guards on foot, their breastplates shining in the winter sun. I wave, I shout until my voice is hoarse but he cannot hear me. The noise, the commotion, is too great. Men scuffle with the guards, scream obscenities, beat on the coach doors, rocking it back and forth. Women jeer, throw mud and stones. 'Traitor!' 'Let us at him! 'Avenge the death of Essex!' 'Tear him limb from limb!' I even see children hurling tobacco pipes.

Oh, God, please let him see me – one loving face among this sea of hate. But he doesn't, of course, how can he? The two guards seated either side of him, cower in terror. But Walter sits straight and defiant, stares out at his tormentors, a contemptuous smile curling his lips.

'Stop it!' I scream, 'you'll overturn the coach!'

At last the coachman, cursing, manages to best the men who would unseat him – lays about him with his whip and the frightened horses rear, then gallop madly on – pulling the vehicle round the bend and out of sight, followed by its armed escort. The crowd surges, pointlessly, after it, still shouting . . . I am jostled, shoved until I fall to the ground to kneel, weeping, in the dust.

Still the best hated man in England, then. What chance does he have?

* * *

Arthur Gorges called again today.

Kate, Alice and I were packing in preparation for our journey to Salisbury. We're to stay with Carew and Dorothy for the duration of the trial.

Leaving Kate to finish, I hurried down to the hall and found him pacing, his round face flushed. Now what can have happened? I thought in dismay, but when he came towards me I saw he was alight with excitement.

'Bess, we need to talk privately. This is important.'

I took him into the garden where I'd talked with Carew (those stout walls must be privy to many a secret). Although there was not a soul in sight he spoke very low.

'I've received a note from Walter, delivered by Cal, the savage boy. It seems Walter managed to smuggle letters to Cobham while they were both still in the Tower - urged him, many times, to speak the truth.'

My heart beat faster. 'And?'

'Cobham eventually sent him a letter retracting his earlier confession – exonerating Walter from all blame.'

'But – that's wonderful!' I grasped his sleeve. 'Does this mean there will be no trial?'

He glanced round nervously. 'Hush! Speak soft! Too late to halt it now. But Walter aims to use this letter – produce it as his trump card during the trial.'

'And when he does, they'll have to find him innocent!' I threw my arms around the dear man in glee.

He hugged me close, spoke into my hair. 'We can but hope, Bess, we can but hope. But this must be our secret – yours, mine and Walter's. He wishes to spring the letter on the jury, catch them unawares...

I laughed. 'Of course he does! He wishes to produce it with a flourish, to gasps of amazement.' So typical of Walter.

'Oh, and Bess – he does not wish you to be present. His enemies are out to draw blood. He thinks it may distress you...'

I nodded meekly but shall pay no heed, of course. Miss the trial? Unthinkable! Especially now.

* * *

Wolvesey Castle, Winchester, November 17, 1603

It's like a scene from a play – colourful, dramatic, intense.

Only the trial in a play might have a happy ending. Whereas this...

They've placed a stool for him to sit on but he scorns it – stands beside it, proud and erect, his very stance challenging his accusers. I am struck afresh by his height; think he looks taller than ever. Then I realise this is because he is thinner, much thinner. He is handsome as ever, though, in dark blue satin slashed with palest silk, jewels winking on the sleeves of his doublet, upon the buckles of his shoes, an enormous pearl droplet swinging from his right ear.

Pride swells within me. The Raleigh pride.

This ancient, high-ceilinged hall is filled with a few friends and many foes, here to see a once-great man brought low. The expectant atmosphere is chill – hostile looks are cast in my direction. The mud thrown today will be verbal and how these onlookers will relish it!

I stand in the gallery, well back where Walter cannot see me, flanked protectively by Carew, Arthur, Nicholas and Thomas Harriot. Below in the hall, near the dais where the Judges, Jury and Commissioners sit, I spy Adrian Gilbert, Henry of Northumberland, Cousin Gorges, Mary of Pembroke's sons. Walter nodded to them when he was brought in, raised his hand and raised a smile – knowing they, at least, are here to support him, to give him courage should it be needed.

'Not guilty,' he says firmly, when asked for his plea, then agrees he takes no exception to any members of the jury.

I take exception to Cecil the Snake, seated among the Commissioners, brazenly facing the friend he has so abandoned. For he cannot, surely, credit the charges just heard against Walter?

'Conspiring to deprive the King of his government.' (Of his very life, they'd have us believe);

'To alter religion and bring in the Roman superstition.' (My husband, the staunch Protestant);

'To set Lady Arabella Stuart upon the throne.' (The King's cousin, who he once called a 'milksop');

'To accept Spanish gold and incite Spanish invasion.' (Sir Walter Raleigh, who stormed Cadiz).

It's so ridiculous it should be a laughing matter. Yet these men, with their scarlet robes and sober faces, are weighing this nonsense against my husband's life.

The prosecutor, Sir Edwards Coke, is as tall as Walter, as handsome as Walter. But he has not Walter's dignity. He shouts, he bullies, while Walter, who is allowed no defence and must speak for himself, answers clearly but quietly, so that all hang on his every word.

Coke calls Walter 'A monster!' 'A viper!' 'An odious man!' 'The rankest traitor in all England!' And Walter answers back wittily but politely, proclaiming his innocence over and over, and asking that Cobham be brought from his cell beneath the hall to accuse him face to face. A request that's refused, of course, because the Commissioners dare not risk it. One small, hunch-backed Commissioner in particular. Cobham is weak – he'd not be able to lie to his old friend's face.So brave is my darling, so composed, that, gradually, a strange thing happens. The onlookers, so against him, so thirsting for his downfall, begin to admire him.

Begin to murmur against Coke, to groan at his insults, to laugh at Raleigh's occasional thrusts that leave Coke red of face.   'You are the most vile and execrable traitor that ever lived, 'shouts Coke.

'You speak indiscreetly, barbarously and uncivilly,' returns Walter mildly. 'I want word sufficient to express your viperous treasons,' shouts Coke.

'I think you want words indeed,' says Walter, 'for you have spoken one thing half a dozen times.'

It's turned into a duel between the two of them. And the best hated man in England seems, suddenly, to have become the favourite.

* * *

The day wears on. We started at eight this morning and it is now well into evening. My head throbs with the strain. I find it hard to concentrate.

An extra stir in the proceedings as the Earl of Nottingham walks forward, the Lady Arabella Stuart on his arm. He proclaims her innocent, insists she knew nothing of the wicked plot to put her on the throne. Too much of a milksop, then, to speak up for herself.

I tap my foot impatiently. I'm waiting for the letter – Cobham's letter – that must, I think, be hidden in Walter's doublet, ready to be produced. The letter that will prove his innocence, once and for all. That will shame Judges, Jury and Commissioners into letting a blameless man walk free.

But wait – what's this? Coke is brandishing a letter, a triumphant smile on his face. 'From My Lord Cobham, 'he shouts. 'Another confession!'

Loudly, he reads it out. Cobham begs forgiveness for himself and blames Walter once again for persuading him into the plot against the King, for being the ringleader, and the procurer of money from Spain.

My head now swims with bewilderment. Was this letter dated before the retraction hidden in Walter's pocket? Surely, it must have been.

My gaze swivels to Walter and I see, by the sudden pallor of my husband's face, that it was not. He appears to struggle for words; sinks down, for the first time, upon the stool provided for him. Sick to my stomach, I am forced to accept that Henry Brooke, Lord Cobham, our one-time friend and good companion, has turned his coat yet again.

'Now Raleigh,' thunders Coke, 'if you have the grace, humble yourself and confess your treasons!'

A hush, as all eyes rest on Walter, who looks drawn, defeated. Then suddenly he rallies – stands and fights gallantly on. He pulls out his own letter from Cobham from within his doublet, as I'd thought, hoping to show the unreliability of the wretched man as a witness, an accuser.

'You have heard a strange tale from a strange man,' he says. 'You shall see how many souls this Cobham has. You shall see that he is a poor, silly, base, dishonourable soul.'

He asks that Cecil read it out, being Cobham's brother-in-law and knowing his handwriting. Cecil does so. He can hardly refuse, though the words proclaiming Walter's innocence must surely stick in his throat.

'. . . I never had conference with Sir Walter Raleigh in any treason,' Cobham has written, 'nor was ever moved by him to the things I accused him of. He is as innocent and as clear from any treasons against the King as any subject living . . .'

Loud murmurs arise from the spectators. Even a ripple of applause.

But I know, Walter knows, the entire Court knows that this cannot be counted as evidence. This letter exonerating Walter was written four days hence, in the Tower. The new confession refuting it and accusing him again was penned only a few hours ago, in Cobham's cell beneath this hall..

Walter asks, yet again, for Cobham to be called and accuse him face to face, and again the request is refused.

There is a ringing in my ears. Walter speaks again, at length, but I am so overcome with dread I cannot take in the words. Again applause, louder now. And when Coke rises to speak he is hissed. Everyone seems to be shouting at once and the Sergeant has difficulty in quietening the courtroom.

'This last letter,' Coke bellows, 'was politically and cunningly urged from my Lord Cobham, whereby the one written here in Winchester is the simple truth, drawn from my Lord Cobham without promise of mercy, hope or favour.'

The Commissioners, the judges, are nodding in agreement.

Proceedings move swiftly now. Of what good to prolong? The members of the jury stand; solemnly depart to another room to decide my husband's fate; return after fifteen short minutes to give the verdict King James and Robert Cecil have all along intended - 'Guilty.'

It is what I expected, yet I gasp, sway and almost fall, my knees having turned to water. ('Water' – the old Queen's name for him. How she would curse this injustice!) Carew throws an arm around me, holds me close. I feel his body trembling and see that his face is tight with rage.

The crowd in the body of the hall are angry also, and loudly make it known. The Sergeant again has to call for order while

Walter shows no emotion, stands calm and even straighter than before. He again proclaims his innocence of all charges and adds:

'I recommend my wife and son of tender years to the King's compassion.' Again, the ringing in my ears which prevents me from hearing properly. The Lord Chief Justice is speaking at length, saying something about thinking it impossible that one so great could have fallen so low. Accusing Walter of 'eager ambition' and 'corrupt covetousness'. There follows a lot more that I do not comprehend, but I hear the last part well enough:

'Since you have been found guilty of these horrible treasons, the judgement of the Court is this: That you shall be taken from hence to the place whence you came, there to remain until the day of execution: and from thence you shall be drawn upon a hurdle through the open streets to the place of execution, there to be hanged and cut down alive, and your body shall be opened, your heart and bowels plucked out, and your privy members cut off and thrown into the fire before your eyes; then your head shall be stricken from your body, and your body shall be divided into four quarters, to be disposed of at the King's pleasure. And God have mercy on your soul.'

✳ ✳ ✳

I walk from the buzzing courtroom dry-eyed, my head held high. He was brave and so shall I be. Cecil was the one who wept, the hypocrite – buried his face in his hands as Walter was led away.

Arthur grips my elbow, seeks clumsily to comfort. 'His sentence will be commuted, Bess. He'll not be drawn and quartered.'

My lips twist in a bitter smile. Hanged or beheaded, he'll still be dead.

* * *

At Carew's house Dorothy, Anna, Kate and little Alice weep – how they weep. They must think me unnatural for I still cannot. I sit straight-backed at Carew's desk and write letters. I am utterly weary of, holding a quill and fear it will do no good. But I have to try. I write a letter to Walter, begging him also to try:

'Do not abandon hope. Write to the King, to Cecil the Snake, to the Queen, to every member of the Privy Council. Forget pride; pride will not help us now. Beg them, plead with them to let you live. For my sake, for the sake of Little Wat . . .'

* * *

The execution dates have been announced. Cobham and his fellow conspirators will die on December the tenth, Walter on December the twelfth. All the sentences commuted to beheading.

Every night I dream of Walter on the scaffold, kneeling, his head on the block. The axe falls, there is blood everywhere. On my face, in my eyes, blinding me.

* * *

December, 1603

A messenger has arrived with a letter from Walter. A last letter. I hold it in my hands, unable to open it.

I remember how Queen Elizabeth kept her last letter from the Earl of Leicester locked away in her desk – took it out frequently to re-read and kiss and weep over. Shall I do the same with this? 'Take the man to the kitchens for some refreshment,' I bid a tear-stained Kate.

'But, my lady - I have not yet finished pinning up your hair . . .'

'Leave it!'

Putting the clasps down, she goes out sulkily.

The morning is dark so I take the letter to the window; force myself to break the seal.

'You shall receive, dear wife, my last words in these my last lines. I would not, with my last will, present you with sorrows, dear Bess. Let them go to the grave with me and lie buried in the dust. And seeing it is not the will of God that ever I shall see you in this life, bear my destruction gently, and with a heart like yourself.

I have much money owing me. The arrears of the wines will pay your debts, and howsoever you do, for my soul's sake, pay all poor men. I send you all the thanks my heart can conceive or my pen express, for your many troubles and cares taken for me, which – though they have not taken effect as you wished – yet my debt is to you nevertheless; but pay it I never shall, in this world.

Get those letters, if it be possible, which I wrote to the Lords of the Council, wherein I sued for my life. God knows it was for you and yours that I desired it, but it is true that I disdain myself for begging for it.

I cannot write much. It is time to separate my thoughts from the world. Beg my dead body, which living was denied you, and either lay it at Sherborne if the land continue, or in Exeter Church, by my father and mother.

Time and death call me away. My love I send you, that you may keep it when I am dead, and my counsel that you may remember when I am no more.

My true wife, farewell. Bless my poor boy for his father's sake, that chose you and loved you in his happiest hour. Pray for me. May the true God hold you both in his arms.'

A second sheet is attached to the letter – a poem;
'Give me my scallop shell of quiet,
My staff of faith to walk upon ...'

Our love affair began with a poem. Now it ends with one.

ROBERT CECIL

Wilton House, December 1603

I pace the bedchamber allotted me in this sumptuous house of Mary Herbert, Countess of Pembroke, confronting my old dilemma. Love and hate.

Weak fool that I am, I do not want him to die. Disgraced, locked up for life, yes. But finished for good – extinguished – snuffed out like a candle flame? That warmth? That vitality?'

'You cannot let it happen!' my mistress insists, sitting up in bed. 'I'm confused about the verdict. I thought him innocent yet you seem so sure of his guilt. But what will it do to his wife? His poor wife . . .'

In the end I go to James. Not to grovel, of course, as Raleigh's supporters are doing, but to reason, with a show of reluctance.

Bowing as low as I can, I say, voice tinged with regret: 'I fear, Majesty, that if you now take Raleigh's head he might afterwards be regarded as a martyr, causing uproar and dissent among your subjects...'

James, munching an apple, waves a grubby hand. 'Credit me wi' some sense, ma little Beagle.'

I try not to wince. I was Elizabeth Tudor's Pygmy, then her Elf. Now I am the Stuart King's Beagle. Can these royals never manage a straightforward Robert?

'Was I not present in the courtroom, concealed behind a curtain?' James goes on. He spits out a pip. It misses me. Just. 'Did I not curse the moment the tide turned, thanks to the knave's crafty wile, his easy tongue? Even one of ma most loyal men, an honest, trusted Scot, was swayed. Told me that before Raleigh's trial he would have gone a hundred miles to see him hanged, but after it he would go a thousand to save his life.' He gulps wine, wipes his mouth on his sleeve. 'So, ma little friend, we think it prudent to exercise clemency – we'll spare the wretch. For the moment.'

I bow again. 'And the others, Your Majesty? The other conspirators?'

He laughs, splutters. Spittle hits me in the eye. 'I ha' plans for the others – a jest, to turn their bowels to water.'

✱ ✱ ✱

On the grey, rain-drizzling morning of the tenth of December, I witness this 'jest'. I stand, with the other dignitaries, on the platform erected beside the raised scaffold in Winchester Castle yard. George Brooke and two priests went to their maker days ago. Now it is the turn of Sir Griffin Markham, Lord Grey, and Lord Cobham.

Markham is led out first – shaking and distraught but struggling to be brave. He kneels at the block to say his final prayers, the axe-man at the ready, when there is, in the crowd, a great commotion as a messenger from the King shoulders his way through, brandishing a royal warrant. The Sheriff reads it aloud – an order from James that Markham should not be executed first, but be allowed two hours respite. And so the bewildered man is marched back inside the Castle, his ordeal postponed.

Lord Grey is led out next, his face betraying surprise to see no blood staining the scaffold. He prays, long and sincerely, then kneels at the block. But before a blow is struck – behold – another messenger comes forcing his way through the murmuring onlookers, presenting a warrant, the same as before. Grey is to have two hours respite. As he is made to retrace his stumbling steps back to the prison he had thought never to see again, he looks towards me, white-faced and questioning. I shrug and shake my head. I know nothing of all this.

Then it is the turn of my brother-in-law, Cobham. He was cowardly at his trial, tearful and pathetic. But today he holds his head high, determined to show his mettle. Before his prayers he makes the speech he has been ordered to make and which I composed– reaffirming his charges against Raleigh. Everyone is half expecting the King's man this time, urgently waving his warrant. Sure enough, he appears, and when the paper is received and read out, a cheer goes up. But Cobham is not taken away. Instead, Markham and Grey are brought back to stand beside him.

By this time we are all soaked and frozen – shivering as much as the condemned and in need of a warm fire and a sup of ale.

'Are not your offences heinous?' the Sheriff demands, teeth a-chatter. 'Have you not been justly tried and lawfully condemned?'

The three near-drowned rats nod miserably and agree.. The executioner (again) steps forward with his axe.

'Stay!' the Sheriff booms, full-voiced. 'Behold the mercy of your King who has sent a countermand and granted you your lives!'

A buzz from the amazed crowd, a few groans from the bloodthirsty, then rousing cheers for the clemency of James. The reprieved trio, meanwhile, stand shocked and trembling, unable to believe they have been spared.

As they are led away – Markham to be exiled, Grey and Cobham to be taken back to London and imprisoned in the Tower – I glance up at a high window that overlooks the Castle yard, spy Raleigh looking down. The distance is too far for our eyes to meet, but I know he must feel as I do about this tasteless comedy; that it sickens him as it does me, this game of cat and mouse played out with human lives.

But his heart must also, now, be leaping with the hope that he, too, might be spared – perhaps even pardoned.

I turn, make my clumsy way down the platform steps without a backward glance. The King, I know, has given order that the scaffold be kept in place – means to keep the Raleighs waiting in suspense for a few more days at least, before Walter is taken from Winchester Castle and escorted back to the Tower.

BESS

The Tower of London, December, 1603

The gaolers smile as they let me into my husband's cell, their smiles turning to grins as we fall into each other's arms and on to the hard little bed. Still grinning, they close the heavy door, turn the key in the lock and clump away, leaving us time – the time we thought we would never have – to be together.

But we don't make love, not yet. It is enough to cling together in relief, in thankfulness, to weep a little and whisper, emotion catching in our throats . . .

'Bess, my Bess! I've missed you so . . .'

'Walter, my dear, my love. I thought never to see you again.'

At last, when he properly finds his voice, Walter asks: 'Have you heard it was Robin Cecil who pleaded for my life? Yet why, when he helped put me here in the first place?

I spread my hands helplessly. 'He wept in the courtroom when you were sentenced to death. And he told little Will that he loves you still. It seems he wants his rival out of the way but he does not want you dead. Perhaps he has a conscience, after all.'

His lips twist in a bitter grimace. 'Or perhaps he knows that being shut away from the world is a worse fate, to me, than death.'

'Don't say that.'

'But what use am I to you now?'

'Your head is still on your shoulders, that's all I care about.'

'Perhaps it would be better if it was not. When I knew I was to be reprieved from death, I asked the Governor how long I was to be imprisoned. He shrugged and said 'Indefinitely.' Indefinitely, Bess! What future have I to look forward to? What future can I offer you? It would be better for you and Wat if the sentence had been carried out and I was in my grave.'

My temper flares, surprising us both. I leap to my feet and stand over him:

'How dare you say that!' I spit. 'How dare you give up when I've fought so hard for your life! They'll release you soon – I'll make them! Your friends, your relatives will make them. You have a wife to live for – a son who needs you . . .'

'Hush, my sweet. Hush – that's enough.'

Unbelievably, he's laughing, pulling me down beside him and kissing me silent. 'I may survive imprisonment after all,' he murmurs, smoothing the hair back from my forehead, 'with you to visit and chastise me. I'm sorry, sweetheart – it's just – I'm so disillusioned, so tired . . .'

He looks tired. There are dark circles under his eyes and he's so very thin.

'At least my apartments will improve,' he grins, determined to be cheerful now. 'I'm told they are enlarging two rooms in the

Garden Tower to increase my comfort. Again on 'friend' Cecil's orders.'

Tenderly, I stroke his pale cheek and come to a decision.

'Ensure there's a double bed, along with a single one. Wat and I will move in with you if the Tower Governor allows it.'

For a moment his face lights up. Then he frowns and shakes his head. 'I can't let you do it. It would be unfair!'

'Would further separation be fair? We'll make it work. It need not be so bad here. Wat and I will not be prisoners, we can come and go as we please, and you, I'm sure, can find a worthwhile occupation. I'll send for some of your books, you'll have more time for reading and writing. You can even pen that history you've often dreamed of doing.'

He pulls a wry face. 'Not if you speak the truth and my imprisonment is short. The kind of history I'm planning will take me many years. But come, wife . . .' he smiles the wicked smile I love so well and pulls me closer, 'I can think of an occupation in which to engage this very minute.'

I giggle as he lies me back. Not so tired, then, after all . . .

~PART FIVE~

BESS

The Garden Tower, Winter, 1604

Some call this the Bloody Tower; claim the two young sons of Edward the Fourth were murdered here, smothered by pillows as they slept. It is even said their bones remain, bricked up within these walls.

I try not to think of it.

Yet it's hard not to feel depressed when I look out through the inner window, beyond the frosted Green, to the chapel of St Peter in Chains where so many ex-prisoners lie —among them Anne Boleyn, Catherine Howard, Jane Grey and, most recently of course, the Earl of Essex – their headless bodies bundled carelessly under the nave or chancel with no memorial.

But at least Walter's head remains where it belongs and I remind myself my task is to remain cheerful, to pin on a bright face, to put away the thought that these cramped quarters are a far cry from the elegant chambers of Sherborne or Durham House. Please God we shall not be here for long and this Tower, in fact, has a pleasant name, since it adjoins the Lieutenant's garden.

And the Lieutenant himself – Sir George Harvey – appears to be on our side. He seems eager to grant permission for anything we need (anything except his freedom, Walter says). He has even offered us the use of the little garden but Walter, at present, is in no mood to enjoy it, saying an enclosed space open to the sky makes him feel more of a captive than ever.

I do my best to make the two rooms we occupy more comfortable and homely. At least we have great stone fireplaces to keep out the damp that seeps up from the river and the moat. I get Wood to hang warm tapestries of classical scenes in glowing, vibrant colours to cover those (sinister) walls. I have Cal lay a thick rug on the floor of the chamber which has become Walter's study, rush mats on the one above, now our bedchamber. I have Walter's desk and other furniture brought up by wagon from Sherborne, together with his trunk of books and papers. He sits there, hour after hour, writing endless letters of appeal and complaint to Cecil the Snake, to our unsympathetic King. (To which neither of them reply.) High, deep alcoves in the walls become bedrooms for Dean, Cal, and John Talbot – Walter's new secretary to replace poor Edward Hancock who will also tutor Wat – but there is no room for Kate, who complains bitterly. I am obliged to find lodgings for her on Tower Hill, so that she can come daily to attend me. Luckily there is a chamber there for Wood, which he can share with Harry the Native, who refuses to abandon us, and an outbuilding and stables for our coach and remaining horses. Also a tiny room for Alice, who begs to stay near her father after almost losing him.

Little Wat is at first bewildered by all this. then angry. 'My father is important, the hero of Cadiz!' he cries, crimson with fury. 'Who dares to lock him up? I will go to the King – demand he is set free!'

Hush, hush!' I soothe.

Perhaps we were wrong to protect him from Walter's troubles – to order his tutor and the servants at Sherborne to allow no unpleasant whispers of the trial to reach his ears. He is ten now, after all. We explain, as best we can, that it is the King who has imprisoned his father, that it is all a mistake and he will soon be released.

But the first, bitterly cold winter passes and there looks to be little hope of it.

✳ ✳ ✳

Money is a constant problem. With the help of Laurence Keymis (who was released on New Year's Day), of brother Arthur and Tom Harriot, I've worked hard at keeping creditors at bay. I've sold many of my jewels and much of my prized plate. But it isn't enough. Still the vultures swoop.

Today I find myself having to bend the knee to Robin Cecil in order to keep Sherborne Lodge and our adjoining land. Having to swallow my pride and beard him in his splendid private rooms at Greenwich Palace.

'Watch your tongue, Bess,' Walter urges, rising from his desk and kissing me as I prepare to leave (from Tower Wharf and by common wherry, because I've sold our barge). 'No matter how hurt you feel, how betrayed, you must not show it . . . We need his help still, if I'm ever to be released. Weep all over him and prey on his better nature, on the guilt he must surely possess.'

So, with anger burning in my throat, I force myself to smile at the wretched dwarf as I curtsey to him (he's Viscount Cranbourne now), to squeeze a tear or two from my eyes instead of scratching out his.

He comes forward to welcome me with open arms – raises me up, kisses me on both cheeks (he's forced to stand on tiptoe) and tells me how 'very grieved' he is at all the torments I've endured.

'Am still enduring,' I remind him.

Holding my hand in his, he guides me to a chair. 'I'll help you all I can, my dear, for the sake of our long friendship . . .'

Hypocrite! He looks unwell. New lines of worry, of weariness, mar his forehead, his face is thinner, hollowed. Once I would have been concerned, but not anymore.

Dabbing at my eyes with the silk handkerchief he proffers (poor, brave, wronged little woman) I tell him what he must surely already know – that the Howard family have been granted Walter's wine patent, that they are seizing the arrears which by law belong to him; that the commissioners have descended on Sherborne, are selling our cattle and even trying to claim the furnishings of the house itself . . .

'Is it not enough that my husband has been stripped of his offices, his good name, but that everything he has accumulated for twenty years should also be swept away and lost?' I demand, tears of anger now falling in earnest. 'He deeded Sherborne to Wat before his arrest, no-one else has a right to any part of it.'

Frowning and looking sorrowful, he explains that, unfortunately, there is a slight stumbling block over the validity of the Sherborne deed.

'What?' I stare at him, bewildered. 'What do you mean?'

He spreads his hands apologetically. 'I fear the clerk Sir Walter employed to draw it up was negligent. The wretched man omitted a word that was essential to make the conveyance lawful.'

I am aghast. 'Omitted a word?'

'An important word.'

'But, surely, you're not saying that Sherborne can be taken away from us for the sake of one word?'

'He tuts dismissively. 'Do not distress yourself, I assure you I will do everything in my power to prevent this happening. I'll strive to have the deed approved, intervene with the Howards, call off the despoilers of the estate, even appoint trustees to protect you and Wat. Despite all that has happened, I am still your ally, Bess, believe me.'

I have no choice but to believe him – to hope, this time, that his own word is not as crooked as his back.

Through gritted teeth, I thank him profusely; manage (without vomiting) to sip the wine and nibble the cakes he presses upon me; even manage to congratulate him on his promotion.

And come away with a sense of unreality. Can this really be me, Bess Raleigh nee Throckmorton, grovelling to keep what is rightfully mine?

✳ ✳ ✳

Scadbury, March 1604

'I'm sure you've no cause for worry,' Audrey says.

We're strolling, arm-in-arm, beside the moat that surrounds the pretty manor inherited by Aud's husband, Sir Thomas Walsingham. The sun shines warmly on our backs and the air is scented with the perfume of early lilies-of-the-valley, growing in dense clusters along the bank.

Last night the Walsinghams entertained in style with a dinner and amusements fit for royalty, though no royal persons were present, thank the Lord – I might spit at King James if I met him. But many people of the court attended and seemed pleased to see me, asking after Walter with genuine concern.

I enjoyed the play we watched, danced with old friends and had a merry time. So I should be grateful for the invitation Walter insisted I accept – happy to be here on this lovely morning. Instead I'm irritable and out of sorts. Too much wine, perhaps, or, more likely, I'm feeling envious because this kind of life – Aud's kind of life and the life I once enjoyed – is not part of my world any more. To rub salt into my wounded discontent, Aud has been talking of the masque she performed with Queen Anne in January.

'At Hampton Court – The Vision of the Twelve Goddesses. We were all Goddesses, the Queen and eleven of us ladies. Queen Anne was Pallas Athena, I was Astraea,' she giggles, 'the virgin Goddess of innocence and purity, can you believe. Penelope Rich was Venus . . . You're looking bored. Perhaps you're not interested.'

I summoned a smile. 'Of course I'm interested. What did you wear?'

'I raided the royal wardrobe, you'll have heard I'm Keeper of the Queen's Wardrobe now. It's housed at the Tower, as you know, so I'll be able to drop in on you and Sir Walter often. The King's giving me a yearly pension, a very generous one. All the old Queen's gowns are still there. Near' five hundred of them. I found cloth of silver and cloth of gold and jewels galore. We looked wonderful. And the set! There was a marvellous mountain, a Cave of Sleep and a Temple of Peace. I think the temple was supposed to represent the peace negotiations with Spain that Cecil and the King are attempting to organise. You're really not interested, you're miles away. What's the matter?'

I can hardly confess I'm jealous of her position at Court, of her security and wealth. Instead, I tell her of my meeting with Cecil, of the doubt hanging over the Sherborne deed.

'I haven't told Walter yet. I'm afraid it will drive him into one of his depressions. Oh Aud, we can't lose Sherborne as well as Durham House.'

'I'm sure you've no cause for worry,' she says.

'No cause for worry?' I give a bitter laugh. 'With Cecil the Snake in charge of things? He probably deleted that "important word" himself.'

'Now that's unfair,' she returns, to my surprise. 'Robin's always working in your best interests. Why, he told me only the other night, in confidence, that he's determined you must keep Sherborne when you've lost so much. He said ...'

'The other night? In confidence?'

I withdraw my arm and halt abruptly, so that she's forced to stop. We face each other. Her blue eyes dance.

'All right, you've caught me. Yes, it was pillow talk.'

'You're having an affair? With Robin Cecil?'

'Is that so terrible? Half the Court are having affairs. We don't all have the happy union you have with Walter Raleigh. Some of us are disappointed in our marriages.'

I recall how mad she was to marry Thomas Walsingham, how she set her cap at him and chased him with single-minded determination.

'I thought you were happy with Sir Thomas. You always appear to be.'

She shrugs. 'Appearances can be deceptive. Oh, we get on well enough – in public and on the surface. But beyond the bedroom door, well, we're not intimate anymore.'

'So you're intimate with Cecil instead?' What would Lizzie think? She didn't much care for Audrey. 'I can't believe it!'

'I don't see why it's such a shock.' She looks cross. 'We were both lonely. And I've always liked him. You used to like him. You, of all people, know how charming he can be. I know he's a bit – well – small and delicate, but we get round that. He's still a man – a very passionate man.'

A successful, powerful man, who controls most of what goes on. And Audrey always did like to know what went on.

'You should drop your grudge against him,' she says sharply now. 'Your precious Walter would be dead if Robin hadn't saved him.'

'What?' I feel my colour rise, my cheeks begin to burn. 'It was your precious Robin who got him convicted!'

She shakes her head. 'So you've always believed. But you're wrong. He would never hurt you, he adores you both. Despite what Walter did.'

I want to slap her. 'Walter did nothing. He's as innocent as the day is long.'

She snorts. 'According to you.'

We glare at each other. 'I'll get Kate to pack my bags,' I say.

'Please do.'

I turn and stride away, leaving her there beside the moat.

She's lucky I don't push her in.

* * *

The Garden Tower, April, 1604

When, at last, I gather my courage and tell Walter about the discrepancy in the Sherborne deed, he shakes his head in disbelief and reassures me.

'It's just another of Cecil's games. He wants us to be grateful to him, to see him as our protector rather than the false friend we know him to be. I swear that deed is lawful. We'll hear no more on the matter, you'll see.'

Certainly we've heard no more as yet, so I dare to believe he's right. Especially as Dolberry, our Sherborne steward, writes to inform us that things have calmed down on the estate, been restored to order, and that John Shelbury (our lawyer) and Robert Smythe (a loyal friend) have been appointed temporary trustees, so Cecil's kept faith there, at least. True, 'temporary' is a little worrying, 'permanent' would be better. But Walter tells me to have patience, that it's a step in the right direction.

And as Easter approaches our spirits rise. It is the custom for the monarch to visit the Tower at this time – to grant amnesties and some releases. Queen Elizabeth did, year after year, so will James follow her example? Most importantly, will he consider releasing Walter? Sir George Harvey thinks it likely.

But on Shrove Tuesday our hopes are dashed. The kindly man comes to us with a long face. He regrets he has orders to remove Sir Walter Raleigh to the Fleet Prison for the duration of the royal visit.

With heavy hearts, we say our farewells. Since Wat and I can hardly be accommodated in the Fleet, we have no option but to join Kate, Alice and the others, to take ourselves off to the house on Tower Hill (thank God I had the foresight to rent a large property).

I tell Wat to leave some of his books and belongings for I expect to move back soon. But it is three long weeks before Walter is returned there, at such time the Lieutenant discovers the townsfolk who were allowed in to cheer the King and Queen have left behind the plague. Walter sends an urgent message bidding us stay where we are until the scare is over.

I write begging him to take precautions, to douse himself in vinegar and chew angelica – no need to remind him to smoke tobacco.

It is two more months before we can be reunited, and by that time things have changed.

* * *

As our coach lurches under the arch of the Byward Tower and along Water Lane my stomach lurches with it.

Kate reaches forward and grips my hand. Are you sick, my lady?'

I attempt a smile. 'Only with apprehension.'

Wood reins in the horses, jumps down to help me alight and looks round a little nervously, still doubtful about the wisdom of driving into the Tower courtyard.

'Should we not leave the coach and horses at the gates, my lady?' he'd asked..

'We should not,' I'd told him firmly.

Driving in with a flourish is my small gesture of defiance, of pride. See, we Raleighs have not lost everything, we are still people to be reckoned with. We have transport, fine clothes, servants (a few), jewels (some left), and our estate of Sherborne (just).

I hold a scented pomander to my nose while Kate sniffs at an orange. The Tower is clear of infection now, but it's best to take no chances. One woman prisoner died, but Walter, thank God, is reported to be healthy. Today, Kate, Wat and I are meant to be moving back in with him, but –

'He'll complain the timing is wrong,' I mutter, as I mount the winding stairs of the Garden Tower, leaving Kate to wait with Wood.

Which it is, of course. It could hardly be worse.

I'm relieved to find him alone at his desk – penning grievances to Cecil, no doubt – Dean, Cal and Talbot all engaged on some errand.

'Welcome back, sweetheart!' Beaming, he stands to embrace me, looks over my shoulder: 'No Wat?'

'I left him behind at our lodgings.' Taking a deep breath, I begin at once. 'Walter, it seems I am with child.'

His smile vanishes. I've pictured this scene so many times over the past weeks. Expected him to be amazed, upset, worried. As, indeed, am I. But the blaze of anger that flares in his eyes as he steps back from me – this I would never have imagined.

'Who,' he asks coldly, 'can be the lucky father?'

I gasp, appalled; gape at him in disbelief. Then I reach up and slap him – hard – across the face. My rings snag his lip, a bubble of blood arises.

In a flurry of skirts I whirl to storm out, but he catches my hand, pulls me back and gathers me to him.

'I'm sorry, I'm sorry. But . . . after all this time . . . All these years . . . no sign. And now, when I'm fifty-two – locked up here with nothing to offer, and you're free to go abroad, to dance, to flirt with younger men if you so wish . . .'

'You encouraged me to accept invitations,' I say bitterly. 'To further your cause. Yes, I dance but I do not flirt. I socialise, now and then, to make sure we are not forgotten, to remind our friends to speak well of us at Court . . .'

He groans. 'I know, I know! Forgive me, say you'll forgive me. It's just the shock, Bess. Something that we wanted once, so very much. It's cruel for it to happen now. The timing—'

'—is unfortunate, I know.' My voice softens. 'But we're not paupers and you won't be here forever. We still have Sherborne to retire to, the moment you're released. And perhaps this babe will help our cause rather than hinder it. The King, they say, is an indulgent father – adores his children almost as much as he does his pretty young men. Perhaps the thought of a babe born in the Tower will soften him towards us, who knows?'

He laughs. 'I doubt that, but I applaud your optimism.'

I kiss him, lean in to him, this most immaculate of prisoners. If he took my advice and doused himself in vinegar he does not smell of it now. He rises at dawn each morning to soak in the tub of scented water Cal acquires from Heaven-knows-where, for Dean to dress his hair, comb his moustache and beard, to dress him in clothes fine enough for Court. Still vain as a peacock, my Walter Raleigh, and I love him for it.

Suddenly, I want this late child – *our* late child – more than anything in the world. But I'm old for giving birth. Forty next Spring! Please God I can safely deliver. Do I still have my lucky eagle stone? I must have kept it somewhere . . .

'One thing I know,' Walter says firmly, 'this child won't be born in a prison cell, no matter how cosy you've made it. It must come into the world at Sherborne, as Wat did.'

'No. Sherborne is too far from you.'

'I insist.'

'Insist away. I will not go.'

He sighs. 'God preserve men from stubborn women. Then you'll remain in the house on Tower Hill. As long as you visit me often.'

I grin, pleased to have won. 'All day and every day. I promise.'

ROBERT CECIL

Hampton Court, August, 1605

'Add it to the pile awaiting replies,' I instruct my chief clerk impatiently, waving the paper away.

Throw it on the dunghill, I would like to say to him, for I am sick to the teeth of receiving complaints and pleas from Raleigh. So is King James.

'Does the knave not realise he is legally dead?' he splutters now. 'Convicted and still under sentence o' death; imprisoned, but not reprieved. Ne'r ha' I received so many letters from a dead mon.'

And never has Raleigh seemed more alive, more vigorous, according to my man at the Tower. Not only has he fathered another child, he's charmed Lieutenant Harvey into giving him a plot in the man's own garden to grow tobacco and other plants; into giving him a hut – an old disused hen house – to turn into a laboratory where he dabbles in such nonsense as making sea water fit to drink. He is permitted frequent visitors, some on the official list, some not, for the guards are encouraged to turn a blind eye, and he's even allowed to take a daily walk on the ramparts that lead out from his upper room, a fact that incenses James.

'People on land point up at him, folk on the river wave to him, while he looks down and bows like a player upon the stage.'

Indeed, he's become one of the sights of London; as popular as the beasts housed in the Lion Tower.

'It has to stop,' fumes James, but he won't openly condemn it because he is afraid of public opinion, if bewildered by it. He fails to understand the English championship of the underdog.

And now the King has another grievance, for that same underdog has won the gratitude of Queen Anne. When, recently, Her Majesty was sick of a fever none could cure, one of her ladies sent for a cordial of Raleigh's, brewed in his hen house. Which, of course, immediately made her well and gained him new fame as a chemist.

'We canna ha' this,' fumes James. 'Keep the mon down, Beagle. Keep the mon down. You must know of a way.'

'The only way that I can see, your Majesty, is to appoint a new Tower Governor. One less susceptible to the Raleigh charm.'

He waves an impatient hand. 'Then do it, Beagle, do it.'

Rising, he pulls on his riding gloves, anxious, as ever, to be off hunting.

'Your Majesty,' I say hurriedly, 'I have another matter to discuss. Concerning the Catholics . . .'

He sighs.

James ignores my warnings about our English Catholics; shrugs his shoulders when I say they simmer with resentment because the golden time of tolerance they foolishly expected under his reign has not come about. As his mother, Mary of Scotland, was of their faith, they hoped for better treatment. But, rightly, the penalties and fines imposed on them under Elizabeth are still in place. For many months I've failed to make him understand the danger these aggrieved people present; failed to convince him their loyalties lie with the Pope rather than with their King.

'Another time,' he mutters now, half-way out the door. 'Another time.'

I shrug. So be it. I'll inform him of my 'discovery' another time. And *then* he'll listen.

His eyes will widen and his face will pale. Oh yes, next time he'll listen ...

BESS

The Tower of London, November 1605

All over the city the bells ring out, the Cryers bellow: 'The King is spared, the King is spared, God be thanked, God be thanked'.

God? Or Robin Cecil? For it was he who discovered this wicked plot before it came to fruition.

The Powder Treason, they're calling it. And they suspect us, the Raleighs, of involvement because my relatives were knee deep in it – Robert Catesby and Francis Tresham again, the same two who were involved in the Essex rebellion. The fools, with other fools, aimed to lead a Catholic uprising by blowing up the House of Lords on the day of the Opening of Parliament, killing the King, the Queen, the Prince and the Government, then placing the Princess Elizabeth on the throne as a puppet Queen who'd be forced to marry a Catholic. Oh, these 'puppet' Queens! First Arabella Stuart, now nine-year-old Elizabeth!

Walter has been ordered to appear before the Council for interrogation – taken to Whitehall by boat and under guard. What assistance do they think he could offer the plotters from his prison cell? Shoot flaming arrows from a Tower window?

While I, to my indignation, am summoned to the Lieutenant's lodging. To be questioned, not by our friend, Sir George Harvey, but by his replacement stern Sir William Wade,

I've already had words with the unpleasant man, who, as soon as he arrived in August, insisted I cease driving into the courtyard in my coach.

I glared at him. 'You expect me to walk, with my attendants and a babe in arms, all the way from the Tower gates?'

He smiled nastily. 'I do. By order of His Majesty, King James, who thinks you too haughty and insolent.'

I intend to be haughty and insolent today. Refusing the chair he offers me, I draw myself up to my full height and demand in ringing tone:

'On whose authority do you dare to question me?'

Again the wide, nasty smile that reveals bad teeth. 'On the Lord Cecil's orders, madam.'

Who else? But surely even Cecil cannot believe me guilty? I'm no fanatical Papist.

'My father turned Protestant before I was even born. The involvement of my relatives does not place blame on me.'

'Nonetheless, you are under suspicion of involvement.' Wade looks down at the notes upon his table. 'You journeyed to Sherborne Lodge in the summer, did you not?'

I nod. 'What has that to do with it? I'm permitted. It's still my house – in trust for my son.'

'But are you permitted to make ready for an uprising?'

I stare, perplexed. 'I don't know what you mean.'

'You had the armour scoured, did you not? Every piece of it. Ready to be worn – by whom?'

God in Heaven! Following his train of thought, I almost swear aloud. 'By nobody! I expected it to be worn by *nobody*. I ordered the armour scoured, yes, because it was rusty. I ordered the entire house cleaned because it was covered in dust – the servants are slack when I'm here in London. Is good housekeeping a crime these days?'

He strokes his beard. 'The readying of armour on the eve of a rebellion, of a planned assassination, could be deemed a crime, yes.'

'Well it was not!' I won't have this, I decide, won't stand here meekly like a criminal for applying a little spit and polish. 'If this is all the 'evidence' you and Lord Cecil have, this examination is at an end.'

Gathering my cloak about me I sweep out, nose in air. I half expect the horrid man to summon me back, but hear only the twitter of the birds as I escape into the winter sunshine. I tell myself that I am not, after all, a prisoner under his command, I reside here with my husband out of choice. All the same I found him intimidating, and realise I am shaking when I get back to the Garden Tower and reach out to take my new little son from Kate's arms.

Carew, named for Walter's brother and baptised in that sinister chapel across the green. He wasn't meant to be born here, of course, against Walter's wishes. For weeks, when my time drew nigh, I'd obediently up and left for my rented house at the hint of any discomfort. But Carew had a will of his own.

Laurence Keymis, Tom Harriot, Cousin Gorges – all were present in the Garden Tower, laughing at some jest of Walter's, when my pains began. They came on without warning, taking me by surprise – strong and crippling from the first, so that I dropped the shirt I was stitching and cried out, startling them all.

'The babe,' I panted, when at last I could draw breath.

'God's blood!' shouted Walter, panic stricken. 'It cannot happen here! Kate, Alice – help her to her coach. Quickly!'

'Too late!' I croaked.

My waters broke, to the embarrassment of all. The flustered men departed hurriedly, in a chorus of good wishes, except Walter, of course, and Cal, who insisted on remaining. Wat, thankfully, was off somewhere with his tutor, while Dean fled with the others.. No time to fetch the midwife, or even the Lieutenant's lady. An anxious Kate attended me, helped by a white-faced Alice and Cal, who was as calm and soothing as any doctor, while Walter stood around barking instructions that everyone ignored.

'We must get her to bed,' cried Kate.

'No!' Cal shook his head. 'Not bed. She must squat. Walk, then squat. My countrywomen squat. Babe come quick. Easy.'

'It's true,' Walter said.

'She can't!' Kate was scandalised. 'She can't squat!'

'I can,' I gasped, as Cal seized my arm and began to walk me round the cell. 'I will.'

And soon, dizzy with pain, with walking, I was glad to squat.

I cannot say it was easy but it was certainly quick. I could scarce believe it was over, that Kate was placing the squalling infant in my arms.

'Look at his blue eyes, his dark hair,' cooed Alice, helping me into Walter's bed. 'I thought all new-borns were ugly, but he's beautiful.'

As beautiful as Wat (as Damerei) was at birth.

'A Raleigh through and through,' I summoned the energy to murmur, with a triumphant smile at Walter who had the grace to look shamefaced. But although he kissed the tiny head and I saw tears in his eyes, he has not bonded with Carew as he did with Wat. He's tender with him always, but seems unable to take joy in him.

'Poor little mite,' he says often. 'What future can he expect, with a shamed prisoner for a father?'

* * *

The shamed prisoner was returned to the Tower the day after my brush with Wade. He says he was examined on account of his friendship with Henry Percy, Earl of Northumberland, whose cousin was a conspirator.

'Henry's innocent, of course, but he'll have a hard time proving it.'

'Because he's a Catholic?'

'A very rich Catholic, whose lands they can seize.'

I've not been questioned again and have only glimpsed Wade at a distance, crossing the courtyard. On his way, no doubt, to oversee the torture of Guido Fawkes, an explosive expert, according to one of the Guards, who was recruited by Catesby, caught storing gunpowder, and was the first rebel to be brought to this grim fortress.

There are others here now, awaiting execution, including Francis Tresham, while Robert Catesby, the ringleader it's emerged, and Thomas Percy, have been shot dead at a house in the Midlands where they fled and took refuge.

'I don't believe either Cecil or the King thought us guilty of anything,' I complain to Walter. 'They simply wanted to frighten us.'

I do not add that they've succeeded where I'm concerned. By dragging Walter again before the Council they've confirmed that he's still under shadow of the axe, kept alive by nothing but the King's pleasure.

My sleep is again troubled by nightmares. The scaffold, the block, my husband's blood on my face ... I awake, in the rented house, sweating, choking back sobs, trying not to disturb Alice or Kate.

✳ ✳ ✳

The Tower of London, December, 1605

I saw Muriel Tresham today, when I was hurrying along Water Lane from the Garden Tower. Alone for once, I was looking for Carew's wooden rattle which he'd dropped on an earlier walk. I'm ashamed to confess I hesitated. It's not a good time to acknowledge my relations. But how could I ignore the poor woman? She was leaning up against the wall, her head bowed, weeping.

I went to her and put my arms around her. 'He's worse?'

I'd heard her son Francis was ill, being attended in his cell by no fewer than three doctors and a nurse – not for any humane reason but in order to make him well enough to be hung, drawn and quartered like his fellow rebels.

'He's dead, passed away in his sleep,' she sobbed. 'But they won't let me or his wife have his body for burial. They've hacked off his head to spear on a spike and display it beside Catesby's for all to see. The rest of him is to be thrown into a hole on Tower Hill.'

I hugged her closer, bereft of words.

'His role was minor,' she said. She looks haggard, years older. 'Catesby drew him into it at the last minute. And Cecil knew. He could have stopped them before my Francis joined. He found out what they were planning long ago but led them on. He even made it easy for them to buy gunpowder.'

Again, I made no answer. Easy to believe anything of Cecil but better to hold my tongue. Even the stout Tower walls might have ears or, more realistically, a Cecil agent skulking in an alcove.

'How is Cousin Anne, Robert's mother?' I asked.

She smiled a bitter smile. 'How do you expect? Distraught, like me. How would <u>you</u> feel if you were unable to bury your son in a proper grave? Give him a proper funeral?'

I thought of my little Damerei, bundled into a plague pit before I was told of his death. And wept with her.

✻ ✻ ✻

The Powder plot has had several repercussions – some good, some bad. It has brought Henry of Northumberland, unable to prove his innocence, into the Martin Tower. Bad for him, of course, but good for Walter, who communicates with him through Tom Harriot, who visits them both.

But it's given wretched Wade an excuse to tighten security. Not content with banning me from driving into the courtyard, he has now decreed, in writing, that 'Wives of prisoners are no longer allowed to lodge in the Tower alongside their husbands.' And 'All prisoners are commanded to be back in their cells at five of the clock each evening, when doors will be locked until the following morning.'

So it's off to the rented house each night for me. There won't be another Raleigh infant conceived in the Garden Tower.

But at least it's not all bad news. We receive some good, and Wade is obliged to be the bearer of it. He comes to us reluctantly, sour of face, and informs us (the words must be sticking in his teeth) that Sherborne Castle, Sherborne Lodge and all its manors and lands, are to be granted by Letters Patent to one of my cousins, Alexander Brett, and George Hall, a relation of Walter's, in trust for myself and Wat..

'Security at last!' I sob to Walter, hugging him. 'Oh, the relief of it!'

'It must be Cecil's doing,' Walter says, when Wade has gone. He pulls a face. 'I'll have to write a humble letter of thanks to him, I suppose. Yet another.'

I'm filled with optimism. 'Perhaps they – Cecil and the King – have decided you've been punished enough. Perhaps they're considering a pardon.'

He shakes his head. 'Too much to hope.'

'You never know. Write and thank Cecil for saving us from utter ruin, and say that if you could only be released you'd be happy to be confined at Sherborne. Or go abroad. Or – oh – go anywhere rather than this gloomy place.'

He laughs at my eagerness. 'It could be worth a try. I'll write something of the sort. But I doubt they'll consider it.'

They haven't.

✳ ✳ ✳

Under the new rules Walter's visitors are supposed to be further restricted, but the guards, eager as ever to accept bribes, still look the other way.

One visitor who often slips in under Wade's nose is little Will Cecil (unknown to his father, I'll wager). Not so little now, he's fourteen summers, and studying at Cambridge University, 'though he admits he spends few hours there.

So when I arrive, rather breathlessly, from the Tower Hill house on a sunny but cold afternoon, I'm not surprised to find Will poring over diagrams of ships with Walter. Then I see he's brought someone with him and, stifling my gasp of amazement, I dip into a curtsey.

'Please, Lady Raleigh,' Prince Henry says, reaching out a hand to raise me up. 'No ceremony. We're all friends here.'

Are we? His father would disagree. And surely no boy was ever less like his father. Younger than Will, eleven, like Wat, he's tall for his age, fair and graceful, charming in speech and manner. I've heard King James is jealous of his popularity – the crowds cheer him wherever he goes – and I'm not surprised. Our shambling, bow-legged king in his bulky padded doublet stirs little admiration. Who would *you* cheer?

'Sir Walter has been explaining his efforts to turn salt into fresh water,' the Prince tells me eagerly. 'And – look – he's drawn a sketch of a ship I'm going to build for my navy when I become king. He's promised to make me a model of it.'

He's gazing at Walter with the same shining admiration I'm accustomed to seeing on the faces of Wat and young Will.

'May I come again?' he asks politely, as if he's visiting us in a palace and we're the royal ones.

'Only my father would keep such a bird in a cage,' we hear him murmur to Will as they clatter down the steps on their way out. 'I'll release him as soon as I'm king.'

I raise my eyebrows at Walter. We have to wait *that* long?

✷ ✷ ✷

The Tower of London, March 1606

Dean waylays me on my way out of the Garden Tower at five of the clock.

'I'm worried about Sir Walter, Lady Bess. He's out in that garden of his, rain or shine, some days it's bitter. And he sleeps badly, without you here, so he stays up half the night writing. He expends so much energy, one way or another. I fear he never stops!'

'But he never has done,' I say, shifting Carew from one shoulder to the other, anxious to leave before the gates are shut.

Dean has always been something of a fuss-pot and Walter looks fine to me. 'Activity can only be good for him.'

'The Master's energy comes from the Devil,' a Sherborne maid once said of Walter, and I dismissed her on the spot, fearful of the atheist slur so many attached to him then. These days I feel it's Heaven sent, for that same restless energy, that vigour and relentless drive, preserves his sanity, staves off his depression, caged as he is within these prison walls.

I encourage him to keep endlessly busy on all manner of projects and experiments. He's planted shrubs from the New World in his part of the garden. He cures his own tobacco. He grows herbs, makes medicines and pills in his laboratory. His Great Cordial is famous at Court, thanks to the praises of Queen Anne.

'And his Balsam of Guiana has been requested by the wife of the French Ambassador,' Prince Henry tells me proudly on his latest visit.

True to his word, he's come again. And keeps coming, with a frequency that pleases Walter and stirs a little worm of jealousy in Wat. He hangs on Walter's every word, especially where ships and sea-faring are concerned. The little hen-house turned laboratory also appeals to him and I often smile to see Walter, Cal, Wat, Tom Harriot, Laurence Keymis, Harry and the Prince all crowded around the furnace in the cramped space, testing metals.

And smile wider when the ringing of Wade's silly curfew bell causes Walter to bang down his tools and almost choke in the effort to swallow a curse. It's well known that Henry detests foul language – perhaps because his father is so coarse-mouthed. But maybe he carries his dislike a little too far – he's even said to keep a swear box for the unwary. Thank God he leaves it at home or we'd be the poorer for it.

But today, when I approach the 'laboratory' (warily, because the chemicals often smell vile), instead of the usual crowd two different visitors are leaving, striding down the path towards me. I recognise Walter's nephew, John Gilbert, and George Percy, the Earl of Northumberland's brother.

They greet me with affection but both are sober of face and quite obviously anxious to be on their way, so I don't detain them.

I'm alarmed to find Walter sitting on the little wooden bench beside his furnace, his head in his hands.

'What is it? What's happened? Did John bring bad news?'

He raises a flushed and furious face. 'He did. By God he did! The King, as you know, cancelled my patent to colonise Virginia. Now he's about to issue it as a fresh charter to the London and Plymouth Companies. They're planning an expedition to plant a new colony where mine failed. John Gilbert and George Percy are hoping to sail with it. They tried to persuade King James to allow me to lead it but ...'

'He refused,' I say bitterly.

'Of course he refused. Bess, they'll be using the maps I had drawn up, the charts I laboured over, all the information Tom Harriot brought back to me – me! George Percy even asked me to aid them – to offer my advice and experience. Only secretly, Bess. I have to be their secret advisor.'

'Did you agree?' I'm worried about the colour of his cheeks, they're almost purple

'Agree?' he laughs. 'I near' threw them out. I said...I said ...I...'

The words he utters next are unintelligible – strange sounds issue from his throat, his tongue lolls to one side and his eyes widen in bewilderment, in fright.

I'm terrified. I whirl to a table where sits a jug of ale, but before I can find a mug I hear him slump to the floor.

'Walter!' I kneel beside him, scream for help.

Cal and Dean arrive from somewhere, with Wade close on their heels (the one time I welcome him). Between them they carry Walter back through the garden gate and up to his bed where he lies unconscious, pale now and breathing oddly.

Wade sends for our doctor – the brisk, efficient Peter Turner. It seems like hours before he arrives, clutching his bag of ointments and instruments. He examines Walter quickly, says he has suffered a seizure and has to be bled.

'My husband doesn't believe in the practice of bleeding,' I say. 'He thinks it weakens the body.'

Turner shrugs. 'I'm sorry, Lady Raleigh, but we either bleed him or leave him to die. Which would you prefer?'

He takes my preference for granted and bids me leave the room as Walter is bled. Cal refuses to leave, but Dean comes with me, down the stone stairs to the study I've made such an effort to look cosy. I blink back tears. Will Walter ever sit at his desk again?

Dean, I believe, is thinking the same. I fancy he looks at me accusingly.

'It wasn't because he was overdoing things.' I say. 'It was the shock. He received bad news.'

'Hmm,' returns Dean.

I know he's unconvinced but I will not, for pride's sake, let him know how guilty I feel. Perhaps it wasn't just shock. Perhaps

Walter has indeed been ailing and, being preoccupied with the baby, I failed to notice. I should have been more observant, more caring. I should have . . .

A great commotion as Wat dashes in, followed by John Talbot, his tutor. Wat flings his arms about me. His eyes are filled with tears he's trying not to shed.

'Is father going to die? Kate said he might.'

Curse Kate! She's usually more tactful.

'Of course he won't die!'

Behind Wat's back I cross my fingers, pray silently;

'*Please* God!'

* * *

His symptoms are, at first, dismaying.

He manages to convey that his left side is cold and numb, but his tongue has been affected and he talks thickly, strangely. We have difficulty in understanding him. The fingers of his left hand are also enfeebled.

'Thank the Lord it's not his right,' says Tom Harriot. 'He'll still be able to hold a pen.'

'He's much too weak to write,' Dean contradicts, protective as ever.

* * *

Slowly, little by little, each day Walter improves. His left hand still gives him trouble but the feeling in his side returns and, thank Heaven, his speech is back to normal.

As soon as he's well enough to sit at his desk, he writes to Cecil the Snake (made Earl of Salisbury now). He doesn't show me the letter, so I suspect it's about the proposed voyage to the New World. He's hoping, through Cecil, to change the King's mind and sail with it after all. And he knows I'd protest just now. He hasn't the strength to travel down his garden, so how he thinks he could command a ship ...

I also write (without showing him the letter) from my house at Tower Hill, describing how ill he's been. Surely Cecil will be moved. Surely he can't be all monster. Surely the King, the Privy Council, all of them, must see that Walter is no threat to them – that it's time for his release. Not to the New World, though, but to the tranquillity of our beautiful Sherborne.

ROBERT CECIL

Theobalds, Hertfordshire, Spring, 1606

'Even the King must take pity on him now,' my mistress says. 'He must be too frail to present a problem.'

Raleigh will always present a problem. Even severe illness has not stopped his flow of pleading letters. He's lost the use of his left hand, I'm told. Would that he'd lost the use of both. He won't believe it, of course, but I'm doing him a favour by turning down his latest request. He'd be lucky to survive a voyage to Virginia. Although maybe I should reflect on that – if he died at sea the 'problem' would be solved.

But I can't do that to Bess. As for her own plea – let him retire to Sherborne? He'd be back at Court in no time, through some pretence or other, meddling, gaining support from all manner of quarters.

No, it can never happen.

'I'll speak to King James,' I say to my mistress, 'do my best to gain him a pardon.'

She beams at me. 'I knew you'd listen.'

I know the King *won't* listen. He, in his turn, is sick to death of petitions from the Queen on Raleigh's behalf. Ever since he supplied her with that damn potion she's been staunchly on his side, urged on by Prince Henry who, like my Will, has fallen under his spell. Perhaps the old rumours are true and he does possess dark powers. Perhaps the potions he brews in that hen-house of his are not all for the improvement of health. Perhaps some are to draw people to him, much as love potions draw couples together.

I smile to imagine what Audrey would make of my thoughts – love potions indeed – as we walk through the Old Privy Garden; at least three feet apart, in case one of my other guests should chance to look out of a window. I suspect there is gossip about us and there's no sense in feeding the fire. But I can never resist showing off the gardens of Theobalds, the estate my father built and left to me – with their fountains and terraces and avenues. I love them even more than the vast park, the great house itself. More palace than house, the King never fails to remind me.

He wants it, of course. Wanted it from the first moment he saw it. His face lit up when he rode up the tree-lined avenue, took in the vast spread of it, noted how the sun shone on the golden bricks, how the stonework glowed. His eyes narrowed with greed when he entered the great hall, looked up at the tall oak tree growing there, the mechanical singing birds among its silken leaves, at the huge planetary clock of gold, silver and jewels (my father's pride and joy), and jested it was too grand for kings.

Only it wasn't a jest. Too grand for the likes of me, he meant. Since that first visit he comes often whether I'm here or not, the enormous park being his favourite hunting ground, even above that of Royston and Newmarket. And drops hints galore about me gifting it to him, to which I pretend to be deaf or stupid.

But I can't hold out forever. No doubt he'll get it in the end. And I dread to think what orgies he might hold here.

Audrey stops to admire a deep red rose, to glory in its perfume. 'It's wonderful to be in the clean fresh air,' she says, 'after last night.'

I shudder. *Last night.* My father must be spinning in his grave.

It was meant to be a grand evening of entertainment. King Christian of Denmark is in England, visiting his sister, Queen Anne, and I considered it my (somewhat reluctant) duty to invite both Kings, their retinues and half the Court, here to Theobalds.

I've spent a fortune on the event – over one thousand pounds. And what have I to show for it? A memory that will haunt me forever.

The lavish banquet I provided was meant to be followed by a graceful masque, 'The Queen of Sheba's visit to King Solomon', with the finest of musicians and the loveliest Court dancers (thankfully, Audrey was not, this time, among them). But both Kings are heavy drinkers and the other guests followed their lead. They all enjoyed my wine so much that the masque was a disaster. A disgusting, repulsive disaster. Dear God, just thinking of it makes my blood run cold! The Queen of Sheba tripped, while carrying a tray; threw cream, wine, jellies and spices over King Christian who, more drunk than she, did not appear to care. Laughing and belching, he led her out to dance and, needless to say, they ended up spread-eagled on the floor. Faith, Hope and Charity retired, quite green of face. Victory slumped down and fell asleep. And Peace? A normally gentle woman, Peace became violent and had to be restrained. And, all the while, King James drank, spat, fiddled with his codpiece and embraced his favourite young man.

One thousand pounds! For this!

Today, a hush prevails, for all are still abed, nursing their aching heads.

Except, that is, for one small page in the Danish livery who enters the garden and bows before me, presenting a note from his royal master.

I'm surprised the Danish King is able to string two words together after his escapades, but he writes a steady hand without one single blot. He requests my help in securing the release of Sir Walter Raleigh from the Tower of London. He wishes to take him back with him to Denmark to head his royal navy. A suggestion put to him, he stresses, by his sister, ' the good Queen Anne'.

He must be more drunk than even I imagined.

'What is it?' asks Audrey curiously.

'Nothing of importance,' I smile, ripping it up.

BESS

The Tower of London, December 1606

Walter has a change of heart and offers advice and assistance to those sailing on the voyage to Virginia. John Gilbert, George Percy and the man leading the expedition – a Captain Newport who has only one arm but is very capable and efficient, according to the others – come quietly and often to the Garden Tower to pick his brains and those of Tom Harriot.

It gladdens *my* heart to see Walter looking so well and happy again – so full of enthusiasm as he pores over maps and charts and diagrams, argues good-naturedly with George Percy and laughs at some jest of John Gilbert's.

But his contentment (and mine) is short-lived. One bitterly cold morning, wrapped in my fur-lined cloak, I arrive to find him pacing up and down like a caged animal, his limp pronounced and his face as white as paper.

'They sail today,' he tells me bitterly. 'I may as well give up, Bess. I'll never see the ocean again, let alone sail on it. It's time we both accept that I'm here for life.'

'I'll never accept it!' I rush to him and hold him close. 'Forget the sea, we'll all be back at Sherborne soon, I promise you.'

✳ ✳ ✳

I remain optimistic for a while, thinking of my letter – of the sway Cecil is said to hold over the King. But when the months pass and I get no reply, I realise what a fool I was to even consider the Snake has a streak of kindness left in his twisted body – that I've merely wasted ink as well as hope.

ROBERT CECIL

Cecil House, February, 1607

Will is a disappointment to me. (I'm sorry, Lizzie, I know this would upset you but it has to be admitted.) Instead of studying at Cambridge he throws away his opportunities by following the King – joining the hunt at Royston or Newmarket. Not for any hope of advancement, for I'm told the King scarcely notices him, but purely for the joy of it, which, to my mind, is even worse. He cannot speak six words of Latin and has no talent, as far as I can see, for any other subject.

Wat Raleigh has started at Oxford and is said to be wild and unruly – yet extremely clever. He always was brighter than Will, which has never failed to irk me.

There is no hope, whatsoever, of Will following in my footsteps as I followed in my father's. No point in training him for a position he would never be able to hold.

Sighing, I summon Will to Cecil House for another of my lectures.

'I'm sorry, my Lord Father,' he says, head hanging, shoulders slumped.

His posture annoys me further as my son is blessed with even shoulders and an uncrooked back.

'Stand up straight,' I say sharply. 'There seems to be little point in you continuing at university, therefore I propose to send you on a tour abroad, in the hope that you might, just might, pick up at least one foreign language.'

His eyes shine at the prospect of getting far away from me and my moans of expectation.

I do not inform him of my plans for his coming marriage. If he cannot gain an important post at Court at least he can have a safe one, which depends largely on the possession of influential friends and relatives. I intend him to be wed shortly, therefore, to the Earl of Suffolk's daughter Catherine – a splendid match that will ensure him a secure and rich future. Time enough for him to be advised of it.

Meanwhile, a trip to foreign parts (under close observation, of course) might keep him out of mischief. And also keep him from visiting the 'glamorous' Sir Walter Raleigh.

✳ ✳ ✳

Whitehall Palace, March, 1607

King James has a new favourite. Robert Carr, a handsome youth of one and twenty – hated by Queen Anne, Prince Henry and most members of the Court. He goes everywhere with James, who holds his hand in public and rewards him with gifts of clothes, jewels and slobbering kisses.

He fell off his horse at a joust, they say (I wasn't present), right in front of the King's box. Some hold that he did it deliberately, counting a broken leg a small price to pay for royal attention. I suspect this to be the case for I detect a slyness in him.

He, too, has a passion for hunting in Theobalds Park, and it's no surprise to me when the King comes out into the open at last – offers me Hatfield House in an exchange. An unfair exchange.

Hatfield House for *Theobalds*! Inferior in every way!

But I shall have to agree. It would, of course, be folly to refuse.

BESS

The Tower of London, 1607

Thank Heaven for Prince Henry. He has his own household now, at the Palace of St. James, and comes to the Garden Tower whenever time permits, which it seems to do a great deal. Cousin Gorges has a position in the Prince's service and sometimes they visit together. But, more often, Henry comes alone – something he's not allowed to do, I'm sure, being heir to the throne. But Henry despises his father's padded doublets and fears of assassination and seems to glory in being different to James in every possible way. (Not that he has to try very hard. No-one would believe they were even distantly related.)

Walter has always thrived on young company, and with Wat at Oxford and Will Cecil in France, Henry's bright enthusiasm for all his pursuits staves off the familiar clouds of dark depression I feared were approaching.

Now that Wade's ridiculous curfew keeps Walter locked in his rooms each evening, he's turned again to his love of reading, studying and writing. Much of his writing is for the instruction and entertainment of Prince Henry, whose lively interest spurs him on. The Art of War by Sea is a particular favourite, but the work that fills him with awe and which he asks to be dedicated to him is a book Walter has been planning in his mind for years; a history. But not just a history of our own times, or of the days of Queen Elizabeth, or even of England. No, typical of my ambitious husband who never makes things easy for himself, he's setting out to write a history of the entire world.

'A story of all ages past,' he says, to a wide-eyed Prince Henry and an open-mouthed Cal. 'Starting at the beginning of the world and continuing up to our own time, or almost our own time. Dangers might lurk in being too topical, in offending people. I shall need more books, of course, for reference, but friends will supply those – Ben Jonson, Francis Bacon – oh, many others.'

His eyes are alight now with enthusiasm. He looks eager as a schoolboy given a holiday.

I've been trying to persuade him to write this history of his for years. Thank Heaven, indeed, for Prince Henry.

ROBERT CECIL

Whitehall Palace, January, 1608

Within months, Carr has been knighted, appointed Gentleman of the Bedchamber and showered with more gifts of land, money, jewels and fine clothes than any young man has a right to expect.

His influence over the King is frightening. Particularly as he dislikes me intensely and stirs up bad feeling about me behind my back.

It's no coincidence, I think, that James has become a little cool towards me. He resents me trying to control the extravagances he and Queen Anne indulge in, of course. But that's been the case since he came to the throne. No, it's something more. Poison of some sort being dripped into his ear by Carr, I'm sure of it.

So when he summons me to his privy chamber one morning, I'm apprehensive. It must be urgent. James doesn't usually rise early unless he's going hunting, and never welcomes business talk before noon.

Indeed, he's still in his blue velvet night robe when I'm announced, and Carr, sitting close – almost on the royal lap – wears an identical one. Carr, of course, looks better in his, blonde and handsome and boyish. While his robe, unlike the King's, is not splattered with food stains.

I make my awkward bow, thinking whatever it is it can't be bad news for they both smile in amiable fashion.

'Ah, ma little Beagle,' says the King. 'We'd welcome your assistance. Sir Robert here is in need of a country estate; a good house with plenty of land. Somewhere a mite special, you know the sort of thing. Put that sharp little brain of yours to good use. What can we give him?'

I hardly stop to consider. It is, after all, in my best interest to oblige.

'The estate of Sherborne, in Dorset, would be suitable, Your Majesty,' I reply, smiling in return. 'Originally owned by Sir Walter Raleigh, he deeded it to his son before he was attainted. But an error has since been found in the conveyance. Which means, in fact, that the said estate is still in Sir Walter's name. And as, by law, all goods and properties owned by a man convicted of treason revert to the Crown, Sherborne now belongs to you.'

BESS

Hampton Court, October, 1608

'Hush, *hush!*' I implore Carew, who sobs louder.

Two stable hands, dressed in the royal livery, turn to stare. What is this woman doing, hovering in the stable yard, holding a tiny boy by the hand? They'd attempt to move me on if I was poorly clad, no doubt. But I'm wearing a silk gown and a fur-trimmed cloak. I may be about to beg, but I'm no beggar woman. At least, not yet.

The King seems a long time coming. Have I got the wrong place? The wrong time?

'Is His Majesty not riding today?' I ask at last, shouting over the clatter of horses hooves.

Both lads stare harder. 'No, he ain't,' shouts one.

'Playing bowls,' shouts the other.

I rush to the gate that leads to the gardens, Carew in my arms since he can't keep up. Setting him down in a leafy archway, I pause to think.

It's years since I came to this palace, I can't remember where the bowling green is...

* * *

Luck smiles on me. James himself comes shambling down the path on his awkward bow legs, his gentlemen in attendance. As he nears us, I step out from the archway, fall on my knees in front of him. He's forced to a halt, looks down at me in amazement, kneeling in the mud in my fine clothes; at Carew, who is tear-stained and tragic.

'Your Majesty,' I say loudly. 'I'm a proud woman but I beg you, I *beg* you, please don't take Sherborne away from us. We've lost everything else, and we don't expect it back, but Sherborne is the legacy for our children, the hope for their future. You're a merciful King, I can't believe you'd expose this little boy, this little boy's brother, to ruin and beggary for the sake of an error in a document ...

James looks at me with anguished eyes. 'I must ha' the land,' he mutters. 'I must ha' it for Carr.'

Red with embarrassment, he brushes past me, almost knocking me off balance.

'I must ha' it for Carr,' he says again, shambling away as fast as his legs can totter.

'Almighty God will punish you!' I shout after him, losing my temper.

The Tower of London, October, 1608.

Walter accuses me of making things worse.

'As if they could *be* any worse,' I say bitterly.

'They'll be a lot worse if you get locked up for cursing the king,' he shouts, thumping his desk.

I thump it too and shout back. We have the worst quarrel of our married life. I accuse him of stupidity, of carelessness in failing to notice that missing word, of selfishness, self-pity, and, oh, many other things I do not mean. Then I remember that he loves Sherborne even more than I do and I burst into tears.

He takes me in his arms and we kiss and make up as we usually do after a falling out. I wish we could go a step further and rush off to bed but we can't. Dean and Cal will be back soon and, anyway, Tom Harriot arrives.

And that wretched curfew bell will soon be ringing.

✳ ✳ ✳

Walter has written to Robert Carr, appealing to him as 'a worthy gentleman' to forget Sherborne and set his sights on another property. His tone is polite, but somehow the distaste shines through.

He receives no reply.

✳ ✳ ✳

Perhaps James was out of earshot and failed to hear my 'curse'. Or misheard it. Or was frightened by it. Whatever, to our surprise he grants me compensation for the loss of Sherborne. Our lawyer, John Shelbury, bustles into the Garden Tower with papers for me to sign.

'I've read through them six times. No flaws or errors, I assure you,' he says with a grin.

The King has granted me a lump sum of eight thousand pounds, together with an annual pension of four hundred pounds.

'Conscience money,' Walter says. 'No amount of it can make up for the loss of Sherborne.'

Of course it can't. But dear God, it's very welcome.

✸ ✸ ✸

Welcome it may be, but we soon find out there are disadvantages to the granting of my compensation. It encourages greedy people to sue for debts, real or imagined. Walter's half-brother, Adrian Gilbert, is first among them (I never liked the man). He has shocked us by suing for a huge amount – the almighty sum of four thousand, six hundred and fifty-three pounds! This sum he has calculated by going back thirty years, even including ten pounds he once lent Walter when they were much younger, and another seven hundred pounds he claims to have spent on the Sherborne improvements (for which I am certain we paid him). With loyal John Shelbury to represent me, I am contesting the case in the Court of Chancery. Walter thinks Adrian's claim will be thrown out as too old and unreliable. But it's one more worry with which we have to contend.

✸ ✸ ✸

The Tower of London, 1610

Walter has been imprisoned for seven years. *Seven years*! Longer than Carew has been alive. And still no sign, no hope, of release. If we'd known, that day I promised to move in with him, how long it would be, what would we have done? What *could* we have done? No point then, and no point now, in sinking into despair.

Somehow we keep our spirits – if not exactly high, at least on an even keel. Walter persuades me to invest in another voyage of exploration to Guiana – six hundred pounds we can ill afford. Sir Thomas Roe, a friend from the old Queen's day, is sailing in the hope of finding El Dorado. I expected Walter to be envious but instead he seems excited.

'If Thomas finds it, Bess, and brings back gold, it can only be to my credit.'

Can it? We'll see. But it's so good to see his enthusiasm I haven't the heart to disagree.

Harry the Native is to sail with Roe. To interpret and, sadly, to remain.

'I miss the warmth of my homeland now, Lady Bess,' he confides, kissing my hand for the last time.

I find I'm the one with tears in my eyes. I shall miss him, the dear loyal man.

'I am getting old.' he says.

Aren't we all?

※ ※ ※

Walter is certainly not getting any younger and I fear for his health. These years of captivity are taking their toll. His face is thinner, there's silver in his hair and beard, and the limp from his old injury is more pronounced.

It's cold in these rooms in winter, no matter how big Dean builds the fires. And damp; I've been forced to take down the ruined hangings from the walls. In hot summers the coolness is welcome, but then there is the more serious worry of the plague which can spread like wildfire. Visitors bring it in (not ours, of course, but those of other prisoners) and the public who visit the lions. So far we've all been lucky, but every summer I pray for our escape from sickness. Especially I pray for Walter, who can never leave no matter how great the threat.

At least I'm thankful he can work outside in the daytime, in the fresh air. (Or is the plague carried on the air?). He grows medicinal plants, still, in the garden. (The little garden, no bigger than a Sherborne flowerbed. Best not to think of Sherborne. I try never to think of Sherborne.)

His evenings, when I'm dismissed by the bell like a school child and he's locked into his quarters, are always spent writing. He's written many essays and tracts while his History of the World is growing fast and is going to be a great success, according to Prince Henry, who has also persuaded Walter into writing essays on, of all things, the subject of his marriage and that of his sister, the Princess Elizabeth. King James, (forgetful of the Powder Plot?) wants them both to wed Catholics – Spanish Catholics, to Henry's great dismay. He's staunchly Protestant and as anti-Spanish as Walter – they both agree we should never have made peace with Spain. Fifteen now, and newly invested as Prince of Wales, he has very strong opinions on most things.

'Sir Walter's arguments against both matches are sound and scholarly,' he confides to me 'And he can express them better with his pen than I can vocally. Once the papers are complete I'll take them to the King. And if he won't back down I'll refuse my bride at the very altar.'

'You can't interfere!' I say, aghast, to Walter as soon as he's gone. 'The Prince should never have asked you. It's a personal decision between the King and Queen, surely?'

'It's a matter of State,' Walter corrects, sharpening his quill. 'Of foreign policy. Parliament will certainly debate it.'

'But you're no longer a member of parliament,' I point out angrily.

He grins. 'No. But I still want the best for England and I enjoy annoying the King.'

* * *

Annoyed or not, the King has given in. There are to be no Spanish matches. The Princess Elizabeth is quickly betrothed to a Protestant (the Elector Palatine), while Prince Henry has won the right to remain single for a while.

* * *

Marriage, or talk of it, seems to be in the air. Will Cecil (now Viscount Cranborne) brings his new wife to see us at the Tower. Catherine Howard, the Earl of Suffolk's daughter. It was an arranged match, of course, they hardly know each other but seem to get on well enough.

'Does your father know you're here?' I ask her, guessing he does not.

'No, but he wouldn't mind,' she smiles. 'He's an admirer of Sir Walter, as are many at Court.'

I smile back. Wryly. Nice to have admirers but what good do they actually do?

* * *

My niece, Arthur's and Anna's eldest daughter, is also getting wed. I journey to Paulerspury for the wedding, taking Carew, who enjoys being petted by his cousins. It's some time since I've seen them for I have to swallow my resentment when I do. I can't help feeling bitter when Anna talks proudly of the entertainments they put on for the frequent visits of King James. Unfair, I know, for I understand that they and my brother Nick, at Beddington, have to kow-tow, are obliged to seek royal favour. What good would it serve if they stood up lustily for Walter and ended in the Tower alongside him? Yet, in my heart, I feel they are being disloyal.

They give me a warm welcome, and I'm pleased to find a special friend among the guests – I'll-Never-Marry-Again Frances (nee Sidney, nee Essex), attending with her third husband, the Earl of Clanrincarde, who bows to me politely then disappears to play cards with the men.

At first we sip wine and nibble bride cake and talk of trivial things. I admire her pretty ruff; 'Such a striking colour. So unusual.'

'They're all the rage at Court,' she says, 'even the men are wearing them. Well, the fashionable ones. A Mrs Turner from Paternoster Row supplies them. She uses yellow starch and stole the idea from the French.'

'I'll get one,' I vow, 'Or maybe even two.' I look at her expectantly. I know her very well and can tell she has some worry on her mind.

'It's Robert,' she confides at last, drawing me to a window seat where we can talk privately. (Her son, she means, the third Earl of Essex; he forfeited the title after his father was beheaded but James restored it.) 'Oh Bess, he's distraught. You know he was married to Frances Howard, the Earl of Suffolk's daughter, when they were children? She's the sister of Will Cecil's new bride.'

I nod.

'After the wedding we sent him on a Grand Tour and Frances returned to the home of her parents. Now they're of age and Robert has come back, expecting to begin their married life. But Frances won't have anything to do with him.'

'Perhaps she's afraid of the marriage bed,' I suggest.

'No!' She shakes her head. 'Not her. She's hard and fearless, a wolf in lamb's clothing. And immoral, it's common knowledge that she's having an affair with Sir Robert Carr.'

I groan. *Him* again! 'That won't please King James,' I say.

She shrugs. The King encourages them. He never seems to mind his favourites having lovers.'

I pull a face. 'Unlike Queen Bitch.'

'And now,' Frances goes on, 'the wretched girl is telling everyone that my Robert is impotent, incapable of performing the ... well ... the *act*. What can I do?'

I cannot think of anything she can do. So I tell her of our worries about Wat, as a kind of solidarity in the anxiety of motherhood. About his pranks at university and his wildness, his recklessness.

'He'll challenge anyone to a duel and, of course, they're now illegal. We've sent him on a tour of the continent in the hope the new experiences will calm his high spirits. With Ben Jonson as his guide and mentor.'

Frances looks shocked. 'The poet and playwright? Is he the right choice? He's a clever man, granted, but he's also a drunkard.'

I shrug. 'Walter trusts Ben. And it's no good sending Wat with someone he dislikes.'

I don't mention that Wat's handsome and clever and loving and I wouldn't change him for the world.

* * *

The Tower of London.

Prince Henry arrives in a rush – leaping up the stairs. His face is flushed and his eyes sparkle. He's carrying a flagon and, for a moment, I wonder if he's lowered his principles and taken to drink. But no, he's also brought a flagon of water.

Walter is at his desk, writing his History, and I'm sewing in a chair by the window. At least, I was. We long ago dispensed with formal curtsying and bowing, but I'm still surprised when Henry grabs me by the hands and pulls me up.

'Come,' he says, 'find glasses, Lady Raleigh. We must drink a toast. We're celebrating! Come, Sir Walter. Lay down your pen.'

'What?' laughs Walter. 'What are we celebrating, my Prince?'

'Sherborne!' cries Henry. 'Sherborne! I've persuaded my father to cancel the grant he made to Carr and give it to me. I made sure to make the request in front of men hostile to Carr, and shamed my father into agreeing. I shall, of course, give the estate back to you, Sir, on the day that you're released.'

We express joy of course, and effusive thanks. Drink toasts of triumph with our wine, Henry with his water.

But the secret glance we send each other speaks volumes.

Will the day of release ever come?

✷ ✷ ✷

A strange thing happened yesterday. It began with a thunderous knocking on the door of the Tower Hill house. Very early, I was still in my shift.

Alice flew downstairs to answer it and, when I heard Dean's voice, I pulled on a robe and rushed down after her.

'What is it? Is Sir Walter ill again?'

'No, Lady Bess,' Dean turned a grim face to me. 'But I thought you'd want to know – Lord Cecil is with him.'

'Cecil?' A visit from Cecil could never be good news. What does he want?'

Dean shook his head. 'I didn't hear. He asked me to leave – said he wanted a private word with Sir Walter.'

A poisonous word, no doubt.

'Wait here. I'll come back with you.'

Kate's fingers were a-tremble with nerves so Alice helped me to dress. She begged to come with me but I forbade it.

'Heaven alone knows what trouble we are in now.'

I hurried as fast as I could, but the Snake had gone when I arrived at the Garden Tower. Walter was alone, standing by the window smoking his pipe, staring out over the Green. (Or perhaps at the Green, place of executions.)

'Walter, why was Cecil here?' I asked sharply. 'What did he want?'

'I don't know.' He turned, frowning. 'I don't know, Bess.'

'But you must know!' Anxiety made my voice shrill. 'What did he say?'

'He said he just wanted to see me. He seemed gentle, kind. Like he used to be.'

'But what did you talk about'

'Of the old days, of the good times we had. Hawking – we talked about our favourite birds, of the good-natured competition we enjoyed with them. Of his stays at Sherborne ...'

'Sherborne!' I gave a scornful laugh. 'The place he cheated from us. That wasn't all, surely? Surely you took advantage of his sudden softness? Surely you talked about your need for freedom?'

'No. It didn't seem the time. He looked so frail, Bess, as if a strong wind would bowl him over. Yet he grasped my hand so hard when he was leaving, he nearly crushed my fingers. And I swear tears stood in his eyes.'

'Tears stood in his eyes when they sentenced you to death,' I said bitterly, 'but he didn't dispute the verdict.'

He said nothing, turned back to the window, but not before I saw that his own eyes glistened with tears.

Men! Women the weaker sex? A myth.

ROBERT CECIL

Bath. May, 1612

I am not long for this world. I know it, others know it. Before I left the Court, where once they bowed and fawned, competed for my favour, I sensed them shy away from me, fancied I heard them whisper: 'Of what use a dying man, no matter how high his office?'

Dying, yes. High office, yes – Lord Treasurer and Chief Minister of State. My father would be proud that I achieved both posts – he taught me well. But he'd also be the first to say that any courtier worth his salt must look to the future. And I, all too obviously, am now a man of the past.

I have never possessed good health, and the effort of steering and advising two difficult monarchs has taken its physical toll. My back has always been troublesome – I've long been accustomed to pain. But this is different – agonising and all-consuming. Impossible to ignore. At times it cuts like a knife, robbing me of breath. At others it's dull and nagging, making me short of temper. While my legs, my poor feet ... They've never worked well, of course, I've long been embarrassed by my dragging gait, but now they swell so badly that at times I can hardly walk.

Queen Anne remarked on my pallor – advised me to see a doctor. I forbore to tell her that I've seen doctors – good doctors – who diagnosed, among other things, growths too large to treat.

Audrey said I looked tired. We have not managed a full relationship for quite some time, I've not been well enough. But we've remained good friends. She contrives to see me, now and then, and I flatter myself it's through fondness.

It was Audrey who suggested Bath. 'The waters,' she said, have helped you in the past.'

True. But not this time, I fear.

She kissed my cheek. 'I wish I could come with you, 'she said tenderly, but that, of course was out of the question.

Instead, I travelled with my chaplain and a retinue of servants. Our journey from London took five days, the spring-less coaches bumping over the rough roads at a snail's pace.

'We're taking it slow to avoid causing you discomfort, Lord Cecil,' Bowles, my chaplain, said.

'Thank you.' I tried to smile. I could have told him I was in agony anyway, that the slow ride only prolonged it.

And, as I predicted, the waters have done me little good. I told Bowles that I think I'm dying, but he wouldn't accept it, wouldn't listen. Or, more likely, he doesn't want me to face the truth.

At least my children are settled. I've made good matches for them.

'I don't wish my son to come,' I told Bowles this morning. 'Our parting would be too painful.'

But he's come, nevertheless, ridden like a demon to get here. He's with me now, telling me, like all the others, that I'm going to get well. And I'm glad to see him, of course. My Will. Lizzie's Will.

'Are you happy in your marriage?' I ask. He may not be a scholar, fit for great things, but I want him to be happy. I worry that it was not a love match, not like mine with Lizzie. 'Your mother and I were lucky,' I tell him.

'Catherine and I are lucky,' he assures me. 'I'm glad you found her for me. You must get to know her better, when we return to London.'

None of them will listen when I say I won't reach London.

We begin the journey back but get no further than Marlborough. They carry me into the Parsonage in a sedan chair.

Will has tears on his cheeks. 'I can't do without you,' he says. 'England can't do without you.'

Can't it? I think it can. James won't miss me – he would have done, once, at the beginning of his reign when he needed me so badly. But now he'll have Robert Carr into my shoes before they're clear of my sweat. And God help them both for Carr knows less of statecraft than James, and has no understanding of managing a monarch. My father argued with Elizabeth then carried out her wishes. I agreed with James, then made sure he changed his mind. What England needs ... but it's no longer my concern.

'I love you, Father,' I think I hear Will say. I attempt a smile. He loves me, even though I'm not glamorous.

My concern is Heaven or (but I hope not) Hell. I've lived a sinful life, as we all do on this Earth, but I pray to be forgiven.

Will Bess Raleigh forgive me? Prince Henry will look after the Raleighs, secure Walter's release, hand them Sherborne like a goose on a golden plate. Will Bess forgive me then, I wonder? Raleigh will. There were so many things I wanted to say to him, yet, when we were face to face, I couldn't say them. But perhaps he knew. I like to think he did.

Two things in my life have been my passion – Lizzie, and the lust for power. Now the cloak of power has slipped from my sloping shoulders and I go to Lizzie. She's there, in the corner, beautiful as ever. Waiting for me.

Will grips my right hand, the chaplain grips my left, as if they would lift me between them, right up to the pearly gates. But I'm rising and walking to Lizzie, to Lizzie in the corner ...

BESS

The Tower of London

'Cecil's to be buried at Hatfield,' my brother Arthur tells us. 'Privately and quietly, according to his wishes.'

'The hand of death was upon him when I saw him last.' Walter sighs.

How can he look so sad? It fills me with impatience. He might be able to forgive the Snake but I never will.

'What difference can this make to us?' I ask. 'To you? That's the important thing. Surely there's more hope, with Cecil gone?'

'A great obstacle removed,' Arthur agrees.

'Write to the King again,' I urge Walter. 'Today. This minute. Ask – *beg* – for your freedom.'

'I'm tired of writing to the King.' he grumbles, 'and I'm certainly not going to beg.' But he takes up his quill.

✽ ✽ ✽

As usual, there is no reply. James is too busy installing Robert Carr as Secretary of State.

'A ridiculous move,' says Cousin Gorges. 'Carr is totally out of his depth, everyone but the King can see it. We all know it's Carr's friend, Tom Overbury, who's doing the work. And few are mourning Cecil; if the King misses him he's hiding it well, and the people in the streets still blame him for the death of Essex. Cruel ballads are being sung about him.'

People once blamed Walter as well as Cecil for the death of Essex, and cruel ballads were sung about him in the streets. But not anymore, thank God. In the past I've deplored such nasty little songs but I might be tempted to join in the ballads about Cecil if I hear them. Quite apart from mothering his son, I once embroidered gloves for the wretched little man, welcomed him into my home, greeted him with affection, ordered his favourite food. Was the Cecil of those times our enemy even then? It's said he was so weak at Bath he had to be lowered into the water in a padded chair suspended from a pulley – that he died a painful death. Should I be sorry? Walter's sorry. I even heard him praying (very quietly) for Cecil. He must have a nicer nature than the one I possess.

※ ※ ※

At least one other person is mourning Cecil. Today I was leaving the Tower at five of the clock when I met Audrey at the gates. She was on her way in to the Royal Wardrobe. I suppose, I thought, she is so important the wretched curfew does not apply to her. She confirmed this by saying she was on an errand for the Queen.

'She wants one of the new yellow ruffs we've stored away for her,' she said. 'I see you're wearing one. Good to see that you're keeping up with the fashion.'

'Even though I'm an outcast from Court, you mean?'

She flushed. 'I didn't mean that.' She was looking older, tired and wan. Not at all her usual ebullient self. And she was wearing black – for her lover, I supposed.

'Bess,' she took my hand. 'He's dead. I'm miserable and you must be happy. We will never agree on the sort of man he was, but does that really matter? Are we truly going to let this ruin our friendship? I apologise for implying Walter might have been guilty that day at Scadbury. I was angry and I know that's not the case. I've always believed in his innocence. I've missed you, and in these back-stabbing times we need all the friends we can get. Surely?'

I sighed. 'We Raleighs certainly need our friends. And I've missed you too.'

We clasped hands briefly, agreed to meet soon and went our separate ways.

I can't forget how lined and strained she looked. I'm older (forty-seven!) and have had a much worse time. I'd best not look too closely in a mirror.

* * *

We meet sooner than I expect since Aud is first with the news. (Just like old times.)

She whirls into the Garden Tower, farthingaled skirt swinging, hat askew.

'Oh my dears, my dears! I had to come!' She hugs me, crushing my sewing, hugs Walter, knocking out his pipe, hugs Carew, who tries and fails to wriggle away. 'It's true! It's true! It's really true!'

'What?' I ask wearily. 'What's true?'

'The Prince has secured Walter's release! Prince Henry, that is of course, not little Charles – it would hardly have been Charles. But Henry stood up in front of the entire Court and made his father give his solemn promise that you, Walter, would be released from the Tower …' (She pauses for effect) this Christmas!'

We hug her back and thank her for coming and say it's marvellous but, in fact, we're dazed and disbelieving.

'You were there, yourself?' asks Walter. 'you heard and witnessed it all?'

'Oh no,' says Aud, 'I wasn't present, I'm part of Queen Anne's Court, not the King's. But I have it from a most reliable source.'

Ah, then it's just another rumour.

Only it is not. Prince Henry himself comes later, bounding in as fast and as flushed as Audrey. And owns himself sadly disappointed to have had his thunder stolen.

'I wanted to surprise you,' he groans.

But the news he adds is even better. 'I made it my business to read the report of your trial,' he tells Walter, 'and found it a travesty. No-one reading it could believe in your guilt. When you're released at Christmas, I shall insist on a royal pardon. As well as returning your home, of course.'

Walter is jubilant. 'I knew Henry would be our Saviour,' he says later, when we're alone. I always knew it. He's England's hope as well as ours. England's hope for the future.' He takes me in his arms and kisses me, long and tenderly. 'Just think, Bess, we'll spend Christmas at Sherborne this year!'

I nod and smile and agree, but I wish I could be convinced. We've had so many disappointments. And Christmas seems a long way off.

CAL

November, 1612

Their prince is dead.

I still cannot say *my* prince. I have lived long in the White Chief's land. I now speak English as well as most and have great liking for meat pies, ale, and the shows the white actors put on in their playhouses. But my prince is Cayoworaco. I will always stay loyal to him and to my tribe for I can never be quite an Englishman however hard I try.

But I am sad because, at eighteen summers, it is too young die. Everyone, everywhere, is sad. The people in the streets, in the markets, beside the river, here in the Tower, all weep and wail and ask why him? Our future king, our brightest hope – why him?

And the saddest of all are *my* people. Chief Sir Walter and Lady Bess, little Carew who I helped bring into this world, pretty Alice who had eyes for no-one else whenever the prince was near.

Alice will never look at me the way I would like her to. Despite my white man's learning, my white man's clothes, I am still a savage to many. But I liked Prince Henry. He did not regard me as a savage, he always spoke civilly, respectfully even, from when he was a child. He claimed to be amazed at my skill in mastering his language. 'For I could never learn yours,' he said. And he could not. He tested his tongue on some words, once, that I tried to teach him, and made us all laugh out loud.

No, at eighteen summers only, he did not deserve to die.

And he was going to release Sir Walter, that's the tragedy. I could weep like the people in the streets when I think of that.

The day we got the news I was with Sir Walter. Dean was tidying up his moustache and beard, the way he does each morn, and yawning behind his master's back because we were talking of Guiana, which Dean finds boring. But we often talk of my homeland, the Great White Chief and I. We discuss his book, The Discovery, which I have read a hundred times, and he asks me what I remember of my boyhood there and tells me what his memories are. And we speak, of course, of the gold mines. Of the riches to be found.

We were speaking of them then, but we broke off our talk abruptly when the visitor arrived. Will Cecil, it was, in a panic.

His face was white as a swan's feather and he was shaking, as if with the sweat. But he wasn't the one ill, he said – no – it was Prince Henry, who'd fallen sick after swimming in the wide river they call The Thames. The King's doctors, he said, anger in his voice, were applying remedies upsetting to the Queen.

'They've shaved the Prince's head and smeared dead pigeons over it. They've cut a live cock in two and pressed it against his feet. They've bled his nose. And when I left they were forcing a syrup down his throat – a syrup made of snails and frogs and crawfish. All this and he's getting worse, Sir Walter. They're killing him with ignorance.'

'Fools!' said the Great White Chief, rising from his chair.

'Your Great Cordial, Sir Walter –' Dean began, before I could form the words. (My speech, sometimes, is slower than my thinking.)

'It's the reason I'm here.' Will Cecil, now, had tears upon his cheeks. 'I come from the Queen, Sir Walter, she's begging for your help. She says your cordial saved her life and she believes it can save her son's. Please, Sir – please tell me you have some brewed for his fever's mounting and I doubt he'll last much longer...'

'I have some brewed.' The Great White Chief was already at his medicine chest. 'It will cure the fever but is no proof against poison, should there have been foul play. And it must be given immediately. Immediately, Will, you hear?'

'The minute I get back,' Will promised.

Only it was not.

Sir Arthur Gorges told us later that no-one would listen to Will or to the frantic Queen. They were doubtful of the Cordial. They tried it first on dogs, even on a member of the Council. When all survived they at last gave it to Prince Henry. But by then more moons had passed. It was too late. The fever abated, the Prince opened his eyes and spoke, but was too weak to recover.

So the country is in mourning. Sad faces everywhere. Alice weeps bitterly, Lady Bess looks pale and ill. While Sir Walter – for the first time since we met I think the Great White Chief looks old.

'What will happen to him now?' I ask Dean, who seems to discover more than I. 'Will he still go home at Christmas, as the White King promised Henry?'

Dean sighs. 'Sherborne's lost. It reverted to the King on Henry's death and he's given it back to Carr. From what I hear of James he might 'forget' his promise of freedom.'

'To his dead son?' I gasp. 'The Gods will curse him!'

'We have only one God,' Dean reminds me. 'And He took Henry from us.'

BESS

March, 1613

Walter has completed the first enormous volume of his History of the World with a touching dedication to Prince Henry. The story is intended to be told in three volumes, beginning with the creation and continuing (almost) up to the present day.

Not trusting anyone else with such a precious cargo, I deliver it myself to the printer William Jaggard at the Half Eagle and Key, Barbican.

He was working on the second volume when poor Henry died – making notes, drawing maps, borrowing books and toiling hard – just as he did with the first. A labour of love, he called it.

Yet when I return to his study in the Tower I find him bending over a great fire blazing in the hearth.

'Stop him, Lady Bess,' Dean implores. 'He's burning his book, the second one – after all that work!'

'Walter, please don't!' I attempt to catch his sleeve as he throws a pile of papers on to the leaping flames. 'You'll regret it later.'

'No Bess, I won't.' He turns to me, that stubborn set to his jaw. 'It was for Henry, mostly, and I've lost all joy in it.'

'But Mr Jaggard thinks the first book wonderful – he can't wait for the second...'

Walter shrugs, reaches for another pile. 'Then he'll be disappointed. Or he can write the thing himself.'

I grimace at Dean and shake my head. Nothing to be done.

✳ ✳ ✳

April, 1613

A letter is delivered to the Tower Hill house, addressed, very carefully, to me. I recognise Wat's writing and open it with trepidation. What's he done now, that he doesn't want his father to know about? It seems he and Ben are in Antwerp, both broke. Wat is sending home for more money. I sigh and wonder what I can sell. Perhaps Frances was right, and Ben is not the ideal companion.

Meanwhile, a new prisoner has been installed in the Tower next door to Walter's – Sir Thomas Overbury, the one-time friend of Robert Carr, now Viscount Rochester. (The man who did all the work for Carr, according to Cousin Gorges. I wonder how Carr will manage now – his ignorance exposed.)

They had a falling out, Overbury told Walter. He has a way of wandering out into the garden, strolling into the little hen house laboratory. Walter wishes he wouldn't – finds him irritating and arrogant, but has hardly the right to stop him. And I enjoy hearing anything bad about Carr.

'King James was jealous of me, a younger man close to Carr,' Overbury said recklessly. (No wonder he's in the Tower!) 'Then the Countess of Essex, Carr's lover, turned him against me. She's a bitch, that Frances Howard. So here I am – an innocent man, held on a trumped-up charge.'

As am I, Walter could have replied but didn't – merely grunted. (He's not been very sociable since we lost Prince Henry.)

'The less I talk to him the better,' he said to me. 'I just don't take to the man.'

Neither do I. He's tall and slim and could be quite nice looking, but he has a slyness about the eyes which is unattractive.

I'm sorry for him later, though, when one of the warders, a Master Weston, tells me how ill he is. 'I've never seen anyone so poorly, Lady Bess. The pain comes and goes, it's true, but he's fair crippled by it at times. It's not the Plague and it's not the Sweat, no-one knows what it is.'

No further visits to the hen house, the man's not well enough. Walter sends him a plaster for the spleen, which might afford relief.

* * *

September, 1613

Poor Thomas Overbury is dead. Master Weston told me this morning and I wasn't really surprised. We've not seen hide or hair of him in all these months and, the last few days, we've heard loud groans whenever we've passed the door. And if the door happens to be open a crack, the stench is terrible. Kate has been urging Walter to complain to the new governor – Sir Gervase Elwes. (Wade, thankfully, has been replaced.) 'It's not healthy for the rest of us,' she said. But now, sadly, there's no need.

Alice tells me there's talk of poison, but I don't take too much notice. I've learned, over the years, that there's often 'talk of poison' whether justified or not.

* * *

The hen-house stands neglected. Walter has taken up his pen again. Not to complete his history, though, or write anything creative. He grieved long for Prince Henry, the poor boy's death depressed him. Not only on account of his love for him (and he did love him, almost as much as he does Wat and Carew) but because all hope of freedom seemed to have died with him. Now he's making a bid for it again. A last bid, he calls it, his face alight – one last throw of the dice.

I'm in favour, of course, of his freedom. I'd give my right arm for it. But not this way, please, not this way, for he wants to organise another voyage – to sail to the place I dread. To the land of floods and swamps and alligators and all manner of dreadful things. To Guiana in search of gold. The old dream resurrected, or did it never go away?

'But you searched for gold before,' I argued. 'And failed to find it. And Sir Thomas Roe returned the poorer, convinced there's no El Dorado.'

'He all but convinced me too,' Walter agreed. 'Perhaps it *is* just a story. But the *mine,* Bess – *two* mines, I believe. 'We know more now, of where the gold mines sit. Every two years I sent a ship, to keep faith with the natives and to gather more information. As you know.'

I should do. Even here from the Tower he arranged these voyages and I helped raise the money for them. Once, I recall, we quarrelled over a jewel he wanted to sell – a great diamond given to him by Queen Elizabeth. I knew he valued it and I said, if he could bear to sell it, it should be for the good of himself and his family, not for more exploration.

'But these doings keep me in the world, Bess,' he explained, rather desperately. 'Shut away within these walls, I'd go insane without some involvement, some control over what's happening out there. Try to understand.'

I did (I do) and I sold the jewel for him. And I know he's been holding out the bait of gold to James for many years – writing to him enticingly, knowing of the King's extravagance over money, of his battles with Parliament to gain more. But Robin Cecil blocked Walter's path, perhaps James never saw the letters. Now Cecil's gone, it might be possible... There are many at Court firmly on Walter's side, people who have always believed in his innocence, who thought, and still think, his imprisonment to be unfair.

Some would need bribes, of course, to help them speak up, persuade the King. And we'd have to scrape money together – nothing new to us.

But Walter's old, he's ill. The damp from the Tower has seeped into his bones, aggravated the wound he got from Cadiz, his left hand is still unsteady, he suffers from chills and ague ...

'It's madness,' I told him. 'Madness!'

'It could be the price we have to pay. The price of freedom.'

Yes. It could well be. King James showers gifts he can't afford on his pretty young men. Where pleas and petitions failed, lure of gold might unlock stout doors.

Oh, but I'm still against it.

I watch them, all in a huddle – Walter, Laurence Keymis, Tom Harriot, and Cal, even little Carew, pouring over maps and charts and drawings, in a fever of excitement.

Disloyally, I pray that James will forbid the voyage, that Carr will persuade him against it.

✳ ✳ ✳

One day I can stand it no longer. I take Alice and Kate off to Beddington to stay with my brother Nicholas and his wife Mary. The menfolk, I'm sure, will not miss me. They'll hardly notice I've gone.

Nicholas and Mary are entertaining guests, so a few more make little difference. I'm pleased to see familiar faces, and here's Audrey, full of the latest gossip.

'Have you heard that Frances Howard has been granted her annulment from young Essex? He's very bitter. He claims she drugged him to make him impotent. I wouldn't put it past her.'

'So she's free to marry Robert Carr?' It's a relief to talk of anything but Guiana.

'He's been raised to Earl of Somerset now, and they're getting married at Christmas. King James is paying for the wedding and I've heard it's to be almost as lavish as that of the Princess

Elizabeth when she wed the Elector Palatine. Oh, and Carr's resigned from his post as First Secretary ...'

'For which we should give thanks,' Nicholas puts in. 'It was obvious he couldn't manage once he got Overbury sent to the Tower.'

I recall the groans, the terrible stench. Poor Overbury, dying in agony.

'Who's to replace Carr?'

'A good man – Sir Ralph Winwood.'

My heart sinks. Winwood's a friend of Walter's. *He'll* help him to Guiana. Walter's probably writing – appealing – to him now.'

✣ ✣ ✣

March, 1614

Walter's appeals seem to be getting nowhere, much to his frustration and my secret relief. But his History is published and is selling very well. It's a handsome book, with Walter's portrait, name, and coat of arms on the title page. Everyone likes and admires it, Cousin Gorges tells us, except King James. He's even talking of suppressing it.

'He fancies himself as a writer,' Cousin Gorges says, 'so it's my belief he's jealous.'

And he can't like the dedication to Prince Henry. It must remind him that the boy thought more of Walter than he did of his own father.

✣ ✣ ✣

December, 1614

Servants of the Archbishop of Canterbury have been seizing copies of the History and further publication is forbidden. King James has declared the book 'Too saucy in censuring the acts of monarchs.'

A poor excuse for spitefulness; he really does hate Walter.

'But the book's selling well on the continent,' Ben Jonson tells us, in an attempt to lighten the mood, for he and Wat have returned at last, penniless again, and not covered in much glory.

They were obliged to run from France, thanks to Ben's drinking bouts and Wat's terrible behaviour. One night, it seems, Ben got more drunk than usual so Wat laid him down, spread-eagled, on a cart and pushed him through the streets, crying out to all he met that here was the best crucifix in Paris.

Walter embarks on a stern lecture – so righteous I can't resist a smile.

'I once heard of a young man by the name of Walter Raleigh,' I said to the room in general, 'who spent a week in the Marshalsea for brawling. And who sealed up a friend's beard to his moustache with sealing wax to stop him talking.'

'Truly?' asks Wat, amazed.

'Father, you didn't!' cries Carew with a look of such delight we all begin to laugh.

※ ※ ※

September, 1615

Scandal is rocking London. Thomas Overbury, it seems, was *murdered*. And by Frances Howard, the new Countess of Somerset (my replacement as Mistress of Sherborne – I can't resist a smug litle smile). She had jellies and pasties and pies spiced with arsenic and sent into the Tower – to be fed to poor Overbury by my not-so-friendly warder Master Weston. He's to be hanged soon. So is Sir Gervase Elwes, the new Lieutenant of the Tower. I thought Elwes a pleasant, kindly man, but it seems he knew all about it, permitted it to happen. But perhaps the biggest shock of all is learning who supplied the poisoned food . . .'

'Mrs Anne Turner of Paternoster Row,' Aud tells me, in hushed tones. (She's visited the Tower especially to inform me.)

I'm stunned. 'The yellow ruff lady?'

Aud nods. 'The very same. She's to be hanged in one of her ruffs, the judge ordered it. They've gone completely out of fashion. I should burn yours.'

I will, I resolve. This very night.

Aud leans forward, widening her eyes. ' Now the question on all tongues, of course, is this – was *Carr* involved? Whether he was or not, he'll have a hard time proving his innocence. And the King won't save him – he's moved on to another favourite, a handsome lad by the name of Villiers. It's the belief of all at Court that both Carr and his wife will hang.'

※ ※ ※

They don't – James spares them execution, sends them both to the Tower instead.

And, after thirteen years, Walter is hastened out of it. His rooms are required for the murderess Frances Howard, Countess of Somerset.

~PART SIX~

BESS

Broad Street, March, 1616

It seems unreal. Dreamlike.

We've worked towards Walter's release for so many years it is hard to believe it's happening. I'm torn between relief on the one hand, fear on the other.

And I'm also full of regret – bitter regret – for his home-coming should be at Sherborne Lodge, not here in this Broad Street house. He'd have time to heal at Sherborne, to get fit in the healthy air. To hunt, to fish, to breed his falcons. But Sherborne will never again belong to the Raleighs. When Robert Carr was convicted it reverted back, yet again, to King James. Who quickly sold it to Sir John Digby (his ambassador to Spain) for ten thousand pounds.

'A bargain,' Walter said with a humourless laugh. 'It's worth more than that now and will be worth still more in the future.'

Years ago, Walter's half-brother, Adrian Gilbert, told me Sherborne had a bishop's curse upon it.

'Saint Osmund's curse,' he'd said spitefully. 'Not on the estate itself, but on the people who live there.'

Adrian disliked me then (and dislikes me still), and no doubt sought to alarm me. So I dismissed it at the time as superstition. But now I'm not so sure. Was it Osmund's curse that descended on us, changed our lives forever? Did the same curse descend on Robert Carr, who owned Sherborne for two short years?

Sir John Digby seems a decent man, from what I can remember, so if there *is* a curse I'll be charitable and hope he will escape it.

Am I being fanciful as Cal, with his heathen omens, when I fear the curse is still upon us?

For Walter is released, yes, but only to sail to Guiana – to bring back gold from the mine he believes to be there. What if he is wrong? His memory could be faulty after all these years. Even if he's right, can he survive the voyage there? Find the mine? Survive the journey back?

And Wat! He wants Wat to go with him. My wild Wat, still in Holland where he went to fight his latest duel. When I took him to task, once, about his hasty temper, he silenced me with this reply.

'Mother, when you have a father imprisoned in the Tower you become the butt of jests and sneers. The only way to combat this is to be first with your fists and your challenges, before others fight or challenge you.'

Now Walter has sent for him. He says the voyage will tame him, be good for him. Will it? Or will his high spirits endanger them both?

These questions rattle in my head, worry keeps me from sleep. But I summon a smile when Carew shouts 'Father's here! They've turned into our road, I see them from the window!'

I fly to the door to welcome him, rush into his arms as he descends, a little shakily, from the coach.

'How does it feel, my darling, to be out in the world again?'

'Bewildering,' he says, looking up at the house I bought with Arthur's aid.

'I hope you're not disappointed.' I try to see it through his eyes – tall, quite large, but ordinary, wedged in between its neighbours. 'It's no Sherborne, no Durham House.'

'It holds you and it spells freedom, that's all that matters.'

Only he's not free, not entirely. He's released without a pardon, forbidden to attend the Court, and he has a keeper with him, to observe his every movement. I recognise the fellow, a cheerful man in service to Ralph Winwood, helping Dean, Cal and Carew unload luggage from the coach.

'You'll not notice me, Lady Bess,' he calls out as he passes with a pile of books, 'I'll be but a shadow in the background.'

I smile, but he's bound to be an embarrassment, dragging after Walter like a chain around his leg.

✽ ✽ ✽

Next day, when he's rested, Walter limps around London (followed by his shadow) seeing sights familiar or built during his confinement. He returns tired but exhilarated.

'I said a prayer beside the old Queen's tomb, Bess, in Westminster Abbey,' he tells me over supper. 'I passed by Durham House but did not linger, though I admired the New Exchange Cecil built in the grounds. Whatever else he was, he knew how to plan a building. I braved Paul's Walk and met many an old friend. My History's out again, despite its ban, did you know that? The title page has been removed, together with my portrait, but the bookmen told me it's selling better than ever, and everyone knows who wrote it. Hats are taller, clothes less fine, and the number of coaches seems to have trebled.'

✷ ✷ ✷

Friends and relatives come to visit – Carew and Dorothy, Mary of Pembroke among them.

Like me, they are worried about this coming voyage.

'But he has to make it,' I explain. 'It's the condition of his release.'

'Walt's too old for it,' Carew frowns. 'I've told him so, but he won't listen. Best if he'd stayed in prison. He had some degree of comfort.'

'Best to sit and write beside a warm fire than perish in a jungle,' Dorothy nods.

I wince. A great comfort.

'He must not go anywhere without a full pardon,' Mary insists. She looks old now, and wrinkled, but she glitters with jewels and is formidable. 'Without a pardon he is still officially a traitor. He must buy one, Bess. If the King won't give it freely, Walter must buy one.'

* * *

It won't be given freely. The royal commission naming Walter as Admiral is issued under the Privy Seal, not the Great Seal, and the King himself has scratched out the words 'Our trusty and well-beloved' – just as Queen Bitch did on the occasion of Walter's first Guiana voyage, when she was furious over our marriage. But at least she had the tact to simply leave them out. James has scored them through so hard he's almost ripped the parchment. And he's written that Walter is 'under peril of the law'.

'We know the king will never trust you and you are certainly not his beloved,' I said. 'But what does this 'under peril of the law' mean exactly?'

Walter puffs on his pipe. 'James is playing a double game. He wants me to bring him gold, but he also wants to keep peace with Spain, which will be difficult for him to do as I am sailing into territory the Spanish believe to be theirs.'

'But it isn't theirs,' I protest. 'You claimed Guiana for Queen Elizabeth when you went there in fifteen-ninety-five.'

'Yes, but the Spanish won't acknowledge it. James wants Prince Charles to marry a Spanish princess, remember – the match is on one minute and off the next, but he's ever hopeful of it. So he's ordered that there's to be no fighting between my men and the Spaniards already along the Orinoco...'

'But how can you avoid it if the Spaniards think the mine belongs to them? Surely they'll fight for it?'

He removes his pipe and grins. 'They've got to find it first. I believe they're still looking. Meanwhile, I've arranged for some French soldiers to join our expedition. They can do the fighting, if it's needed, while we locate and work the mine. If I succeed it will make James rich – enough to compensate for the loss of the Spanish alliance.'

'And if you fail?' We both hear the tremble in my voice.

His smile fades. 'I'm still under shadow of the axe. He can say I've broken the law and send my head to Spain in an act of appeasement.'

If I was worried before, I'm terrified now.

'We have to buy that pardon,' I say. 'We'll raise the money somehow.'

Walter sighs. The expense of this voyage grows daily. He'll need to bring back plenty of gold to reimburse us for the gold we've already spent. So far, Walter has sold many of his personal belongings and parted with £10,000, some of which he's borrowed. I've given him my Sherborne compensation money, sold my farm in Mitcham for £2,500 and called in £300 which I lent long ago to the Countess of Bedford. The Crown, by law, is obliged to give 700 crowns in tonnage money and Walter has asked each gentleman volunteer sailing on the expedition to contribute up to fifty pounds. There will be investors, of course, but not as many as we'd hoped. Times have moved on, and it's hard to get the City Companies involved. The Muscovy Company and the East India Company are all the rage at present, offering less risky rewards than an expedition to Guiana.

'Mary's son, the Earl of Pembroke, would lend something towards a pardon,' I urge now.

Walter spreads his hands. 'The Earls of Pembroke, Huntingdon and Arundel are already investing. And, between them, are providing £15,000 to ensure my "good conduct and return". I could not, with clear conscience, ask any of them to pay another penny. I'll take advice on the matter before we part with more money we don't have.'

* * *

He decides to visit his old friend, Sir Francis Bacon, now Attorney General.

I beg him to take my coach to Gray's Inn (I'm determined not to sell it whatever else we lose), but he refuses in disgust.

'Women and children travel in coaches. When I left the Tower I rode home in one to please you. But never again.'

'You haven't ridden a horse for thirteen years,' I protest.

He scowls. 'No need to remind me.'

He mounts his black stallion shakily, knocking away Wood's helping hand. But he sets off confidently enough, followed by his 'shadow' on a plump grey mare. I watch them as they trot down Broad Street and turn right into West Cheap, the Shadow hunched and awkward in the saddle, Walter tall and straight-backed, doffing his hat to folk who stare at him, as he did from the walls of the Tower.

Sir Francis, he told me later, greeted him warmly. He visited Walter in prison and helped to supply books and information for the History. Both scholarly and with a passion for science, they have long shared common interests. Bacon was kept down by his cousin Cecil the Snake during the reign of the late Queen, but has risen under James to Lord Keeper of the Great Seal, Lord Chancellor, Baron Verulam and Viscount St. Albans. The number of titles stick in my throat when I consider what has happened to Walter, an equally brilliant and able man. But Bacon, obviously, is a good friend to have on our side.

They strolled in the Gray's Inn gardens, along one of the pleasant walks, and the counsel offered to Walter was exactly what he was eager to hear – Bacon advised him to go ahead with the voyage without wasting money on a formal pardon. He declared the pardon to be 'a mere formality' and 'quite unnecessary'.

'Upon my life, you have a sufficient pardon for all that is past already, the King having made you Admiral, and given you the power of martial law.'

'Then why,' I ask Walter, 'did the King not include the pardon in actual words?'

Walter shrugs. 'I questioned the same, but Bacon insists my commission as Admiral is as good a pardon for all former offences 'as the law of England can afford'. Don't look so worried, Bess. Francis knows the law, none better. This is good news.'

I hope so, but I still have doubts. Especially when Sir Ralph Winwood comes to the Broad Street house with a further royal command.

He accepts wine and cakes and takes his time coming to the point of his visit. At last, he says awkwardly:

'The King requests Sir Walter hand over his private list of ships, armaments, and proposed ports of call for examination.'

'Examination by whom?' Walter demands, flushing angrily.

'By the King himself.'

'But I can't comply,' Walter retorts. 'The Admiral's list is always kept secret. Shown to no-one.

Sir Ralph looks uncomfortable. 'The King knows this, and he assures you of his sacred promise to impart the information to none other. He says he will "hold the secret on the hand and word of a King." And the papers will be returned by me the minute he has perused them.'

Against all his principles, Walter has no choice but to hand over the various documents.

He shoots a despairing glance at me.

Does King James ever honour his promises? If he should reveal this information to the Spanish Ambassador …

But of course he won't. He wants gold. It would be against his best interests to betray such secrets.

* * *

Doublets, shirts, hats, ruffs …

Dean and I work together in silence – packing chest after leather chest. Both miserable, both afraid of this coming voyage.

Medicines, books, quills, ink …

Both aware the practicalities still have to be carried out.

* * *

Plymouth, Devon, June, 1617

Walter receives a hero's welcome. We're cheered wherever we go.

Crowds gather to call out greetings, rejoice that he's free of the Tower.

The mayor gives a dinner to honour him. Speeches, eulogies, bring a tear to his eye (and to mine). A grand feast follows, with meats and pies and jellies by the score. But I cannot enjoy a morsel, thinking of the morrow.

And now it's here. The day I've been dreading. A glorious day, to mock my heavy heart. Fourteen ships ride at anchor, waiting for the tide. The sun sparkles on the sea, gulls circle above us as Wat kneels for my blessing on the deck of the Destiny, the great ship his father designed and had built at Deptford. People have come from miles around to gaze at it. But I shudder whenever I think of the thirty-six guns it carries.

I murmur something – anything – more prayer, I think, than blessing, and stroke Wat's curly hair. He leaps to his feet and hugs me, crushing me to him.

'Mother, darling Mother, take care while we're away.'

'I shall take care of her. She's in safe hands,' Carew says, with dignity.

I hide a smile and Wat is careful not to grin. Carew begged to join them on the voyage, but we persuaded him against it.

'Thirteen summers is too young,' Wat said.

'Much too young,' Alice agreed.

'Father takes cabin boys who are younger,' Carew pouted.

Walter laid an arm about his shoulders. 'The life of a cabin boy is hard and not for you, my son. Do well at your books, practise your swordplay, and in a few years you can be a Captain, like your brother, and order cabin boys about.'

I said nothing, but swore to myself I'd lock up my younger son before I'd let that happen. Carew is sensitive and studious, more gentle than the brother he adores. He's been accepted at university and will go there soon. A life on land is the one I'll choose for him.

'It's you who've to take care,' I tell Wat now. He's glowing with excitement, with eagerness to be off. He's captaining The Destiny, with his father on board as Admiral. To my mind he looks too young – more like sixteen than almost twenty-two, but he paces the deck like one born to it (as I suppose he was). 'She's the best ship ever launched!' he enthused when first he saw her. 'Four hundred and forty tons! Think of that!'

And Walter, in command again, barking orders, is just as flushed and eager. Released from his keeper six months ago, he too looks younger, fitter, vigorous. Even his limp was less pronounced, I noticed, when, a while ago, he proudly boarded this flagship to the sound of the drummer's tattoo

'We'll bring back gold, Bess, never fear,' he says now, hugging me to him. 'And silver, wait and see. Two fifths, the King demands. There will be plenty for the rest of us.'

The cost, in all, of this expedition – the building, provisioning and manning of the ships – has swelled to thirty thousand pounds. Of which we've personally paid one fifth. We're left with one hundred pounds between us – fifty-five for Walter to take with him, forty-five for me to survive upon at home.

'All I want is your safe return,' I say, swallowing a sob.

'I'll look after him, Lady Bess,' vows Laurence Keymis, appearing at my elbow. 'And our young wild Wat, as well. I'll guard them both with my life, depend upon it.'

'I know you will.' I kiss his cheek, this tall, thin, loyal friend with the wandering eye. Watch him fondly as he climbs nimbly down the ladder, jumps into the rowboat carrying him to his own nearby ship, the Convertine.

I bid farewell to others – George Raleigh, Walter's nephew, John Talbot, Wat's old tutor, Cal, the native boy who towers above us all, Captain King ...

In the end they become a blur of faces and smiles and good wishes.

Then, suddenly, we're in the way, Carew, Alice and I. The tide has turned, the crew leap to their various tasks. Time to take our leave.

Alice hugs Walter, then Wat, and bursts into floods of tears. Carew shakes hands with both and solemnly wishes them luck. I cannot speak – my voice dries up, as it used to do at the start of other voyages.

Walter kisses me, holds me close for too short a moment, Wat bows, laughing, and kisses both my hands. They see us down the ladder, a sailor steadies us into the waiting boat, a rough-looking fellow, as many of the crew seem to be.

'Scum!' Walter sighed to me when he'd recruited them. 'Bought out of prisons, some of them. Others thieves, cut-throats, fleeing justice. Few truly decent men are willing to risk a voyage with an Admiral fresh from the Tower – a so-called 'traitor' lacking a pardon.'

'But Bacon said you'd no need of a pardon.'

'He did. Let's hope he's right.'

We're being rowed further and further from the Destiny, where Wat blows kisses and Walter waves his hat.

Small figures now, they turn away and go about their business. On shore, the great crowds cheer as the billowing sails carry the squadron out to sea.

A line from a poem echoes in my head, Walter's poem:

'To seek New Worlds for gold, for praise, for glory'

Will there be glory in this venture, this last 'throw of the dice'? Will there, indeed. be any gold?

CAL

Ireland, August, 1617

The omens are bad. There was a rainbow over the house in Broad Street just before we left. At sea, this is good, on land it is bad. But I mentioned this to no-one for the White Chief brooks no doubts. He cannot afford to have doubts if he wants to keep his freedom.

I knew he would be released because he stood on a beetle without noticing – a very good omen. Then he rescued a butterfly trapped in his room at the Tower – let it out through the window so that it could fly free. A sign, I told him, that he would soon be free.

Dean laughed at me then. Dean hates the sea, so we've left him at home with Lady Bess, which is just as well. Although I miss him sometimes, I confess. But I scowled when he made fun of me.

'No sense of humour, you,' he often said.

The White Chief has a new man to look after his needs aboard ship. Man, I say, but in truth he is more of a boy – Robin, a cheery soul who loves the ocean as much as he loves adventure. Robin respects me, he never pokes fun. Sometimes I think he is afraid of me – in awe of my great size.

I have lived in England for twenty years. I wear English clothes. I speak the language perfectly. I even think in English. But Dean used to say no-one would ever take me for an Englishman.

'Not with your dark skin and great height. But of course, your height comes from the Amazons, you say.'

Dean does not believe in the story of my birth. He used to laugh about it, as my brother once laughed. I do not care. I know it to be true.

'The Great White Chief wrote of Amazons in his book, "The Discovery", I tell Robin, who nods agreeably.

'Then they must exist,' he says. 'For Sir Walter would certainly know.'

The White Chief never laughs at me. He listens to all I tell him with interest, not scorn.

But when he told me I was to come on this voyage with him, this voyage to my own country, he thought I would be pleased. As pleased as Robin, with his thirst for adventure. So I pretended to be pleased but I am not pleased, I am frightened. Frightened because of the bad omens, frightened because of the Water Spirits who spared me when I travelled the ocean to come to England, but may not wish to spare me ever again.

This voyage was doomed from the start. When our ships reached the Channel the weather changed. The storms, so many said, were the worst since the summer of the Great Armada, near thirty years ago.

Shamefully, I, the son of an Amazon, hid in the White Chief's cabin, held onto the furniture there, while they fought the storms on deck. I felt sure we would be wrecked, cast into the raging sea and devoured by the Water Spirits.

Three times we were driven back to port. But somehow we have survived and are here in Ireland where the ships can be repaired, the victuals replenished.

The White Chief is happy in Ireland. Cork, they call this place. We're staying in a great and elegant house, guests of the Lord Boyle, so Wat has told me.

'Father sold him his Irish estates. We'll live like kings here, Cal. Rest our bones in comfort.'

The comfort, for me, is having both feet on solid land. Chief Sir Walter rides out hawking, talks for hours with this Lord Boyle, who is big and jovial with a loud and hearty laugh.

I ask the Gods to keep us in Ireland but, in two months, the ships are mended, and we are off to sea again.

✳ ✳ ✳

September, 1617

The weather seems accursed, sent by the Water Spirits. Storms drive us off course, tear away our sails, spring leaks that drown the men baling out the hold.

Then, at times, there is the mist – thick, yellow and very hot, with never a breeze to lift the sails and no rain to fill the buckets, to pour down our poor parched throats.

Then, worse, a sickness strikes. None like I have ever known. Many die, forty on our ship alone. Many friends and loyal servants of the Great White Chief – among them Master Talbot, a gentle, kindly scholar who lived with us in the Tower. I weep for him as, with prayers and hymns, we send his body overboard. So does Wat – so, too, does Chief Sir Walter.

I daily ask the Gods to spare Wat and Chief Sir Walter.

'Oh worthy God of the Sun, God of the Moon, God of this dreadful Ocean, keep the Sickness Devil from them, and from the good Captain Keymis on his ship the Convertine.'

✳ ✳ ✳

October, 1617

The Gods have dismissed my prayers. Perhaps I have offended them with too many requests of late, for the Great White Chief is ill.

Wat, pale as a ghost, begs me for my help. 'The ship's doctor is at a loss and is feeling ill himself. Robin, too, is ill, but knows naught of medicines anyway. You're as good as a doctor, Cal. Better, even.'

But this is a mystery sickness and I have no remedy.

I bathe his face and body when, at last, it rains. Change his shirt three times each morning, three times every night. Apply Balsam of Guiana, force sips of his own Great Cordial between his cracked dry lips, a trickle of lemon juice...

I do the same for Robin, who seems a little better.

But the White Chief raves in fever.

'The Admiral is dying,' I hear a sailor say.'

'Sick unto death,' Another one agrees.

* * *

November, 1617

Early this morn a rainbow shimmered in the sky. I fell on my knees and thanked the Gods, but Wat cursed in dismay.

'We'll have yet another drought, Cal,' he groaned. 'A rainbow means the rain has ceased, we'll be baked by the sun again.'

But he was wrong. In my country it is different. The rain, sent by the Gods, came down in torrents, and the good omen prevailed for the White Chief's fever broke. He knew Wat, and he knew me, before he drifted back to sleep.

'A good, feverless, healing sleep,' I said to Wat, who clapped me on the back and thanked me, with tears in his eyes.

'It was the Gods, not me,' I smiled.

'Then I praise your Gods with all my heart,' Wat said, smiling back.

I love his smile, so bright and wide and mischievous.
'His father's smile,' Lady Bess once told me. 'When we were young, that was the smile that won me.'

After the White Chief and Lady Bess (and Alice), I love Wat most in the world.

* * *

Robin recovers quickly, being young and strong. The White Chief also mends, but his recovery is slow. He is weak, still, and lying in his bunk when, at last, we drop anchor in the Cayenne River. He insists on being helped on deck, so Wat and I support him for he cannot walk alone.

He gazes at the shore of my homeland, Wai Ana, land of Many Waters.

'Guiana, Cal,' he says softly. 'I feared I'd not live to see it.'

I am not sure I want to see it. I have been away, I think, too long. It feels so alien, now. I may not be an Englishman but I am no true India, either. I could dream of Wai Ana, back in London, at Sherborne, but that is how it seemed – a dream. So much I have forgotten. I do not even remember the way to my village now.

But the Great White Chief knows this. He will use me as an interpreter, not rely on me as a guide.

'Harry,' he says now. 'You remember Harry, who lived with us for so long? Who I sent back some years ago, to rule over his own people? His village lies nearby. We'll send a message to him.'

✷ ✷ ✷

Harry comes in haste. He comes in a painted canoe, at the head of a fleet of others – a great Cacique now, in his ceremonial robes, bright with jewels and beads and parrot feathers. Aboard the Destiny, he greets the White Chief joyously, bows and clasps his hands, hugs Wat and beams at me. Three other Caciques come with him, and many of their tribes. They, too, hail the White Chief, smiling and clapping to show they welcome his return.

Harry has forgotten his English, but for the occasional word. So I prove useful now. Although his language is not quite mine, we understand each other. He tells the Great White Chief, through me, that his name has lived among them; that his kindness, on his first visit to Wai Ami, after the cruelty they had suffered at the hands of the Spaniards, is remembered with grateful affection.

'I'd hoped to liberate you from the Spaniards,' Sir Walter says, through me. 'Set up an English Colony here, that was my aim, as you know. It's still possible. If we can find the mine and take back gold, my king will show more interest.'

Harry says he has heard of the mine, though he has never seen it. He knows the White Chief will find it but, first, he must be made more comfortable, so that he can recover his strength again. Wrinkling his painted nose at the stench of the disease-ridden ship (a stench we've long got used to), he orders his men to set up a tent for Chief Sir Walter on the beach, has him carried to it. The women of his tribe bring cassava bread, roasted mullet, plantains, pistachio nuts and pineapples to tempt him, but he can still eat very little.

The rest of our men, those recovered from their fevers, are kept busy by Wat in the sweet fresh air, burying the latest dead (please the Gods, there will be no more), cleaning out the ships, repairing the pinnaces, mending torn sails and rigging ...

'And we need them to fill the water-casks, collect fresh fruit and meat, and build a forge to repair metal gear and tackle,' says Captain Keymis, newly arrived from the Convertine. (I am happy to see the Sickness Devil spared him, passed over him as it passed over Wat and me.)

Meanwhile, I recover ink, quills and paper from the White Chief's cabin so that he can write to Lady Bess.

'Sweetheart,' I see him begin. 'I can yet write to you with a weak hand...'

I move away in order to give him privacy.

※ ※ ※

Robin tells me the White Chief's letter is to be taken to England by a Captain Alley, who suffers from a weakness of the head and needs to be sent home. He takes passage on a Dutch ship.

Most of our remaining men have now recovered their health and strength and are ready to go on. Chief Sir Walter has not fully recovered but insists we hoist sail.

'This venture has already taken twice the time I planned,' he says.

So our fleet sails north, then west to the Triangle Islands, off the mouth of the Orinoco River.

The Water Spirits sleep, this time. The weather is warm and pleasant.

'At last!' rejoices Wat, when we drop anchor. 'From here we trek to the goldmine, Cal.'

He throws his hat into the air and his eyes shine.

He cannot wait.

But George Raleigh, the White's Chief's nephew, is not so happy. 'Four more ships were meant to meet us here,' he says uneasily. 'French ships, with French soldiers to protect our backs from the Spanish, if there be need. Two men – Faige and Belle – were put in charge of their arrival. Yet there's no sign of them.'

'Who cares?' cries Wat. 'Who needs 'em?'

* * *

It is clear to all that the Great White Chief is too weak to make the journey up the Orinoco since he still cannot walk without aid.

But who, then, can lead the expedition?

'My trusty senior officers lie at the bottom of the sea,' the white Chief groans to me. 'While others I might choose are, like myself, too frail to go at all. Wat clamours to be chosen but lacks experience. My good friend Laurence Keymis knows the country well. Having explored here twice before, he knows where the goldmine is thought to be. We rely heavily on his memory. But, though fit, he is no longer young. My intention was for him to take the role of guide and advisor rather than be in command.'

In the end, he has no choice. He names Captain Keymis as commander, George Raleigh, second-in-command, and Wat (doing his best to look serious and responsible) one of the Captains.

I pray the Great White Chief will not choose me to journey with them on account of my strength and sure-footed-ness. I do not fear the jungle. I know the tricks of survival will soon come back to me. But first the path leads past the River of Lagartos where my brother met his end. Although so many moons have passed, I still recall the horror with shivers down my spine. But my prayers are answered for the White Chief keeps me with him – to help nurse him and the other convalescents back to health, he says.

He issues strict instructions to the expedition leaders.

'You must make your way westward to the Mountain called Aio. From there you have no less than three miles to travel to the mine. Place your forces between the mine and the Spanish town – if there be a town there – as a defensive measure while you make note of what depth and breadth the mine holds, and whether or not it answers our hopes. If the mine is found to be royal, and the Spaniards attack, you have permission to repel them and drive them off as far as you can. But you must not, I stress not, attack first. If the mine is not rich enough to be worth defending, bring back a basket or two of gold or silver. Just enough to satisfy King James that the mine exists.'

'Is there not a second mine somewhere near the village of San Thome?' George Raleigh asks.

The White Chief nods. 'There is held to be, yes, but San Thome is occupied by the Spaniards and the mine is too near the Spanish settlement for us to approach it safely. The Mount Aio mine is the one we are after.'

'We will follow your orders to the letter,' Captain Keymis says earnestly. 'We will not betray your trust, Sir Walter. I am confident that I know the exact whereabouts of the mine and we will be successful, I feel sure of it.'

In the middle of the preparations, Wat comes to me and grasps my hand. 'I know you'll look out for my father, Cal.'

I nod, blinking a sudden tear from my eye. Little Wat, off on a dangerous mission. He may be tall as Chief Sir Walter, with a moustache that curls up naturally, but he will always be a little boy to me.

'Look out for yourself, young sir.'

He laughs his merry laugh as he turns on his heel and strides away. 'Oh, don't worry about me, Cal. I'm invincible.'

I think to myself that Lady Bess is right – he is very like his father.

* * *

December, 1617

Today the party set out upriver in five of the shallowest draught vessels, containing 250 soldiers, 150 sailors, and carrying provisions to last one month.

The White Chief, meanwhile, ordered the Destiny and our other large ships toward the southwest coast of Trinidad. We now cruise up and down, keeping a watch day and night, in case of a Spanish attack.

'And if they attack, how can we defend ourselves?' I worry to a gentleman volunteer who clutches the ship's rail, still feeble from the sickness. 'We have only weak men left aboard.'

He shrugs. 'Let us hope the sight of our ships will deter the Spaniards from coming close. The French were meant to be supporting us, fighting for us. But they've let Sir Walter down – I don't know how or why. You'd better pray to your Gods the others return soon – weighed down with gold.'

* * *

January, 1618

This waiting is hard. We wait for a Spanish attack, wait to hear from Captain Keymis. The crews, fretful from their sickness, grow restless, quarrelsome.

The White Chief sets an example, pretends patience. He reads, writes in his journal, strolls the deck of the Destiny. He can walk unaided now, leaning heavily on his cane. But he wearies quickly, and although he snaps at me when I insist he rests on his bunk, he submits eventually, with poorly disguised relief. I know him well. He cannot hide from me. I see he quietly grows more anxious as the days, the weeks, go by.

'He sleeps badly, too,' says Robin. 'I hear him tossing and muttering.'

Every passing canoe he hails, has me question the natives paddling it. Have they news of the expedition up the Orinoco river? They shake their heads and look surprised. No. They've seen nothing out of the ordinary.

And then, one day, a canoe bears three excited natives who call up to me eagerly. They've heard a rumour that Englishmen have sacked a Spanish Fort – San Thome, they think it is. At least four officers have been killed. Two Spanish and two English. They do not know their names.

'What is it?' the Great White Chief demands. 'What do they say? Tell me!'

With a chill around my heart I interpret for him.

✽ ✽ ✽

Aboard the Destiny, February, 1618

The waiting, now, has become unbearable Bad omens abound. We thirst for news yet dread it. But at last a messenger travels downriver, with a letter from Captain Keymis.

I am with the White Chief, in his cabin, when he sits down to read it. The omens rang true, I can see. His face grows whiter and grimmer until, suddenly, he throws the paper from him.

'Read it, if you will,' he says in a strangled voice. 'For I cannot tell you of it.'

He rises and stumbles out – up to the deck and the fresh air, forgetful of his cane.

I pick up the letter. I do not want to read it but know I must.

It is full of excuses, but the facts are clear: Captain Keymis has been a fool. Disobeying the White Chief's orders, it seems he sailed on towards the second mine, near San Thome, before looking for the Aio mine. He put most of his men ashore just below the village, where they set up camp for the night. A number of Spaniards, hidden in the woods, attacked them while they slept. They awoke in wild confusion, but Wat and George Raleigh rallied them and they pushed the Spaniards back into San Thome itself. There they found themselves confronted by the Spanish Governor with a force drawn up in formation of a battle. They paused, outnumbered, unsure what to do, but Wat hurled himself forward, crying 'Come on, my hearts!' He fell almost immediately, but continued to shout 'Go on! The Lord have mercy upon me, and prosper your enterprise!' His handful of men, enraged by his death, thrust on as if they were a thousand, drove the Spanish right out of the village. On each side, five men were lost, one of them the Spanish Governor.

I find myself in tears. Weeping, the son of an Amazon! But Little Wat is dead, he was not 'invincible'. And English have killed Spanish, against the orders of their King. Will the White Chief's life be forfeit?

* * *

'If Keymis can find the mine – either of the mines,' the White Chief says, 'the gold therein will placate the King and all may not be lost. He and his men are pushing forward at this very moment in an attempt to do so.'

He is composed, now, on the surface, although his eyes are very red. He has gathered together the crews from all his ships on the poop deck of the Destiny, to impart the news to them in a flat, but steady voice.

Then he retires alone to his cabin to write, I think, to Lady Bess. How will he find the words?

* * *

Later, he shows me a parcel of papers that were delivered with the Keymis letter.

'These, Keymis found in the Spanish Governor's quarters.,' he tells me bitterly. 'They are the lists I was forced to give King James – copies of the expedition plans in every detail. His Majesty promised me he would show them to no-one, yet he must have taken them straight to the Spanish Ambassador. The dates on the copies show that, even before we sailed from Plymouth, our strategies were known. Small wonder the Spaniards were everywhere Keymis went in the jungle. They knew of our every movement.'

'But why then, Sir,' I ask, bewildered, 'did King James let us sail at all?'

The White Chief sighs. 'God only knows the workings of his mind. I, for one, will never understand him.'

* * *

March, 1618

Captain Keymis has returned with his men – one hundred and fifty only of the four hundred who started out. Weary, disgruntled, disheartened men – arguing among themselves and abusing Captain Keymis. They have failed to find a mine. Some say there was never one to be found.

'They feel let down, as well they might,' George Raleigh grumbles. 'Keymis has been saying he knows where the goldmines lie for more than twenty years. But, if he did, his memory proved faulty. He acted lost, confused, nervous. He was hopeless as a leader. After Wat died he was even worse. I'd not be in his shoes when he has to face Sir Walter.'

* * *

At first they hardly speak. Greet each other like strangers, then dine together in the White Chief's cabin, both pale and drawn and silent.

I hover near the door, I cannot help myself. It is not honourable, I know, but I am amazed at how quiet they seem. I had expected loud voices, recriminations, the excuses I read in the letter and more besides.

Then, suddenly, the storm breaks..

'Why,' I hear the White Chief demand, 'did you not follow my instructions? Why did you go first to San Thome, which you knew would be well guarded, and not to the Mount Aio?'

'Sir, the Spaniards were all along the Orinoco,' Keymis replies. 'Hostile. Sniping at us. I thought it best, rather than face a long trek through a jungle swarming with enemies, to continue upriver, make for the other mine. It seemed more practical ...'

'Practical?' the White Chief thunders. 'Practical, indeed, to lose half your men, including my son, in a venture that should have been straightforward! You burned San Thome to the ground, you killed a Spanish Governor! You have not only killed my son, you have undone me. King James will have my head for this, or hand me over to the King of Spain to be hanged.'

'Sir, I was sure you must be dead already, we left you so sick and weak. Dead either from the fever or from a Spanish attack. I feared you would not be alive to read my letter, but I wrote it all the same. I lost heart, but I tried. God knows, I tried. The village of San Thome has been moved, I swear, and has grown, become a town. It was not where we saw it last. I had thought to skirt round it, but the Spaniards attacked and we fought back in self-defence! Surely if you explain this to King James, even though we have no gold ...'

The White Chief's voice sinks low again. I have to strain to hear it. Then it rises, cutting as a sword thrust.

'I will say nothing in your defence. Not to the King, nor to the Council, nor to any of our investors. The blame, entirely, rests upon your shoulders.'

A silence now, so long I turn to walk away.

Then Keymis asks: 'Is this your final word?'

'It is.'

A sigh, from Keymis. 'Then I know, sir, what course to take.'

I step back guiltily from my eavesdropping post as he strides past me, unseeing, white as a ghost.

I wonder if I should I go after him as he makes for the cabin allotted him. But what could I say? I, too, blame him for our present trouble, but he has been kind to me since I was first taken to England, to Sherborne and to Durham House. And it is surely the White Chief's grief for Wat that makes him so cold and hard and unforgiving to his oldest, most loyal friend.

I hear a key turn in the lock. He wants no company. Sadly, I walk with heavy steps to the ladder that leads up to the deck, but before I place my foot on it the crack of a pistol shot rings out. Shocked, I rush back down the passageway, but Robin is there before me.

'It's alright,' he says with a grin, 'The Captain's called out that he discharged his pistol by accident.'

'Nonsense!' Chief Sir Walter is behind me. 'Charge the door,' he commands.

We break it down.

Captain Kemys lies on his back in his bunk. His eyes, without life, stare at the timbered ceiling. Thick blood spreads over his chest. The bullet failed to kill him. He has finished himself off with a knife.

~PART SEVEN~

BESS

~Broad Street, London, May, 1618

Last night I dreamed the dream again. Only it was different. When Walter knelt to put his head upon the block his body shrank – became that of a boy. Little Wat!

'No!' I cried, struggling frantically through the crowd before the scaffold. 'You can't! He's too young! Only a child!'

But the axe came down with a brutal thud and I awoke, as I always do, in tears.

✻ ✻ ✻

Soon after breakfast, the letter comes. William Herbert, one of the gentlemen from the Destiny, brings it. I know what it contains. William's strained face confirms my fears as I take it from him. His hand is shaking, mine is not. He's explaining how he got here, which ship he took, what his journey was like – babbling because he's embarrassed. I silence him.

'I'd like to be alone, if you'll excuse me.'

I take the letter out into the walled orchard behind the house. Sit on a stone seat and stare at it. My name, on the outside, is in Walter's hand. It is sealed with the imprint of Walter's ring. The sun blazes down on my shoulders, yet I feel cold. The trees are weighed down with blossom, but I smell only death.

I sigh. Refusing to open it will not bring Wat back. I steel myself. Sentences leap up at me –

I was loath to write, because I knew not how to comfort you and, God knows, I never knew what sorrow was till now ... Comfort your heart, dearest Bess, and I shall sorrow for us both... My brains are broken, and it is torment for me to write. The Lord bless you and comfort you that you may bear patiently the death of your valiant son...

He has been dead four months. He died bravely but rashly, as I would expect. He was buried, with full military honours but without the presence of his father, before the altar of a church in a town called San Thome. The town was sacked later, burnt to the ground, but his body will be safe because it was buried deep.

Wat, buried beneath a ruined town in Guiana. Damerei, buried in a plague pit field.

Why does God take my sons?

I sit in the orchard for a long time. After finishing his letter, Walter broke it open again and wrote a detailed postscript of all that happened. I will have to read it later for though my eyes follow the words, I take few of them in. Wat is dead. I shall never see him again. Nothing else matters.

When Kate comes out to find me I am surprised to see that dusk is falling, I had not noticed.

'We must send for Carew,' I tell her. 'He must not hear this news from anyone else.'

She nods. 'I will tell Wood to travel to Wadham College. Bring him home.'

Her eyes are blood-shot from weeping. Why do I not weep? I wept after a dream, but now I feel numb, dead as Wat. The tears will come, I know. But not just yet.

✻ ✻ ✻

Today a messenger arrived from Devon. The note he brought spurred me into action.

My dear Bess,

'Word has it that Sir Walter's fleet has docked at Kinsale, in Ireland. Winds permitting, he should be sailing for Plymouth in the next few days. You are very welcome, as always, to come and stay with us should you wish to be here to greet him...

Your friend

Christopher Harris

I summon Dean and begin to pack:

Food for the journey.

Drink for the journey.

Fresh clothing for Walter:

Doublets, shirts, hats, ruffs ...

Money ...

✱ ✱ ✱

Plymouth, June, 1618

The rain comes down in torrents as Carew, Alice and I stand on the wharf of Plymouth Sound, watching for the sight of Walter's fleet on the horizon. We can't be certain it will arrive today, of course, but Carew insisted we come 'just in case'.

The last time we were here it was a scene of celebration – flags flying, drums rolling, cheering from the crowds. Today there is a crowd, but only a small one – hunched against the weather, subdued, sorrowful even. Sir Walter Raleigh is their hero, one of their own sons. They would like to welcome him back with a salute of cannon, a blaze of fireworks, but news of his failed venture has spread, become common knowledge. And they realise that this, his last voyage, is likely to cost him dear. Already, a warrant is out for his arrest. And rumour has it that King James has promised the Spanish Ambassador that, once captured, Walter will be handed over instantly – shipped, in chains, to Madrid for public execution.

'My guess is he'll not come back,' I overhear Wood mutter to Dean, from their position a little behind us.. 'He'll have the sense to jump ship. Be off in another direction.'

My brother Arthur said the same before we left. And they could, of course, be right. Maybe Walter won't return to face, first a king who betrayed him, then a jeering Spanish throng who will relish watching him hang. Maybe he'll remain in Ireland or is on his way to France. He is valued in both places, and he can send word, when he's settled, for Carew and me (and Alice) to join him.

But would I wish to join him? I want him to escape, of course, but ...

For the first time in thirty years of marriage, I am questioning my feelings, my loyalty.

I begged him not to take Wat, but he wouldn't listen. Wouldn't listen to the doubts of any of our friends. Now he has sacrificed our son on this mad venture. He has lost our money, other people's money, our hope of any future here in England. Why didn't he stay in prison, where he was safe? Where we were all safe?

Walter, in the postscript I eventually made myself read, blamed Keymis for Wat's death. Poor Lawrence Keymis, who loved Wat like a son. But if Walter had stayed in the Tower, had given up his golden dream, Wat would still be alive.

Since I opened that last letter I've walked, conversed, smiled even – like a wooden puppet without a heart. But when I'm not numb I am angry. Angry and bitter. Can any marriage survive such bitterness?

I hear Dean's reply. Dean, who is ever loyal. 'If he runs he looks guilty and he's committed no crime. His friends paid a fortune to ensure his promise of return. He'll not let them down. Sir Walter is a man of honour. Whatever he may face, he'll come back.'

No sooner have the words left his mouth than Carew shouts 'I see them! I see the ships!'

We strain our eyes, peer into the distance. There are sails, to be sure, but –

'Only one ship,' I say. 'Where are the others?'

'Does it matter?' cries Alice. 'As long as it's the Destiny?'

'It is!' Carew grasps my arm. 'It is the Destiny. I'd know her anywhere.'

I'd know her too, I think, with a wrench of the heart. Four hundred and forty tons. Wat's pride and joy. Returning without him.

'But is Sir Walter aboard? That's the question,' Wood frowns.

'Of course he is,' shouts Carew. 'I can see him – I'm sure I can see him!'

'It's too far away to see him,' scoffs Alice.

A light touch on my elbow and Sir Christopher bows before me, his kind face creased with concern.

'Bess, I fear the Destiny will be arrested once she berths. A mere formality at this stage, Sir Walter will not be detained. But I suggest you return to the comfort of my home – get warm and dry – and I will bring Sir Walter to you as soon as I am able.'

✳ ✳ ✳

Radford House, 1618

Alice and Kate help me into fresh clothes, then retire to get dry themselves. I sit by the fire in the cosy parlour.

'Imagine needing a fire in summer,' Lady Harris exclaims, struggling to make conversation. 'Hail one day, rain the next. What has happened to our weather?'

In the past we've got on well, have never been lost for words. But today is different. I can tell she wants to mention Wat but fears to do so. I'm thankful when, sensing my need to be alone, she takes Carew under her motherly wing, sees that I am served with food and drink, then leaves me undisturbed. One hour passes, two, three. Tense, nervous, on edge, I sip a little wine but can eat nothing. Was he on board? Will he come? And if he does, what will I say?

'Bess ... I am so very, very sorry ...'

At last he hovers on the threshold. Looking worse than I have ever seen him – bone thin, grey of face, haggard. A broken man.

A broken man who needs his wife. More, now, than ever before. What have I been thinking? Grief, surely, has addled my brain, I am filled with remorse and a rush of overpowering love.

I hold out my arms. With a sob, he limps into them and we cling and weep together.

'I feared you might blame me,' he says, dashing an arm across his eyes when our tears are spent. 'That I might lose you too...'

'You'll never lose me – never!'

'But you argued about Wat...'

'Wat would have stowed away if you'd refused to take him.' I realise this is true. Of course it's true.

'He was brave to the last, so I'm told,' his father says. 'And he was wonderful with the crew, Bess, they all loved him, even the roughest among them.'

'We must remember him as he was,' I attempt a smile. 'Bright and merry, full of laughter and love. And we must be brave for Carew's sake. He's grieving terribly. He strives hard not to show it, but I hear him crying in the night. We must all go on for each other. Wat would have wanted that.'

Walter leads me to the window seat, sits beside me, puts his arm around my shoulders, holds me close. 'I may not be allowed to go on, Bess. You understand that?'

'The King, you mean?' My heart sinks. 'I know he's out for your blood. He's even issued a proclamation condemning your actions, condemning the voyage, although he approved it. Copies are plastered all over Plymouth.'

'I've seen them.'

'And Secretary Winwood is dead, Walter. It happened suddenly, without warning.'

He sighs. 'Our best ally. Lord Boyle told me of it, in Ireland. Also that some of the rats who deserted and returned have been bleating lies about me to the Privy Council.'

'They have, but others will support you,' I say stoutly, clutching at straws. You still have loyal friends at Court ...'

'If they can be relied upon.' He sighs again, more heavily. 'Some of my 'loyal friends' turned their backs on me on the voyage, Bess. A lot of the men were scum, we knew that from the beginning – not the sort I would usually choose to take with me. But they were not alone in causing trouble – some of the officers I trusted, some of the gentlemen volunteers I've counted my friends for years, turned against me when they thought I was doomed to fail. Deserted, even. Then there was a mutiny, coming home. I had but four ships left to me, after all our misfortunes, but the crews of three of them remained in Ireland. From an outgoing fleet of fourteen ships and one thousand men, one ship and twenty-two loyal men have returned. Among them Samuel King, Cal, young Robin...'

He pauses as a fit of coughing takes him – a harsh, racking cough that leaves him weak and trembling. I pour him some wine, but he waves it away.

'It's nothing. It comes and goes.'

'Oh my dear,' I stroke his hand. 'You're not fit enough to face all this trouble. You should have stayed in Ireland. Or sailed to France. You should not have come back ...'

'I would not have done, not yet. I would have refitted, tried again to find the mine, but with deserting, discontented crews the task was hopeless. As for France or Ireland, it is not in my nature to run, Bess. And I pledged my word, did I not, to return? In success or failure.'

'The King never keeps his word, why should you?'

He smiles wryly. 'I like to think I have more integrity than the King.'

'Write to Cousin George Carew ...'

'I have done so. Also to the Queen. I know she'll try to help but the King takes little heed of her opinion.'

'So...' I'm in tears again. 'What are you going to do?'

He shrugs. 'Smoke tobacco. Rest. Wait for the knock on the door by whoever comes with the warrant. I'm so weary, Bess. I was afraid to sleep on board in case some ruffian thought to murder me.'

Despite the warm fire, he's still shivering. 'You must indeed rest,' I say. 'I've brought my cordial of Horehound and Germander which will ease your cough. And if someone comes with a warrant they can kick their heels until you're better.'

He smiles. 'I'll soon recover with my Bess to nurse me. But first I must greet Carew. And Alice. Are they here? Can you call them?'

'Of course.' I rise to do so. To my shame, I'd forgotten them.

Carew bounds in like a puppy, then bows and shakes hands like a man. Walter laughs and hugs him, then turns to Alice who, looking shocked, kisses him gently.

'He looks so frail,' she whispers to me. 'So ill!'

'He's worn out,' I whisper back, and call Dean to help him to bed.

* * *

Later, I look down on him sadly, his face so gaunt, whiter than the pillows. He sleeps, I can't help thinking, like one already dead.

* * *

The days pass. Walter is looking better, still frail but more himself. He rests, he smokes, he reads, he writes more letters – to the Lords Arundel, Pembroke, Huntingdon and others of import – explaining his actions. He plays chess with Sir Christopher, draughts with Carew, cards with Alice and Lady Harris. He tries to include me – 'Come, Bess, you enjoy Primero.'

I refuse impatiently. How can he behave as if he hasn't a care in the world?

My ears ache from listening out for the bearer of the dreaded warrant. My nerves are strained to breaking point. I can't sew or read. I certainly can't play cards.'

'Relax, Bess,' Walter says. 'At least we wait in comfort.'

Relax!

✱ ✱ ✱

Two weeks! We've been here at Radford Hall fourteen slow days, fourteen long nights. And still the knock on the door fails to come.

Perhaps the King wants you to escape,' I say to Walter in desperation.

He laughs. 'Why would he? No, he's playing one of his twisted games – dragging the whole thing out to make me shiver in my boots. Then, just when I think maybe I won't be arrested after all, he'll swoop. Send me off to Spain like a trussed lamb to the slaughter.'

'And is that what you want?' I ask bitterly. 'To be shipped off in chains? To be hanged, like a petty criminal, in a Spanish square? To be jeered at by Spaniards, spat at by Spaniards? To be cut down and butchered in front of a hostile Spanish crowd?'

He flushes. 'Of course I don't want it but turning my face from it is not going to make it go away.'

'But you *can* make it go away,' I point out. 'By going away yourself.'

He sighs. 'How many times do I have to repeat myself, Bess? I will not run. I will stay and face whatever music confronts me.'

'Funeral music,' I say. 'To be played to your grieving widow.'

* * *

Tonight, as I lie beside him in the room allotted to us, he groans and tosses, mutters in his sleep. Most of what he says is unintelligible, but I recognise one word – 'Guattaral'. The name the Spaniards call him.

* * *

I waylay Sir Christopher in the Great Hall after breakfast. 'What do you think Walter should do?' I ask quietly.

'Escape,' he replies instantly. 'I've told him so, but he refuses to listen. Sam King has also tried to reason with him, but he won't listen to him either. Sam's even arranged for a passage to France – bribed a Huguenot captaining a barque. But Walter won't hear of going.'

Captain King, I know, is staying at a nearby inn with Cal and young Robin. When Walter is taking his afternoon rest, I send for him.

'Is the French ship still available?'

He nods. 'It rides at anchor in Plymouth Sound, but it won't delay much longer.'

'Can you get word to the ship's captain that Sir Walter will board tonight? Under cover of darkness?'

He spreads his hands. 'There's no need to send word, Lady Bess. He's been expecting us for the past three nights. But the problem is Sir Walter himself ...'

'Leave it to me.' I say stoutly.

* * *

I use a low weapon. One he can't combat. I use Carew who, in his distress, forgets to be a manly thirteen, reverts to a tearful eight-year-old who begs and pleads – tells Walter how much he loves and needs his father, how much I love and need him.

'We want you alive, Father,' he wails. 'Not dead, like Wat. He'd want you to save yourself, you know he would. We've lost Wat, we cannot lose you too. Please, Father. Please.'

With a sigh, a muttered oath, Walter gives in. As I prayed he would.

'Unfair,' he mutters to me, as he summons Captain King. 'Unworthy of you, Bess.'

I shrug. Who cares if I'm unworthy? As long as he escapes. As long as he lives.

* * *

Cal and Robin are to go with him, as well as Captain King, who's arranged for a boat and two fishermen to row them to the French vessel.

'They'll wait at Radford's private quay,' he tells me, 'then, when the tide is full, they'll sweep us out into Cattwater and on to the ship'.

'And you're sure these men can be trusted?'

He smiles. 'Sir Walter is worshipped hereabouts. They'll not betray him.'

* * *

They leave in the early hours, while our hosts are still abed. We've agreed Sir Christopher and his wife should not be involved, for fear of repercussions. But Sir Christopher will help me later to buy passages for Carew, Alice and me. And Kate, of course. I could never leave Kate behind. She'd never permit me to leave her behind.

I told her once, in our happy Sherborne days: 'Should you ever wish to marry, to create a home of your own, you'd always have my blessing and a hefty marriage portion.'

She grinned at me. 'The only man I've ever fancied is Sir Walter Raleigh.'

Now that same Sir Walter Raleigh fastens his heavy cloak, straightens his hat on his greying hair and turns to me. The time has come. Our farewells are emotional. It's hard to part so soon after being reunited. I weep, Walter weeps, Carew weeps, Alice weeps ... Even Captain King and Cal have tears in their eyes. Robin turns his back. He's not the type to weep.

'Guard my husband, Cal,' I murmur to the tall bronzed native who's been loyal to us for so long.

'With my life, Lady Bess,' he answers in that solemn way of his. 'He'll come to no harm with me.'

'Soon,' I keep repeating to Walter. 'We'll join you very soon.'

'You'd better,' he says grimly,' Since this was all your doing.'

He kisses me one last time and then they're gone. Out into the night. Four stealthy figures,

Swallowed up soon by darkness.

* * *

Before it's light, they're back. I'm disturbed by muffled voices, rush down the stairs and stare in disbelief at the sorry group crossing the Hall.

'I couldn't do it,' Walter says, wearing his stubborn look. 'Cowards run.'

'But the warrant ...' My voice comes out in a squeak.'

He scowls. 'To Hell with the foolish warrant. I'll wait for it no more. I'll ride to London, plead my case to King and council. Insist they give me a trial.'

'It won't be a fair one.'

'No matter. I'll have my say as I did at Winchester.'

I clench my fists to keep from hitting him. 'And then he'll send you to Spain.'

Carew weeps. Alice weeps. I rant. All to no avail. Walter stamps upstairs to bed.

'We leave tomorrow,' he shouts back over his shoulder.

'A quarter of a mile further,' Sam King moans, 'and we'd have boarded the ship for France.'

* * *

The Road East. July, 1618

Bumping along in the coach with Walter, Alice and Kate, I simmer with resentment. This is madness, suicide. London instead of France! If he wants to die who can stop him? Certainly not his wife.

The others surround us on horseback – Cal alongside Carew, Sam King riding with Wood, Dean just ahead of young Robin – all as glum as I. The only one cheerful is Walter, who sits there humming a tune.

He even boarded the coach in good humour. The despised coach fit only for "women and invalids." He sank back against the cushions with an invalid's sigh of relief. (Too unsteady to mount a horse, yet ready to fight for his life.) He catches my eye, stops humming and pretends to fall asleep. I purse my lips. He need not bother, for I've given up. I'll argue with him no more.

We rattle over the River Plym, skirt Dartmoor and are heading for Ashburton when, to our surprise, more horsemen join us, overtake us and wheel about. Our coachman pulls the horses to a halt. Carew, King and the others are also forced to halt. The leader of the strangers dismounts and approaches the coach.

'It's Cousin Lewis,' Walter says, 'awaking' with a start.

'Who?'

'Stucley. Sir Lewis Stucley. A kinsman. Knighted by James just before I went to the Tower. He rose, I fell. I've told you of him. His father held I cheated him over the spoils from the Virginian voyage. I didn't. Lewis was only a boy at the time.'

'Sir Richard Grenville's nephew?'

'The same. Vice-Admiral of Devon, now. D'you think he's come to arrest me?'

He has. A big man – about forty, I judge – with an oily manner. I dislike him instantly. He sweeps off his hat with a flourish, bows lower than there is need.

'Cousin Walter,' Stucley says, with a smile that reveals big teeth. 'I would like to say it is a pleasure to greet you, but I wish 't'were in happier circumstances.'

'My circumstances are far from happy, Lewis,' Walter replies. 'But that's no fault of yours. Have you a warrant?'

'Alas, no formal warrant. But I have letters ordering me to apprehend you and escort you to London. The warrant will be sent to me later.'

'Don't trust him,' I hiss to Walter. 'If he hasn't a formal warrant he has no authority.'

'I can show you the letters,' Stucley says, with an unpleasant glance at me. 'From both the Lord Admiral and Sir Richard Naughton, acting for the King.' He fumbles in his coat.

'No need, Cousin,' Walter smiles. 'I trust you as my kinsman. As for taking me to London, I can save you the trouble for we're on our way there now.'

'Indeed?' His smile is more oily still. And more toothy. That's good of you, Sir Walter, and brave, if I may say so. But I have business in Plymouth – your business. Your ship, The Destiny, is anchored there, I'm told.

Walter nods. 'In Sutton Pool. I put her sails ashore the day we moored.'

'But her cargo is still on board?'

'Mostly tobacco, to my bitter regret.'

'Of course, of course.' Stucley looks grave. 'I'm sorry for your misfortunes in Guiana. But tobacco, as you know, is valuable and can fetch a good price. Since you are not at liberty to dispose of it yourself, I thought I could be of service. If we return to Plymouth now, you and your good lady can rest in comfort for a few more days while I sell your cargo for you.'

'You'll not see a penny from it,' I warn in a whisper.

'But I thought we must hasten to London,' Walter says. 'Surely your orders must be obeyed?'

Another oily smile. 'My orders were to take you to London in easy stages, for the sake of your health. A small delay enabling you to enjoy more rest is permissible.'

And so, with little choice, we turn coach and mounts and head back the way we've come. Not to Plymouth itself but to Radford again, where Sir Christopher welcomes us warmly but looks puzzled (as well he might).

※ ※ ※

Radford House

More aimless days of waiting. Only now we're no longer visitors but under house arrest.

'You're still honoured guests as far as I'm concerned,' Lady Harris clucks. 'It's disgraceful you should have this Stucley fellow breathing down your necks.'

But 'Cousin Lewis' bothers us little (he's asked me to call him this and I suppose I should not offend him). He's out mostly, selling tobacco.

'Have you received profit from it?' I overhear Sir Christopher ask Walter

Walter laughs. 'Lewis is "keeping it safe" for me.'

Hah! Safe in the depths of his pockets.

* * *

A relief, almost, when the warrant comes. Cousin Lewis shows it to Walter who, in turn, shows it to me. I only scan it lightly. I would like to rip it up.

"We commend you, Sir Lewis Stucley, upon your allegiance, that, all delays set apart, you do safely and speedily bring hither the person of Sir Walter Raleigh to answer before us such matters as shall be objected against him on his Majesty's behalf."

It's signed by the Privy Council and sounds, I think, reproving. "*All delays set apart.*" Perhaps they know of the tobacco theft.

Lewis thinks so, too, he's looking a little pink. 'Right,' he says. 'No more loitering.' We set out this very day.'

And so, once more, our little party boards coach, mounts horse, and sets out for London, but this time under armed guard. Cousin Lewis has brought reinforcements (does he think we'll make a run for it overland?) He's also brought his page, Cuthbert, and a funny little French physician named Manoury who, he says, is along for Walter's benefit.

'For I observe, Cousin, that you're still a trifle delicate.'

How perceptive the man is, I think, as Walter's cough racks him again.

Still, the physician's welcome. We may have need of this Manoury. It's a long, tiring journey to London. Walter needs all the help he can get.

* * *

Stucley keeps his word and we indeed 'journey by easy stages'. We cross the River Axe, join the Roman Road and enter the village of Musbury to lodge with John Drake of Ashe House.

Next day, we pass from Devon into Somerset and head for Clifton Maybank, just over the Dorset border, to stay with the Horseys, who do everything possible to make us feel welcome and normal, knowing we'll never be normal again.

'It's humiliating,' I complain to Walter, 'this lodging with friends yet being under guard.'

'I'm the only actual prisoner,' he points out, puffing on his silver pipe. 'You remain free as a bird.'

'Yes, a sparrow watched by a hawk. I all but fall over Stucley – Cousin Lewis – wherever I turn.'

Walter shrugs. 'I could have a worse keeper. At least he makes a show of being on my side.'

He does indeed.

'I wish I could be of more service, Cousin Walter,' he declares over supper, tears in his eyes. 'I grieve for your situation, but I have no influence in Court circles, as I'm sure you are aware. Being your official escort in this manner brings me no pleasure. I beg you to believe I volunteered for this post purely to ease your travel and ensure you are treated with the respect owing to you.'

'I do believe it, Coz,' Walter says, smiling. 'And I thank you for it.'

'Do you like the man?' I demand later, in the privacy of our guest chamber.

Kate has helped me get ready for bed but Walter is undressing himself. He's dismissed Dean and Robin who, both jealous of each other, compete over attending him.

'Go to your own quarters, the pair of you,' he said, losing patience. 'And squabble there.'

'Liking has little to do with it,' he says now, struggling into his night shirt. 'It's in our best interest to be agreeable.'

I suppose he's right.

'I'm more worried about Doctor Manoury,' he goes on, his eyes twinkling. 'I think he aims to steal my wife.'

I laugh. 'Don't all Frenchmen have an eye for the ladies?'

'This one makes far more fuss of you than he does of young Alice.'

He does. It's ridiculous – Manoury's ridiculous, with his little tubby figure, his short and stocky legs. It's true he's often at my side, helping me in or out of the coach, passing me my fan if it's hot, my cloak if it's wet or cold. All with a kiss of my hand and an admiring, sunny smile. And I, too, am ridiculous, for his attentions give me a spark of pleasure on this journey that can have no pleasant end.

I brush my hair. Walter meets my eyes in the mirror as he knocks out his pipe. His hands are less shaky, I notice, there is colour in his too-thin cheeks. Healthy colour. And he hasn't coughed once today. Our trek, so far, seems to be stimulating him rather than taking its toll.

He sighs. 'You know where our route takes us tomorrow?'

I nod, feeling suddenly sick. 'Through Sherborne.'

We sleep badly. Walter tosses and turns, moans occasionally. I lie awake for hours and then dream of Little Wat riding through

Sherborne park on his pony, fishing with Will Cecil, climbing Jerusalem Hill with Cal, sitting with his father on their favourite walled seat, wriggling impatiently on our pew in Sherborne Abbey... ...

* * *

Our coach sweeps round a corner and we're in sight, now, of the town. Of the abbey. And there's the old castle, high on its rocky hill.

Walter turns his eyes from it, but I gaze, with an ache of longing, recalling our early days there. This view, I know, was Walter's first glimpse of it. A tale that Wat loved well.

'Father – tell us the story of how you first saw the old castle.'

'I've told you a thousand times,' but Walter would relate again how, on a journey from London to Plymouth, he caught his breath when he spied the castle, glowing in the sun; flung out an arm to point to it and –

'Fell off your horse!' Wat would roar. 'And Uncle Adrian Gilbert said it was an omen – that you'd soon own the ground you had kissed!'

And now the Digbys own it. Passing the drive to Sherborne Lodge, it's my turn to look away.

We rattle through the town, past the New Inn and The George, out onto the Shaftesbury Road, bound for Poyntington Manor, home of the Parhams. More old friends to embarrass.

* * *

They are not embarrassed in the least. Sir Edward and his wife make a great fuss of us - wine and dine us in royal fashion but treat Stucley coldly, with a touch of contempt that causes his colour to rise, makes him defensive.

'If it were not me escorting my cousin, Sir Edward, it would be someone with less regard for his well-being.'

Sir Edward snorts. 'And escorting him to his death is good for his well-being?'

Stucley turns away without bothering to reply. He retires to bed directly after supper – early, for once. Kate and Alice chose to eat in their room, and Carew, exhausted, now also begs permission to retire. Which leaves us at liberty to talk as we sit around the table.

'Why, oh why did you not escape while you were still in Plymouth, Walter?' Sir Edward groans, pouring more wine. 'All your friends expected you to make for France – wagers were taken on it.'

Walter sighs. 'It would not have been honourable. I gave my word ...'

'To Hell with your word!' Sir Edward thumps the arm of his chair. 'When did the King honour his word? You expect a trial? For all you know he won't give you one, fair or unfair. He might well have you clapped in the Tower the minute you reach London, before shipping you off to Spain in the middle of one dark night.'

Walter sips his wine. 'I knew before I went it was a case of perish or prosper.'

'But there was no need, surely, to put your head in the lion's mouth?'

Lady Parham leans forward eagerly. 'I heard today that the King is due to visit Salisbury in four days' time on his summer progress. You pass through there, don't you? You have such a way with words, Sir Walter. If you could obtain a face-to-face audience, you might be able to sway him, to make him see reason...'

Walter smiles and pats her hand. 'I thank you, dear lady, for your concern. But King James would never grant me an audience. I have met him but the once – when he first set foot in England ...'

'And he was most ungracious,' I put in. I've heard rawly of you. 'Hostile, even. For no reason at all. I don't know why, but he truly hates my husband.'

She tuts impatiently. 'Then your husband must take up his pen and write to him, stating his defence in detail. You're about to say he wouldn't read it, Sir Walter, but members of the council will be with him, good friends of yours among them. If they get to read it, at least you'll have put your case before them. Perhaps they will be able to demand you are given a trial. And a fair one, this time.'

For a moment I am hopeful. This makes sense. Then I remember. 'But we're due to arrive in Salisbury tomorrow and stay for one night only. Stucley won't dare to let us linger.'

'He's already been in trouble for dallying in Plymouth,' Walter nods. 'He's so anxious to make up time I worry for the horses. No, I'm sorry, my friends, but there's no solution. The lion's mouth it will have to be.'

✣ ✣ ✣

In the middle of the night I sit up suddenly, wake Walter.

'I know what you must do,' I gabble. 'You must be taken ill in Salisbury. Then Stucley will have to give us time there – time in which you can quietly write your defence.'

He rubs his eyes, yawns long and loudly. 'Feign illness, you mean? Stucley thinks I'm ill already. He's always saying how frail I appear.'

'You do look frail – you are unwell. But I'm talking of severe sickness.'

'He'd never believe it. What are you suggesting? That I fall down in a faint, clutch my stomach and groan? He may be many things but he's no fool. He'd know in a moment that I was playing for time.'

He lies down again, pulls the covers up to his chin. 'Go to sleep Bess. We've miles to cover in the morning.'

I shake his shoulder. 'You could maybe have a rash. Or boils, perhaps. Sores? Something so grotesque dear Cousin Lewis wouldn't dare move you from your chamber lest you infect the whole of Salisbury.'

He groans. 'And how am I to achieve these sores and boils? This terrible rash? If I had access to my laboratory in the Tower, I could manage something of the sort. If you had access to your stillroom at Broad Street, it could be possible. But as we're here, journeying under guard with nothing to hand but cough medicine, your idea is nothing short of insane. Now let me go to sleep or I will indeed be ill.'

I lie down beside him, defeated. Then shoot up again.

'I have it! Walter, I have it! Doctor Manoury! He must have many remedies in his little bag of tricks. Remedies, mixed together, that can do all manner of things. Produce all kinds of 'symptoms'.

He sits up again, wide awake. 'Emetics. Ointments.' He stares at me. 'It could work. But how can we get him onside? He might run straight to Stucley who brought him along in the first place.'

'Not if I use my womanly wiles.' I bat my eyelashes at him, making him laugh.

'Well, it's true he does seem sweet on you. But I doubt he's sweet enough to risk his reputation.'

'A bribe along with my honeyed tongue? Could any man resist? If only Stucley had given you that tobacco money. But we must have something we can offer ...'

He thinks for a moment. 'There's the purse of gold your brothers kindly sent.'

'No.' I shake my head. 'That could be useful later.'

'I have a ring,' he sounds reluctant. 'One the Queen gave me...'

'Keep that too. I still have my pearls, we'll offer him those...'

'Well, if you're sure...'

'I am.'

I'm not. I hate to part with them. But needs must.

* * *

Doctor Manoury refuses the pearls. I manage to snatch a few words with him next morning while Stucley is bossing his men, preparing to leave. I expect the little Frenchman to be reluctant at first, to need persuading. But he agrees at once, his dark eyes twinkling merrily.

'For you, Lady Bess, it will be a pleasure. We fool them all, non?'

'Yes.' I glance around to make sure we can't be overheard. 'No-one else must know the illness is not genuine. Just you, Walter and me. But I'd be happier if you accepted some payment...'

'Non, non.' He waves his hands dismissively. 'I need no reward. I 'ave much sympathy for your 'usband. You can rely on Guillaume Manoury.'

'I hope we can trust him,' I whisper to Walter, as we board the coach once more. 'He is, after all, in Stucley's employ. It's a lot to ask of him.'

He shrugs. 'We must hope for the best. And we must also confide in Robin and Cal. I will have need of their help if I'm to be convincing.'

'And Dean, of course.'

'No. Dean is too honest. The deception would show on his face.'

※ ※ ※

We begin our performance on the way to Salisbury. Stucley rides ahead with his men instead of in the coach, which makes it easier. I halt our progress four times, to Stucley's frustration, saying Walter is feeling faint and in need of fresh air.

'He needs to alight, Cousin Lewis, and walk awhile.'

Later I demand a blanket: 'Because his teeth are chattering.'

The day is extremely hot, so Walter has no difficulty in working up a sweat, which alarms the kindly innkeeper when we (finally) arrive at The King's Arms, on St. John's Street. He brings Walter a cold drink and advises he go straight to bed.

Walter, however, 'bravely' sits down to the lavish supper that awaits us. He eats little but appears, to the vast relief of everyone except Manoury and me, to recover a little.

'Still, Cousin Walter,' a worried Alice says, 'you frightened us in the coach. You need to rest.'

Walter agrees, but when he rises to go up to bed he staggers, hits his head on the door post. Carew leaps to his feet to steady him while Alice gives a little shriek. Stucley, looking vexed, shouts for Cal and Dean to help him upstairs.

I follow them, assuring Carew and Alice that Walter is merely exhausted from travelling. 'He'll be fine in the morning, I'm sure.'

✳ ✳ ✳

In the privacy of our chamber (which, luckily, is furnished with a table containing quill, ink and paper) he begins 'Sir Walter Raleigh's Apology for the ill success of his Enterprise to Guiana'

'Less of an apology, in truth,' he explains, 'than a justification for all that passed. My men fought the Spaniards – yes – but in self-defence. And Guiana, I maintain, belongs to us rather than to Spain ...'

When Kate knocks, expecting to help me undress, I stand in the doorway, blocking Walter, and tell her I need no assistance tonight. She is surprised but, being a poor traveller, is grateful to retire herself.

Walter, already in his night-robe, pauses to help me undo my laces and hooks. 'Go to bed yourself,' he advises. 'For I aim to write all night.'

* * *

I open my eyes in the morning and find him fast asleep, slumped over the table, balls of screwed up paper at his feet and his 'Apology' scarcely begun.

'It will take time,' he yawns when I wake him.

'Which proves the importance of our plan,' I smile.

To my surprise he frowns, comes to me and takes both my hands. 'Bess, before Kate and Dean come in, I have a request, one you won't like.'

'Oh?' I'm wary.

'I aim to be a little better at breakfast and, later, I shall 'collapse' in earnest, as we arranged with Manoury. But before I do, I want you to leave – to travel on to London with Carew, Alice and Kate.'

'Leaving you here?' I'm amazed. Indignant. 'No! I can be of help. And anyway,' I add childishly, 'it was my idea.'

'Yes,' he nods, 'and I'm grateful for it. But you must think of Carew, of Alice. They are already upset enough. If we confide in them they might smile, giggle, laugh even – give the game away. If we do not, they are going to be alarmed and distressed because I aim to appear at death's very door.'

'But...'

'No buts, my sweet. Do this for me. Apart from all else, I do not wish you to see me covered in every blemish God could send, playing the buffoon.'

I argue long and stubbornly, but he is adamant and, eventually, I submit.

* * *

Carew and Alice are not happy about leaving Walter. They think I am being uncaring and unreasonable until Walter persuades them this is what he wants.

Kate is thrilled, she can't get home fast enough. But Stucley, of course, is surprised by my sudden decision to go on ahead. I am forced to spin some tale about things that need my attention in Broad Street.

'And Carew should not be too long away from his studies.'

He frowns. 'But Cousin Bess, Sir Walter's health ...'

'Doctor Manoury is in charge of his health. You were so thoughtful in bringing him along. And you look to my husband's welfare so caringly yourself I feel I can safely leave him in your hands.'

Mollified, he gives me a toothy smile and performs a little bow. 'I will continue to do all I can for him.'

I smile also, sweet as sugar. 'I know you will.'

Walter instructs Captain King, Dean and Wood to ride with us for protection, and I manage to snatch a private word with Cal and Robin before we depart, explain the situation. Robin thinks it a great jest (I hope he'll take it seriously when the time comes). Cal looks anxious.

'I do not like this Frenchman, his eyes are set too close. Can we trust him not to poison the Great White Chief?'

'Yes, Cal,' I assure him firmly. 'He refused a bribe, which proves him an honest man. I'm sure we can trust him'

Behind my back (and his), I touch the wooden door frame.

✲ ✲ ✲

Bidding farewell is painful as ever. 'Supposing,' I say, clinging to Walter in sudden panic, 'that they do take you straight to the Tower? And they won't let me see you?'

'Lewis assures me we'll come first to your house in Broad Street. He's promised to arrange it, so never fear.'

I'm awash with fears. It seems I've been fearful for centuries. My handkerchief is soaked by the time I'm seated in the coach, but Walter looks cheerful waving us off, although he does not forget to totter a little, as if unsteady on his feet. He's enjoying this playacting, I think resentfully.

I'm amazed and rather ashamed to realise that, for a while, I enjoyed it too.

CAL

I beg the Great White Chief to wear my armband – an alligator's tooth, strung on a beaded cord. A gift from a Medicine Man when I was very young, it is proof – strong proof – against poison. The White Chief refuses. Kindly. He says it is not needed. Doctor Manoury, he says, is trustworthy.

I do not trust this white, French, Medicine Man.

This eve he gave the White Chief a liquid drink – bluish, murky-looking. And now the White Chief is flushed and sweating. His skin has a purplish tinge. Poison? I'm sure he's been poisoned!

Robin, playing his part, calls the Cousin who is a Guard. The Cousin who is a Guard stands in the doorway, worried.

'I'm sorry you're unwell, Cousin Walter. Hopefully, you will be better in the morning. For we must move on, we have no choice.'

As soon as he is gone, the White Chief leaps out of bed – demands his quill and paper. Writes, furiously, this document to King James that he has set his heart upon.

'Will it help?' I ask Robin. 'Help him to be forgiven?'

Robin shrugs. 'It's worth a try.'

※ ※ ※

We stay in his room overnight. He vomits twice but appears bright and merry as soon as the sun is up. The sweat has gone, and also the purplish tinge. I was wrong. He has not been poisoned but now he looks yellow as parchment. He climbs out of bed, still in his nightshirt, and again sends Robin to the Cousin who is a Guard.

'Don't be alarmed by what you see, Cal,' he whispers with a wink. 'I am about to act the fool. I will need you to restrain me soon. Do not be gentle but, again, do not use too much force.'

I stare at him, not understanding, until he begins to moan and tear at his hair. He drops to his knees and crawls about the chamber. Still moaning, keening, he even starts to chew the rushes on the floor.

'What in the name of Heaven!' Still clad in his night-robe, the Cousin who is a Guard stands in the doorway once again, a gaping Robin behind him.

The Medicine Man bustles in: 'A fit he is having – restrain him!'

I recognise my cue and leap forward, Robin beside me. Together we seize the White Chief's arms – try to return him to the bed. But he fights us, then glues his legs firmly to the floor. We lift them, one at a time, but he stamps them down again. At last we lift both legs together, wrestle him to the bed. He throws himself from side to side, hits his head upon the bed post, then rolls onto his back and shakes from head to toe. We hold him down while he thrashes and whimpers.

'A cloth!' the Cousin calls out. 'In his mouth, or he'll swallow his tongue!'

But now he becomes still, gives a great sigh and closes his eyes.

The Manoury man grips his nose so that his mouth opens – pours a yellow liquid down his throat. What is it? Is it safe?

'Bien! 'E will sleep now, poor soul. For a long time.'

'How long?' The Cousin is white as chalk. 'We must travel today. No more delay, the Privy Council expects ...'

'Non, non!' The Frenchman waves his arms. 'You cannot! I forbid it! My patient could die.'

'Delivering a dead man to London would displease the Privy Council, Sir Lewis,' Robin says. He's trying not to grin, but the Cousin is too distressed to notice.

He gnaws at his thumb – a nervous habit. I've noticed him doing it before. 'Very well,' he says at last. 'We will wait one more day. But tomorrow we must travel, no matter what state he is in.'

* * *

Today he appears even worse. Last night he wrote again, as furiously as before. But at dawn the Frenchman painted his face and chest with a stain unknown to me. It stirred memories of the paint we used in my homeland. My brother painted me and I him – red, usually, but sometimes many colours. But it was not like this. This is not good. It makes the Chief break out in sores and pimples. Some purple, some yellow with touches of green. I cry out in protest, but the White Chief laughs.

'For show only, Cal. It will wash off, never fear.'

The Cousin who is a Guard gasps when he enters the bedchamber. He staggers back, holds a kerchief to his nose.

'What the devil is it, Manoury? Not the plague!'

The Frenchman shakes his head, spreads his hands. 'Sir Lewis, I do not know. I 'ave not seen such a thing before.'

The White Chief moans. 'Water,' he gasps. 'Water. God help me, Lewis, I think I'm dying.'

'Another physician,' the Cousin decides, gratefully escaping the room. 'If you can't cure him, Manoury, I must find someone who can.'

* * *

Two new doctors stride over – from the big building beyond the cobbled Close.

That's the Bishop of Winchester's palace,' Robin tells me gleefully. 'Stucley went bleating to the Bishop for help and he's sent his own physicians.' He rubs his hands. 'This is all working out just as Sir Walter hoped.'

The doctors declare themselves baffled. Horrified by the rash and the pimples, their examination is swift. They retreat downstairs as soon as they can, and demand yet another opinion.

Before the third doctor arrives, the White Chief beckons me urgently.

'Quick, Cal, fetch Manoury to me. This one may examine my water.'

He does, and whatever the Frenchman did – I could almost come to admire him – the water the White Chief passes is jet black and very foul-smelling.

'God save us!' the doctor cries, and all but runs from the chamber.

Downstairs, the three men confer.

'He cannot be moved.'

'The fresh air could kill him.'

'He is mortally sick.'

'But what, sirs,' asks the Cousin impatiently, 'what do you think it is?'

They spread their hands. Shake their heads. It is a mystery.

'La l'epre?' Manoury suggests. 'Leprosy?'

The Cousin who is a Guard turns green and sways on his feet.

✽ ✽ ✽

It is important, Chief Sir Walter has told us, that he appears unable to eat. For three days, he is thought, by the Cousin, to have kept down nothing but water. But every night, at supper, Robin and I save him scraps of food. This eve, 'though, we can smuggle in little, and his hunger pangs are great.

Summoning the Frenchman to him, he gives him coins from his leather purse. 'The White Hart,' he says, 'is a few doors down. Buy mutton and two large loaves.'

Later, wiping his mouth, he smiles in satisfaction. 'Tonight I finish my Apology. And tomorrow the King arrives'.

* * *

The King is to stay in the Bishop's palace. We hear the cheers as he rides in. But the White Chief is stricken with panic.

'My writing,' he cries, 'is deplorable! I was scribbling in too much haste. Robin, you must copy it for me – a fair copy, without any blots.'

Robin turns pale. 'I cannot, Sir. Your work would only look worse.'

The White Chief looks at me, but I shake my head. 'I am slow with a quill. I'd need days.'

The Frenchman bows. 'My hand is clear, readable and fast. Pass me the pen and the ink.'

* * *

The Cousin who is a Guard delivers the script himself. Goes, willingly, to the Palace; gives it into the hands of one of the King's own men.

'It was written, I assume,' he smiles, on his return, 'before our travels began.'

'Yes indeed,' Chief Sir Walter agrees. 'So fortunate the King's come to Salisbury. He can read it before we reach London and it may aid my defence. I thank you for your kind assistance…'

'I'm happy to help you, Cousin,' the smile becomes a beam. 'And happier still to observe you are so much better. We can resume our journey today.'

* * *

He hires a coach for the White Chief and we ride in it also, Robin, the Frenchman and I. Bound, once again, for London, and the troubles that wait for us there.

~PART EIGHT~

BESS

Broad Street, London. August, 1618

Walter's nature is such that his spirits have always been either up in the clouds or down in the depths. And so it is no surprise when he arrives back home in a dark, pessimistic mood.

When we parted in Salisbury he was elated, in his element, enjoying fooling toothy Stucley with his feigned illness, hopeful of the success of his Apology to the King.

But now he's convinced this is the end.

'What was I thinking, Bess? Wasting time and energy for nothing? Time we could have had together? I was a dolt to think James could be swayed by anything from my poor pen. I doubt he'll even glance at the rubbish I've written, assuming it gets anywhere near him. More like, it will end up on a bonfire somewhere, naught but a heap of ashes.'

'Cousin George Carew won't let that happen,' I assure him. 'He, at least, will read it and pass it to other Councillors.'

He shakes his head. 'Stucley thinks they'll never give me a trial. We must prepare ourselves for the worst now, Sweetheart. Accept that I'm bound for that square in Madrid you described so vividly, to be hanged and mutilated before a bunch of foreigners. If I'm allowed to address them on the scaffold, they'll not understand a word of it for I'm damned if I'll blather in Spanish. Five days I'm allowed to have here with you, before being dragged first to the Tower and then to Spain. Five days only, in which to put my affairs in order, in which to say our last farewells.'

I smile. I'm feeling smug. 'A lot can happen in five days. Captain King and I have been busy.'

* * *

For all his talk of defeat, of being finished, he still takes a deal of persuading.

'You know how I feel about fleeing like a criminal.'

'But you're being treated like a criminal! You'll be hanged like a criminal. This is your last chance to save yourself. I will never forgive you if you don't take it.'

'You're being hysterical ...'

'I'm feeling hysterical!' I bang my fist down on the table. The crockery jumps, for we've only just finished supper. (A meal for two. The others are tactfully giving us time alone and Stucley, for once, is nowhere to be seen.)

'The French will welcome you.' I play my winning hand. 'Le Clerc says he cannot understand why you haven't landed in Calais already, when his government are falling over themselves to offer you sanctuary.'

Walter looks startled. 'Le Clerc? The acting ambassador? You've been in touch with him?'

'He's coming here tonight to try to convince you.'

'But Stucley …'

I grin. 'Sam King will look after him. He aims to get him drunk.

* * *

Le Clerc does a good job. A dapper, lean Frenchman (very different from funny little Doctor Manoury who said goodbye to Walter at Staines), he makes Walter feel so valued, so much his old, respected self, that he agrees – at last – to run.

'I believe your good Captain King has seen to the practicalities of your actual departure. It is only left to me to ensure your warm welcome when you disembark, which I shall do with the greatest of pleasure.'

Taking his leave, a satisfied smile on his face, Le Clerc kisses me on both cheeks.

'I look forward to seeing you in Paris, Lady Raleigh,' he says. 'You will follow Sir Walter soon and meet 'im there, I trust? With your son and your servants?'

'Indeed.'

I have to refrain from hugging him. After he's left I weep with relief.

* * *

The arrangements Sam King and I made so hopefully are all in place. Walter, thank God, approves them. Walter, Cal and Robin are to make their way at midnight to Tower Dock. There, on the Thames, at the foot of Tower Stairs, Sam will have two small wherries moored, along with the men to row them. The wherries will take them to Gravesend and hence to the ship bound for France. And freedom.

But – suddenly – a fly in the ointment. It seems we've been too pleased with ourselves, too careless. For as the three of us sit in the parlour explaining our plans, whispering them to a thrilled Carew and Alice, a familiar strident voice startles us out of our wits.

'So you're off to France, Sir Walter. May you have a pleasant crossing.'

None of us speak, we're struck dumb as Stucley moves out of the shadows to stand before us in the candle-light. His teeth gleam larger than ever as he smiles his oily smile.

'You overheard us?' I ask stupidly. Of course he did.

He nods, gives a little bow in my direction. 'And earlier I saw the Frenchman leave. Your ale is not as potent as you believe it to be, although Captain Kidd here may have a sore head come tomorrow.'

'So,' Walter sighs wearily. 'it seems we are defeated before we even begin.'

'No need to be.' Stucley moves closer, puts his hand on Walter's shoulder and lowers his voice. 'I desire to be in on your plot, Coz. To escape to France with you.'

I gasp, and so do the others.

'But why?' I cry. 'Why would you wish to go?'

He turns to me, looking suddenly grim. 'There is little to keep me here, Cousin Bess. While you were still in Devon a Spanish diplomat ran over a child in his coach.'

'That's sad,' Alice says haughtily. 'But what has it to do with us?'

'This.' He pulls forward another stool, sits beside her at the table. 'A mob of several thousand Londoners stormed the embassy gardens, seeking his blood.'

Alice shrugs. 'I'm not surprised. Most Londoners hate the Spanish. But I still don't see ...'

'The diplomat hid from the mob, refused to face them. And, suddenly, their shouts of rage turned into shouts of praise for Sir Walter. Crowds in the streets took it up and also shouted for him – howled their disgust at the present treatment of him. It appears he's become a symbol of the anti-Spanish feeling. And I have become the un-feeling villain who holds him captive. Despised. Reviled. Only this morning mud was thrown at me. I'm already in trouble with the Privy Council for dawdling in Devon – being too lax a keeper. My future looks somewhat bleak. Can you blame me for wanting to get away from it all – for needing to start afresh? Accompanying Sir Walter to Calais seems as good an option as any.'

Another silence. Longer, this time. We look at each other. Can we trust him? Dare we trust him?

At last Walter rises, holds out his hand. 'Cousin Lewis, your presence will be welcome. I can't deny it will make the first part of our flight easier with you on our side rather than against us.'

Stucley stands also, grasps his hand gratefully. 'When do we leave?'

'Tomorrow. At midnight,' Sam King says gruffly. He does not look happy and neither am I.

Yet Stucley's tale about the diplomat is true – Kate told me of it, and of the support for Walter. So perhaps the man's wish to get away is genuine. At all events, now that he knows our plans we have no choice but to believe him.

CAL

The swirling London mist is a good omen for men who don't wish to be seen. Men like us. Chief Sir Walter limps in front of me along the narrow back alleys. His cane taps evenly on the cobbles, his footsteps are muffled, thanks to the softness of his shoes. Yet I can only just make out his form, unfamiliar in his drab, ill-fitting clothes.

Robin giggled when we first saw him dressed for the journey and I, who seldom laugh, was forced to hide a smile. Who was this stranger? Surely not Chief Sir Walter, with his fancy hats and ruffs, his velvet cloaks and breeches?

It was not his clothes that caused amusement, 'though they were strange enough. The White Chief's doublet was a dull, plain, brown affair. No lace. No jewelled buttons. His breeches. also brown, billowed out from his long thin legs. His shirt was white but unembroidered, his ruff small and commonplace. His cloak was thick but undistinguished, his hat old-fashioned in shape, with a cheap green band around it. But the most startling thing of all was his beard. His neat and pointed silver one was hidden under a thick black bush, completely altering the shape of his face.

Lady Bess laughed aloud – laughed until she cried.

'Too much?' the White Chief asked her with a grin. 'Sam found it for me. Should he have bought a smaller one?'

'No, no,' she mopped her eyes. 'A smaller one would not have covered your own. You've been called a pirate often enough. Now you look like one.'

'If we're stopped, he'll never be recognised,' Robin spluttered to me.

'He'll not be stopped,' the Cousin who was a Guard said stoutly. 'I'll see to it, 'though he may need the disguise.' He frowned. 'But the savage here will be recognised. Whatever he wears he'll stand out. He should not be allowed to come.'

I ignored him, turned away. I dislike this man who calls me a savage behind the White Chief's back yet smiles on me in his presence. It is up to the White Chief who goes with him and who stays. He wants me, which makes me happy. But I am wary of this land called France. The thought of it frightens me. But I was frightened of London, at first. Bewildered by the noise, the traffic, the people who gaped and pointed at me. Now I'm used to the horses, the carriages, the street criers and the great barges on the river. People still stare and point but it bothers me no longer. And if I can get used to London I can get used to this place called France.

Before we left, Lady Bess took me aside. 'If my husband changes his mind again, Cal, knock him senseless and carry him aboard the ship.'

I nodded. I'm prepared to do it, but I think I'll have little need for he wants to survive now – he admitted it to me.

'I may be old, Cal, and not in the best of health. But I still have a life to lead – things to write, things to do. Things that can make a difference. I don't fear death, just the waste of it. I'm not ready for it yet.'

Quietly we go, wrapped in the fog. Wrapped in our private thoughts. Few are about at this late hour and the ones that are skulk in the shadows, stay close to the darkened walls.

'Up to no good,' Robin whispers. 'Too set on their own business to bother with the likes of us.'

Robin walks behind me, his feet clatter on the cobbles. I make no sound for I walk barefoot – pleased to have the chance for once.. The Cousin who was a Guard strides ahead of the Great White Chief. I hear him coughing now and then – a dry, uneasy cough.

We're nearing the river, I smell it. I hear the Cousin's voice, chatting to Chief Sir Walter. I hate that Cousin. A pity we had to bring him. I walk now, almost on their heels, I can see them more clearly in the fog, and hear Robin's breathing, behind. There was much talk of how we should get here. Horses? Carriages? In the end, the White Chief said we should take neither to attract the least attention. But it's a long trek for him, with his lame leg. He's panting now, relieved we've arrived. When he stops I 'near crash into him.

'Tower Dock,' he says with satisfaction. 'Where's Sam?'

'Here.' The broad form of Captain King looms up from the greyness. 'I have the two wherries waiting, Sir, along with the men to row them. I've told them you're a gentleman in a hurry, but not, of course, who you are. Mind how you go on the steps – they're more treacherous than ever in this foul mist.'

The Cousin who was a Guard moves to take the White Chief's arm, but he turns and takes mine instead.

'Nearly there, Cal,' he says softly, as I help him down to the boat. 'You'll ride with Lewis and me, Sam and Robin will follow. You recall our route? The wherries will take us downriver to Gravesend, and there a waiting ketch will sweep us out of the river's mouth into the ocean and the Channel.'

I nod, suppressing a sigh. The sea again. I never can escape it. Still, this Channel is narrow, the White Chief showed me on his map. We'll soon be done with it. ('Though Robin said the crossing can be rough and feigned an attack of vomiting.)

✻ ✻ ✻

Nothing, now, but the splash of oars, the heaving of the rowers as we glide past landmarks unfamiliar in the fog.

'Can the rowers see where they're going?' the Cousin asks nervously.

The White Chief laughs. 'Experienced oarsmen, these. They've rowed in worse conditions.'

'Still, I wish they'd slow down,' the Cousin whines. 'There's no need for such great haste.'

I wish they would go faster. I've a bad feeling, suddenly.

✻ ✻ ✻

On, on through the mist. All seems strange – other-worldly. A shiver slides down my spine. Do the Water Spirits like mist? If they reared up, would we see them?

The White Chief is looking back. He stiffens, sits up straight.

'There's a third boat! Following us!'

I turn my head, peer into the gloom. See nothing but fog. Even the boat carrying Sam and Robin is hidden from my view.

'You imagined it, Walter,' the Cousin says. 'Your nerves are all on edge.'

The White Chief snorts. 'I have nerves of steel. I tell you I saw a boat.'

'Well then, is that unusual? the Cousin asks, his voice calm, reassuring. 'The Thames, after all, is not our private thoroughfare. Others are allowed upon it.'

'You're right, Coz.' The White Chief sighs. 'I'm being over-cautious. Pay me no heed.'

He relaxes back into his seat in the stern but, tense now, I keep a watch.

When, a short while later, the fog lifts slightly, I make out Sam's boat. And behind that …

'There is a third boat! Larger than both of ours and directly on our tail!'

'God's wounds!' the Cousin snaps. 'Another boat. What's that to us? Have faith, the pair of you. We've covered our tracks full well. No-one suspects us. No-one follows us. I've put it about you're too ill and weak still, Walter, to even leave your house. No-one believes you well enough to make a run for it. There is nothing at all to fear.'

A craft pulls alongside us. Our rowers rest their oars. Sam's voice calls from the gloom

'Do you see it, Sir? A great barge follows us. They've twice our number of oarsmen, so, if we're their quarry, they'll overhaul us fast. The tide will soon be on the turn, already the water's slackening. We'll never reach Gravesend. D'you think we should turn back? If it's not after us, the barge will carry on.'

The White Chief swears beneath his breath. 'We'll return to Greenwich, Sam. Then, maybe, take horse.'

Our wherry turns, and so does Sam's. The oarsmen row full out. But soon –

'It's still on our tail,' the White Chief mutters. 'I do not like this, Lewis.'

'Nor do I,' the Cousin admits. 'It's my neck, as well as yours. Think, man, think! What can we do?' He snaps his fingers. 'If they're truly after us, we could pretend you're still my captive. They might then leave us alone and we can still get ourselves to France. Quick, hand over the money and jewels you have in your pockets – the funds for your new life. If I have them 'twill be more convincing...'

I expect the White Chief to refuse but no, he hands over all that Lady Bess has worked so hard to get – has begged or borrowed from friends and relatives to help him survive in France. Hands over, too, some of his own most treasured things – a ring Queen Elizabeth gave him, a miniature of Lady Bess, a small, carved idol from Guiana...

Our rowers, followed by Sam's, turn in at Greenwich dock. And the great barge turns in also.

The White Chief gives a bitter laugh. 'That's it, then. All is lost.'

'Stick to the plan,' the Cousin breathes. 'Trust me. I'll save us, Walter. Have I not been a friend to you? A true kinsman with a kinsman's love and a kindly guard when I was forced to be, looking out for your every comfort?'

He leans forward suddenly, embraces the Great White Chief. Even, to my horror, kisses him on the cheek.

The White Chief does not return the kiss. He pats his cousin's hand. 'You've done all you can, Lewis, and I thank you for it.'

The barge pulls up alongside. A voice hails us. Orders us to disembark.

I help the White Chief up the steps. He limps up proudly, back erect, head held high. When we reach the top armed guards surround us, seize the White Chief, Captain King, Robin and me, pull our hands behind our back, remove swords from the others and my dagger from its belt. The Cousin steps forward – to explain, I think in relief, that the White Chief is his captive and we have the right to proceed. Instead, he places his hand on the White Chief's shoulder.

'Sir Walter Raleigh,' he says, in ringing tone. 'I arrest you in the name of the King.'

BESS

Broad Street, 10th August, 1618

Too worried to sleep, I am about to give up and go downstairs when the hammering on the door begins.

Alice meets me in the corridor outside my room, her eyes wide and her face as white as her night-robe.

'Are they back, do you think? Has he changed his mind again?'

I try to smile. 'They would hardly knock on the door and awaken half the house.'

My legs tremble as I descend the stairs, Alice following.

'Stop!' No need for that!' I shout, as the hammering increases. 'I'm coming.'

Dragging the door wide, my worst fears are confirmed. A short, plump man stands on the threshold, behind him three armed guards.

He steps forward, his chest puffed out importantly. 'Lady Elizabeth Raleigh, you are under house arrest by order of the King. I, Sir Thomas Lowes, am appointed your keeper.'

Alice gives a little scream. A pulse throbs in my throat. I find it difficult to speak.

'My husband?' I gasp at last.

'Is on his way to the Tower.'

* * *

The wretched days pass. I am allowed to keep Carew, Alice and Kate by my side. I fight for Dean and keep him but lose Wood, my cook, and all my other servants who, mostly, leave in tears. They are replaced by blank-faced strangers who perform their duties coldly.

I am not allowed to visit Walter or, indeed, to step outside the house, not even to walk in the garden. 'Are you afraid I'll scale the wall?' I ask Sir Thomas angrily. He has made himself comfortable in my house and watches my every movement. I detest having him here.

The guards search every room.

'Why?' demands Kate. 'What do you think we're hiding?'

They ignore her; continue turning over cushions and looking in cupboards. Dean walks behind them, clucking crossly, putting the things right that they disturb.

'Perhaps they think Cousin Walter did find gold in Guiana and has hidden it,' suggests Alice. She shouts at the guards. 'He brought back only tobacco! And that worm Stucley took it.'

I am not allowed to visit friends. Friends are not allowed to visit me. I am expected to sit meekly at home and not be a trouble to anyone.

'Blessed are the meek' the Bible tells us. But I am Elizabeth Raleigh nee Throckmorton who is anything but meek. I refuse to be bullied by a fat little no-account who lays down ridiculous rules.

When Francis calls I insist she be let in – she insists she be let in. The guards have been told they must not be violent. They shrug helplessly and in she comes. The same occurs with Audrey Walsingham, Arthur and Anna, my brother Nicholas, brother-in-law Carew, Thomas Harrington and a host of other friends and relatives. They come, Heaven bless them, to prove their concern for Walter, to show their concern for me.

Sir Thomas Lowes throws up his hands and despairs of me, of his ability to subdue me. He asks to be relieved of his duty as my keeper. Lowes is replaced by a city merchant called Wollaston. (He does not reveal his Christian name and I do not bother to enquire it.) My friends continue to visit me and, after three weeks and many arguments, Mr Wollaston writes to the Privy Council pleading release from 'this difficult woman'.

Another city merchant by the name of Richard Champion arrives at my door. He is tall and thin with a forbidding manner. He has strict instructions, he says, to admit 'Only the visitors I think fit.' My visitors call as before, and, tired of my 'tantrums', Mr Champion opts for a peaceful life and declares most of them fit.

My visitors, of course, are my lifeline to the news. Walter, they tell me, is more popular than ever in the city.

'People are disgusted with Sir Lewis Stucley,' Audrey says. 'They're calling him Sir Judas and jeering at him wherever he goes. He's as much a prisoner in his own house as you – afraid, now, to step outside.'

Cousin Gorges nods. 'Support for Walter is passionate and widespread.'

'But will this support do any good?' I ask wearily.

'Public opinion must count for something,' Frances says. 'Surely?'

No-one replies. We all know that it does not.

'There is support for him on the Privy Council,' George Carew assures me. 'Not all of us are afraid to stand up and be counted. I believe Arundel, Pembroke and I have convinced James not to send Walter to Spain to be executed.'

'But does that only mean he is to be executed here?'

He frowns. 'Not necessarily. By common law, a man indicted for treason cannot be charged with a new crime.'

So there remains a glimmer of hope.

✣ ✣ ✣

September, 1618

I take up my pen and write to the Queen. Her opinion, I know, also usually counts for nothing. But I have to try. She's always admired Walter and, as a mother, I feel an affinity with her; she lost her lovely Henry, I lost my lovely Wat. I know she'll help if she can.

Carew comes to me as I'm sealing the letter. He clutches a sheet of paper and looks shy.

'Mother, I've written to the King.'

Touched, I take it from him. Tears sting my eyes as I read. In his best handwriting he pleads for his father's life. He writes of his father's loyalty to the crown, of his years of faithful service to Queen Elizabeth. He reminds James that his mercy once saved Walter from destruction and asks for 'the redeeming hand of your princely goodness' to do the same again.

I doubt mention of Walter's loyalty to Queen Elizabeth will do anything but annoy James, who has always been jealous of her popularity. But I do not say this, of course. I embrace Carew and tell him his letter is wonderful and that I am proud of him.

'You have the same fluent way with words that your father has.'

He flushes with pleasure. 'How can we get it to the King? Mr Campion won't let us leave the house.'

'He lets Dean out to deliver letters,' I tell him. 'He even lets him go to the Tower to deliver my letters to your father and bring your father's letters back to me.'

Not that we say much of interest in these letters. I quickly realised by the tone of Walter's first short note that he believes our correspondence is being scrutinised. Why, for God's sake? What the Privy Councillors think we have to hide is beyond me. But because of this interference our communication is dull and disappointing.

✳ ✳ ✳

Captain King comes to see me. My stupid heart leaps when Kate ushers him into the parlour. If Sam is free, then ... But he's only been released, he says, because he's considered of no account, not particularly useful to the authorities. Walter remains in the Tower while poor Cal is detained in the cell next to him and Robin somewhere nearby.

'But they won't let either of them attend Sir Walter,' Sam says angrily. 'Things were better at first, when he was 'lodged' in the Lieutenant's house'

Did he look out through the window, I wonder? At the garden where he planted his herbs? At the hen house that became his laboratory? Did he think of the happy hours we all spent on that little patch of land?

'Sir Allen Apsley, as you know, fought at Cadiz,' Sam goes on. 'And he and his wife treated Sir Walter like an honoured guest. But then he was moved to the Wardrobe Tower and now he's in the Brick Tower with no servant to so much as comb his hair.'

He combed his hair in the Brick Tower after we wed and we were both imprisoned. Is he remembering how he bribed the warders and used to visit me?

'And now the Council have sent a fellow called Wilson to interrogate him. I'm told he does so day and night, giving Sir Walter little peace.'

'But why?' I ask, bewildered. 'What do they expect him to confess? He's told them – and even written down – all that happened.'

'They're at a loss,' shrugs Sam. 'James wants to hang him quickly to appease the Spanish Ambassador and the Spanish King and secure the marriage of the Infanta to Prince Charles, but now they've got him in the Tower they can't find a lawful way to do it. He wasn't present at San Thome, he killed no Spaniards and the men that did so acted against his orders.'

Men – young men – like Wat.

'So – that hopeful leap of the heart again – do you think they might let him go?'

Sam scowls. 'Not if they can help it.'

* * *

October, 1618

Arthur and Anna visit. I ask Kate to bring refreshments. I can tell from their strained faces that the news is bad and they don't know how to impart it. But eventually, out it comes.

Despite their best efforts the Council can find no treason. Not a whiff of it. But this has not deterred them. The old treason will suffice, from fifteen years ago. According to Sir Francis Bacon, there was, after all, no pardon.

'But it was Bacon who assured Walter he needed no pardon.' I cry. 'Who advised him against applying for one.'

'Bacon,' Anna says bitterly, 'turns his coat to serve only the King and Francis Bacon.'

'There has been no trial,' Arthur goes on. 'Just a private hearing held by toadies of the King.'

Anna pulls a scornful face 'The King feared a public trial would make Walter still more popular. He was heard to say it would be Winchester all over again – that Walter's wit would sway public opinion.'

'I'm sorry, Bess.' Arthur takes both my hands in his. 'Deeply sorry. But Walter is to be taken to Westminster Hall tomorrow, to be brought before the justices of the King's Bench. And the verdict of execution is a foregone conclusion.'

'The original one,' sobs Anna. 'Of hanging, drawing and quartering.'

* * *

He dies tomorrow. Lord Mayor's Day. The King has chosen this date in the expectation that the annual lavish celebrations will draw the public away from the city, away from Westminster and Old Palace Yard, where another spectacle will be taking place.

Walter was found guilty of four ridiculous charges; of never intending to discover a gold mine, of planning to start a war between the Kings of England and Spain, of abandoning his men and behaving unfaithfully to his king. When Cousin Gorges told me we both broke into bitter laughter. How could anyone who knew Walter believe such nonsense?

The sentence has been commuted to beheading, as it was fifteen years ago.

Walter has been moved, for this one night, to an upper chamber in the Gatehouse adjacent to Westminster Abbey. Cal and Robin may now attend him, and Dean stormed the Gatehouse and made such a fuss he's been allowed in also.

I am to see him later. For the last time in this world.

Poor Carew has not been given permission to visit. Nor has Alice. Thank God it has been granted to me.

Can I hold myself together?

I must.

* * *

'Bess – my love!'

His eyes light up as brightly as they did on our wedding day when he beheld me in my finery. I'm dressed finely now, in the gown he calls his favourite, deep rose silk with a petticoat of silver. But I was young then, full of hope, and he was the handsomest man I'd seen – his hair and beard as dark as night.

Now I'm fifty-three and look it on days like these. I'm older, by two years, than Queen Elizabeth was when first I went to Court. But Walter Raleigh is handsome still. His face may be lined and his hair and beard white, but nothing can dim that spark in him, that vitality that so attracts.

He limps to greet me, takes me in his arms and we embrace as passionately as we did on that wedding day of ours, all those years ago.

Then we sit on his narrow bed and talk of many things. Of anything but tomorrow. Of Wat and our happy times. Of Damerei and our sad ones. Of Carew and of Alice (poor Alice; always an afterthought, yet she's been a daughter, now, to both of us, for very many years). We even speak of Lawrence Kemys.

'I regret now, Bess, my harshness to him. I hope soon to meet him and tell him so.'

And now we can't avoid it, it's staring us in the face.

'I asked for two concessions, Bess,' Walter says soberly. 'One, that I might be given a few more days to put my affairs in order. Two, that I should be given leave to speak on the scaffold. They granted me the second but refused me the first. So we have much of the practical to discuss and little time in which to do it.'

He goes on and on – I'm to do this and I'm to do that. It would be best if I write to so-and-so, demanding what they owe me. Nicholas will help me with this, Arthur with that. Tom Harrington will advise me. Also Cousin George Carew. Some of it I take in and most of it I do not. But I nod as if I agree and am conscious all the while of the time ticking by, of the hammering, outside, of the men erecting the scaffold.

At last, Walter's aware of it also. We speak, again, of personal things – of our life together with its ups and many downs. Of our love that has endured.

'We were lucky to find each other, Bess. Few couples have such a bond.'

'And we'll be together again, won't we? I have to believe that.'

I weep now, into his doublet. I can't help myself.

He smiles down at me, but tears shine in his eyes. 'I'll be waiting for you, be sure of it. With Wat at my side and Damerei in my arms. But I hope you'll have many years yet. I hope you will remarry…'

'Never! You know I never will!'

'I want you to be happy. But remember, only marry him for his money, Bess. Don't dare to love him.'

We attempt a shaky laugh. And I find I'm able to bring myself to tell him I've been granted permission to have his body buried in the church at Beddington, on my brother Nick's estate.

'Where, eventually, I shall rest. Beside you.'

'Good.' He smiles. The old, twinkly, wicked smile. 'It's well you'll have the disposal of it dead, for you did not always have it at your disposal when it was alive. Your sour face, at every departure, waving me off to sea, near un-manned me.'

'It was *sad*! Never sour!'

A cough, behind us. The gaoler's here.

'Now get you gone,' Walter says. 'Before you un-man me again.'

I will not weep. Not now.

We cling together one last time. Then he holds me a little away.

'One promise, Sweetheart, before you go. I don't want you there tomorrow, I don't want you to watch me die. Let this be your last sight of me. Your last memory of me.'

I nod. 'I promise I won't watch.'

Then, with an effort, I tear myself away. Without looking back, I allow myself to be led down the steep stone stairs and out into Old Palace Yard. Past the scaffold that is now almost built.

How will I live without him?

CAL

*The Abbey Gatehouse /Old Palace Yard,
October 29, 1618*

Dean insists on being the one to brush his hair. To comb his moustache. To trim his beard. To assist him into the black taffeta breeches, the ash-coloured silk stockings, the silk shirt and white crisp ruff. He then makes a great business of brushing the black embroidered waistcoat, of shaking imaginary creases from the elegant fawn doublet before elbowing Robin aside and helping the White Chief into these also.

Robin only succeeds in holding out the long black velvet gown while I approach with the hat – high-crowned, wide-brimmed, sporting one bright peacock's feather.

'A tribute to Guiana, Cal,' the White Chief smiles, as he adjusts the brim. 'Although it should be a parrot's feather, should it not, like the Caciques wear? I wish I'd thought of it.'

He's full of smiles, seems light of heart, while our sadness sits on our faces, pulls down our mouths, drags at our feet. Perhaps he's relieved the end has come after hovering over him for so long.

He's eaten a hearty breakfast, smoked his silver-barrelled pipe, taken communion and said his prayers with a solemn High Priest called Dr. Tounson, who thinks him too cheerful for one about to die. I heard him say as much to one of the two sheriffs present.

And now it's time to go. The Gatehouse gaoler steps forward with a cup of sack.

'Drink this, Sir Walter, it's cold out there. It's my own brew, I hope you like it.'

The White Chief takes it and downs it thirstily. 'As a fellow on the way to Tyburn said, "it's a good drink if a man might tarry by it."'

The gaoler laughs, the sheriffs laugh. Dean, Robin and I cannot.

We descend the stairs and step out into the bright frosty morning. The two sheriffs of London either side the White Chief, followed by the High Priest, muttering prayers, and the three of us bringing up the rear. Armed guards surround us. Why, I wonder, do they think we need so many? Then I hear and see the crowds – a seething mass of people, rich and poor, pedlars and noblemen, men on horseback and on foot, faces at every window, crowds on balconies, children on the shoulders of their parents, babes in their mothers' arms . . . The guards are forced to push their way through a sea of bodies in order to get us to the scaffold – past folk who shout out messages of affection, of blessings, of regret.

'So much for the Lord Mayor's show,' mutters Robin with satisfaction. 'King James will not like this.'

At the foot of the scaffold, as the guards drop back, the White Chief pauses before a very old man with a head as bald as an egg.

'This is too raw a morning for you to be out, good sir.'

The old man bobs his head in an awkward gesture. 'I've come to pray for you, Sir Walter.'

'I thank you. But you're more in need of this than I. You'll get more wear from it.'

Removing his hat he pulls off the lace cap Dean insisted he wear for warmth, tosses it to the man, claps his hat on again and leads the way up the steps onto the wooden platform.

Several of the nobility – the White Chief's friends – are waiting there to shake his hand. The Priest, still quietly praying, and the sheriffs stand back respectfully. I turn my face from the sight of the block, the black-hooded figure leaning on the handle of a wicked-looking axe.

One of the sheriffs calls for silence as the White Chief steps forward. He smiles down and around at his expectant audience. 'I thank God in his infinite goodness that he has brought me into the light to die and not suffered me to perish in the darkness of the Tower,' he begins.

He speaks then, for a long time (five and twenty minutes, Dean tells me later), but I take in little of it. I realise he is defending himself from all the charges against him – the new and the old. I sense that the people watching and listening with such rapt attention are entirely on his side, murmuring among themselves about the unfairness of his treatment. Convinced, all of them, of his innocence.

But I hear only snatches of the rest because I spy Robin staring into the distance, beyond the mass of upturned faces, and it dawns on me suddenly that he is hoping for a horseman, a royal messenger, to come thundering through the crowd waving a reprieve. It happened in the year sixteen hundred and three. I stood beside the Great White Chief at the window of his cell in Wolvesey Castle, watching three men accused of treason prepare themselves for death, only to be saved at the last moment 'by the mercy of the King'. A favourite game of King James, the White Chief told me.

So perhaps, once more, this strange King of theirs' plays games. Like Robin, now, I stare out hopefully beyond the mass of faces, beyond the bobbing heads. But all I see is a black coach, its curtains drawn, two white horses standing patiently before it. Lady Bess, waiting to receive her husband's body

'I entreat you all to join with me in prayer,' the White Chief is saying. 'For I have many sins for which to crave God's pardon. I have been a seafaring man, a soldier and a Courtier, and in the temptations of these there is enough to overthrow a good mind and a good man. Pray, therefore, with me, that He will forgive me, and that He will receive me into everlasting life.'

Now the scaffold is clearing. Behind the White Chief only we three loyal servants, the High Priest and the headsman are left upon its wooden boards.

The White Chief turns and beckons us. Dean steps forward, streaming with silent tears, and helps him slip out of his robe, untie his ruff. Robin unfastens his doublet and removes it, while I take the hat he hands me, with its jaunty peacock's feather.

In his shirt sleeves now, the White Chief turns to the headsman and asks to examine the axe. The man hesitates, uncertain, then passes it to him. The White Chief turns it over, runs his thumb along the blade.

A sharp medicine,' he nods, smiling. 'To cure all ills.'

The headsman drops to his knees, asks forgiveness, according to custom.

'I forgive you freely,' the White Chief says. 'When I stretch out my hands, despatch me.'

He turns again to the watching crowd. 'Friends, pray heartily, for I have a long journey to travel.'

The headsman offers him a blindfold but he waves it aside. 'Think you I fear the shadow of the axe when I fear not the axe itself?'

He kneels down with some difficulty, due to his lame leg and the stiffness of his joints. I ache to help him but know he would not wish it. He lays his head upon the block. Dean, sobbing, turns his back. I glance at Robin who is staring in disbelief. No reprieve then, all hope gone.

The headsman takes out a knife, rips the white shirt that Dean prepared so carefully, the better to expose the neck.

The White Chief prays quietly, then stretches out his arms. The headsman hesitates. I think I hear him sob.

'Strike, man. Strike!' The White Chief shouts, with all his old impatience.

The axe crashes down. Once. Twice. The blood spurts – so much blood! And the head, that handsome, white-haired head, falls onto the straw, lips still moving in silent prayer.

The headsman, as his job demands, lifts it up, holds it aloft, displays it to left and right. But he does not cry out the traditional words: 'Behold the head of a traitor.'

A low murmuring only, from the crowd. Until one voice shouts: 'We have not such another head to be cut off.'

At once the air is alive with angry shouts, protests and noisy weeping: the shaking of fists and a loud outcry against the Privy Council and King James.

Guards rush onto the scaffold, pushing us aside, covering up the White Chief's body, rolling it into the folds of his own black velvet gown.

'It's to go in a coach to Beddington,' I shout, grasping one of them by the arm. 'I'm to take it. Give it to me.'

'Change of plan.' He shakes me off. 'We're to take it to St. Margaret's Church just over yonder. The head an' all. By royal command.'

He turns away, with the others, intent upon their task. Looking wildly around, I see that the head – the White Chief's poor head – has been thrust into a red leather bag. Without more ado I snatch it up, leap down the scaffold steps and push my way through the noisy crowd. If there are shouts of protest behind me, orders for me to halt, I hear them not.

At last I reach the coach. Lady Bess flings open the door.

'They won't let you have his body, after all,' I gasp. 'But I've stolen his head.'

She nods her thanks. She's too overcome to speak. Without a word she takes the bag, hugs it to her.

I spring into the coach. 'Drive on!' I call to Wood, installed in the coachman's seat. 'Drive on as fast as you can!'

* * *

* * *

~EPILOGUE~

* * *

* * *

BESS

The Manor, West Horsley, 1645

Twenty-seven years I've lived without him, yet I've felt his presence every day. Guiding me, protecting me.

I have his head with me still. It sits in its red leather bag and is never far from me. I had it embalmed to preserve it but do not show it to visitors as some ghoulish folk report. How do such tales take root? Who begins them?

Never once have I looked at it since it was severed from his body. Cal stole it to ensure it did not end up on London Bridge, nailed to Traitor's Gate. I doubt the angry Londoners would have stood for that, but better safe than sorry. The bag, with its contents, will be buried with me when I die. Buried in the church at Beddington, where they said I could bury Walter's body and then denied it to me.

It won't be long, now, until we rest together, the red leather bag and I. Kate and I accept wagers as to which of us will go first – two silver-haired old ladies who yet remain young at heart.

We've outlived so many friends, so many relatives – my brothers, Anna, Audrey, Frances, Tom Harriot, even Alice (poor Alice who died of the sweat before I could find her a husband). I miss them and pray for them all. And more, when I can remember their names. Names escape me sometimes.

Of my loyal servants, my companions, Wood and Dean died of old age, but Cal and Robin are with me still. Also Samuel King, who's ancient now but says he refuses to die.

We manage well enough for I've discovered I have a talent for business, for piling up the pennies, for suing people who owe me and people who owed Walter. I'm known as a 'difficult woman', which rather pleases me. The difficult woman is quite a wealthy one now, living in comfort in this pleasant house in Surrey.

Our enemies are long gone, too. 'Judas' Stucley complained to King James of the hostility served him by the public after Walter's death, and James replied: 'If I hung everyone who speaks ill of you there would not be enough trees in all the land.' They tell me the wretched man fled to Lundy Island and died alone there, driven mad. I don't pray for *him*.

James remained spiteful to the end.

When Carew came down from Oxford, the Earl of Pembroke (Mary's son) tried to present him at Court but James turned pale at the sight of him, said he was 'too much like Raleigh's ghost' and ordered him to leave.

Then, tired of my badgering, the House of Lords passed a bill restoring Carew in blood, renouncing Walter's attainder, but

James would not allow it. Thankfully, he died of dysentery at the age of fifty-nine. Taken ill while out hunting – what else would he be doing? Some say he was poisoned. The tired old story. I don't pray for *him*, either.

His son, Charles, is now King and he approved the bill (swayed by the four thousand pounds I donated to his war fund) provided Carew gave up the fight to get back the Sherborne estate, which I persuaded him to do.

He didn't want to – he fought long and hard for it but there are some fights you cannot win. 'There will be Raleighs here for generations,' I remember Walter saying, when the Queen bestowed it. But it was not to be.

'The attainder is lifted,' I reminded Carew. 'That's our greatest triumph. The Raleigh name restored.'

And Walter's innocence accepted, that's what it means to me.

'No longer the traitor's wife,' I said, and Carew looked shocked.

'I'm sure no-one ever called you *that*.'

Carew is a good, loyal son. He married well – his wife's a wealthy heiress. But it's a love match, which pleases me. They have three children, almost grown. It's true he has a look of his father now (but is not as handsome). And he writes sonnets and poems which are almost as good (not quite) as the ones that Walter wrote. I've published some of Walter's, together with many of his papers, his letters, his treaties, to keep his memory prominent in the world.

'He'll never be forgotten,' Carew assures me. 'Folk speak of him more than ever, more respectfully than ever, in these uncertain times.'

Horrible times! Walter would abhor them. Charles, who was a weak child and is a weak king, has embroiled us in Civil War. Neighbour against neighbour, brother against brother. Charles clings onto his throne by his finger-tips, holed up in his base at Oxford. God alone knows what will happen. Carew is with him, supports him. He was appointed a Gentleman of the Privy Chamber, so he can do no other, but I know he often disagrees with the way Charles handles things. If Prince Henry had lived ... but he didn't, and that's that. I once cursed James, a Stuart king. Has my curse affected them all?

I've heard that Oliver Cromwell, the leader of the opposing side, reveres Walter's memory, considers him a hero, takes his History of the World with him wherever he goes. I'm pleased that he admires the book, but Walter would not be flattered. Walter was a royalist through and through, despite his criticism of kings. And he nursed a hatred of civil war.

Cal and Robin tell me of the battles, of the horror and the casualties. But, in truth, though I nod and pull sad faces, I don't really pay attention. Living quietly as I do, it all seems far away – unreal. The past, now, is more clear to me than the present. Twenty-seven years since I lost Walter, yet it seems like yesterday. I miss him every day. Read, every day, the poem he wrote on the eve of his execution, in the flyleaf of his bible:

> Even such is Time, which takes in trust
> Our youth, our joys, our all we have,
> And pays us but with earth and dust;
> When we have wandered all our ways,
> Shuts up the story of our days.

> But from this earth, this grave, this dust,
> My God shall raise me up, I trust.

Voices, rising up from the courtyard. Carew's wife and my grandchildren are here. I'm always thrilled to see them but I shall fall asleep, no doubt. I sleep so much, these days, little naps here and there. But I welcome sleep. I like my dreams, always such pleasant ones. I shall dream of Little Wat, galloping on his pony. Of strolling in the gardens at Sherborne on a summer afternoon. And of splendid Walter Raleigh, dancing with the Queen . . .

* * *
* * *

AUTHOR'S NOTE

Fact or Fiction?

No record exists of how or when Bess and Walter met, but it's assumed their relationship began at Court. Historians are divided over their wedding date, but there was a lawsuit over Bess's inheritance and a deposition states, according to John Winton, one of Raleigh's biographers: *'On the 20th day of February in the thirtieth year of Queen Elizabeth, or thereabouts, the aforesaid Elizabeth Throckmorton accepted as her man Walter Raleigh, knight.'*

Which, if accurate, seems clear enough. Many couples have married in haste with the threat of war hanging over their heads. Why not the Raleighs?,

Historians, in fact, are divided over most of Walter's activities and motives (although all agree that he was brilliant, handsome and charismatic), but I make no apology for portraying him in a sympathetic, somewhat heroic light. This novel is, after all, expressed through the eyes of Bess, who obviously loved him very much, and Robert Cecil, who was undoubtedly a mixed-up friend/enemy.

Apart from their letters to each other (a mixture of practical details and affection), little is known of the Raleighs' personal relationship, so their thoughts, feelings and conversations expressed here are, of course, fictional. But the important events throughout are rooted in fact.

There are many contemporary versions of the spelling of Walter's surname. The popular modern one adopted in the UK now is Ralegh, because it was the signature he (eventually) used most. However, as the capital of North Carolina is called Raleigh, and in view of Walter's close association with the Americas, I decided to stick with the more traditional one which is still preferred by many people both sides of the Pond.

Little, again, has been discovered about Bess's intimate women friends. Therefore I have given her close ties with some of the women she would certainly have known well – Audrey Shelton, Mary Herbert, Frances Walsingham, Elizabeth Cecil etc.

Cal, the native from Guiana, is based on fact. A baptism register discovered in the London Metropolitan Archives (and reported in newspapers in 2009) reveals that a native boy was baptised in the Parish of St. Luke, Chelsea, on February 13, 1597. The child, named Charles, was aged between 10 and 12 and is thought to have been one of the earliest and youngest natives brought to Britain from Guiana during Raleigh's first voyage there. He is understood to have settled in Sir Walter's household, but nothing more is known about him. He takes the place, in the novel, of several natives known to have been close to Raleigh, taught to speak English and introduced to Anglican Christianity. On his first trip to Guiana, one of Raleigh's party was eaten by an alligator. He was *not* Cal's brother. Harry the Native, Leonard the Native, and Prince Cayoworaco all existed and lived in the Raleigh household.

Raleigh's illegitimate daughter by Alice Goold also existed. She was first mentioned in his will which I have moved forward a fraction in time to fit the story. (He could easily have made an earlier will at the time I mention). Her name is not known. She is thought to have died in London, but whether she ever lived with the Raleighs, or met Bess, is a mystery.

Lastly, that cloak. *Did* Sir Walter Raleigh spread his expensive cloak over a muddy puddle for Queen Elizabeth to walk upon? In *The Traitor's Wife,* Bess refers to the incident as a rumour she thinks unlikely. Sadly, it *is* unlikely, as the story first appeared some forty years after Raleigh's death, in the Reverend Thomas Fuller's *History of the Worthies of England.* No other mention of it has ever been found.

Further reading

There are many excellent biographies which have been of great help and interest to me. These include:

Raleigh Trevelyan: *Sir Walter Raleigh,* The Penguin Group 2002

Stephen Coote: *A Play of Passion,* Macmillan 1993

John Winton: *Sir Walter Ralegh,* Michael Joseph 1975

Robert Lacey: *Sir Walter Ralegh,* Weidenfeld & Nicolson 1973

A.L. Rowse: *Ralegh and the Throckmortons,* Macmillan 1962

Agnes Latham & Joyce Young: *The Letters of Sir Walter Ralegh,* University of Exeter Press 1999

Anna Beer: *Bess, The Life of Lady Ralegh,* Constable & Robinson 2004

Lord David Cecil: *The Cecils of Hatfield House,* Constable & Company Ltd. 1973

NB: A new Raleigh biography by Anna Beer: *Patriot or Traitor,* Oneworld Publication 2018, came out just as *The Traitor's Wife* was being published.

Snippets of Information

Venus Glove:

A type of condom made of lambskin and originally from Italy. Expensive, so mostly used (illegally) by men of means and without effective results, judging from the amount of illegitimate children in Tudor England.

Spiced Caudle:

A warm drink of thin gruel and wine, sweetened and spiced. Given to sick people, especially women in child-bed.

Eagle Stone Talisman:

A hollow stone containing a pebble, sand, or other material inside so that it rattled when shaken. It was a very ancient talisman, believed to prevent miscarriage and help relieve the pains of childbirth.

The Lord's Tokens:

Marks or spots appearing on plague victims.

The Twelve Days of Christmas (sung by Bess's cousins):

There exists a theory (disputed by some historians) that the carol was one of the 'catechism songs' used to help young, persecuted Catholics learn the tenets of their faith by memory, rather than by the written word, which was dangerous.

The songs' 'gifts' are thought to be hidden meanings spelling out the teachings of the faith. The *True Love* is God. The receiver of the presents is a baptised person. The *Partridge in a Pear Tree* represents Christ.

The rest:

2 Turtle Doves, the Old and New Testaments.

3 French Hens, Faith, Hope and Charity.

4 Calling Birds, The Four Gospels

5 Golden Rings, The first five books of the Old Testament.

6 Geese a'laying, The six days of Creation.

7 Swans a-swimming, The seven sacraments.

8 Maids-a-milking, The eight beatitudes.

9 Ladies Dancing, The nine fruits of the Holy Spirit.

10 Lords a-leaping, The ten commandments.

11 Pipers Piping, The eleven faithful apostles.

12 Drummers Drumming, The twelve points of doctrine in the Apostles' Creed.

True or not, it's interesting.

THE BACK-COVER PICTURE

Present-day Sherborne Castle. Sir Walter Raleigh built the original house, which is now its central core, on the site of a hunting lodge in the deer park opposite the Old Castle. He renamed it Sherborne Lodge.

Rectangular in shape, four stories high, with large windows filled with diamond-paned glass, it was considered very modern and sophisticated.

Later, he added four hexagonal turrets to the four corners. When Sir John Digby acquired the property, he copied the style, adding four wings with identical hexagonal turrets.

During the Civil War the Old Castle was reduced to ruins and the name Sherborne Castle transferred to the new building. It is still owned by the Digby family.

THE TWO POEMS MENTIONED

Now what is love first appeared in *The Phoenix Nest*; an anthology compiled in 1593. The contributing writers were all 'anonymous' but Raleigh is thought to have penned this one.

Even such is time is said to have been found on a sheet of paper inside Sir Walter's bible the morning after his execution.

ABOUT THE AUTHOR

Anna Rossi is a former journalist who now concentrates on her first love – writing fiction.

She lives in Warwickshire, UK, with her husband and family.

The Traitor's Wife is her second historical novel. Her first, *Black Damask,* although set in Tudor England, is a supernatural story and different in style and content from the story of Bess Raleigh.

Anna is currently working on her third novel.

If you would like to get in touch, please visit her website at www.annarossiauthor.com.

* * *

* * *

Printed in Great Britain
by Amazon